DAGGER OF THE MIND

"What can I do for you, chief?" Lacey asks, dropping into the armchair behind her desk.

"There's been a third murder. A human—and one of my best officers, damn it."

"I'm sorry." The sympathy in her voice is as genuine as her earlier anger. "What happened?"

Bates keeps his voice low and steady as he tells the story. As he talks she types, her fingers moving fast over the old-fashioned equipment, the screen casting odd flecks of glare into her face.

"Oh, hey!" she says abruptly. "Thanks, Buddy." She turns to Bates. "My computer just reminded me of something that might fit in. Remember Mulligan's fit when he tried to do a reading over the first carli corpse?"

Bates nods.

"Buddy found a paper demonstrating that it's possible to put a psychic block on someone, to interfere with their psi functioning and—this is the telling detail—*to keep them from remembering that they were blocked.*"

Bates swears briefly but vilely. When he glances Mulligan's way, he finds his face dead-pale, his eyes kid-wide.

"It's someone who broke his oath," says Mulligan. "When they register you, you got to sign an oath that says you'll never hurt nobody with your talent."

"Someone who goes around cutting people's throats no is going to worry about a lousy oath."

POLAR CITY BLUES

An Entertainment

Katharine Kerr

BANTAM BOOKS
NEW YORK • TORONTO • LONDON • SYDNEY • AUCKLAND

POLAR CITY BLUES

A Bantam Spectra Book / September 1990

ISBN 0-553-28504-1

Published simultaneously in the United States and Canada

Bantam Books are published by Bantam Books, a division of Bantam Doubleday Dell
Publishing Group, Inc. Its trademark, consisting of the words "Bantam Books" and
the portrayal of a rooster, is Registered in U.S. Patent and Trademark Office and in
other countries. Marca Registrada. Bantam Books, 666 Fifth Avenue, New York,
New York 10103.

PRINTED IN THE UNITED STATES OF AMERICA

OPM   0 9 8 7 6 5 4 3 2 1

The lines of poetry on page 128 are from "All the Earth, All the Air," by Theodore Roethke, in THE COLLECTED POEMS OF THEODORE ROETHKE, Doubleday Anchor, 1975.

For Stephen W. Dakin, wherever he is.
He knows why.

AUTHOR'S NOTE

The dialect in which the characters speak, called Merrkan in the text, is a future projection of the changes going on all over the American Sunbelt as Middle-class White (often called Standard) English, Black English, and New World Spanish fuse together. Since most of the settlers on Hagar came ultimately from California, this emergent dialect forms their everyday speech. Anyone who lives in the Sunbelt will also know that Merrkan is a very-much-watered-down-for-publication version of this dialect, which even now seems to be incomprehensible to English-speakers in the rest of the country.

Chapter One

Hagar's enormous sun sets in an opalescent haze, the sky brindled a metallic red-orange that seems insultingly gaudy, as if a cheap holopix director were designing an alien sky. As the red fades into an offensive little-girl pink, the real show begins above Polar City. The northern lights crackle, hang long waves of rainbow over the skyline that resembles nothing so much as egg cartons set on end, and at times wash the high gantries of the space-port in purple and silver. Although most of the inhabitants (just getting out of bed, checking their kids or their incubating eggs, brushing their teeth or washing their beaks) ignore them, tonight police corporal Baskin Ward stops on his downtown beat and leans against the blue plastocrete wall of the public library to watch the sky. He has a lot to think over, and it is very hot, as it always is in Polar City. In an hour or so, the town will come alive, but he wants to take it easy so he'll be fit for the sergeant's exam on the morrow. If he passes, he'll be able to marry the woman he's loved for three years, a clerk/comp-op over in Traffic Control who wants, as he does, two children and a transfer off this goddamn low-tech desert world with the continually gaudy sky. If he does well as a sergeant, he'll be able to request posting to Sarah, his home planet, a world of rains and jungles—if, of course, he passes the exam in the first place.

The blue-arc street lamps wink on, floating in their maglev field some six meters above the pale gray sidewalks and the shiny black movebelts that flow beside them. The Civic Center Plaza in front of him is empty except for a woman hurrying across, her high-heeled boots echoing and slapping on the rammed-earth tiles, the sound competing with the

1

endless snap of magnetism in the sky above. In a little while, office workers and bureaucrats will pour in from the underground condos rimming the city proper. Ward hopes for an easy beat. Most likely it'll be a few drunks and more than a few dreamdusters, all to be lectured, ticketed, and entered into the rehab computer via the terminal on his belt, while the most exciting arrest is likely to be a pickpocket. Basically, Ward is there to be seen in his kelly green uniform with its imposing gold braid and shiny silver stun gun, a visible symbol of the Republic's power to protect and punish.

He settles his cap, peels himself off the library wall, and steps onto the movebelt that runs across the plaza toward City Hall, an enormous black basalt building as glum as a tombstone. In the center of the plaza is a roughly defined square bordered by holm oaks. Just as the belt carries Ward inside this square, some unseen worker far below the surface turns on the public hologram in the center. A tall fountain snaps into being, the illusionary water spraying in dead silence for a minute before the hiss-and-splash tape goes on. When the ion generator joins in, Ward can almost believe that it's cooler near the fountain. He steps off the belt and ambles over to the real railing that keeps lids, lizlets, and pets out of the imaginary water. In the middle of the big white plastocrete pool, he sees his first drunk or druggie of the night, lying half-hidden in the murk of the illusion.

"Okay, amigo, need a little help, huh?"

As Ward wades through the holo, he's irrationally irritated that his legs stay dry and thus hot. The doper never even moves, merely waits, lying on his back with his hands folded over his chest. Then Ward sees the stain, more black than red in the arc light, spreading over the whiteness.

"Jeezchrist!"

Ward kneels down fast, reaching for his combox. He sees that he's dealing with a male carli, about one and a half meters tall, even skinnier than most of his species, the three fingers on each hand like long twigs and tufted with pale gray fur. The dark gray fur visible on his face, arms, and neck is dull and matted. His eyes are wide open; the skin flaps around each ear, fully extended and rigid; his thin slit of a mouth, shut tight. Since Ward knows carli ways, he realizes that these particular facial expressions indicate a certain mild surprise and nothing more. The victim must have suspected nothing, seen no danger coming, until the exact moment that someone slashed his throat open to the spine.

"Since he's a carli, sir, he got to be part of the Confederation Embassy."

"Safe enough bet, Ward."

Chief Al Bates, an enormous, burly man whose skin is so dark that it glitters with bluish highlights, and his corporal, about half his size and on the pale side, stand off to one side of the plaza and watch the 'grammers and techs swarming around the corpse. Since the fountain has been shut off, they can see the body clearly, dressed in luxurious blue robes of natural fiber. On its left wrist is a multifunction chrono with a solid gold band, its expensive presence eliminating a nice routine robbery-with-bodily-harm. Although the chief wants to find a simple motive—unpaid gambling debts, say, or an affair with some other carli's female—deep in his heart he suspects that politics lies at the root of this killing, simply because major crimes on Hagar almost always have something to do with politics. Just six blocks to the west of them stands the embassy of the powerful Interstellar Confederation; eight blocks to the east, that of the enormous Coreward Alliance. Polar City Hall, seat of the provincial administration of this portion of the pitifully small Republic (seven inhabited planets in four systems, two asteroid belts, and a couple of minable moons), stands symbolically in between, caught, as the citizens like to say, between the Cons and the 'Lies. This joke is not meant kindly.

By now the office workers are arriving, popping up like sandworms out of the Metro exits, and of course, they stop to gawk. Without waiting for orders, Ward trots away to keep them moving—a good officer, in the chief's estimation, and one worthy of a set of sergeant's stripes. He also sees the Vulture Detail weaving through the crowd: a medic and two body techs, with a maglev platform bobbing along after them. Bates wonders why the killers left the body in the middle of the plaza, especially in the fountain, a damn strange place to dump a corpse. Perhaps the killers were new to Polar City and didn't know about the fountain? Perhaps they were deliberately insulting the dead man? The carli are extremely touchy about the disposal of their corpses. He reminds himself to access a databank on carli burial customs to see if water might be a source of ritual pollution.

"It looks horrible, chief."

"Jeez! Mulligan!" Bates swirls around, his stun gun half-drawn before he catches himself. "Will you stop creeping up on me like that? One of these nights you're going to get a skull full of shock waves."

Mulligan merely smiles his open, boyish grin, one of the things that the chief particularly dislikes about him. Although Bates is willing to admit that a free society should tolerate psychics, and that indeed, the Republic often finds them useful, he has never felt at ease around psionic jocks and particularly not around Mulligan. Tonight Mulligan looks even messier than usual, all skinny two meters of him dressed only in a pair of filthy white walking-shorts and a green shirt open to the waist, both of them much too large. His hair, though permanently shaggy, is temporarily turquoise blue, a color that clashes with the bright red mandatory P tattooed on his left jaw, just beside the ear. (While the Republic tolerates psychics, it also brands them to protect its other citizens.) In the streetlights, his eyes glare like a reptile's—reflective gold contact lenses, the chief notes in disgust. He cannot quite stop himself from thinking that, after all, white people, los Blancos, are mostly this way, out of touch with hard reality, caught up in some faked image of themselves. Then he feels ashamed of himself for lapsing into old prejudices.

"Can I help?" Mulligan waves vaguely at the corpse.

"What do you want the bucks for? Dreamdust?"

"Never use the stuff. How about, like, rent? My landlord's going to throw me out. Y'know?"

Bates snorts in skepticism, then hesitates, thinking. Mulligan has the virtue of being right there on the scene, and early, before whatever vibrations it is that psychics read have weakened or even dissipated completely.

"Yeah, sure. Follow me."

Mulligan trots meekly behind as the chief shoves his way through the crowd to the coroner's techmen around the corpse. They are just loading the gray-shrouded bundle onto the maglev platform.

"Got a registered psychic here," Bates says. "So hold off moving him for a moment."

Obligingly the techmen let the corpse fall back onto the

fountain floor. Mulligan kneels down, slumps back onto his heels, then holds his long-fingered pale hands out over the body. For a moment he sits quietly, while one techman gets out a recorder and primes it to catch whatever he says and the other corpse-handler gets himself a pinch of chewing spice out of his shirt pocket. Then Mulligan goes rigid, his head snapping back, his back arching, and howls once, a high-pitched shriek of pain. One techman swallows his spice and rushes away to puke it back up in the privacy of the gutter. The other, who is apparently more familiar with psionic techniques, flicks on the recorder and yawns. Bates hunkers down close.

"What do you see?"

His mouth half-open, Mulligan turns his head to look the chief's way. Because of the reflective contacts, it's some moments before the chief realizes that something is badly wrong, that Mulligan's acting blind, that he's desperately trying to force out a few words and to raise his hands. When Bates grabs him, he howls again, but this time he sounds like he's choking. For all his big-bellied bulk, the chief can move fast when he has to. Dragging Mulligan with him, he jumps to his feet and leaps back. The result appears to be exactly the same as dragging someone away from an electrical shock. At first Mulligan spasms, then faints in the chief's arms. Turquoise sweat streaks down his face.

"Medic!" Bates's voice booms over the murmurs of the gawking crowd. "Get me a medic! Pronto!"

Mulligan wakes up on an examining table in a cubicle down at Polar City Emergency Center. The bright pink walls are stained along the baseboard by the urine of two different species, and the smell of disinfectant makes his dry throat constrict further. A strong overhead light stabs his eyes. When he tries to roll over onto his stomach, the pain in his head makes him moan aloud. In one corner of the room is a sink: water if he can only reach it. His legs and shoulders ache so badly that he doubts if he can. For some minutes he lies perfectly still and tries to remember what sent him to the hospital. The only thing he can think of was that he was knocked down by an errant skimmer or even by some hobbyist on an antique bicycle. He can remember walking across a street to talk to Chief Bates; then nothing.

From out in the corridor he hears footsteps, big, shuffling, slapping footsteps, and another mind touches his.

Okay little brother, Nunks now. My home>safe my home>safe my home>safe.

Tears form in Mulligan's eyes. When he goes to wipe them on his sleeve, he realizes that someone has taken out his contacts. He finds this infuriating for a reason he can't verbalize to himself. A soothing warmth touches his mind.

<Nursewoman give< Nunks pocket now.

At that the door opens, and Nunks pads in. Well over two meters tall, vaguely hominoid in that he has two legs, two arms, and a head all coming off a central torso, he is wearing a pair of striped black and white overalls, cut off at the knee, over his thick coat of curly gray fur, but as always, he's barefoot. Bluish fur covers his skull, which is bifurcate, that is, it looks as if he has two wedge-shaped skulls, each striped with a pinkish ear-strip, that join in the middle lump of bone and flesh, about the size of a baseball, where his perfectly round mouth and three eyes reside. He gets Mulligan a plastic cup of water, helps him drink it, then lays one huge, bare-palmed hand on Mulligan's forehead. The pain disappears.

Cure\block it? Mulligan asks.

Block. Not-know cure.

Okay. Thanks.

Go home> Lacey know? Buddy know?

Lacey maybe.

Go home> Nunks nods in a firm, paternal manner. *Find nurseman, go not-here>*

The nurse, however, finds them, slamming into the room as if he expects to find Nunks murdering his patient. His dark brown face is set in grim lines. In one hand he carries a comcube; in the other, a typer.

"Okay, white boy," he snaps at Mulligan. "Does your . . . ah . . . friend speak Merrkan?"

"He no speak anything, but he, like, understands Merrkan."

"Well, you no should be in here"—this last addressed to Nunks. "Who let you in, anyway?"

Nunks regards him with two of his large, green eyes for a long moment; then he steps forward and raises one hand.

"You no should be in here! Hey, what are you doing? Dunt touch me, you jerk! Dunt . . ."

The moment Nunks' hand reaches his forehead, the nurse smiles, sighs, and falls unconscious to the floor.

Little brother walk\ not walk?

Not walk. Mulligan lets some of his body pain flow outward. With a wince, Nunks acknowledges that he understands.

Little brother mindshroud\ not mindshroud?

Can do.

When Nunks picks him up, Mulligan wraps his arms around his neck and lets his friend carry him like a child. They link minds, then send out a vast and misleading amount of pure signal that acts as a virtual screen of invisibility as they go down the hall. Past the gray and silver triage station, where four sentients in white coats are standing around gossiping, through the crowded lobby, outside to the plaza and down to the robocab stand—no one notices them go by; no one says a word to stop them, not even when they have to wait a good five minutes for an empty cab to swing their way. Although Nunks can open the door and get Mulligan into the seat, Mulligan has to punch in the coordinates of Porttown, because Nunks' fingers are too broad. The effort leaves him gasping.

Porttown proper begins about two miles from Civic Center where First Avenue dead-ends into the customs building, and that's where the robocab stops to let them off, because its programming forbids it to go any deeper into the neighborhood. By then, Mulligan's muscles have relaxed enough that he can stumble along, provided Nunks keeps one arm around him for support. They amble down D Street, past the gray plastocrete facades, the pawnshops and the cheap hotels, the drunks in doorways, and the dreamdusters sprawled openly on the sidewalk. Every now and then a tired whore calls down a bad joke from a window, or a Fleetman in full uniform staggers past on his or her way to the skyport after a night of liberty. Twice they are followed by lizzie gangs, but not only is Nunks very large, he is also broadcasting a psychic projection of danger and hostility that makes all the passersby instinctively feel that he's a bad sentient to cross. After a block or two, the gangs fade away.

They're within sight of the port gates when they turn down an alley that dead-ends against the side of a faux-brick warehouse taking up the entire city block. It sports slide-up cargo doors and a loading dock, but the doors are padlocked and rusty, the windows painted over, the dock heaped with wind-blown trash. At one corner is an ordinary door and a faded, three-dee block sign that reads A TO Z ENTERPRISES. Although Mulligan doubts if the sign ever fooled anyone but the occasional Outworlder who had the ill luck to wander this way, the setup was never truly intended to deceive. Rather, it announces to the authorities that Lacey is willing to pretend that she's trying to make them believe she runs a legitimate business, so that the authorities can go on pretending that they've been fooled. On Hagar, there are proper ways of doing things.

When Nunks presses his palm into the autolock, the door slides back with a clogged groan. Just stepping inside makes Mulligan feel better. What looks like a solid block's worth of warehouse from the outside is in fact a hollow shell, only one room or corridor thick. Inside blooms a garden, green row after green row of fruits, vines, and vegetables. All around the edge of the open space are trees, mostly Old Earth apples. Although a good many government officials might wonder, if they let themselves, where Lacey gets the extra water rations to keep this paradise alive, none asks hard questions. If they did, where would they go when they wanted exotic fruit to impress a lover or fresh greens to pamper a pregnant wife? The apple brandy that Nunks and Lacey brew is too valuable a bribe to risk losing it to a fuss over regulations. Besides, much of the water comes from legitimate sources, because Lacey is a fanatic about recycling every drop the household uses.

At night, under the ever-shifting colors of the northern lights, the garden seems to breathe as the iridescent shadows flicker and swell. As they make their way carefully between two rows of grayish-green bread ferns, Mulligan notices a young woman standing in a spill of light from an open doorway behind her. About sixteen, she's a lovely child, small and slender with her bleached white hair, just frosted with purple, setting off the perfect smooth darkness of her skin. One side of her face, however, is bruised as purple as her hair, and even in the bad light he can see red marks on her neck that are about the size and shape of fingertips.

Big brother? New girl/Lacey friend/live here?

Yes/no/yes. <Street find\ last noon.

When she sees them the girl ducks back into her room and slams the door. Mulligan hears old-fashioned bolts being shot and the rattle of a chain for good measure. Feeling her fear takes his mind off his own physical pain long enough for him to struggle up the outside stairway to the second floor. Nunks shoves open the heavy door at the top and half-carries him into a corridor purring with air conditioners. About ten feet along, Lacey's door stands open, and he can hear her husky voice snapping with anger.

"Listen, panchito. I told you that if you want to stay here, you have to follow the rules. Rule One: when Nunks gives an order about the gardens, you obey him. Get it?"

"Yezzir." A boy's voice, but soldier crisp.

"Okay. One more chance. Another snafu, and you're gone."

The boy trots out, glances their way, then runs down the hall. Maybe twenty, if that, he crouches as he runs, ducking unseen laser fire. Mulligan vaguely remembers that he's a deserter from one space force or another—Alliance Marines, he thinks, but by then his head is swimming so badly that he doesn't really care. Nunks picks him up and carries him the last few feet into the room, then lays him down on the gray foam-cube sofa that stands by the far wall. Lacey looks up in surprise. She is sitting in a gray vinyl armchair with her feet up on a royal blue comp desk and watching a baseball game on the three-dee hanging on the wall. Because of his condition Mulligan indulges himself with only a brief, abstract pang of the hopeless lust that he usually feels at the sight of her. Although she's only of average height, Lacey always seems taller because of her ramrod-straight posture. Thanks to rejuv drugs, she looks about twenty-five and rather girlish, with her big blue eyes and quick, triangular smile, but she is, in fact, a thirty-year veteran of the Republic's deep space fleet, as one might guess from the cut of her blond hair, an efficient military bob. Although she would have risen to a high rank in any fleet bigger than four frigates, three cruisers, and one aging battleship, she recently retired as a lieutenant commander. Those who don't know the true story say that if only she weren't white she would have gotten that last promotion to full command rank. Be that as it may, she lives on her pension in this warehouse, a property inherited from an uncle.

"What in God's name's happened to you?" Lacey flips off the sound on the game and comes over to the couch. This particular night she's wearing a pair of cut-off jeans and a loose blue shirt that says OFFICIAL ZERO-GEE BOWLING LEAGUE across the back. "You in a fight?"

"No remember," Mulligan mumbles. To his surprise, voice-speaking hurts his mouth. "Thought you knew."

Puzzled, Lacey looks at Nunks, who shrugs, turning his hands palm up. Although his naturally psychic race never developed suitable speech organs for talking aloud, he's learned to mimic a wide range of human and lizzie gestures. For her part, Lacey has learned to ask the correct questions.

"Let's see," she starts out. "You knew Mulligan was in trouble."

Nunks nods yes and taps his skull to indicate that he picked up his friend's pain psionically, then raises a hand to suggest that he wait.

Little brother>tell Lacey. <strong force< {evil} break mind <you scream{there<<way back} <murder/carli/police-friend<.

<Not-remember >how tell?

Try>

With a little groan Mulligan nestles into the cushions and tries to send his memory backward. Immediately he encounters a wall of pain, sheeting through his mind. When he gasps, Nunks hurries over and lays a hand on his forehead, but not even he can block the agony. Mulligan draws back, away from the hidden memory; the pain eases.

<Blood smell<< Nunks says. *Only thing{there<<way back} I feel now> tell, little brother>>*

"There's something, like, blocking my mind," Mulligan says, his voice little more than a whisper. "It hurts when I try to remember. But Nunks think I was doing a police job, a murder, maybe, cause he picked up a blood smell."

"For Chief Bates?"

Police-friend now, Nunks prompts.

"Yeah, must've been." *BUT\ not-friend mine now <not-friend< >not-friend> Just know-police now.*

[surprise] Sorry.

"Well, I can give him a call easy enough. I take it you want to know what happened."

"I'm no sure if I do or not."

Yes, little brother. Must know now, must know>

"I take that back, Lacey. Yeah, sure, course I got to know."

"Okay. Want a drink? I've got some honest-to-God Old Earth whiskey."

"Please, oh jeez, please."

She goes over to the wet bar, a gleaming, spotless thing of gray and royal blue enamel. In the midst of a collection of bottles and glasses, all precisely arranged by size in neat rows, is an electric ice-maker. She rations Mulligan out two small cubes into a glass, then pours a generous amount of whiskey over them. When she hands it to Mulligan, Nunks shakes his head in sour disapproval.

[*irritation*] *Please big brother, I now feel need to >blunt mind edge.*

[*resignation, mild contempt*]

"You want to get real drunk?" Lacey says.

"To the max. I'll, like, pay you for the booze when I get some bucks."

"No problem. But after that glass, I'm going to pour you the cheap stuff. You won't know the difference anyway."

"Sure. Swell by me."

Mulligan takes a long sip of the whiskey, then sighs in anticipated pleasure. In just a little while and for just a little while, he'll be able turn off the mental "gifts" that have poisoned half his life.

"Hey, Lacey? Who's the kid with the purple hair?"

"Name's Maria. She got beaten by her pimp when she tried to leave his stable. He left her for dead in an alley close by here. Nunks found her and hauled her in."

"Jeez. Poor kid."

[*Rage*] *>Find, beat him> BUT* [*fear*] */police trouble>*

Yes, big brother. There> big police trouble. Pimp pay now big money/ police protection>

Nunks abruptly leaves, striding out of the room and banging the door behind him.

"What's he mad about?" Lacey said.

"We were talking bout the girl, Maria, like how her pimp probably pays off the cops."

"Nunks has a real low opinion of our species sometimes."

"He's usually right. Y'know?"

With a shrug Lacey sits back down at her desk and begins running her fingers over the touch-sensitive toggles sunk into the edge.

"You're going to input what I told you?" Mulligan says.

"Yeah, a murder's always important to the old biostat scheme of things. And I want to cross-file this story of something blocking your mind. I can maybe pull up some explanation for you."

"Guess I want one. Oh, yeah, for sure. Jeez, Lacey, you sure love gossip."

"I never. You know the old joke: you gossip, but I exchange significant data. In this city, pal, the right kind of data means bucks. My stupid pension dunt keep me in the kind of luxury I deserve."

Mulligan has another sip of whiskey, watching as she flips up the pale green screen. A panel in the desktop slides back and her keyboard rises—an old-fashioned, practically museum quality piece of hardware that only she can keep in working condition. Although her comp unit of course operates by voice like everyone else's, Lacey has installed this antique keyboard so she can enter data privately while someone else is in the room with her. After all, Mulligan reflects, any sentient who could access Lacey's comp banks could become a very rich being indeed. Unfortunately for anyone with such a larcenous turn of mind, she's also programmed the unit to respond in some peculiar language. Mulligan suspects that it's her own invention.

"Say, think the news I brought you's good for, like, some breakfast tomorrow?"

"What, you broke again?"

"I'm always broke, y'know."

"You ought to get a regular job. Your civil service needs YOU!"

"Have mercy! I tried that for a while. You no savvy how damn boring it gets, doing past life readings for job applicants. Nobody who wants a desk job ever's got any like interesting karma. I dunt know why they even bother to keep a psychic on the staff. Y'know?"

"If you tried it again, maybe you'd find out."

Mulligan feels a sudden stab of guilt. Here he is, trying to sponge off Lacey after he promised himself that he'd never do it again. He decides that the least he can do is tell her the truth.

"Well, y'know, I no can go back to the civil service. They fired me."

"Oh."

"Yeah, well, I just dint fit in. Like, I mean, that's what they said, though I had to kind of agree with them."

"Let's see, translated that means you were always late and always a mess, and you talked back to your supervisor."

"Jeez, if you'd've known her you would've talked back too. She was, like, one of those psychic donnas who wear gauzy scarves and dresses with flowing sleeves and sort of sweep around real mysteriously while they talk about Other Realms and their Sensitivity and Talents—all with capital letters, y'know?"

"Yeah, I savvy." Lacey favors him with a smile. "But hell, when I was in the Fleet I had lots of superior officers that I no could stand. You just follow your orders and ignore the bastards best you can."

"You got a military mind. I dunt."

"We will now award Señor Mulligan the prize for best understatement of the year."

"Ah, lay off! But I really did, like, try at that damned job."

Lacey raises a skeptical eyebrow, then gets to work. Although he can't see the keyboard, Mulligan can see her face, her mouth slack, her eyes half-shut, as if she's daydreaming about an absent lover, or perhaps communing with a very much present one while she works the keys. At times he hates her comp unit.

"Okay," she says at last. "Now I'm going to call the chief himself and feed his data right into the file."

"Always efficient, that's you. Say, before I drink myself blind, there's, like, something I want to ask you. I no want to forget it."

"Sure. Fire away."

"That deserter. It's safe to have him here?"

"You and Nunks both vetted him, told me he was legit."

"I no mean that, I mean if that old Alliance catches you harboring him, they'll pull every string they can to get their hands on you. Y'know? Then it'll be, like, the old fatal injection and the recycling lab. For sure."

"Yeah, I know, I know. I'm arranging fake papers to get him off-world with the merchant marine."

"Jeezchrist! That's how many thousand bucks?"

"Oh, I'm just calling in a few favors. Listen, the pobrito panchito in his innocent way has already repaid me about six times over. Here I am, a brother officer though ex, right? So he likes to sit and talk to me, babbling everything in his little head about the Alliance fleet's disposition and their new weaponry and all the special deep space maneuvers he saw when he was in training. I can sell each byte of that about three ways."

"Jeez! Nunks and I agreed that the kid's, like, too dumb to lie, so it must all be straight dope."

"You bet. Basically the Alliance is better off without a software-deficient dude like him. He'll do okay in the merchant service."

"What made him jump ship, anyway?"

"One flogging too many. His captain sounds like a sadistic bastard, and that's no way to run a goddamn navy anyway, flogging personnel."

"You know, like, if worse ever comes to worst, I think I'd like rather get conquered by the Cons than the 'Lies. Y'know?"

"Dunt say it aloud! But yeah, you got a point."

"Yeah, glad to know he's all right," Bates says, but his image on the screen looks suspiciously indifferent to Mulligan's state of health. "It scared the holy crap out of me, Lacey. Thought he was going to die on me. Did Nunks figure out what Mulligan did wrong?"

"Fraid not, but he's working on it."

"Let me know if he does. It's maybe relevant."

"Will do. Hasta la vista."

As Lacey powers out of the tie-in, Mulligan holds out his empty glass with a small piteous moan. She gets him a refill, makes a drink for herself, then stands up to sip it and watch him as he gulps whiskey like a greedy child.

"Nunks was right. There was a murder, a carli, and you were walking by at the time. Bates asked you to help, and boom! Something blew your circuits good and proper."

"I hate it when you talk about my mind that way, like circuits and shit. It's flesh and blood, y'know, not wiring."

"Ah, it's all the same principle."

"No! Wish it was. Then I no would be a damn psychic."

"Say, man, a lot of people'd give their eyeteeth to have the talent you do."

"Then they're like loco or stupid or both. Ah jeez, Lacey, all I ever wanted was to play ball. Y'know? For chrissakes, I could've been in the major leagues."

"Yeah, I savvy. It sure was a tough break, pal."

Mulligan looks away with tears in his eyes while Lacey

hopes that he isn't going to tell her the story yet again. Sometimes when he's in these beery moods he seems to have a real need to repeat it, like picking at a scab or biting on a sore tooth. When Mulligan was in high school he was the star of his baseball team, confidently expected to go to the big leagues as soon as he graduated. Then, as the hormone changes of adolescence began to settle down around eighteen, all his latent psionic talents surfaced. Although he did his best to hide them, some of his classmates reported him to the proper authorities, and he was corralled, sent to the National Psionics Institute for testing, registered, and branded. That was the end of his chance at pro ball. Even though Mulligan has absolutely no psychokinetic ability, no hope in hell, in short, of influencing the movement of a baseball, he would have always been under suspicion of somehow changing the course of play. No team wanted to spend money drafting him only to have a public outcry make the league officially prohibit psionic players the way it prohibits bionic ones.

"It's no fair," he says, his voice thick. "I mean, jeez, even if I could have, like, read the pitcher's mind and seen he was going to throw a curve, like, I'd still have to hit it, y'know. It's no fair."

"Well, yeah."

"Like, it ruined my life." He has a long gulp of whiskey. "Whole damn thing ruined my life. Y'know? Here I am, stuck playing semi-pro ball for a lousy five bucks a game when I could've been in the majors."

"That team you were telling me about—it took you on?"

"Yeah. Dint I tell you? They no care about my goddamned mind, they need a shortstop so bad. Y'know? Lousy semi-pro ball. Mac's Discount City Appliances Marauders, and I could've been in, like, the majors."

Lacey goes tense, afraid that he's going to cry. She never knows how to deal with someone in tears. After a minute, though, he merely sighs and mutters something under his breath.

"You're real articulate tonight."

"I just want to be like left alone." His voice is a bare mumble.

Out of sympathy, not pique, Lacey does just that. First she gets the bottle of local whiskey and puts it where he can reach it, then goes back to her desk and armchair. Up on the viewer, the Polar City Bears are thrashing the New Savannah Braves eight to two in the seventh inning. Since the Bears have the best bullpen in the Interplanetary League and the Braves one of the worst, she decides there's no use in watching further carnage and switches it off.

Soon, she knows from experience, Mulligan will drink himself into a stupor. Since in the meantime he can be safely ignored, she switches her comp unit over to voice op, but she doesn't quite trust Mulligan enough to speak in standard Merrkan where he can overhear. Instead she uses Kangolan, a language so obscure that only about two million sentients in the Mapped Sector even know it exists and only about five hundred thousand of those actually speak it. Lacey learned it during a tour of duty spent as comp officer on a frigate guarding against pirates at a hyperspace entry nexus that happened to be near the planet. She had plenty of time to study local customs because in the entire five years only two pirate vessels ever appeared, and one of them turned tail and ran as soon as its sensors picked up the frigate.

"I am awake and operating." Buddy's voice is a pleasant if somewhat brisk tenor, Lacey's own programming, overriding the seductive female voice provided by the factory.

"I am pleased to hear it, Buddy. Did you dream of the new data I gave you while you were in silent mode?"

"I did. It is incomplete in its current state."

"I know. I am hoping to access more sources as time goes along. File it and cross-reference with all murders in Polar City during the last year period. Then search and collate any instances of psychics being unable to access their memory banks because of pain. Both searches in the first extension only for now."

The unit makes a soft sound which Lacey always describes as "humming under his breath."

"I am finished. The cross-reference command is complete. The search and collate command is incomplete. I have no more examples of such instances in my current files. Is it possible that the Mulligan unit is providing false data?"

"It is impossible. Why do you think the data would be false?"

"The Mulligan unit is unsatisfactory."

"In what way?"

"In every way. It is messy, ill-regulated, and prone to neural breakdowns."

"Say 'he,' Buddy, not 'it.' Mulligan is a human being."

"If my programmer insists, I will categorize him so."

"I do insist. As for the neural breakdowns, the proper term for that is intoxication or getting drunk."

"Only a previous neural breakdown would lead the unit to desire to drink himself to stupefaction."

"Well, maybe, but still, he's also useful, even if what you say about him is true."

"If my programmer says so, I will define him as useful."

"Do it, yeah."

"Command executed. Mulligan unit is redefined as a useful human being. Next command?"

"Go into waiting mode while I think about this."

Leaving the unit on, Lacey gets up and strolls over to the wet bar to make herself another drink. Mulligan has already passed out, his empty glass half-overturned in his fingers, a thin trickle of watery whiskey staining his shirt. When she plucks the glass away, he sighs in his sleep and squirms like a restless child. Most of the turquoise hair coloring has ended up on his face in long streaks, letting the normal straw color of his hair show through. She gets a damp towel from the sink and wipes his face, but even though the water's cold, he stays asleep, merely squirms again and sighs.

"Poor bastard," Lacey remarks. "He's just lucky he was born in the Republic."

"My data banks tell me that psychics are killed in worlds dominated by the Alliance."

"Usually as children, yeah. They're not exactly welcomed with open arms by the Cons, either."

"Checking that assumption. I have found the file. In the Confederation those with psionic talents are considered mentally ill and are confined in comfortable if restricted nursing homes until those talents are destroyed by psychotropic drugs."

"As I say, he was lucky to be born here. Though, I don't know, Buddy. Mulligan keeps saying he would have been happier with a mind-wipe."

"The Mulligan unit is inherently unstable. No rational intelligence desires the loss of some area of its prime programming."

"I wish you'd stop insulting Mulligan. He's my friend."

Buddy hums for a brief moment.

"I have recalled the definition of that term. Why do you care about his inherent welfare above and beyond his usefulness to you?"

"Come off it! You know damn well that understanding feelings like friendship has been built right into your CPU. Who do you think you are, Mr. Spock?"

"No. I am not in the habit of defining my personality module in terms of characters from ancient literature."

"You just watch it, pal, or I'll flip you into automode so fast—"

The monitor screen flashes half a dozen colors, then subsides to its normal dark gray.

"I am ready to complete another command if my programmer so wishes."

"That's better, yeah. Okay. Define relevant memory banks for carli burial customs and laws governing murder, the current political situation in Polar City, past murders, so on and so forth; search said banks and collate all information to the fourth degree of extension relevant to first the murder, second what happened to Mulligan when he attempted to perform his reading. Print the collation."

"Do I understand this implied directive? Relevant memory banks are to be defined thus: not only those in my immediate possession, but also those that I can access using assorted passwords and entry codes."

"You are correct. When accessing banks beyond those that belong to us, use a false ID."

"That was understood, programmer."

While Buddy hacks, Lacey paces restlessly around the room and wonders just why she does put up with Mulligan. He drops in at all hours of the day or night to interrupt her work; he drinks large quantities of her alcohol and barely says a thank you; he's always scrounging meals or turning up without a place to sleep for the night; he has even on occasion borrowed money that he's never paid back. She feels sorry for him, she supposes, a psychic fighting against a talent that he never wanted and that has quite literally branded him as a semi-outcast in society. Yet beyond the pity, she has to admit that she genuinely enjoys his company. Mulligan sober can turn any ordinary morning into a party or a trip downtown into an adventure. There have been moments, usually when she's had a couple of drinks herself, when she wonders if she might possibly be fonder of him than simple friendship would explain. For a Blanco, he's a very good-looking man, with his soft full mouth and flat cheekbones. Usually, as she does now, she dismisses such thoughts the second they appear.

"Say, Buddy, check the comm channel listings, will you? If there's another ballgame on, put it on screen. I need a distraction."

"There are no ballgames." Buddy sounds both annoyed and absentminded, as he always does when someone asks him to fulfill one of his multifunction subprograms. "This might interest the programmer."

"This" turns out to be a news special, the President of the Republic standing at her imposing lectern in the bare press room of her residence, her hair hastily swept back into a messy braid and her makeup a little off, too—a carefully calculated effect, no doubt, to convince people that she has rushed away from something crucial in order to read this bland, soothing prepared statement about the murder of a member of the Confederation Embassy. His name, or rather his special name of the kind that carlis pick when they are forced to deal with aliens, turns out to be Imbeth ka Gren, roughly translatable as He who Smooths the Way, fitting since he was an undersecretary of protocol. The President also assures everyone that the police are working full time, and with the aid of the Public Bureau of Investigation, too.

"Bet Chief Bates will just love that," Lacey remarks in Merrkan. "A couple of PBI boys hanging around at his elbow."

"Indeed," Buddy says. "The chief has made his views on the Bureau well known in the past."

"And so," the President looks straight into the camera, her large, dark eyes so utterly sincere that Lacey feels like throwing something at the screen. "We're calling on all our fellow citizens to aid the police in this matter. It's super important that we get this here mystery solved just as soon as we can."

"So the Cons don't bomb the hell out of us, she means." Lacey grabs the remote and mutes the sound.

"Do not agitate yourself, programmer. The Alliance would not allow it."

"One of these days, one empire's bound to call the other's bluff over us. Then we'll be well and truly liberated—blown to hell for our own damn good."

"It will not occur over this murder. I estimate that we have at least fourteen point six years left before escalating tensions make confrontation inevitable."

"You are a true comfort and joy."

Since he's been programmed to recognize the subtle voice changes that indicate sarcasm, Buddy merely hums at her. On the screen, the camera zooms in for a shot of the Great Seal of the Republic, a large predatory bird of some sort, with a bunch of leaves clutched in one claw, a stylized space cruiser in the other, and a striped shield across its belly. In a band round the edge is the motto E STELLIS PLURIBUS UNA.

All at once the screen flickers in long bands of ice-blue static. From outside she hears a rumble that rises first to a roar, then a shriek. She gets up and strolls to the window to watch as a shuttle launches from the port and cuts a swath of silver across the lambent sky. She seems to have picked up something of Mulligan's mood, because her eyes fill with tears, just briefly before she wipes them away. Although Mulligan may have had a chance at the majors, she's had something greater taken away: the endless freedom of deep space. Trite images of birds in cages come to her mind; she dismisses them with a stoic act of will and has another swallow of whiskey.

Since carlis, the dominant race of the Confederation, value the visual arts highly, the Cons' embassy is a beautiful building, a graceful half-circle made of pale beige plastocrete scored to look like stone blocks. In the embrace of the crescent are small diamond-shaped flower beds, filled with red and blue blooms native to the carli home planet, and thorn trees pruned and shaved into some semblance of symmetry. On guard by the enormous double door, made of a rich brown wood imported from Sarah, are two humans in stiff gray uniforms. As Chief Bates strolls up, just a bit after midnight, they salute with great precision, then open the door.

Stepping inside the big reception room makes the chief feel twenty degrees cooler. The walls are pale blue-green, the thick carpet a darker shade of the same, and in the center of the room a real fountain murmurs and splashes as it runs over purple tile into an ivory basin. All along the walls are metal sculptures, the carli race's most famous art form—thin twisted plates of gold, silver, oxidized copper, and the occasional jewel or piece of precious stone arranged in amazingly complex patterns, each one a good three meters by two. Bates is sincerely glad that the security of these treasures is someone else's responsibility. Just beyond the fountain stands a heavy desk of imported rosewood, so highly polished that the comp unit is reflected down to the last toggle switch and key.

Sitting at the desk is another human, a young woman, this time, with red-blond hair and green eyes. Although many of the humans that live in the confines of the Confederation (and there are over twenty systems' worth) are white, Bates always finds them different from what he thinks of as "his" white people. The Con lot all seem to have thin lips, cold eyes, and no sense of humor. This young woman is no exception. When he gives her his best reassuring smile she merely looks him over as if making a mental inventory of the pieces of his uniform.

"You must be the Republic policeman."

"I'm the chief of police in Polar City, yeah."

"I have orders to send you straight in." Her tone of voice implies that she thinks this order is a big mistake. "If you'd go through the door on your left?"

The door in question bears a sunken brass plate with both carli and Merrkan lettering, announcing that here officiates the chief secretary of protocol. Since he was hoping to see the ambassador himself, Bates is briefly annoyed; then he remembers that in the carli world no high personage is readily available in any emergency short of total war. That the chief secretary is willing to see him without making him wait for an hour in the lobby bespeaks a great willingness to cooperate. With a quick knock he steps into another huge room, this one decorated in sandy pale browns and tans except for a four-meter-square tapestry that's mostly turquoise on the far wall. The chief secretary's desk is even larger and shinier than the receptionist's. Pacing restlessly in front of it is a golden-furred male carli in the long green robes of the warrior caste. His ear flaps droop at half-mast, indicating a real sadness.

"Your Excellency," Bates says. "Allow me to tender my sincere sympathy for your loss."

"Thank you, sir." His Merrkan is startlingly good, without the slight growls on the r's typical of carlis, and Bates reminds himself that formal speaking is the order of the day. "Ka Gren was developing into a fine officer. My name is Hazorth ka Pral li Frakmo."

"Ka Pral, I am honored. I am Albert Bates."

"Bates, the honor is mine."

They bow, then consider each other warily for a moment. The chief is inclined to like this carli. Since his chosen name means He who Walks Narrow Bridges, the equivalent of the Merrkan phrase He who Splits Hairs, the secretary apparently has a strong sense of humor about his job, and senses of humor among the carli are rare. His ear flaps gradually stiffen to full extension, a sign that he finds Bates reassuring.

"Will you sit and take a drink?" The secretary gestures at a low green divan under the vast tapestry.

Refusing would be rude, so Bates bows and perches gingerly on the edge of the piled cushions while the secretary rings for a servant. A young female carli in a plain gray jumpsuit pops in like clockwork with a crystal decanter and two glasses on a bronze tray. She sets the tray on the waiting stand by the divan, then bows so low her nose almost touches the carpet. When the secretary snaps out a word in their language, she turns and rushes out of the room.

"She is learning," the secretary says approvingly. "When she first arrived, she was slack."

"Ah," Bates says. "Perhaps being so far from her home world was disorienting."

"You know, I never considered that. You may well be right."

The secretary pours out a pale green liquor, hands Bates a glass, then takes the other and sits on the far end of the divan. They each raise their glasses, consider the color, then have a small sip. Bates is profoundly thankful to find the drink sweet and only slightly alcoholic; there are some carli liqueurs that can knock a BetaPic dragon flat on its many-spiked back with a single sip.

"His Excellency has exquisite taste in tapestries," Bates says, with a polite nod toward the turquoise monster. "I would assume that this one was not produced here on our humble and unworthy planet."

"It comes from our homeworld, truly." With a sigh of satisfaction Ka Pral settles himself among the cushions. "It was woven in a most unusual way."

About an hour later the conversation finally drifts toward the reason for Bates's visit. After the chief learns that the murdered carli was just beginning to put together a fine collection of flat-woven rugs in the Old Earth style, Ka Pral remarks that

Ka Gren was missing from the embassy yesterday, that he left on some mysterious errand two hours after sunrise and never returned.

"Since he was off duty, of course I had no complaint, but it was distinctly odd. Like most of our young men, Ka Gren needed a great deal of sleep. Normally he went to bed immediately after his dinner and stayed there until woken for breakfast."

"I see, Your Excellency. Would it be presumptuous of me to ask who was in the habit of waking him?"

"Our head housekeeper, Kaz Trem. Her main comp terminal is programmed to send automatic wake-ups to the auxiliary units in the rooms of our various personnel, but she always waits by the monitor until they've all punched in a response. As I say, our young people sleep very heavily; it is a function, or so I understand, of our being carnivorous. When Ka Gren didn't answer, Kaz Trem went to his room. All the locks are keyed to her palm, except, of course, those in the ambassador's suite and offices. When she opened the door, she saw that Ka Gren's bed had never been slept in, and she came straight to me. We were just discussing what to do when we received your commcall." His ear flaps turn flaccid and droop in grief. "As soon as you said that you had one of our personnel, I was sure it was Ka Gren. He was the only one unaccounted for."

"And of course, your security head came down and identified him. I am both sorry and humiliated to have been the bearer of bad news."

"I share your grief but I wipe clean your humiliation."

"Your Excellency has my humble thanks. I realize that I presume greatly to question you and yours during this time of mourning, but it is necessary that we—"

"We will be glad to answer what we can. Bates, my species is like yours in savoring revenge. I want whoever murdered Ka Gren found and brought to your justice—well, if this sentient can ever be tried in your courts, of course."

Bates hesitates, then finally sees the subtle meaning. Ka Pral is hinting that the murderer may be part of the Alliance Embassy by implying that he, she, or neuter might have diplomatic immunity.

"I am glad to hear it, Your Excellency. Then do you know of any reason at all that young Ka Gren would have gone into town without telling anyone?"

"I *know* nothing, but I do have two speculations. The first is that he might have found somewhere to gamble. As I'm sure you know all too well, our young men are usually fanatically fond of human-style card games. The other speculation is much more complex. One reason that Ka Gren was such a good officer was that he was very zealous, what you humans would call gung-ho, I believe. He always took on duties above his strict obligations. Now, of course, for all of us here in the embassy our prime duty lies in establishing and maintaining good relations with your glorious and admirable Republic."

"Of course."

The carli hesitates, his ears at half-mast as if he's wondering whether or not he was too subtle for the chief. Since Bates isn't quite sure if he's understood the implication or not, he decides to try a subtlety of his own.

"Of course there are other sovereign states that are not so admirable."

"Of course."

Again Ka Pral hesitates. It's obvious that there is something that he wants very badly to make clear without ever having to say it aloud.

"When something dishonorable lies in our midst," Bates says, "it is important that we stay on guard with open eyes."

Ka Pral sighs in profound relief.

"That is very true, Chief Bates, and very beautifully expressed."

So, the kid he was doing some junior-level spying on the 'Lies, was he? That can be dangerous as all hell.

At the door comes the low whistle that conveys the same message to the carlis as a knock does to humans. Ka Pral's ear flaps tighten and furl in annoyance.

"You will excuse my rudeness and that of my staff, Chief Bates?"

"Of course, Your Excellency. I wipe clean any stain of discourtesy."

In a rustle of robes the secretary sweeps across the room and throws open the door. So frightened that she's stammering, the young servant female blurts out a message in their speech. The chief secretary throws both hands out to the side in surprise.

"Chief Bates, we have a new development." With a flick of one hand he sends the girl away and shuts the door. "One of our staff, a cook named Gri Bronno, has disappeared, and one of our skimmers seems to have gone with him."

Bates heaves himself out of the soft cushions and hurries over.

"If you'll just give me a description of the car, Your Excellency, I'll get my men right on that."

Chapter Two

Two hours past sunset Little Joe Walker is hiding his beaten-up old skimmer in the scrub about fifteen kilometers southeast of Polar City. Although he has a couple of keys to go and he hates walking, the road quite simply stops cold on the edge of the tract of land set aside for the planetary rehydration project. Muttering to himself he gets out, locks the cabin, then opens the trunk and takes out a light-sucking cammi cloth, a piece of equipment that civilians are not supposed to have in their possession. Little Joe, however, owns a lot of high-tech things that are supposedly out of the reach of the citizens of Hagar; even though the top brass refuses to admit it, plenty of officers as well as ordinary crewmen in both the Fleet and the Ground Forces use a lot of dope, and they're always willing to trade away any government property that's not nailed down.

Once he's got the cloth lashed over the skimmer, Little Joe backs away from it to consider the effect. When he's about two meters away, the car seems to melt and disappear into the twisted thorn-tree shadows; from four meters, he would swear that there was nothing there. He allows himself a rare smile. Although the cloth cost him a kilo of his best weed, it was obviously worth it, and he makes a mental note to ask Quartermaster's Clerk First Class Ismail Inballah if he can get his hands on a lightweight jacket made of the same stuff—one cut long with a hood. In Little Joe's business such an article of clothing would come in handy.

With the skimmer secure he leaves the roadside and finds a small path, barely wide enough for his massive shoulders, through the tangled chaparral that's the only native vegetation in this part of the planet. Thorn tree and grabber shrub, low creeping dirt vine and the ubiquitous fleshy "grass" that crunches in a disgusting way when you walk on it—they grow twined together in a smothering blanket down the long ravines, dark stripes marking the presence of underground water in Hagar's barren hills. In the tangle live insects, mostly, a few pseudoreptiles, a few flying, warm-blooded creatures, and small rodents that bear such a startling resemblance to Old Earth gray rats that most people simply call them rats and leave the precision of fancy names to the scientists. Although the fossil record shows that the usual profusion of species once lived on Hagar, most died off when the planet lost the greater part of its water to the mysterious cataclysm that devastated it a million years ago. The comparatively few species that survived are thus oddly disparate, seemingly unrelated to each other and the planet's ecology. Only the fossil record can show their proper relationships.

The trail leads along the lip of a vast crater that was a lake bed before the disaster and that will, if the Republic gets its way, be a lake once again and soon. Way out in the middle of the crater under bluish-white maglev floods, Little Joe can see the work crews, cutting away the protective chemical film from huge chunks of comet ice, caught on the fly in orbit and brought down by grav net to melt into the ground or evaporate into the air; the engineers don't care which, just so long as the precious water molecules are back in circulation. After forty-seven years of hard going, the project is beginning to show some results; last winter it actually rained in the polar region for the first time in a million years, give or take a few. Although Little Joe went out with all the other citizens to stand solemnly in the brief drizzle as if they were getting blessed by Allah himself, he felt profoundly uncomfortable the whole time. He was born and raised in Polar City, and water falling from the sky strikes him as both wasteful and somehow frightening, an act against nature.

About half a key onward the trail turns away from the crater and plunges downhill through a particularly rabid ribbon of chaparral to the long, dusty valley that's the site of the original colony on Hagar. Now the extruded foam and slabbed stone structures stand in ruins, some thousand hectares of rubble, augmented by a hundred years' and another thousand hects' worth of dumped junk. As he picks his way downhill, Little Joe can see pinpricks of light moving around in the Rat Yard, as the area's called. Beings of several races, maybe a hundred individuals all told, live out there in huts cobbled together out of old skimmer doors and leftover foam slabs, or dugouts furnished with the leavings of the city nearby. Most of them are crazy; a few are on the run. Before he goes much closer Little Joe checks the laser pistol in his shoulder holster. Although the Ratters know he has a legitimate reason to be there, it pays to be careful in the Yard.

And yet, when it comes the trouble isn't from the crazies in the rubble. He has almost reached the edge of the Yard proper when the sky brightens to a sudden silver; long beams of light sweep past, just barely missing him. All at once he hears the screeching whine of police airspeeders, a pair of them, slicing down from the sky and sweeping the valley. With a really foul oath Little Joe starts running, keeping as low as he can, zigzagging back and forth as he desperately tries to get to the shelter of the Yard. Ahead of him he can hear screaming and howls of rage, the occasional metallic chink as one inhabitant or another heaves an accurate rock at the speeders. He finds himself panting for breath, his chest heaving in great sobs, his legs aching, but on he runs, feeling nothing but desperation— if they want him, they've got him now.

A light beam catches him, hesitates, then sweeps on indifferently; the speeders curve, hover, then race away low to the ground, heading for the far end of the Yard, but as they sweep they fire a long burst of plastic slugs that—theoretically—can only stun, not kill, a sentient. Since Little Joe doesn't trust the theory in the least he puts on one last burst of speed, heading for a two-meter pile of old plastofoam packing material. All at once he feels the ground bounce under his feet. With a yelp he tries to pull back, but it's too late. Rumbling and sliding, the ground caves in under him, dropping him at least three meters down in a long cascade of garbage. Grunting, swearing, he rolls to one side just in time to avoid being hit by the battered remains of an air conditioner.

For some minutes he merely lies there, gasping for breath and feeling for broken bones. Although he's going to have some spectacular bruises, he realizes that he's basically unharmed and gets to his feet. Above him he can see the crackling splendor of Hagar's night sky through a hole whose edge is a good three meters if not more above him. Since Little Joe is exactly two meters tall, that leaves a considerable gap to

be accounted for. He finds his light pen, mercifully unbroken,
switches it on narrow beam, then trains it on the broken lip of
the hole above him. Through the dirt he can see rotting
wooden planking; apparently some sentient roofed over this
pit for shelter a long time ago, then abandoned it.

Moving the narrow beam slowly and steadily, he looks over
the pit, which smells of a hundred different rank things.
Fortunately, there's a lot of rubble lying around. Besides the
air conditioner he finds several thick if shattered plastocrete
slabs, a substantial hard foam carton, and a variety of rocks and
remnants that can be piled up together to give him a way out
of this trap. He decides that a pyramid shape would be the
most stable and searches for a small niche or ledge in the wall
where he can prop the light pen. Down in one corner, behind
a lump of decaying rags, something shiny catches his eye.
When he picks it up, rats scatter and rustle. He shudders.

His find turns out to be a smooth metal box, painted gray,
about twenty by twelve by four centimeters. Embossed on one
side are letters in some strange alphabet; on one narrow end is
a thin slit. Since Little Joe has never seen anything like it, he
slips it into his shirt to keep it out of curiosity as much as
anything. Then he finds a place to set up his pen, on wide
diffusion beam now, and gets to work. The first meter or so is
easy to build out of the slabs and the carton, which he fills with
small bits of rubble for stability. When he stands on it, he can
touch the edge of the pit, but the rotting boards crumble away
as soon as he puts any weight on them. He climbs back down,
picks up the air conditioner, and uses it as a bludgeon to clear
away the cheese-soft rot until at last he finds solid wood.

This hard edge, unfortunately, is now an awkward lean away
from his pile of rubble. He gets down, swearing under his
breath, moves the heap piece by piece into position, then adds
the air conditioner on top. When he climbs back up, he can
feel a nervous sweat running down his back. If he can't get out
of this pit, he might very well starve to death before anyone
finds him—anyone sane, that is. Starving to death might be
better than what some of the crazies would do to him if they
decided to take his presence wrong. Although he can reach the
edge now, his angle is still awkward, and he decides to have
one last look around for something stable to add to the pile. In
the same corner where he found the mysterious box is what
appears to be a damp plastofelt carton. When he picks it up, it

crumbles in his hands with a dry, musty stench like old mushrooms. He lets the remnants drop and steps back, wiping his hands on his jeans in disgust.

"Oh shit! Mama, what's that?!"

The "that" in question is lying on the ground in a pile of silvery ooze or slime that stinks like rancid vinegar. About a meter long, it looks like the leg of a giant insect, chitinous, jointed, ending in a pair of mandiblelike pincers. Just above the pincers is a strap made of some sort of metal, and set into the strap is a circular object that looks a lot like a chronometer. Although Little Joe never went to college, he knows his world well enough to know that the leg, if leg it is, belongs to no known species of sentient in the Republic and its environs. Visions of three-meter-long insect men rise in his mind, nightmares crawling out of the bowels of the planet, old horrors bent on vengeance and a creeping death. In his youth Little Joe was a thoroughgoing fan of the cheapest kinds of holopix horror tales. Then he found them funny; now he's lost his sense of humor.

With a strangled sob he leaps onto the pile of rubble and heaves himself up, catching the edge, dangling there, struggling to get some purchase with his feet on the side of the pit so that he can work his way up and out. His arms are aching; sweat runs into his eyes. He can feel the edge slipping, threatening to crumble under his pain-wracked fingers, and from behind him he hears a rustling, a scraping: chitinous feet maybe, scrabbling upward through the earth. With all his strength he heaves again, managing to pull himself halfway up, head and shoulders into the cool night air, but the edge is giving way, and his aching arms refuse to pull any further. Groaning, half in tears, he falls back. When he looks over his shoulder, he sees the red eyes of rats, bright in the beam from his pen.

Another grab, another heave—and this time something catches his wrists from above. Little Joe screams aloud.

"It's just me, for chrissakes!" Sally's voice, and she sounds amused. "Me and Ibrahim saw you and came to help. Now grab on. Grab on to me, you asshole, not the dumb boards and stuff."

Gasping and choking, Little Joe does as he's told. A tall woman, especially for a Blanca, and hard muscled from long karate workouts, she's kneeling at the edge and reaching down, and she tells him to grasp her arms just above the elbows. This time, when he heaves himself up he comes free of the pit, scrabbles with his feet on the side, and walks himself up in Sally's strong grasp. Behind her, clutching her tight around the calves for stability, is Ibrahim, whose sloppy fat has finally come in handy for something, ballast in this case.

"She-it," Little Joe says. "I mean, she-it, man."

"How the hell did you get in there?" Sally lets him go and sits back to dust off the sleek pleats on the front of her lavender shirt. "The police raid chase you in?"

"The roof gave way, man, when I was running from the greenies. Someone must have lived in there once. Or something."

"We was looking for you," Ibrahim says. "Saw you pop up out of the hole like a sandworm catching bugs. Figured something was real wrong."

"Yeah. Brilliant deduction, man. I mean, like really brilliant."

"We maybe can shove you back in again if we piss you off or something."

"Oh for chrissakes, you two, shut up!" Sally intervenes sharply. "You got the bucks, man?"

"I do. Republic twenties, just like you wanted. Where's the stuff?"

"This way. I got a thermos of coffee, too. You look like you need some."

"May Allah bless you, yeah."

"Thanks. I need a cup myself. Been a gonzo night so far, man. When I was scoring, I saw some dude, this Blanco, taking off his clothes right on the public street! He had another set on underneath, and it looked like he was planning on shoving the first set into this big old public recycler. Gonzo."

Little Joe nods his agreement. Although he considers telling them about the box with the strange writing and the insect leg, in the end he keeps it to himself. He's been dealing dope with Sally Pharis and Ibrahim for three years now, but in Polar City it never pays to tell anyone everything you know, unless, of course, they're planning on paying you for it.

The autopsy report on Imbeth ka Gren is straightforward: the carli was in perfect health; there was no trace of any sort of drug in his system, not so much as a beer; there were no bruises, either, indicating that he was lowered to the ground rather than falling hard. His throat was cut from right to left by a very strong being (or, one might suppose if one had an extremely farfetched turn of mind, an Alliance warbot) who never wavered: the cut was straight and true. Since Bates could figure out most of this simply by looking at the corpse, he clears the comp screen in disgust and brings up the report from the admissions tech at the morgue. Although most of the dead sentient's possessions are perfectly ordinary, one detail stands out: he was carrying over a thousand bucks in Republic cash, shoved in a rather cavalier wad into an inner pocket of his robes. Since the Republic is the only place in the Mapped Sector where cash is legal, most citizens of other jurisdictions treat it carelessly, as if they refuse to believe that once lost or stolen it's gone, unlike the electronic credits they're used to.

Bates considers briefly Ka Pral's two speculations of gambling and espionage. The cash would fit either, but the chief is inclined to agree with Ka Pral's hints and consider the cash a payoff for some informant. Since the money is now in a sealed envelope down at the morgue, it seems obvious that Ka Gren was killed before he could connect with his contact, probably on the way to their meeting place. A line drawn from the Con Embassy through the site of the murder points like an arrow straight into the worst part of Porttown. Bates sighs; he should have known, he supposes. As he clears comp, he finds himself thinking of A to Z Enterprises and Lacey, who always seems to know everything there is to be known about the action there in the mostly white ghetto. Out of simple pride, he's determined to find out what he can on his own before he breaks down and goes to see her. He needs an undercover cop in the area fast.

As he reaches for the comm unit, he hesitates, wondering whom he's calling. Although his logical choice is the Vice Squad, since they know Porttown very well indeed, the entire unit is corrupt beyond his ability to clean it up—political appointees, mostly, rewarded by the higher-ups for sleazy favors with a chance to make an equally sleazy buck. When Bates was being hired for this job, the police commissioner made it clear in the very first interview that the Vice Squad was a department independent of his control. Then he remembers the special communication he received from the President's office, and he smiles in gentle delight. So the PBI boys are supposed to have a hand in this case, are they? Fine. Let them hit Porttown and try to find out who was selling Ka Gren data valuable enough to be worth a sentient's life.

This time of night Kelly's Bar and Grill is just beginning to turn lively. Right on the edge of Porttown proper, it gets a mixed crowd: the more prosperous Porters on the one hand and on the other respectable black and lizzie businesspersons who enjoy both a touch of slumming and Kelly's undeniably good food. In one half of the double room is the restaurant, rather nicely done with real cotton cloths and napkins on the tables and a wraparound mural of asteroid belt yacht racing on the walls; the other is dominated by the bar, an expensive production of plastocrete hand-textured to look like wood. Kelly himself is a stout man frozen by rejuv at around thirty with just a trace of gray in the temples of his dark hair. As usual he's pacing nervously around, adjusting tablecloths and napkins in the grill, glaring at the servobots behind the bar as if they could somehow break out of their programming, stopping to flick a bit of dust off the chewing spice dispenser here or to straighten a holo on the wall there.

At the bar are a scattering of people Kelly's never seen before—drop-ins, as he calls them—but most of the patrons are regulars, including a pair of underassistant something-or-others from the In-system Revenue Service, each with their data-comps locked to their belts in a somewhat ostentatious manner. Like all of Kelly's regulars, they are devoted to baseball, even the semi-pro teams of the Park and Rec League.

"Hey Kelly," Nkrumba says. "I hear Mac's Marauders just signed Jack Mulligan."

"Jeez, you had to say it, dint you?" Kelly says, grinning to cover his very real disappointment. "I dint know he was available, or I would've gotten him for my team."

"I hear he's a psychic. Maybe you can protest."

"Naw, who cares? So what if he reads the damn ball two seconds ahead? Still got to catch it, doesn't he? Besides, you could look at it this way, it's kind of a handicap, seeing what's going to happen. You've got to keep your eye on the ball right now, not be thinking ahead."

"You're right about that. Besides, I sure do like to watch him play. He's real good for a Blanco, real good."

Kelly's smile turns thin. In his opinion Mulligan is as good a shortstop as any black player, but since he wants to keep the business of the ruling class, he declines to say so aloud. One of the drop-ins turns idly to listen, a Blanco and blond, about medium height but showing off his muscles in a sleek maroon jumpsuit; a spacer, probably, Kelly thinks.

"Scuse, but what team just signed Jack?"

"Mac's Discount City Appliances Marauders." Kelly rolls off the full name of his chief rivals in the Park and Rec League with a certain sourness. "Bastard. Mac, I mean, not Mulligan."

"Far out." The stranger nods to himself. "When are they going to play next?"

"Season no start for a week, pal. Where you been?"

"Out on the Rock Belt." The stranger flashes him a grin, a spacer, sure enough. "Next week, huh?"

"Yeah, on Fiveday. We play'em, my Big Shots, that is. Should be a good game."

"Swell. I'll try to make it." He looks away with a smile. "I kind of know Mulligan. Be good to see him again, if I no catch up with him before that, anyway."

"He's always worth watching," Nkrumba says. "Should've been in the majors, poor panchito. But if we're talking white shortstops, there's never going to be nobody like Wally Davies of the old Republican League."

Somewhere in the long argument that follows, the stranger in the jumpsuit pays his bill and slips away, leaving a slight unease in Kelly's mind. Later he remembers what bothered him about the fellow; on his left sleeve were some stains that looked like spilled beer, maybe, or coffee. Since Kelly values cleanliness second only to a good slider, he shakes his head in annoyance. Damn spacers—they're always slobs, and this one's giving white folks a bad name, too.

Since everyone in the less respectable parts of Polar City knows that Lacey is always willing to pay for interesting data, she's not surprised when Little Joe Walker turns up at the warehouse with the remark that he's had something real peculiar happen to him. By then, round about midnight, Mulligan has managed to roll off the couch and work his way in a fit of bad dreams into the corner; Lacey considers waking him up and making him go into another room, but since Little Joe is willing to ignore him she decides to leave him there, curled around the pillow in his arms with his head at a twist-neck angle like a sleeping cat. She can tell from the fast and choppy way he talks that Little Joe is sincerely upset, and once she's heard the story, she agrees that *peculiar* is one of the better words for it.

"But c'mon, man." Lacey leans back in her chair and swings her feet up onto her desk. "If you thought something was going to come out of the earth after you, you must've had some reason. You're no the kind of dude who just gives in to fantasies."

"Gracias." He sounds sincerely grateful. "I was beginning to wonder about myself, down there."

"Ah man, anyone would get creeped out, stuck in a hole with the federales buzzing round and part of a corpse—well, I guess it qualifies as a corpse, if it was wearing a chrono or something like that. But come on, think. Try and see it all again."

Little Joe bites into an apple and settles himself on the sofa while he considers the problem. With the keyboard in her lap she punches up input and opens a new file for Little Joe's story. Buddy flashes her an on-screen message.

"We are remaining silent? Is there a sentient in the room?"

"Yes. He is a friend, but not a completely trustworthy friend."

"Understood. Ready for input."

While Little Joe thinks, she types in half a page of data, a bare description of his adventure up to his panic-stricken attempts to get out of the pit.

"Got it! You're right, Lacey. Right by the leg, y'know? The dirt was all soft, like maybe it'd been dug up and then smoothed down again."

"Thought so."

"Look. I found this gonzo thing out there, too."

When he hands over the box, Lacey studies it for a long time, but the markings mean nothing to her. She slides it into the slot in her desk that connects with Buddy's visual sensors, then hits the keyboard.

"Define embossed characters as meaningful writing. Search, identify, and translate. Define function of artifact."

For a long moment Buddy hums and whistles.

"Commands impossible. I have no data with which to obey."

"None, Buddy?"

"Not one byte, programmer. I can make the following logical deductions. This artifact is alien. It comes from an advanced technology, but one that is still using silicon chips as part of its comptech. Its owner is of a race previously unknown to us. It—"

"That's enough. I can make such deductions on my own. Please go into waiting mode. I have to do some more dealing with the sentient in the room."

During all this Little Joe is watching her with an anticipatory greed.

"Kind of interesting, huh?" he says.

"Kind of. What do you want for it?"

"Depends on what it is."

"Buddy no can tell us a damn thing."

"Oh." Little Joe looks briefly worried. "Uh, you think this thing is dangerous?"

"I no trust it, no."

"Neither do I. Look, Lacey, everyone knows you play straight. Can I like leave it with you on credit? I mean, you pay me for it if you want it when you figure out what it is."

"That way if it blows up it'll be in my face, not yours, right?"

"Hey, I dint mean it that way!"

"Yeah, sure, but I'll keep it anyway. In the meantime, Nunks just bottled some fresh cider."

"Yeah? Say, if I could maybe get a gallon of that for telling you the story . . ."

"Sounds good to me, amigo. And thanks."

Lacey takes him downstairs and pays him off, then comes back up to find Mulligan awake, sitting up in his corner and rubbing his face.

"You okay?"

"I no savvy yet. Jeez, I just had the lousiest rotten dream. Someone was beating me to death, like smashing me up with these big sticks."

"Oh yeah? Who?"

"I no savvy. I no could see'em clear, but they were like weird, with these slug kind of faces, all squishy, and they were wearing gonzo clothes."

"Humans?"

"Two were, but one was a lizzie and like real nasty."

When he looks up she sees that his eyes are red and puffy, and the rest of his face, a peculiar sallow color.

"You want to take a shower?"

"Jeez, can I? I'd, like, really appreciate it. The old sono-cleaner just no is the same, y'know."

"Yeah, you look like you could use some hot water. But I warn you, I got the housekeeping comp set up to measure it out. No long rinses. Okay?"

"Sure. I'll be a good boy."

Alternately yawning and swearing, Mulligan pries himself up off the floor, then merely stands there for a moment, rubbing the back of his neck.

"I got a clean shirt of yours, that one you left here last time you drank yourself blind."

"Thanks. That'll be swell." He looks up with the ready grin that turns his asymmetrical face handsome. "I'm real grateful, y'know."

"Yeah? Well, I guess you're welcome." She stifles the answering smile she feels threatening to bloom. "You've been here often enough to find yourself a clean towel."

While Mulligan is taking his shower, she has Buddy do an optiscan on the box and print out a drawing of the mysterious characters. There are six of them in all: a thickly drawn right angle intersecting a thin half-circle; another with the right angle perched by its point on top of the half-circle; then one formed of two elaborate squiggles like three-headed snakes mating; the same two squiggles separated by a few millimeters; and a final pair, two squared-off spirals winding in opposite directions.

"Three pairs, huh? I wonder if they signify off and on, or stop and go."

"A reasonable guess, programmer. They are also simple symbols."

"Right. So easy a hatchling could use it. Maybe. At any rate, some sentient with a pair of pincers on the end of each arm could push on them easy enough. Or they just could be a name. Big Buzz's patented chitin polisher." She puts it away in the top drawer of the desk. "Put a lock on this drawer, Buddy."

"Command completed. Force field on. Do you think this box is a valuable object?"

"I don't know. Better safe than sorry, that's all."

The feel of hot water and real soap is so luxurious that it wipes Mulligan's hangover away. To Mulligan, his mind is a place, as concrete and solid as the streets of Polar City, though quite a bit larger. Using any mental ability, ordinary memory, say, as well as his psionic talents, involves walking to the right place in his mind and using the tools he finds there. To read a person's past life, for instance, he always pictures himself walking down a long dark corridor to a door marked ARCHIVES. Inside the room are millions of data cubes, but he only has to think of the person whose reading he's doing to have the correct cube appear in his hand. He can then sit down at a viewer and insert the cube, but he sees nothing so prosaic as words on the screen. At that point, the untrained part of his talent takes over, and he finds himself watching events and persons as if in a dream.

So it is with the hangover. He experiences pain as a solid thing in his mind, a long sliver of glass, say, and when he gains control of such a pain, he feels as if he's physically picked it up and pulled it out. (Unfortunately the trick is sometimes beyond him; the strength of his talents seems to wax and wane by some mysterious law of its own.) This morning he saw the hangover as a lot of garbage floating around his mind, and the shower has—to him quite literally—washed it all down the drain along with the last remnants of the turquoise hair color. In relief he's whistling to himself as he borrows Lacey's brush and combs out his shaggy hair, as pale as dead grass and just as wild with neither color wax nor pomade in it. Without their contact lenses his eyes are gray. Like most Blanco men, he long ago had the hair on his face permanently removed. Reluctantly he puts his dirty shorts back on (he never has the money to buy underwear) and wanders into Lacey's bedroom to find his clean shirt. The room is spartan: a narrow bed, covered with a gray blanket so smoothly tucked in that you could bounce a coin off it, a chest of drawers, also gray, and a closet, the door always neatly shut. The only wall decoration is the saber from her dress uniform, hung casually from a nail. He finds his shirt, this one plain white with a couple of rips in the back, on a hook on the back of the closet door, puts it on, then stands there for a moment looking at her clothes. He gently strokes a couple of her shirts just because they lie next to her skin. With a sigh he turns away, leaving the closet door open behind him and his dirty shirt on the floor.

As he goes down the hall he hears voices in Lacey's room, hers, Buddy's, and then another woman's—Carol. He stops where he is and considers hiding in the bathroom until she's gone, but since Carol is Lacey's best friend—they served in the Fleet together—she's likely to stay for hours, and the bathroom is very small. Bracing himself he walks on, striding into the room as if he had every right to be there. Since she is still wearing her pale blue medic's pantsuit, Carol must have come straight from work, and she sprawls on the couch as if she's tired. She's a tall woman, strong enough to turn a recalcitrant patient over by force if she has to, and her black hair falls to her shoulders in a cascade of dreadlocks and beads around her dark brown face. She glances at Mulligan with profound disgust, as if he were a new species of intestinal parasite.

"Hanging round here again, are you? It must be time for dinner."

Mulligan forces out a weak smile and sits down on the floor in the corner near Lacey's desk. He suddenly realizes that he's just acted like a pet dog, but it's too late to move because Carol has also picked up the resemblance.

"Jeez, Lacey, if you want a puppy I can buy you one for your birthday."

"Ah, lay off him, will you!" But Lacey is smiling at the joke as she turns his way. "How's your hangover?"

"Gone," he snaps. He doesn't want his drinking discussed in front of Carol's big ears. "I no got that hungover anyway. I'll run a couple of kilometers later and feel fine."

"Good. After dinner you're coming with us to the Rat Yard."

"Where?! Are you like out of your mind?"

"Nah. Oh yeah, I forgot. You dint hear Little Joe's story yet. Listen up. This could be real important."

The long night is already stretching toward dawn when Sally Pharis reaches her usual stand, a very expensive bar not too far from Civic Center. Already the worknight is winding down; pols and business executives are drifting in for a quick drink and a last important conversation before heading home. Near the back, in a tasteful gray silk mini-dress and thigh-high black boots, Sally perches on a barstool, sips mineral water, and watches Ibrahim pouring drinks for a class of men and women who would be insulted to be served by a machine. Her regular customers (and those they recommend) know that this is one of the places they can find her if they're interested in the special kind of excitements Sally can provide. In the vast mirror behind the bar she can just see her reflection through the ranks of bottles and siphons and cranes her neck to get a good view of her new hairdo: a sleek roll just lightly frosted with royal blue highlights on top of her natural blond. Unlike many Blancas in her line of work, she's made no effort to darken her skin or dye her hair black; she's found that paleness has its own exotic appeal to a certain kind of man.

The usual crowd dresses conservatively, gray or dark blue knee-length shorts, precisely pleated or creased, crisp white or light blue shirts of the sort that button up the front rather than pull over. Here and there she even sees an older sentient stubbornly wearing a vest or a necktie in spite of the summer weather. The nicely muscled blond Blanco in the maroon jumpsuit, therefore, strikes a discordant note the minute he strolls through the revolving glass door. Sally watches with a certain anxiety as Ibrahim waves him over for a small lecture. The fellow looks like a spacer, and drunken spacers have been known to trash high-class bars in simple fits of pique at being ordered to leave them. After a few words, though, Ibrahim relaxes, even smiles, as the spacer orders a glass of water and stands back out of the way in a dark corner. Apparently he's sober enough to play by the rules.

Sally finds herself wondering about him, simply because he has such a good body so well displayed by his clothes. He also looks very vaguely familiar, on the order of someone met once a long time ago. He glances idly around the bar, his eyes pausing often on a young woman, then looks her way—and keeps looking with a wondering sort of tilt to his head. Ibrahim talks to him briefly, then hurries down to her.

"Hey, got you a john."

"The spacer? You're kidding."

"Nah. He's just back from the Rock Belt, and he got bucks. About six months' worth of pay, I bet. That's the usual, anyway."

"Okay. He might be a fun change. He got quite a body."

When Ibrahim looks hurt, she pats his hand.

"Nothing personal, gordito. You've got other kinds of things to offer."

She takes her handbag and, with her eyes cast down and a demure little smile, walks over to the spacer, who watches her the whole way down.

* * *

The police staff hypnotist, Linda Jefferson, is a middle-aged Blanca, a bit thick around the middle, who wears her adamantly dyed red hair up in a towering chignon held together with hair spray—the better to gain her subjects' attention, maybe, Chief Bates thinks to himself. In her dimly lit office she sits on a straight-backed chair in front of Corporal Ward, who lounges comfortably on a sofa. Soft music, a featureless whisper of synthesized strings, blocks any noise from the hall. Bates turns on a three-dee recorder and takes a chair to one side of them as she pulls a crystal droplet on a gold chain from the shirt pocket of her uniform.

"Okay, Chief, dunt you look at the focus crystal, or you'll end up going under with him. Ward, did you sign the official release already?"

"Sure. This is only a memory aid, anyway." He turns to the chief. "I know I must've looked at that woman on the plaza, but I sure no can remember anything about her."

"That's what I'm here for." Linda's voice is soothing, like a favorite aunt who's offering to intercede with his parents on some sore issue. "You just relax now, Corporal; sit back and look at the spinning crystal."

In a few minutes Ward is completely under. Except for a certain slackness to his mouth and eyes, and a certain mechanical quality to his voice, he seems completely awake as Jefferson slowly, one step at a time, takes him back to the moment when he was leaning against the library wall and hearing footsteps made by high-heeled boots slap across the plaza.

"It's still nice and cool," he says in an oddly prim voice. "Nothing's happening yet. Oh, the lights are going on now. Yeah, there she is, and she's sure in a hurry."

"What does she look like, Corporal? Can you see her?"

"Yeah, she's tall and looks like she works out a lot. She's wearing blue jeans and a gray blouse—no, maybe it's lavender, I forgot about the arc lights—but it's got folds all down the front. And high-heeled boots. Wait—I know her. It's Sally Pharis. I arrested her once. The case never came to trial because—"

"It no that case that matters, amigo." Jefferson's voice is slower, softer than before, like syrup across a cold plate. "You sure it's Sally? The light's no very good, y'know. You've got to be sure—real sure."

Ward's face screws up in exaggerated concentration.

"Well, I'm no courtworthy sure. But it sure as hell looks like Sally."

"That's enough to go on for now," Bates breaks in. "We'll haul her in and have a little chat with her. Bring him round, will you? He's taking the sergeant's exam in a couple of hours."

Once Ward is on his way to the cafeteria in the police station for some dinner and a little last-minute cramming, Bates takes the tape of the hypno session down to Data to check it in. The excited clerk has some news for him: the team that was scouring the area has found, about ten blocks from the murder site, a single man's or male lizzie's brown boot with a splash of carli blood across one toe.

"Is the lab done analyzing it yet?"

"Nah, Chief. They just brought it in."

"You route the results up to my comp as soon as you get'em."

"Yessir. No problem"

Bates returns to his office, a stuffy cubicle on the third floor that sports three chairs, a comp desk, and a set of storage shelves crammed with data cubes, paper files, and holograms from old cases. A privilege of his high rank, a water cooler stands in one corner. Bates pours himself a tall glass of imported spring water and sits down, leaning back in the swivel chair and contemplating the view out the long windows. Between two tall, pale green buildings the plaza spreads out, bright and bustling under the crackling, pulsing sky. He suspects that he's in for a long day of it, but then, he's used to working till noon, catching a siesta in the worst of the afternoon's heat, and getting back on the job by an hour after sunset. Ever since his wife left him, just eight months ago now, he's had nothing to go home to. For a few minutes he sits there, wondering whatever possessed him to take her to a backward planet like Hagar that lacks all the automated luxury she was used to. How in hell did he ever think it was going to work? After twenty years he should have known that if Leona was missing one thing, it was the pioneer spirit. With a shake of his head he shoves the grief away and turns to the problem of Sally Pharis.

Although he's as sure as he can be without hard evidence

that she's a small-time dealer in Sarahian weed as well as being a high-priced call girl, he finds it impossible to believe that she had anything to do with the murder of Imbeth ka Gren. Sally has always struck him as entirely too prudent to be involved in any sort of violent crime. Most likely she—if indeed the woman Ward saw was Sally—was down on the plaza on some business of her own. The trouble is that since that business was most likely illegal, she will probably deny that she was there at all, even though she might have inadvertently seen or heard something valuable to the investigation.

Bates gets on the comm and puts out the order to bring her in, then checks with the Air Unit dispatcher to see if the sweep of the Rat Yard turned up the embassy's missing cook. When he comes on screen the AU man refuses to look him in the eye.

"All right!" Bates snarls. "How did you fuck up this time?"

"Well, uh, Chief, we got the carli for you."

"That's the good news, yeah. Go on. What's the bad?"

"He's dead."

"Crap. How?"

"Well, the speeders picked him up heading out of the Rat Yard, and they followed, ordering him to pull over both with the lights and the loudspeakers, but he hit the power. So they—"

"Wait. Did they bullhorn him in carli or just in Merrkan?"

"Carli, course. Jeez, Chief, the right tapes are standard issue. So anyway, they chased him, and I'm afraid he no was much of a driver. His skimmer hit some rubble or something and bounced over the edge of the rehydration crater."

"Crap. He was already dead when they reached him?"

"Broken neck, yeah."

Although a broken neck is a perfectly logical result of a fall of three hundred meters in a runaway skimmer, Bates is troubled. The other carli died of a neck wound, too.

"Is he at the morgue?"

"Yes sir." The AU man looks at his chrono. "Oh yeah, they must've gotten him there by now."

"Think I'll go take a look. You tell your hell-for-leather flyboys that I want a full formal report on this incident. I mean I want to know if they picked their damned noses. Get it?"

"Yes sir!"

With a growl Bates punches out of comm. He is not looking forward to telling Ka Pral that another member of his staff is dead, especially since taking a job from someone in the carli world is tantamount to being adopted into his family. Although Ka Pral is of a high caste and Gri Bronno was of a low, they would both consider themselves the ambassador's sons and thus brothers in a very real way. Bates decides that he'll postpone that grim duty until he's had a full report on the corpse. Whether it's intuition or just long experience, he finds something very fishy about Gri Bronno's accidental death.

Carol's bright red van is really a traveling clinic, crammed with diagnostic equipment, basic drugs and supplies, data cubes for the ignorant on every subject from birth control to Sarahian fungus infections, a big cooler of purified water, and even a small birthvironment in case she gets caught delivering a premature baby or presiding over the hatching of a sickly lizlet. Even though space is at a premium, Lacey manages to wedge Mulligan and a pair of suncloaks in the back between the medicomp and stacked boxes of synthiskin, then clears a pile of patient records and a bag of mysterious vials off the passenger seat so that she can sit next to Carol.

"Why are we taking Mulligan?" Carol seems indifferent to whether he can hear her or not.

"A psychic might come in handy, that's why. Look, you sure you want to help me with this? It might be real dangerous."

"Hey, it'd be a helluva lot worse for you guys to go out there alone."

Lacey knows she's right, which is, of course, the reason she asked Carol to take them; she merely feels that she should give her friend the chance to back out if she wants to. Even though Carol is the only doctor in Polar City who'll go anywhere near the Rat Yard—she actually drives out there once a week to treat whoever needs her—it took her months to gain the Ratters' confidence, and she at times doubts that she has it even now. Except for those few denizens of the Yard who are on the run and thus afraid only of being arrested, most Ratters live in terror that they'll be dragged back to a hospital and drugged into obedient passivity with psychotropes. All it would take would be one paranoid soul with a knife to bring her medical career to an abrupt end.

When Carol starts up the skimmervan, it jounces into the air and takes off at an alarming speed as she squeals it around the corner and settles in over D Street. In the back Mulligan yelps once; Lacey skews around to find him rubbing his forehead.

"You okay?" She has to yell over the noise of the engine.

"Yeah, considering something just, like, bounced off my skull."

"Be careful back there, will you?" Carol calls out. "That stuff is expensive."

Mulligan makes a face at her behind her back.

Since the sun is beginning to rise, a long process on Hagar since the red giant fills forty-five degrees of arc, Lacey flicks the switch on the dash that controls the polarizer. As the light brightens, the windows will darken in automatic balance. They careen through Porttown, then head out on the southeastern road, deserted except for the occasional freight train roaring along in a mini-hurricane of forced air. Although most skimmers only operate above reasonably smooth surfaces, Carol's van is an off-roader, bought for her by bureaucrats grateful that she'd ease their consciences by doing something about both the Ratters and the poor white trash of Porttown. In about three kilometers she leaves the road and heads straight out through the barren hills.

"We no want to get there too long after sunrise," Carol yells over the grumbling, wheezing engine. "They'll all be asleep."

Down brown hillsides, across the valleys that once were riverbeds, skewing round the beaches of dead lakes, the van whistles along at a good hundred kilometers an hour while Lacey clings to her shoulder harness and wonders if she's going to be airsick, a degrading fate for a veteran of zero-gee battle maneuvers. She doesn't even want to think of how Mulligan is doing, crammed in the back. Since conversation's impossible, Carol sings to herself. "Oh, oh, baby, there ain't no cure, no baby, there ain't no cure, no cure at all, baby, for the Polar City blues"—looping endlessly round in her husky voice.

At last they come screaming along to the rehydration project's mucky red-brown crater, and Carol somewhat reluctantly slows down. The workmen are just going off shift, strolling over to the trucks some meters away from the dirty white ice chunks. As the red van swings by, some of them look up and wave. Lacey assumes that Carol must be well known out here. Her driving style is certainly distinctive enough. About a kilometer past the work station, at the very lip of the crater, is a little clot of vehicles, a pair of police airspeeders, a big crane, and a tow-skimmer. Carol slows down to a bare crawl so they can gawk as they pass. The crane is bringing up a blue-green skimmer with its front smashed in.

"Hey, that's a Con Embassy car!" Lacey says.

"Sure thing. Look, they probably got the victim out hours ago, but I've got to stop and make sure."

"Okay by me."

Carol lurches the van around, flings it into a patch of shade under a pair of thorn trees, and lets it drop to the ground. In the back Mulligan swears violently.

"Ah, you're such a weakling!" Carol says with a grin. "Know what you need? A good fitness regimen—long brisk walks, some weightlifting, a solid vegetarian diet, and lots of cold showers. Come see me down at the clinic, and we'll work out the details."

Mulligan's reply does not bear repeating.

Somewhat unsteadily Lacey climbs out, then lingers behind to help Mulligan unwind himself while Carol trots over to the policebeings, two humans and a lizzie, whose pale gray skin looks particularly good with the kelly green uniform. As they stroll over to join her, Mulligan suddenly stiffens, tossing his head back and arching his spine as if his lower back hurt.

"Whatthahell?"

"Someone died in that wreck. I no want to go near it."

"Well, okay. We can wait here."

Carol is already trotting back toward them, shaking her head as sadly as if this anonymous victim had been a patient of long standing.

"Nada. I no can do anything for the poor bastard. A carli, they say, and his body's already in the morgue."

"What happened to the other one?" Mulligan says. "There was two sentients in that car. Even if only one of 'em was like killed, the other must've been hurt pretty bad, y'know."

"Oh yeah?" Suddenly Carol is all serious interest. No matter what she thinks of Mulligan as a person, she respects another professional when she sees one. "The greenies haven't picked up on that. You better tell'em."

"I no go any closer. I no can."

Carol is about to grab his arm and drag him along when the lizzie cop comes over, all squat, stocky six feet of him hurrying along with the shuffling walk of his less-than-limber species. In the hot sun he's almost manic-lively, his long snout creasing in a toothy grin as he holds out his hand, the claws at the tips of his fingers all nicely polished a dark blue.

"Hey, Mulligan, you came along at the right time, huh? What have you got to tell us? I'll make sure you get paid the going rate."

"There was two beings in that car before it went over." Mulligan's voice is very soft, and he looks away with unfocused eyes. "They hated each other. They fought. I no can read no more than that from here, and I no going to try. Last time I did a job for you guys I ended up in Central Emergency."

"Yeah?" The cop's third eyelids, the transparent ones, slip down over his bright yellow eyes, then flicker—a sure sign that he's puzzled. "Well, it's a free planet, huh? I'll get you some bucks for that information, anyway. Two guys, huh? Bet the chief'll be interested in that."

Bates is still at the morgue when Officer Zizzistre's call catches up with him. He listens with great interest to Mulligan's insights, has Zizzistre repeat them so he can record them into his belt comp unit, and then adds a note to himself to get Zizzistre a commendation for quick thinking.

"Only one thing, Izzy. What in hell was Mulligan doing out there, anyway?"

"I no savvy, Chief. He was with Doctor Carol. I guess someone needs a psychic out in the Rat Yard, huh?" He allows himself a small hissy chuckle at his joke. "Oh yeah, and that Lacey woman was with'em."

"Jeez. Now that's really gonzo! Well, no problem of yours, Izzy. Thanks for the good work. Signing off now."

As he leaves the grimly gray morgue building and walks back to his skimmer, Bates is feeling rather smug. His intuition about Gri Bronno is being handsomely confirmed on all sides. The coroner's report is perfectly clear: most of the bruises on the corpse were inflicted after death, not before, which is courtworthy evidence that he was dead long before the skimmer hit the crater bottom. Whoever murdered him, then, is a clumsy amateur, unaware of the most basic forensic techniques. Mulligan's evidence about the fight between two sentients amplifies that bare fact nicely. All at once it occurs to Bates to wonder if the two murders are related after all. Whoever killed Ka Gren was no amateur. On the other hand, the likelihood of there being two random cold-blooded murders of embassy personnel on the same night is improbably low. Two murderers, maybe—but there has to be a connection.

Bates climbs into the skimmer and punches in the coordinates of the embassy. It's time he faced Ka Pral and told him this latest piece of bad news.

Chapter Three

The Great Psionic Mutation, as they call it, happened about two hundred years ago in, as far as historians can tell, the Old Earth nation called California. All through humanity's history a few persons carried the naturally occurring though recessive genes for psionic powers, and here and there the occasional couple who both were carriers got together and produced a child with some degree of talent. Usually these psychics ended up being persecuted by one dominant religion or another in the old days or dismissed as charlatans by scientists in more recent times. Even those who survived rarely developed their talents, because, isolated by fear and long distances as they were, they had no way of pooling their experiences and thus of learning how to control and expand their skills.

At the end of the century called the twentieth in the old dating system, however, California was a densely populated place, settled by immigrants from quite literally all over the planet. As you might expect, with so many gene pools to draw from the pairing of recessive genes became more and more common, until by the middle of the twenty-first century a respectable percentage of its people had developed psychic talents. Since this country was one of the most tolerant in history, these psychics could work openly, meet others of their kind, and finally begin exploring this long-neglected human potential. Although there were plenty of frauds and self-deluded souls, the genuine talents tended to sort themselves out and migrate to the northern region, particularly to a mountain named Shasta and a city called San Francisco.

As the situation on Old Earth worsened during the twenty-first century, these psychic communities had warnings of the coming disaster long before the biosphere was finally destroyed. After the First Contact, when young humanity learned the secrets of star travel from the preexisting alien cultures in the Mapped Sector, a good number of them managed to qualify for interstellar immigration, often in unified groups, and when the final disaster came most of the true psychics were safely off-planet in the various territories of the human-dominated Republic, which needed immigrants badly enough to take these psychics in when the alien-controlled Alliance and Confederation turned them away. Since ordinary people tended to shun them, those with the talent generally married among themselves, especially at first, thus strengthening the bloodlines—but not all psionic children have psionic parents. Mulligan's father and mother, for instance, have never shown a trace of any talent, and neither have his four brothers. Apparently he inherited the recessive genes in the old-fashioned way.

There's no doubt, however, that his talent is first class. Even crammed into the back of Carol's skimmervan, with his stomach twisting itself into ropes of nausea, he is receiving a strong amount of what he calls "background signal," vague visual impressions, touches of emotion, snatches of voices, and occasionally a strong pictorial image or sudden stab of feeling: terror, mostly. Although he wishes that he'd never come along, he also realizes that he doesn't want Lacey out there alone, that in spite of Carol's low opinion of his usefulness he would rather be around to offer what help he can than go off somewhere in safety. Yet even so, his fear remains, so strong that he finally decides he's picking up the emotions of another psychic as well as merely being frightened himself. As he focuses in, he gets a strong impression of a blurred, dual mind—or perhaps two minds closely linked? He can read that one of them seems to be very hungry; then the skimmer swerves and dips, breaking his concentration. When he tries to pick up the twinned minds again, the signal's lost, faded into the general background.

Near the center of the Rat Yard, the cracked gray remains of a runway stretch out like a scar through the vast strew of garbage and rubble, shimmering with heat in the midmorning sun. When Carol finally sets the van down there, near a rusty metal light standard, Mulligan hears Lacey sigh aloud in relief.

"This's where I always put down," Carol says. "You have to

establish a routine when you're dealing with people like this. They no like surprises, and some of them just plain no can remember if you change the pattern."

At that Mulligan's sense of relief turns to dread. Being around mentally ill people is very difficult for him, simply because he can feel their pain and fear like a stab at his own heart. When Carol and Lacey get out, squabbling vaguely about what to do next, he crouches in the van and wishes that he was good at karate instead of baseball.

"Hey, Mulligan!" Carol snaps. "Don't just sit there on your narrow ass! Get out the suncloaks, will you?"

He hands over the blue cloak Lacey brought, looks around and finds Carol's, white with a red cross, that ancient symbol of healing. He gives it to Carol along with her medical kit, then hesitates, merely watching while they duck into the stiff helmets in the middle of the cloaks and drape themselves in the long flow of reflec cloth.

"I brought one for you, too," Lacey says. "It's right there by your feet."

This is the moment. He could announce that he's having nothing to do with this crazy idea, that he's staying in the van with the doors locked, but Lacey is looking at him quizzically through the polarized faceplate in the helmet of the cloak. If he cops out now, she will despise him just that much more.

"I'm on my way, yeah. It's just kind of like cramped in here. Hard to move, y'know?"

"You can sit in front on the way back."

"No, I dint mean that. You can sit in front."

"Would you two stop bickering and come on?" Carol says. "I want to lock the van. I no want anyone trying to steal the drugs. Some of these dudes and donnas will swallow anything that even looks like a pill."

Dragging the voluminous cloak with him, Mulligan jumps out. He finds the stiffened, cylindrical helmet and slips it on in a hurry. Hagar's sun can blister fair skin like his in only a few minutes. Once he has the folds of white reflec properly arranged all the way down to his feet, he flicks on the power switch just inside the helmet. As soon as the solar packs that run in strips down the back of the cloak are charged up, the mini-fans switch on and keep the air circulating inside the helmet. For a minute or two, though, the moisture from his sweaty face fogs the faceplate.

"Mulligan, come on!" Carol snaps. "Dunt just stand there, will you?"

"Hey, lay off him!" This time Lacey sounds genuinely annoyed.

For a moment Mulligan is delighted that she would defend him; then it occurs to him that he probably should be defending himself. Feeling more like a pet dog than ever, he follows them as they set off down the cracked runway, pointing like an arrow into the heart of the Rat Yard.

"Someone will see we've arrived," Carol remarks. "The Ratters always keep up a good guard, and some of'em have learned to watch for me. There's one donna here named Del, and she got a niño name of J.J. She usually shows up every time I come. Nothing like mother love to overcome paranoia, I guess."

"A baby?" Lacey sounds genuinely shocked. "Will it be okay?"

"Who knows, man? It's healthy enough now. I think if she thought it—he—was going to die or even get real sick, she'd give him to me to take back to the city."

"I dunt mean his health. I mean, what he's going to be like mentally after growing up out here?"

Carol merely shrugs with a rustle of reflec to admit her lack of a prognosis.

"Who's the father?" Mulligan says.

"This big Blanco they call John Hancock. His name's some kind of joke, I think, but I wouldn't laugh at him. He looks like he could twist someone's head off with one hand."

"Oh jeez," Lacey says. "What do these people live on, anyway?"

"I'm no totally sure. They hunt rats. Sometimes they trade stuff to the rehydro gang. They find artifacts in the rubble from the old colony days, and those are pretty valuable. Some of'em grow things in the ravines where there's a little water. But even all that no is enough. Like I say, they no tell me their secrets. I did get the City Council to pop for vitamin-mineral supplements, though."

"Job and a half," Lacey mutters.

"You bet. Pols—a bunch of selfish bastards all of'em. Oh well, I got to have someone to bully. That's why I took this project on. Without any med techs to push around, my retirement was getting super boring."

Hearing Carol talk so matter-of-factly about her self-imposed mission of keeping these crazies alive and as healthy as she can plunges Mulligan into an orgy of guilt. What's he ever done for anybody, besides his high school baseball coach? The question makes him want a drink, especially since he's sweating inside his suncloak and his hangover is threatening to return. He finds himself walking slower and slower until he's trailing about five meters behind as they pick their way through broken appliances, junked skimmers, indistinguishable packing material, and the occasional heap of fresh garbage.

All at once he realizes that he can no longer see or hear the two women, that not only is he alone but he's also no longer in the Rat Yard. He's up high in mountains of a type he's never known, the slopes covered with tall green plants that he recognizes as trees from the holos he's seen of Old Earth. Down below him in a gorge a wide river runs silver over rocks, and when he looks up he can see higher peaks capped with a white substance that he assumes is snow. The sunlight is all wrong, too, a pale yellow-white. When he steps back from the edge of the precipice, he hears someone cough politely behind him and turns to find an old man leaning on a tall, crooked stick.

"Buenos dias," Mulligan says, because he can't think of anything else. "Nice view, huh?"

The old man smiles, then vanishes, turning transparent first, then melting away. All at once Mulligan realizes that he's having a vision.

"Damn it, Lacey might need me. I no can stay here."

Since the vision refuses to break, Lacey or no Lacey, he decides to walk on, heading downhill away from the precipice. The farther he goes the faster the sun begins to set, until at last he comes to a flat plain or meadow—it's hard to see how big it is in the purple twilight—with a stream running through it, clear water, trickling over rock with a pleasant little sound. In something like awe he kneels down, scoops up a handful, and drinks. Although it tastes clear and cold, he knows the moment he swallows it that he shouldn't have tasted it, that he's now condemned to wander here forever, under the watchful eye of the old woman who suddenly appears, kneeling beside him, patting him on the face, then trickling still more rancid-tasting liquid into his mouth from an old cracked cup.

"He's coming round now, Doctor Carol. See? He's coming round. Old Meg knows what to do."

The woman certainly looks old, with her face lined like a crumpled grocery sack, the pouches under her eyes as big as thorn tree nuts and her skin just as dark. Her gray hair winds round her head in a thin, greasy braid. Just beyond her shoulder he can see Carol, hovering anxiously with a syringe in her hand.

"Lacey?" he whispers.

"I'm right here."

Then he realizes that she is sitting next to him on a lumpy, stinking pile of cushions and holding his hand. That she would hold his hand, that she would look at him in such sincere concern makes this whole miserable trip to the Rat Yard worthwhile.

"Mulligan, you feel okay?" Carol says. "I can give you a shot if you need it."

"He no needs your shot, Doctor Carol," Meg says, sucking stumps of teeth. "I brought him round."

"Well, yeah." Mulligan tries sitting up and finds it easy. "Sure did."

"Least I could do, boy. Caught you in the cards, I did. Sorry bout that. Dint mean to catch anyone in my cards. I was just looking, that's all."

Lacey and Carol both arrange fixed smiles.

"What cards?" Mulligan says. "Can I see?"

"Can you see?" Meg laughs, a pathetic attempt at an arch giggle. "I can bring'em out, sure enough, but I dunt know if you can see or not."

When she gets up and shuffles away, Mulligan realizes that they are in a hut, dug out a meter below ground and roofed with a patchwork conglomeration of junk and chunks of plastocrete slabs. The cushions he is sitting on were obviously scavenged at one time from scrapped skimmers; there is a cooking stove of sorts made out of a big metal drum. Meg herself is dressed in several loose layers of rags, all filthy. She opens a battered hard foam carton while Lacey and Carol watch in utter bewilderment.

"When we get back to town," Carol whispers, "I'm going to get a good look at you, boy."

"Lay off." Mulligan is surprised at how good talking back feels. "Just lay off."

Before Carol can snap at him, Meg comes back. Although the bundle she's carrying is wrapped in a dirty, decaying undershirt, Mulligan sees—in a visionary sense, that is—power streaming from it like waves of light. When he reaches for it Meg snatches it away.

"You no touch'em, white boy. I said you could look. Dint say you could touch."

"Sorry. I'm real sorry. Course I won't."

With a grunt of satisfaction she kneels down again and unwraps the bundle to reveal what looks like a pack of playing cards, all greasy and well thumbed.

"Tear oh," Meg says. "These are super old, boy, and they're called tear oh cards. They come from Old Earth."

With a riffle like an expert gambler she shuffles the cards and reforms the deck, then sets it firmly down on the bit of old canvas that stands her for a rug.

"Well, maybe you can cut'em if you want," she says with an almost flirtatious wink at Mulligan. "Just about in half."

Reluctantly he lets go of Lacey's hand. When he reaches for the deck he realizes that his hand is shaking, as if he's afraid that the cards will burn him. With a little toss of his head he cuts the deck exactly in half, and Meg giggles again, a screechy parody of a young girl. She turns the cut upward and shows him his vision with him in it: a white-haired young man stands at the edge of a precipice in the high mountains.

"But there no was no dog with me," Mulligan says, pointing to what seems to be a spaniel under a smudge of dirt.

"No? You sure, boy?"

All at once Mulligan remembers that he himself is the dog, or so he'd been thinking just before the vision began.

"You're right. It was there."

"Thought so."

Lacey and Carol exchange such a startled glance that Mulligan realizes they're frightened. Since he isn't, he feels briefly smug. Meg restores the cut and begins dealing the full deck into four packs facedown, the cards whispering as they slide, greased, over one another. Once she's done she turns over the top card on each pack, starting from her right and going to the left. On top of the second pack is the pale young man again, but this time he's riding a horse by a vast body of water—an ocean, Mulligan supposes.

"That's you." Meg lays a bony finger on the rider. "Your trouble is Love, ain't it?" Next she points to the card to its right, ten long sticks crossed in the middle. "Never did amount to much, did you, boy? Always losing before you could even start playing." To the left of the blond rider is a peculiar figure indeed: a goat-headed man squatting on some kind of stone with a pair of naked humans in front of him. Meg hesitates, then skips on to the last pack, topped by five old-fashioned coins. "You're never going to have money of your own, neither, unless you marry it."

When she starts to sweep up the cards, Mulligan grabs her wrist and hangs on even when she yelps and tries to twist away.

"Who's the dude on the stone, Meg? You've got to tell me."

"Dunt want to. You let me go, white boy! Doctor Carol, make him let me go!"

When Carol starts forward Lacey gets up, moving fast, and blocks the way with a warning toss of her head. Mulligan gives Meg another shake.

"You got to tell me!"

"He's the Devil. There—now I said it, and we're all in real trouble now." Her voice drops to a whisper, and she leans forward, suddenly friendly and conspiratorial. "They killed him, you see. About two days ago now, I guess. John Hancock and the Wild Man and Blue-beak Bizzer. They seen him crawling along, and they killed him. Smashed his head in, and it stank to high heaven, Wild Man tells me. They buried him, too. Buried the Devil!" She begins to laugh. "Ain't that a good joke, white boy? Burying the Devil?"

With a grunt Mulligan lets her go and sits back, letting her sweep up the cards and begin a slow ritual of wrapping them just so. Although he can hear Lacey and Carol whispering together in what sounds like excitement, he can't take his eyes off the greasy pack.

"Find your own," Meg snaps. "You no can have mine."

"I'd never steal 'em, but I no mind admitting I sure do, like, want a pack."

"Good luck. Like I say, they come from Old Earth. No can be a lot of them left, but you got to find your own. Hear me? No can have mine!"

Since he can see that she's growing agitated, Mulligan forces himself to stop staring and gets up, suddenly aware of his head aching with a dull throb at the base of his skull. Lacey and Carol are both watching him with mingled admiration and concern.

"Vamos," he says to them. "Meg, thanks."

"Welcome. Maybe it was a good thing, me catching you in my cards. I sure do feel sorry for the Devil's wife, losing her old man that way."

Grabbing his suncloak from the floor, Mulligan climbs out of the hut, not so much because he wants to go as because he knows that Meg will start getting paranoid about her cards if he stays. It's obvious to him that she's a very strong psychic who merely happens to be stark raving mad; she knows perfectly well that he covets that deck of cards in a way he's never wanted anything before, not even the two-hundred-year-old baseball signed by Willie Mays that he once saw in an exhibit in the Polar City art museum. Utterly distracted, he walks away in a hurry, navigating almost blindly through the rubble until Lacey yells at him. Obediently he stops to let the women catch up to him, but he is thinking of antique shops that might have a pack of those tear oh cards and wondering how he can possibly get the bucks to pay for them, since he's already had to sell everything of value that he ever owned.

Although she hates to admit it to herself, Lacey is genuinely worried about Mulligan. She's seen him go into trances before, but never while walking. She glanced back once, saw him coming along after them, then looked back not two minutes later to see him lying on the ground and Old Meg crawling out of her underground hut to snatch him like a prize. From what she could follow of the conversation after Mulligan came round, she assumes that somehow or other Meg made him faint, but by mistake. She decides to wait until they get back to Polar City to question him, and after he's had a chance to rest, too.

"Carol, think we should take Mulligan straight home?"

"Ah, he's tougher than he looks. Besides, it's pretty damn obvious to me that this Devil character has something to do with the leg Little Joe found."

"Yeah, I kind of drew the same conclusion." Lacey's brought a crude sketch map of part of the Rat Yard along with her. She gets the map out of her shirt pocket, then brings it out through the arm-slit in the cloak so that Mulligan and Carol can see it. "Little Joe's no artist, but it's pretty clear that he walked in on the southern road right here. Since he was running hell-bent for leather from the police speeders, he's no sure exactly how far he went, but after Sally and Ibrahim got him out, he took a good look round and saw this broken tower about twenty meters away. We ought to find this pit of his pretty easy."

"Easy?" Carol snarls. "I no believe that any of this is going to be easy. You're the one who keeps telling me how dangerous everything is."

"Well, yeah, you're right." Lacey pats her cloak, approximately over her heart. "I got my officer's service laser with me, and it's fully charged."

"Oh jeez!" Carol rolls her eyes heavenward. "Just don't go drumming up any business for me, will you? Between here and Porttown, I got enough hardship cases already."

In this part of the Yard, big slabs of pale gray plastocrete rise out of the ground at odd angles, and tumbled faux-brick walls lie in long moraines. Since there's always the possibility of a cave-in from a hidden cellar, they go slowly, Carol in the lead, Lacey bringing up the rear with one hand inside her cloak near her laser pistol. She keeps her eyes moving, turns constantly, looking for other Ratters who might be less hospitable than Old Meg. If this unlovely trio, John Hancock, the Wild Man, and Blue-beak Bizzer, happens along, she doesn't want her party mistaken for the Devil's minions.

After about a kilometer they top a small rise and see below them the broken tower, a jagged rise of white plastocrete that once was probably a signal tower for shuttle landings. Even after over a hundred years of bleaching sun and scouring winds Lacey can still pick out a cryptic inscription painted in letters two meters high: part of an *N*, an *A*, an *S*, and part of another *A*. Those particular letters appear all through the Republic on ruins and antiques; probably some scholar somewhere knows what they mean.

"Okay." Lacey pulls out the map again. "There's the tower, so the pit ought to be to the south over there—yeah, hey, look—you can see it."

Right next to a two-meter pile of old plastofoam packing material gapes the dark hole, some three meters across. They approach cautiously, testing the ground with each step forward, but the surface holds. At the edge of the pit Lacey flops onto her stomach and peers in.

"I bet someone else's been here since Little Joe. I can see gonzo tracks, and the rubble's been piled even higher. I'm going to go down, guys. You stay here to pull me out."

Before either of them can object she sits up and slides down, landing on the convenient rubble heap with a bounce and spray of minor garbage. She takes out her laser pistol in the spirit of better safe than sorry, then jumps down and begins prowling around. The smell guides her, a vinegar-sharp rot hanging in the air about where Little Joe found the leg, if leg it was. Now that corner is empty, the ground obviously swept clean and packed down, ringed by long but narrow oval prints—a hand, patting down the dirt? a foot, walking round a grave? Embedded into the dirt near the wall of the pit is a plastocrete slab with symbols burned into it by some kind of beamer.

"Omigawd," Lacey says. "They've murdered a sentient."

"Think we ought to dig the poor bastard up again?" Carol is on her hands and knees at the edge of the pit.

"Nah. We've got to let the federales know and let them do it legal."

"Lacey, get out of there!" Mulligan's voice is almost a shout, sharp and urgent. "Get out now! The eaters are there! They're going to get you. Oh please, get out of there!"

"What? You picking something up?"

"Hell yeah! Lacey—"

"Okay, man, okay! Be cool, will you? Help me up."

Between the rubble and Carol's strong hands it's easy for Lacey to flip herself back up to solid ground even in the enveloping folds of the suncloak. She brushes off the worst of the dirt while she considers Mulligan, who is dead-white and shaking.

"Now, what's all this noise about eaters?"

"Dunt know. There's a mind down there, man, a real weird one, like, some kind of animal, not a sentient." He pauses, trembling. "I've blocked it now, but man! it creeped me out. Y'know? Eating, eating, eating—all it thinks about, if you can even call it thinking."

With one last shudder he turns away and walks a few paces back toward the skimmer. Lacey thinks hard, chewing on her lower lip. By rights she should call the police the minute she gets home, but they may well ask awkward questions, for instance, how she knew there was a corpse there in the first place. All at once she hears Mulligan sob aloud.

"Oh for chrissakes," Carol snarls. "What's bugging you now?"

Mulligan flips the helmet away from his face and settles to the ground under the folds of the cloak like a parachute hitting the earth. Even though she can't see him, Lacey can hear him crying and steps back in a sudden fit of cold helplessness. With a visible effort Carol controls her dislike and kneels down next to him.

"Hey, man, come on, tell me. I'm sorry I snapped at you. What's wrong? You tired? You've been through a hell of a lot today."

"No my pain." His muffled voice is thick with tears. "Whoever buried that dude loved him a whole damn lot."

And with a cold shudder Lacey remembers Meg, babbling about the Devil's wife.

Nunks is worried. Mulligan's grief woke him out of a sound sleep, then left him as suddenly as it came. Since he's very tired after a hard night of gardening, he's also annoyed. Sometimes it seems that the little brother is always in one kind of trouble or another, and that no one but him can pull him out again. For a while he burrows around in his bed, a huge square mattress stuffed with big, deliberate lumps, but try as he might he cannot get back to sleep. He gets up, adjusts the polarization on the window to let in a little light, then brushes his fur vigorously with a pair of stiff brushes until he feels halfway sentient again. In his tiny kitchenette he makes himself a cup of strong herbal tea while he wonders what to do next. Without words he's incapable of simply calling a friend on the comm and asking for help. Being on a verbal planet can be frustrating in the extreme, but as a political exile he can't go home again—not, at least, until the current ruling house on his homeworld has been toppled, an event which unfortunately lies in the distant future, if indeed it will ever happen at all.

The tea drunk, he puts on a pair of old green shorts and pads out into the garden, shaded from the burning sun by long muslin panels on computer-controlled frames. Nunks checks the angle of each one of them. Even though Mulligan translated his thoughts into Merrkan so he could tell Buddy exactly how he wanted the panels set, Nunks mistrusts the comp unit, as he would any mind with absolutely no psionic ability or deep feelings. Buddy he dislikes more than most AI's, because this particular comp unit does have some shallow emotions, such as arrogance and an entirely too strong attachment to Lacey. To Nunks' way of thinking, if one is forced to deal with intelligent machines, they should stay machines and nothing more.

He sits down in the deepest shade under an apple tree, leans back against the comfortable bark, and goes looking for Mulligan. Although he's fully conscious and perfectly aware of everything around him, he detaches part of his mind, using the image of a beam of light, and sends it roving around on the track of the overwhelming sob of grief that woke him. In a few minutes he picks up Mulligan—sound asleep. By engaging his own in empathetic contact, he can tell that Mulligan's body is curled up into a cramped position, automatically compensating for shifts and drops as some flying vehicle carries it along. Nunks reflects just how much like Mulligan it is, first to wake him up, then to go right back to sleep himself.

There remains, however, that piercing cry of pain that now seems to have been something Mulligan was reading and transmitting rather than feeling himself. He sends his mind out farther still, following back the traces of Mulligan's outburst. Very distant, very faint—but the grief is still resonating in another sentient, still carving deep a bitter loss into another psionic mind. Nunks tries sending a wave of sympathy only to feel the other mind shrink back in a bleak terror that carries with it overtones of despair. Why bother to fear, why bother to preserve your life, the mind seems to be saying, in a universe as cruel and horrible as this one? Nunks tries to send back hope, and love, and the joy of the coming of the light. The other mind cuts him off.

He comes back to himself, then merely sits for a while, thinking. Not even little Maria, sold into prostitution by a drunken father and beaten half to death by the pimp she trusted, radiates a despair such as the one that mind has sent to him. As he analyzes his memory of it, he reads mourning at the core, but a doubled mourning, made into twisted thorns by some ghastly . . . He struggles with unfamiliar thoughts, then pinpoints the feeling at last. A ghastly joke. Somehow this sentient is thinking of its loss as a hideous, warped joke played on it by the universe as a whole. Nunks feels pity rise within him until his chest aches and heaves. He begins composing his thoughts into a form that Mulligan can translate to Lacey. Somehow or other, they have to find that sentient and get it some help.

Just before noon Bates is sitting at his desk and reading over a stack of paper on the two murders, including the coroner's full report, and a write-up on the Confederation Embassy skimmer that carried Gri Bronno over the cliff in the Rat Yard. Bates's intuition that the cook was murdered has been conclusively confirmed; someone first set, then jammed, the skimmer's autopilot all the way back in Polar City before sending the car out into the night with a dead man at the wheel. The fight, therefore, that Mulligan read from the vehicle must have happened nearly an hour before the "accident."

The most troublesome report is a quick call-in from a squad car to let him know that Sally Pharis doesn't live at her currently listed residence anymore; theoretically all patrols are on alert, looking for her, but after the miserable job they did finding Gri Bronno, Bates has little faith in them. He wants to see her more than ever, because the lab report on the brown boot shows that the blood on it is indeed Ka Gren's, and it was found about where Ward saw Sally walking.

The most interesting file is the write-up of Sergeant Parsons' interrogation of the personnel at the Confederation Embassy. Although as chief of police Bates is willing to supervise an important case like this, he sees no reason to waste his time doing the routine field work. As usual, Parsons' report is meticulous. With the help of two other officers, he has uncovered and collated an amazing amount of detail, including the link Bates has been hoping for. As underassistant cook, Gri Bronno was taking out the garbage after dinner at the same time that Imbeth ka Gren was leaving the building by the back door. Another servant happened to be looking out a window at the time and noticed Ka Gren speaking to the cook, although she couldn't hear what was being said. Bates is willing to bet that it was some innocuous remark that just happened to indicate where Ka Gren was going.

Parsons draws the logical conclusion that the murderer must be someone in the embassy who knew that Ka Gren had spoken to Gri Bronno, but Bates refuses to jump to any conclusions. He calls up a map of the embassy grounds on his comp unit and sees confirmed what he'd been suspecting: the recyclers are right by the back gates, which would have been standing wide open. Since those gates front onto one of the main streets in the neighborhood, it's quite possible the murderer could have been hanging around, unnoticed in the crowd of sentients on the movebelts or sidewalks, watching his victim leave. If so, he might have also seen Ka Gren speak to the cook—and thus hand him his death sentence. On the other hand, Bates remembers the look on the murdered carli's face, his lack of any real terror. He must have known the murderer, must have had no reason to think he was about to die.

At that thought, something that's been nagging at Bates falls into place. The carli's throat was deeply slashed. He must have seen his murderer not only draw a knife but swing hard. Why didn't he run, or scream, or at the least look frightened? It occurs to Bates, too, that since the veins in a carli's throat are as big as the ones in a human's, the murderer must have been practically bathed in reddish-purple blood. Even given that the plaza was nearly empty at that time of day, surely someone would have noticed if a sentient dripping carli blood strolled by. Or is that why Sally Pharis is missing?

"Crap. If he killed Gri Bronno over some small-time remark . . ."

Bates punches into comm and practically screams an all-points alert to every officer on duty. This time he emphasizes that the subject's life is bound to be in danger. Once he's a little calmer he realizes that he's back to thinking that the same sentient murdered both Ka Gren and Gri Bronno. After all, if someone was clever, a professional, even, what would be easier than to fake an amateur-looking job? A professional. For a long time he sits at his desk, staring out the window, letting his mind roam through his memory as he tries to dredge up the fact or facts that nag at him, just out of reach.

He is considering hanging it up and getting something to eat when the comm unit buzzes. He flicks it on.

"Bates."

"Hello, Chief." It's Akeli from the PBI. "Have you any data of moment to impart?"

"I no was aware that you're my superior officer."

Akeli's fat face smiles on the viewer.

"My official designation is, of course, only that of a liaison between you and the President."

You got to rub it in, don't you, you bastard. Aloud, he says, "Well, you're going to have to tell her I got nothing new on my end. What about yours? Anything on the Alliance Embassy or Ka Gren's contact?"

"Nothing I have gleaned is suitable for transmission over a comm line. Perhaps you might appear at my office around eight tonight? Adios."

And he powers out before Bates can say another word. For a few minutes the chief sits at his desk steaming over the multiple layers of insult in that brief exchange, particularly the implication that any facts he gathered would of course be so trivial that they could be said openly, unlike Akeli's deep secrets. Then he forces himself to be calm and leaves the office, shutting the door quietly behind him instead of slamming it as his heart desires.

Here in the middle of the day shift the station building is nearly deserted. Although the cafeteria's open, it's serving only synthicoffee, stale sandwiches, and soy sticks in a gravy left over from the midnight main meal. Bates gets a couple of eggo-paste sandwiches and the big size on the coffee and sits down near the door while he watches the human attendant wiping down the servobots with a wet rag that's probably less sanitary than any spilled food could be. He's just finished the first sandwich when he's aware of someone watching him. He slews round in his chair to see a young woman in the doorway, slender and pretty with deep bronze skin and jet-black hair, done up in severe corn rows. She also looks vaguely familiar.

"Chief Bates? I dunt mean to disturb you, but I'm so worried, and I no can find anyone else."

Her soft voice jogs his memory: Cindy something-or-other, Corporal Ward's fiancée, and he met her at the annual Independence Day picnic last winter.

"No trouble. What's wrong?"

"Well, I no can find Baskin. He took the exam today, and he was going to go home and change, and then call me. Y'know, we've been seeing each other for two years, and he's never missed calling me before when he said he was going to. So I thought maybe the exam went overtime, and I came here to look for him. The exam's been over for hours."

The sandwich he's just eaten turns to an indigestible lump in Bates's stomach. Shoving the plate away he gets up fast.

"Come with me. We'll put out an all-points on him and then drive over to his place. I no suppose his lock just happens to be keyed to your palm, too?"

Her complexion turns an ashy gray, but she tries to make a brave little joke.

"It sure is. Just don't tell my mama, will you?"

"You got my word on that. Vamos."

In the end, though, it turns out that Ward never made it home. A beat cop finds him in an alley about ten blocks from the station, shoved under a debris box with his throat slit from side to side exactly like Imbeth ka Gren's. While the medics wrap him up, Bates stands in the blazing sun and swears revenge. In the squad car Cindy weeps quietly, her shoulders heaving as if she'd been running a long long way.

By the time Carol drops them off at A to Z Enterprises, late in the afternoon, Mulligan is so tired that he can barely stumble after Lacey as she leads the way inside to the shady-cool garden. She'll have to let him sleep there for the rest of the day, she supposes; after all, she's the one who's been running him so hard, and the least she can do is give him a place to recover. Although he hasn't actually said so, she's beginning to suspect that his landlord's thrown him out again. With Nunks' help she gets him upstairs and settled onto the sofa, then pours herself a drink while Nunks hovers restlessly by the door.

"Something you need to ask me?"

He shakes his head yes, his enormous hands working in frustration.

"It's so complicated we've got to wait until Mulligan wakes up."

Another yes.

"But it's so urgent it no can wait."

Exactly. She should have known. Although she's tempted to shake Mulligan awake, he's dead pale and snoring, twisted round a cushion as usual in what looks like a hideously uncomfortable posture. She yawns, tired herself after a day without sleep.

"Well, you'll know when he wakes up. Want to wait up here

with me? We can maybe find a replay tape of an off-planet ballgame on the screen."

With a negative shake of his massive head Nunks clumps out of the room and down the stairs so loudly that she knows something's severely wrong. Sipping the drink, she wanders over to her desk to find Buddy's message light blinking wildly. She settles into the armchair with a sigh of pleasure for the comfort of sitting down in something other than Carol's van and flips a couple of toggles.

"I am very pleased to see you back, programmer. We have had an influx of data."

"Triage, then lay it on me."

"Subject headings in chronological order so that my programmer may triage data. I have found a possible cause of the Mulligan unit's pain. Chief Albert Bates of the Polar City Police Force called. Sally Pharis's life is quite probably in danger. Mulligan's life may be in danger. The security of the Republic is just possibly threatened."

"Jeezchrist! Start with Mulligan's life, then Sally's life."

"Both lives are threatened because of their connections with the murder of the carli Imbeth ka Gren. The Mulligan unit attempted a psychic reading over the corpse. The Sally unit was most likely an innocent bystander at the scene of the crime."

"Was this the substance of Bates's call?"

"You have deduced correctly. He also desires a meeting before eight this evening if at all possible. He did not say why."

Lacey feels a prickle of irritation. If Bates were only something other than a police officer, she would like him, but like all Fleet personnel, most of whom supplement their meager pay with smuggling, she has an instinctive dislike of on-planet police. On the other hand, she knows that she has to do something about the murdered sentient out in the Rat Yard.

"Call Bates for me."

For a few moments Buddy hums and clicks.

"I have reached his comm unit. He himself is unavailable."

"Leave this message. Lacey is home and will see you whenever you drop by."

"Completed, programmer."

"Good. New command. Check with the port and see if the

merchant ship RSS *Montana* has arrived in-system yet. If so, contact Sam Bailey—you remember him, don't you?"

"Of course. A friend of yours, admirably efficient as well as clean in his personal habits."

"Coming from you, I suppose that's a compliment. Anyway, ask Sam if he's noticed anything unusual in-system, particularly anything that could be construed as evidence of an alien ship. If he has any data, tell him to send it immediately in Green-oh-four. And tell him I'm looking forward to buying him a drink."

"Your command is entered, but may I remind my programmer that code Green-oh-four is fifteen years out of date."

"That's why I'm having Sam use it. We know it by heart, but anyone listening in will have to use the code keys, and what do you bet they dumped them out of comp years ago?"

"That is a logical assumption, programmer."

All at once the last of her energy deserts her, and she yawns hugely, shaking her head to stay awake.

"Jeez, Buddy, I got to sleep. Put a sensor beam on Mulligan and sound alarms if he tries to leave before I wake up. Wake me when Bates gets here."

"As my programmer desires."

Buddy sounds vaguely disappointed. It's not until she's falling asleep that she remembers that he had other news to tell her. By then she's too tired to get up and hear it.

FIRST INTERLUDE:
The Hunter

Wherever he walks, rage walks with him. Rage is the prime reality of Tomaso's life, no matter how tightly coiled he keeps it, no matter how deeply drowned in the dark ocean of his nighttime mind. Rage will never make his hand tremble at a killing moment, nor drive him to a curse when he hides in absolute silence, nor twitch his lips in any revealing ghost of a snarl, but when he walks abroad, it strolls beside him and turns cold eyes on the passersby, marking them for possible victims, enjoyable victims, if only his work would allow. At times it tries to speak to him, but he always refuses to listen, because he hates its voice, the high, shrill whine of a frightened child. He would prefer to think that the child was chewed, swallowed, and subsumed into the man he has become, not that it is alive and whole, still whining and begging for its mother, still crying and spitting at the news that its mother is dead, killed by the same hands that drag it along cold corridors and throw it into a locked room, still banging on a metal door and screaming hatred in a venomous stream. The room is still there, too, in his mind, and the bloodstains on the door from the small hands that banged and banged and banged as the voice howled terror.

The room had a frayed blue carpet on the floor and no window, though on one wall was a big holo of a mountain view with a waterfall, the white foam pouring down endlessly in illusionary motion just as the white clouds endlessly rippled through the sky without ever really changing their position. There was nothing else: no bed, no three-dee viewer, no chair, not a book or tape, nothing. Once he stopped screaming, a servobot slid through a slot in the door and brought him a tray of food. Although it turned its sensors on his bloodied hands,

71

no one ever came to bandage or tend them; eventually he washed them in the sink in the bathroom attached to the room and wrapped them in toilet paper. It was the first time that he had to heal himself, but not the last.

The food was a chunk of bread, a bowl of soup, a glass of watery white liquid that he couldn't name. It wasn't quite enough, but since he'd never been hungry before, he assumed that the servobot would give him more when he asked. It merely took the empty tray away and slammed the door-slot shut behind it. Although he waited by the door for some time, there was no more food until approximately the next day. All night, as he tried to sleep on the floor, his stomach growled and tormented him. When he did sleep, it was only to dream of his mother, and he would wake in tears.

As the time passed in the room, food became an obsession. He could never predict when the servobot would come or how much it would bring. At times he would get several good meals in a row; at others, he would lie hungry for what seemed like days. Next to food, he became obsessed with time, with trying to count out some sort of unit that would let him mark the passing of hours. He never found one. At times he wept, at times he screamed; mostly he was silent, wrapped in a ball in one corner.

Eventually two humans came in, one a guard with a stun gun, the other an important official, to judge from his shiny black suit all trimmed in red braid. Although Tomaso wanted to hate them, they were people, faces, human faces, someone there with him in the room. The guard never spoke. The official had a neat black beard that waggled when he talked.

"You going to be a good boy for me, Tomaso?"

"You killed my mom."

"I dint. Our Masters did. You going to be a good boy? If you dunt, they'll kill you just like they killed her. She was psionic. So are you. You know what that means?"

"I felt it when they killed her."

For a moment the official wavered, his mouth parting slightly, a moist pink thing in the beard, his eyes briefly sad. When the guard looked his way he hardened himself.

"Then you know what it'll feel like if they kill you."

He would not scream, he refused to scream, he wrapped himself tighter and tighter into the ball. Although he held the scream back he couldn't stop the voice, pouring into his ears.

"Now if you're a good boy, they won't kill you. You'll be special instead, real special. Know what the Masters are going to do? They'll send you to a big old private school, and you'll learn to use your talents right. This school is so private that most folks dunt even know where it is. You'll be part of a big, big secret. I bet you'll like that."

Anything would be better than the room, any sight better than the waterfall, nauseatingly familiar, endlessly rushing to nowhere. He unwound himself from the ball and turned over to lie on his back and look up at the official from the floor.

"Is there food at this old school?"

"Sure. Lots and lots." He hunkered down close by. "Know something? Your mom tried to lie to the Masters. That's why they had her killed."

"She told me they kill any donna if she got psionics. She told me they kill us dudes, too."

"Now, now, that no is true."

"You're lying. I can always tell when someone's lying."

"I should've figured that. Okay. She was right. They did kill her once they found her, dint they? But they dunt kill all the dudes, just the weak ones. You're pretty tough, and you're going to be a big dude someday. So what are you going to do? Get killed or do what they say?"

"You tell me something first. This old school, what's it going to teach me?"

"You're pretty brave, kid, bargaining when you've got no chips and no cards neither." The man smiled in sincere humor. "Okay, it'll teach you how to kill people on the sly. Ever hear the word *assassin*?"

In sheer surprise he sat up, drawing his knees close and wrapping his arms around them.

"I heard the stories. You mean they're true?"

"Real true. Hey, do you think your mama would want to see you die, too? I bet she'd tell you to go for it."

"Yeah. Bet she would."

And the boy's voice cracked into a waterfall of weeping.

It was later that same day, when he'd had a bath and a big meal and been given new clothes, that he got his first look at a Master. In the Alliance human beings were kept strictly isolated on their own pair of planets unless they'd proven themselves trustworthy servants, and while he'd heard of the

Master Race all his life (all seven years of it), and of course had seen pictures, he'd never come face to face with one of its members. (That he and his mother had lived in hiding on his grandmother's farm until the day when the police came for them doubtless had something to do with that, because the H'Allevae refuse to hide from their human subjects in spite of the regular murders of one official or another.) The man with the black beard, Señor von Hartzmann, told him to mind his manners and took him to a big domed room crowded with strange furniture made of aluminum: bars and platforms and ladders all joined together and marching up the wall. Sitting on the platforms or perching on the bars were some twenty H'Allevae, each about one and a half meters tall with long skinny arms and short, peculiarly jointed legs, all dressed in elaborately decorated suits, embroidered and crusted with gems and seashells, dangling with fringes and beads. Their hairless faces bulged with multilens eyes and extruded out to the long, semi-mobile noses, dead white and drooping over mouths that bore such a resemblance to human lips that at first Tomaso thought they were humans wearing masks. Sitting on the lowest platform, which always belongs to the leader because it's the most vulnerable position, was a particularly bejeweled H'Allev'jan. When he spoke, although the words were perfectly clear, no one could mistake that lilting, sniggering whine for a human voice.

"He no was broken by your methods, Señor von Hartzmann?"

"This little dude, sir, has more guts than most adults. He's tough. He'll do fine."

The Master flicked his head this way and that to stare at Tomaso with the pair of emerald-green secondary eyes set just above the hair-fringed holes in his head that collected sounds. From his red and purple coat he took an atomizer and sprayed a sweet and flowery scent in a soft mist over the boy. Only years later did Tomaso learn that the scent signified he'd been marked as a member of that particular Master's clan-pack. In primitive times, when the H'Allevae were still gathering fruits and seeds and insects as they swept through the mountains in a wave of constant chatter and howls, he would have been marked with the leader's urine every morning to ensure that in the evening he received a share of whatever food had been gathered during the day. With the Master Race (a term they themselves had proudly taken from Old Earth history) in firm possession of over a third of the Mapped Sector, food was to be had for the asking, and the ritual was only done once and with fine perfumes. At the time Tomaso was only aware of wanting to sneeze, of hating the cloying stink and the encrusted being who sprayed him with it. That night, when he cried himself to sleep in a proper bed, the smell wound itself up with his own furious voice, so that even years later, whenever he hears the small boy screaming inside, he can smell the sweetness, too.

But he doesn't listen to the voice anymore, except some-times when he's falling asleep. For a brief second then he feels the abraded pain in the small hands and hears the cracking hoarse hatred, in the merciless intervals before his trained mind snaps itself off like a comp switch and falls to restful oblivion. When he's awake, as he is now, strolling down H Street after stuffing Sally Pharis's body into an organic refuse pickup bin behind a restaurant, he doesn't remember, he refuses to remember the child. But the rage is another matter. The rage is a friend, a useful companion who keeps his mind hard and sharp and centered on death. When the time came this noontide he regretted having to kill Sally after the pleasure she'd given him; it was the rage that bit out her life with a knife for teeth.

He stops in front of the mirror-dark polarized window of a closed shop to adjust the helmet of the suncloak that muffles him in perfect obscurity. As long as he speaks to no one he is for all practical purposes invisible, just another white ghost drifting along the semi-deserted street in the glare of late afternoon. If the police should find Sally before her dead flesh is pulped to strip it of its precious water, who will be able to remember or tell which of the suncloaks concealed the sen-tient responsible? The blunt boots showing beneath the hem could as easily belong to a lizzie as a human, though he is too tall for a carli or a Hopper, as other races so inelegantly term the H'Allevae. With a grin invisible behind the reflective faceplate he goes on, walking slowly and deliberately like a tired sentient with nothing to hide. As he turns down the alley leading to the cheap hotel where he stowed his gear, he wonders if anyone *will* find the body. Perhaps so, if the recycling crew is alert, because there was an odd smell about that bin. He didn't notice it until he had Sally safely tucked inside, but as he left a waft drifted after, a scent like rancid vinegar that will probably make the crew decide to check the contents carefully for something that might be spoiling the batch of reusable proteins. As he thinks about it, he can still smell it, clinging perhaps to his hands or jumpsuit. He decides he'll have to pay the fine for an extra shower, even though he hates doing any of those small things which get a person entered into comp logs and remembered by clerks.

By the time he reaches the small, spare room the smell is noticeably stronger. He tosses the suncloak onto the bed, kicks off his boots, then strips off the maroon jumpsuit. Since the silky fabric is tightly woven, he's been sweating all day, and the moisture seems to reek of vinegar with an overtone of Sally's perfume. He drops the suit onto the blue tiled floor of the closet-sized bathroom, out of the way in a corner to prevent the smell from getting into the frayed carpet, while he gets a plastic bag out of his duffel. Like most spacers' gear, the suit rolls up to a light and tiny wad that he can slip into the bag for a later jettisoning.

The shower and some strong soap wipe the smell away and leave him feeling as relaxed as he ever is. By then he can barely remember Sally's face, and the rage has eaten the last of his regret. As he gets dressed, this time in a pair of gray shorts and the plain white shirt of a businessman, he finds himself thinking a lot about eating. Not that he's hungry—it's merely that images of biting and chewing and digesting seem to be running through his mind. When he focuses on them, he realizes that he's picking up a psychic signal from somewhere very close to him. He sits down on the edge of the bed, opens his mind, and listens carefully. Whatever being is sending the signal has such a primitive mind that words seem to be beyond it. Only images come to him, and dim confused sensations, all of eating, sucking, dissolving. Although the room is empty except for himself, the mind is close: very close, this eater, scraping, slurping, an inexorable scavenger.

For the first time in years the cold mouth of panic brushes across his skin and nibbles at—he cuts the thought, the damned rotten image of eating (chewing, sucking, swallowing, always searching for food to nip and gnaw) off clean in his mind. His long training taught him to empty his mind, to feel nothing, image nothing, verbalize nothing, to focus on his breath and that alone, but now he feels taking a breath as an eating, stripping the air of oxygen and sucking the precious gas deep into his self. The panic begins to chew at the edges of his mind. He jumps to his feet with an audible curse, but even the curse draws its force from excrement, the outer and visible result of inner and invisible digesting.

The signal seems to be getting stronger. He begins to tremble, standing alone in the room with the frayed gray carpet and the purple flowered curtains rippling endlessly without really changing position. The vinegar smell is back; he's sure of it.

Although he doesn't realize it, all the conditions have been met for his madness to start chewing its way through his skull.

Chapter Four

Lacey's message reaches Bates an hour before sunset, when he returns to his office after personally fetching the preliminary coroner's report on Ward. Although he's been considering getting a little sleep, instead he goes to the locked drawer in his desk and retrieves a couple of illegal pills, leftover evidence from a bust some months back, that will keep him awake and functioning all night. After he washes them down with mineral water, he checks in with the duty desk.

"Okay, Ricardo, I'll be at A to Z Enterprises on a tip. That's in an alley off D Street, right by the port gates."

"Sure, Chief. I'll route any news straight to your beltcomp."

As he drives toward Porttown, a little too fast, taking the corners a little too widely, he wonders if he's doing the right thing by bringing Lacey into this. He hates asking, simply because her help is so valuable that he doesn't want to overuse it. He knows perfectly well that she dislikes cops and might simply decide to have nothing further to do with them if he makes a nuisance of himself. Besides, if she should get known as a copbot, half her sources of information would dry up. On the other hand, since Mulligan is a friend of hers, he can stress the very real danger that the psychic's in and maybe enlist her help that way.

When he reaches the warehouse Nunks shows him straight in and leads him across the garden to the staircase up to Lacey's rooms. Walking through the green and growing things gives the chief a brief but much-needed respite, a welcome reminder that most sentients have pursuits other than murder on their minds. Down at the far end, assiduously tying young tomato vines to wire supports, is a strikingly beautiful young girl with a purple frost to her hair. When Bates hesitates, admiring her, Nunks growls under his breath and points firmly onward.

"I take the point, yeah, pal," Bates says. "She's off-limits, huh? Too bad."

Nunks' growl rises to a snarl. Bates lets the matter drop.

In Lacey's sitting room Mulligan snores in the corner, wadded up like an old shirt on the floor. Bates briefly wonders how any human being can sleep in such an impossible position, then turns to Buddy, who's blinking and humming in his butler mode.

"Good afternoon, Chief Bates. I have sent a signal to Lacey's alarm. She will be with you shortly. Please help yourself to an alcoholic beverage if you should wish."

"Thanks, Buddy, but I'll skip it. She got you working on this carli murder case?"

"My programmer has not authorized me to impart those data."

"Course not. She'll get her pound of flesh out of me first, huh?"

Buddy blinks in what appears to be alarm.

"I am unaware that my programmer possesses cannibalistic traits."

"Just a joke. Forget it. Can you tell me if Mulligan's been here long?"

"Oh yes. Those data are open file. He has been here, off and on, for the last twenty-nine hours."

"Good. When he wakes up, make sure that he stays here."

"My programmer has already given me a similar order."

At that Lacey herself comes staggering out of her bedroom, her hair an unbrushed blond thatch and her eyes red-rimmed.

"No sleep today, Lacey?"

"Just two hours, two and a half maybe. Sit down, Chief. I see Mulligan no is using the sofa anymore."

"Does he always sleep twisted up like that?"

"How the hell would I know?"

"Hey, sorry, I dint mean anything risqué."

She shoots him a genuinely furious look and stumbles over to the wet bar to splash water on her face while he curses himself for his lack of tact. The hyper pills, he assumes, are beginning to take effect.

"What can I do for you, Chief?" She comes back and flops into the armchair behind her desk. "The two-carli murder?"

"Just that, but now there's been a third—a human, and one of my best officers, damn it."

"I'm sorry." The sympathy in her voice is as genuine as the earlier anger. "Losing a good man hurts."

"Yeah, it does." He glances away. "I'm no going to ask you how much you know or where you learned it."

"Gracias. Then we maybe can do business. I assume that's what you're here for."

"Yeah, but I no can bargain over the price. The department's got fixed rates for information."

"Oh, I dunt want anything crude like cash."

"Yeah? What, then?"

She gives him a small, amused smile that makes her look about fifteen years old.

"Just having you obliged to me is enough. I might need to call a favor in someday."

Trapped, Bates hesitates. The last thing he wants is that kind of sword hanging over his head, but if he refuses, he risks having her turn him away.

"We'll leave it at that, then. You know what's wrong with you, Lacey? You're bored, being retired. Why the hell dunt you just come work for us?"

"Maybe I will—someday. What do you need?"

"I'm no even sure, but let's start with Sally Pharis. She might be an important witness."

"Yeah, Buddy told me you thought she was in some kind of danger. You got her in custody?"

"No, we no can find her."

"Oh sweet jeezuz."

"Yeah. Damn right."

"Well, I'd better see if I can find her, then."

"I was hoping you'd say that, yeah. Now, Mulligan's involved, too, but he's probably safe enough here. Nunks no would let in anyone who was trying to hurt his friend."

"Mulligan could pick up an enemy coming for him, too, probably. But what happened to your officer?"

Even though it hurts, Bates keeps his voice low and steady as he tells the story, including the coroner's statement that whoever used the knife must have been exceptionally strong to slash that deep with one cut. From there he moves on to tell her everything he knows about the case. As he talks, she types, her fingers moving fast over the old-fashioned equipment, the screen casting odd flecks of glare into her face.

"Are you going to put a release on the evening news?" she says at last. "There no is a lot of people around in broad daylight, but your killer must've been one hell of a sight. Madre! Of all the messy ways to off someone! If anyone did see him, I bet they remember it for years."

"Hell, for the rest of their lives! Makes me wonder, does he have a reason for using a knife? They're quiet, but so are military lasers, and I'm willing to bet that anyone could buy one on the black market if he had the right connections."

Lacey smiles briefly and goes on studying the screen.

"Oh hey!" she says abruptly. "Thanks, Buddy." She turns to Bates. "He just reminded me of something that might tie in. Remember Mulligan's fit? When he was trying to do a reading over the first corpse?"

"Yeah. Did Buddy figure out what went wrong?"

"He's made a superguess. Found a paper from the National Psionics Institute demonstrating that it's possible to put a psychic block on someone, to interfere with their psi functioning and—this is the old telling detail—to keep them from remembering that they were blocked. Mulligan no remembered a damn thing once he came round."

"Jeez! But wouldn't someone have to be close by to do that to another psychic?"

"Real close. Like standing in the crowd of rubberneckers at the scene of the crime."

Bates swears briefly but vilely. When he glances Mulligan's way, he finds him wide awake and sitting up to listen, his face dead pale, his eyes kid wide.

"Trying to remember, y'know?" Mulligan says. "It hurt like hell."

"Buddy says that pain is the usual outcome, yeah."

"So it's someone who broke his oath." Mulligan is beginning to get excited. "I mean, when they register you, you got to sign the oath, and the first thing it says is, like, you'll never hurt nobody with your talent."

"Someone who goes around cutting people's throats no is going to worry about a lousy oath," Bates says with some asperity, then is immediately sorry when Mulligan shrinks back. *For chrissakes, why does he have to act like a kicked* dog?" "Well, that's assuming it's one person and not a pair of accomplices."

"Yeah, but I think Mulligan's on to something anyway, Chief. Look, the Institute's paper is strictly theoretical, not a how-to manual. What if we're dealing with a psychic who no was trained here in the Republic?"

"Where, then? Some planet we never even heard of? Fat lot of good that going to do me! Hell, sorry—I'm running on no sleep, and I no mean to keep insulting you guys."

"No sleep and a purple pill, I bet." Lacey gives him a smile. "You got to watch those things, Chief. That's why they're illegal, y'know."

Bates merely glowers.

"But look," Lacey goes on. "It fits, a murderer with psionics. That's why he left the body out in the middle of the plaza, so it'd be found right away, and he'd get his chance to zap the police psychic. I mean, the longer he hangs around there, the more likely it is that someone's going to notice him, so he's got to get the body discovered by the police fast. Sure enough, poor Ward comes along, calls the squad, and Mulligan appears—just what the dude wanted. He zaps Mulligan and fades away into the crowd, and there you are, afraid of asking another psychic to run the risk."

"Yeah, I sure was. Jeez, Mulligan, you scared the crap outta me. Anyway, sure, and then he killed Ward cause he realized that Ward saw Sally Pharis and could get her as a witness . . . no, it breaks down. How would he know that?"

"You put out an all points, dint you? Lots of hams listen in."

"Yeah, but there's no use in killing Ward once he named the witness."

"Right. Damn!"

"If he got psionics," Mulligan puts in, "he no needs no comm tap to know who Sally was."

When they both slew round to look at him, Mulligan cringes again.

"Go on," Lacey says. "What do you mean?"

"Well, let's say he's walking away after the murder, y'know? He picks up that Sally sees him, but he no can stop to take care of her right then. Maybe Ward is coming along, or someone else, too many people to kill or something. So he like registers her mind. It's hard to explain mind-prints, but they're like a smell, some kind of thing like that. Everyone's got one, and you can like pick it out in a crowd. So after he takes care of me, he goes looking for Sally. There's no way he can know that Ward's already told the chief her name."

"And so we're coming right back to a killer with psi," Bates says. "She-it."

"Ugly, yeah," Lacey says. "But it does mean we got to find a motive for only one murder, Ka Gren's. The others are just covering that one up."

"Well, if we're right, and I think we are, mind. I don't suppose I got a hope in hell of swearing you to secrecy."

"Why? Cause Ka Gren was spying on the 'Lies for the Cons, and you no want an interstellar incident?"

"How the hell did you know that?"

"I dint. It seemed logical, and I just tricked you into confirming my guess."

For a moment Bates is speechless with mingled rage and admiration.

"Hey, man, anyone could draw the same conclusion. The whole damn planet knows that the 'Lies and the Cons come here mostly to spy on each other." Lacey pauses to type Buddy some message. "Dunt get so uptight."

Bates takes a deep breath and reminds himself that she's right. For some minutes she reads from the screen while Mulligan watches her with abject devotion.

"Okay, Chief," she says finally. "I got something to tell you if you swear on a stack of Bibles that you won't ask me where I learned it. No, two things."

"Two stacks and a Koran thrown in."

"Swell." She pauses, types, reads, types some more. "First, for the past couple weeks the 'Lies have been tracking something in a solar orbit in-system. My informant dunt know what it is, exactly. From what he could pick up on his sensors it's either a comet or something traveling with a comet. Suppose Ka Gren knew about it and was trying to find out more? It's a long shot, yeah, but it's also the only shot we got."

"It's enough so I can try dropping a hint or two at the Con Embassy, anyway. What's the other thing?"

"It might not be related to the murders, but I'm willing to bet it's related to item number one. Out in the Rat Yard there's a fresh grave. Some of the crazies murdered a sentient yesterday, and I'm willing to bet anything you want that it's a species we've never seen before. Think you can get an order to exhume?"

"Damn right! Would you ask Buddy to tap into comm for me? I want to get right on that. How'd you find—no, sorry. I meant what I said."

"Good. Then I'll give you a map that'll take you right there. Oh yeah, you better have a couple of guys along with riot guns. The crazies are going to think you're digging up the Devil."

Nunks is surprised at how hard Maria works. There is something ferocious about the way she crouches over each delicate tomato plant, her face skewed in concentration as she coaxes the tendrils onto the wire mesh supports and traps them there with cotton string, as if this job is for her a drug to wipe away the memory of the rest of her life. Since she's latently psionic, he can read something of her mind, a welter of fear that this idyll of normality will end with her pimp dragging her back to their smelly little flat on the other side of Porttown. Nunks wants to reassure her, but she cannot read his thoughts in return, not yet, anyway. In some irritation he casts around for Mulligan's mind, finds it awake, then realizes that Bates is still up in Lacey's office with the little brother. After Mulligan's revelations about pimps bribing the police, Bates is a person that Nunks never wants to see again.

Mulligan, however, has registered his contact.

Big brother >need me?

>Need talk Lacey> BUT| >cop goes away.

Okay\ BUT\ >cop goes, Lacey goes>>

[aggravation] She can wait\ not wait?

Not wait. Big brother, woman Sally name/Lacey friend\ real danger [fear] >>throat slashed open. >Lacey find/must find\ before then.

[shock] Understood, little brother. >talk later Lacey>Talk you sooner\ talk you wait long time?

Talk me sooner. >They go, I stay here.

[satisfaction]

Leaving the tomatoes to Maria, Nunks walks slowly down the length of the garden, breathlessly quiet in the last of the sunset. Soon he will send the maglev lamps floating out so his helpers can do their night's work in something more reliable than the flare and crackle of the northern lights, but for the moment he merely enjoys the orange and apricot sunset, stippled here and there with red. Young Rick, the deserter from the Alliance Marines, comes yawning and stretching down the staircase to join him—on time this evening, after the dressing down Lacey gave him last night. Although Nunks cordially dislikes the fellow, he reminds himself that in a day or two Rick and his forged papers will be gone, on board the RSS *Montana* as a comm tech.

"What do you want me to do tonight, Nunks?"

Nunks points to a shovel leaning against a wall, then to the compost heap, which needs turning. Although Rick groans in an unnecessarily dramatic manner, he does follow the order. Nunks watches him for a minute or two: a very large young man, with well-muscled shoulders and long arms. Since he also owns a laser pistol, stolen from the 'Lies when he deserted, he should be perfectly capable of guarding Maria from her drug-sodden pimp, a necessary precaution because Nunks intends to take Mulligan and Lacey out to the Rat Yard as soon as she's finished with this other business. He can still feel the despair of that distant sentient mind like a taste of poison in his mouth.

In a few minutes Bates and Lacey come clattering down the stairs. Although the chief hurries on ahead, she stops to talk. From the tense set of her mouth Nunks can tell she's more worried than he's ever seen her. With a light blue shirt and gray shorts she's wearing a dark blue vest, part of her old Fleet uniform, so she can carry her laser pistol in reasonable secrecy.

"Nunks, look, I remember that you need to tell me something. Can it wait?"

He nods a yes and makes a sweeping hand gesture to indicate that she's not to worry about it.

"Gracias. Mulligan told me that you know about Sally, but this thing goes way beyond her. I think we got some kind of homicidal maniac running loose in town. Look, take real good care of Mulligan, will you?"

Nunks nods again and pats her reassuringly on the shoulder. He decides that he'll have Rick lock the only door to the garden and stand guard there, gun in hand. From what little he's heard on the subject, he can assume that maniacs look for easy prey, not fair fights.

Porttown has two shopping areas. One, not far from A to Z, caters to visiting spacers with all the usual tawdry attractions:

overpriced restaurants, souvenir stands, bars, sexual partners in a wide assortment, and here and there a store that sells more respectable things like towels and other travelers' necessities. Sentients who live in Porttown call it the Outworld Bazaar and rarely go there unless they're employed by one of those businesses dedicated to parting spacers from their treaty-credits. Round the other side of the port, on North F Street mostly, you can find sonocleaners, foodmarts, skimmer repairs, and other such sensible if mundane services, including neighborhood bars and the everyday sort of recreational drugs, legal and illegal. Since parking is generally impossible on North F, Lacey takes the Metro and leaves her skimmer back at the warehouse.

Little Joe mentioned that Sally has just moved into an apartment over a slice'n'fry place, but he neglected to say which one. Since that particular kind of lizzie fast food is also popular with humans, there are slice'n'fries all over the North F neighborhood, and a lot of them have apartments above. Lacey gets off the Metro at Twenty-third and walks down a block to the Freefall Inn, a tavern owned by her aunt Maureen, a big, bony woman whose blond hair sweeps upward into a ribbon only to cascade down again in curls and whose lower lip is generally stained purple from chewing spice. Since Maureen was forty when rejuv drugs were finally perfected, she has crows' feet wrinkles around her eyes and deep lines at the corners of her mouth, but as she likes to remark, it's not bad for a boozy old broad of seventy.

Lacey finds her behind the bright red plastocrete bar with polished brass railings that makes the Freefall such a cheerful sort of place. Since there's a replay of an off-planet ballgame on the enormous three-dee viewer that fills one wall, most of the patrons—and the place is crowded with regulars—are nursing alfalfa beer and watching with the occasional muttered oath for an error or bad swing. Lacey finds a place at the bar, orders whiskey and water from a servobot, and waits until Maureen notices that she's there.

"Bobbie! Whatthahell? You sick or something?"

"Nah. What makes you think so?"

"You watering your whiskey. Put the damn card away—this one's on me—no, I no arguing about it. What are you doing over our way?"

"Looking for a friend. She just moved, and I no got either her comm number or her address, but I got to find her."

"On business, knowing you."

"Sort of." Lacey leans over and whispers. "You know Sally Pharis."

"I heard los verdes were hotlining her."

"Look, they only want to save her little ass. She's in big trouble, man, I mean el mucho grande. Someone's gunning for her."

"Oh." Maureen pauses to scratch her upper lip with the bright red nail of her little finger, carefully avoiding the mole at the corner of her mouth. "Well, no one knows where she is. Ibrahim came in here when I opened round sunset and had a couple shots of gin. He was pissed as hell, saying she never did come home yesterday. Maybe she got an all-day trick, I tell him. Yeah, he goes, but she supposed to call me if she does. Look, man, I go, it's no romantic, having a girl tell her john that she's got to use the comm so just hang on a minute, okay? So Ibrahim drank his gin and left. Dunt know where he went."

From overhead comes a long low rumble: a ship getting ready to launch from the port. They both pause automatically, Lacey sipping her whiskey, and wait, holding their thoughts in mind easily through long practice, until the ship is gone and they can hear each other again.

"Anyone else seen him since?"

"Nah, not that I know of."

"She-it."

Since Lacey rarely swears, Maureen looks appalled.

"That bad, honey?"

"That bad. They could both be dead by now. Look, if Sally or Ibrahim comes in, or anyone else who knows where they are, you tell'em to get the hell to the police."

"Jeezchrist. Sure will. Hey, Sally's living over a place called Crunch'n'Chat. Down on Fifteenth, just off F. No bet she's there now, though."

"Neither do I, but I'll give it a look anyway. Thanks for the drink."

"Welcome. You ought to come visit your poor old auntie more often."

"Yeah. Well. Y'know."

With a wave Lacey leaves, walking fast, wondering why it still gripes her soul to have one of her many relatives call her

Bobbie, which is, after all, her given name. At least Maureen refrains from retelling family stories, a common practice in the rest of the clan and the reason that Lacey rarely visits them. Over the years she's done her best to bury her childhood memories deep in her mind. Although in Porttown it's no real disgrace to have a father who's always in and out of prison, she hated it and hated him for it, too, with his endless big talk and big schemes that always came to the same tedious end: the police showing up at the door either to take him away or to tell his wife that they already had. Twice the authorities declared him rehabilitated and sent him off to another city in the polar region with a respectable job and a clean start; twice his family ended up coming back to Polar City to live with relatives while he was in slam. When her mother finally had enough, Lacey was only thirteen, but she still can remember her feeling of relief that Dad would never come home again. Aunt Maureen took her out for a real meat hamburger to celebrate the divorce.

She pauses for a moment, looking at the stacks of used clothing in the window of the charity store: discards, most in good shape, from the well-off black folks who live far from the noise and fumes of the port. Her mother dressed her kids out of that store, as so many mothers in Porttown do. Lacey hated that, too. She saw the Fleet as her way out of the ghetto, enlisting young, serving well, getting her chance at an education in Officer Candidates' School. As she looks down the dirty street, at kids playing ball and picking their way around a drunk sprawled in front of the post office, a gaggle of women with tired eyes talking on the street corner, she wonders why she came back to Porttown in the end when she could have retired on any planet in the Republic. Maybe, she supposes, she would have felt ill at ease elsewhere, always wondering if she was good enough for her fancy neighbors, or maybe Bates spoke more accurately than he could have known, and she quite simply would have been bored in some quiet city where sentients mostly play by the rules. When she glances up at the endless flicker in the gaudy-colored sky, she realizes that Polar City is also one of the few places in the Mapped Sector where the stars are always invisible at night. Maybe that had something to do with it, too. She never has to stare up at the night sky and remember what it was like to be free out in deep space.

With a shrug to throw off the melancholy mood she walks on, past the tiny store that sells chewing spice, sodas, and odd lots of whatever Mr. Chen has managed to pick up cheap (children's socks, special today; writing paper and pens for sentients who'll never be able to afford a private comp unit), past the liquor store where they cash welfare vouchers in the back room for a ten percent commission, the tiny storefront mosque for those few true believers in this nest of infidels—all the places that seem utterly unchanged from her childhood, even though that was thirty years ago. She wonders if her memory's playing tricks or if this neighborhood truly never does change, if change is only for those with the bucks to open new businesses in newly built shops rather than passing the old counters and stock and debts down in the family year after year.

The most prosperous shopkeepers, too, have scraped together the money for rejuv and thus look no older than she remembers them, all those years ago, just as she still has the face and body of a young ensign rather than a woman in her late forties. As she passes, some of them hail her: Bobbie Lacey, ain't it? Fancy that, good to see you, still have your Uncle Mel's warehouse? And the answers: sure is, sure is, sure do, as she walks on with a smile and a wondering if any of these men, women, and lizzies have done or seen something that's brought them to the attention of Ka Gren's murderer. Like Chief Bates, Lacey is scared, not for herself, but for Polar City, where a highly skilled killer is determined to cover his tracks no matter how many deaths it takes.

The Crunch'n'Chat is just two houses down on Fifteenth, a big place for a slice'n'fry with a shiny clean window in front. When Lacey pauses she can see the breakfast crowd going down the line, piling their trays with soy sticks, sliced onions and squash, whole sandworms, insect-meal cakes and imported fish-flake patties, taking them to round tables where a pot of oil sizzles at the ready in the sunken center. The lizzie owners rush around frantically, their scales gleaming as they refill bread baskets and vinegar cruets, pass out napkins, and dole out meager cups of water, so busy that they never notice her looking in. Most likely they never would have noticed either if some stranger had stopped by, stalking Sally to her death.

The stairs leading up to the apartment are just round the

side from the restaurant, and the door itself is in a shadowed bay, redolent with fried starch. When Lacey rings the bell, she sees the scan light of the housecomp unit glowing above the door as it records her presence. No one answers, and she knocks hard, just in case there's been a partial malfunction in this rundown building. Again nothing. Although she hesitates for some minutes, thinking that she might as well leave, she's genuinely afraid that Sally is lying dead inside. She takes her portable comp link off her belt and flicks it on.

"Hey, Buddy?"

"I am on line, programmer." Buddy's voice sounds thin and shrill over the palm-sized link box.

"Good. I have a door to open here and an unfriendly housecomp."

"Allow me to contact the unit, programmer, and we will change its attitude."

With a quick glance behind her at the street (empty, mercifully), Lacey places a tiny transmission module on the unit flush against the door's lock plate. She hears a soft hum as Buddy activates the other comp's circuits; lights flash briefly in the scan panel.

"I have erased the record of your visit. Please try the door."

At her touch it slides open. When she steps into the tiny entry hall, the door closes behind her, and a soft yellow light comes on overhead with the air-conditioning.

Sally's apartment is its usual mess, a profusion of purple plush furniture, empty liquor bottles, china knickknacks, and cartons crusted with the remains of take-out food. In the middle of the living room a dustbot mutters under its breath as it circles in a valiant fight against filth. Otherwise everything is entirely too silent.

"Looks like she never came home this morning, Buddy."

"My optiscans are certainly picking up evidence of disorder. Would you place me in contact with her comm unit? There may be revelatory messages."

"About the end of the universe?"

"I beg my programmer's pardon?"

"Just a joke, Buddy. Sorry."

The pale pink comm unit stands on the kitchen counter in the middle of a welter of dirty plates and glasses. Lacey places the link box over its digit pad, then gathers up her courage and goes down the hall to the bedroom door. She stops for a quick glance into the bathroom—perfumed and spotless in spite of a vast litter of cosmetics bottles. Since the bedroom door is standing open she strides in briskly and lets out her breath in a long sigh of relief. There's no corpse on the heart-shaped bed with the purple satin sheets, nor is there one on the lavender twelve-centimeter-long shag carpet. A pair of dirty jeans, a lavender shirt with a mini-pleated front, and a couple of plastofilm bags of Sarahian weed, about five kilos in all, are lying in front of the closet, clear evidence that Sally came back to her apartment after being in the Rat Yard.

Evidence. Some small fact is nagging at her mind, a detail of Bates's long recital, but she can't quite place it. On a sudden instinct she retrieves the comp link from the kitchen and brings it back to the bedroom.

"Buddy, set your sensors to record a visual of this room. How much can you see at one time?"

"Only forty-five degrees of arc. If my programmer would make the necessary adjustments?"

While they get the bedroom and bath on tape, Buddy repeats the messages recorded by Sally's comm unit: nothing of interest, except that someone called and left no message, not so much as a single word, only forty-five minutes ago. Although it could well have been a client afraid of leaving a trace suitable for blackmail, Lacey finds this ominous, because, as she tells Buddy, she's really beginning to think that Sally is dead.

"Although it is a logical deduction, programmer, we have no actual evidence. In that gap between deduction and proof lies what you humans call hope."

"Well, so it does, yeah. Okay. I'm going to leave here now."

"I will sign off. Oh, programmer?"

"Yeah?"

"Remember to wipe away all traces of your fingerprints, and please, be careful."

"I'll do my best. I'm going to Carol's clinic next. If I dunt check in from there, call the cops."

It takes Chief Bates a couple of hours to arrange everything he needs for his trip to the Rat Yard: a ten-man riot squad on choppers, two armored vans, (the coroner's van plus a laborbot to do the actual digging; his own van with Sergeant Parsons, two techs, and their equipment), and finally the exhumation order itself, signed in a scribble by a judge at breakfast. With the order in hand he stops back at his office to send a message to Akeli. He makes it as cryptic as possible, announcing that he'll be late for their meeting due to interesting developments. As he's leaving, he gets, through Buddy, the message that Sally Pharis left her flat some five hours after midnight and never returned.

"My programmer is afraid that she has been killed by this assassin."

"I'm afraid I agree with her. Hey, Buddy, wait a sec. Explain the word, assassin."

"A professional killer dedicated to a specific cause or government rather than being available for hire by any unscrupulous individual. Certain obscure memory banks indicate that the Alliance has long been suspected of maintaining assassins, although hard proof is utterly unavailable."

"Certain obscure memory banks?"

"I may not reveal the source. Any attempt to make me do so will cause a disabling malfunction."

"Okay, okay, then. Any chance that these assassins are psionic?"

"Many sources of data indicate that the Alliance kills all psychics the moment it identifies them."

"I know that. What I'm wondering about are those obscure banks you mentioned. Anything different there?"

"Not that I have found, sir. Are you working on what my programmer calls a hunch?"

"Just that, and there's something nagging at my mind, too, an old story or pic. I tried to find it on my comp, but it no could comply." Bates pauses, switching off the oral input on his unit so as not to hurt its feelings. "Say, Buddy, I bet you're a helluva lot smarter than some standard-issue police comp."

"Specifications generally available would indicate so."

"Would your programmer let you do something for me?"

"She has indicated that I am to cooperate with you as far as possible."

"Swell. Find me every reference you can to psionic assassins, even in fiction and the holopix. Collate these references and try to trace them to common sources that are not fictional."

"I will comply. The collation will take some time."

"Of course. I'll get back to you later."

Bates switches his own comp back on, then hurries downstairs to his expedition, all lined up in the echoing gray bowels of the police garage. Sergeant Parsons is waiting in the driver's seat of the lead skimmervan, with the techs in back. Bates gets into the passenger seat and slides the door shut.

"Okay, Sarge, roll'em out whenever you're ready."

With the roar of forced air the van heaves itself up and glides forward. On cue the garage doors slide up, and they are outside, gaining altitude fast. Bates settles back and tries to think, but by then the purple hypers are making the veins in his temples throb. Solving this puzzle would be difficult enough without them. It's one thing to conjure up the idea of a psionic assassin and give him/her a motive and an M.O., quite another to put a face and name and warrant on an actual murderous sentient. At the moment, the assassin could be anyone in Polar City, whether a Republican citizen, a 'Lie, or a Con—close to a million suspects, not counting kids and lizlets. That's the problem with professional killers of any sort, he thinks: they have absolutely no personal motive in a killing, and so you don't have anywhere to start your investigation, no unhappy marriage, no gambling debts, no hated brother-in-law or rich old aunt. An assassin is as essentially anonymous as the knife in his murdering hand.

And now he has still another death to investigate, one that might have an incredible political impact. If Lacey is right, and this grim event marks a first contact with a new sentient race, Polar City is going to be swarming with spies and media beings from all over the Mapped Sector. Although he hopes that he can keep the discovery secret until he's finished his investigation, considering the larcenous mind-set of every sentient in town, he supposes that one of his own men will sell the news long before he's ready to make an arrest. At times he's sorry that he accepted this posting to Polar City, but he can certainly understand why the Republic prefers to staff the city's police force with Outworlders whenever it can.

Carol's clinic takes up the entire basement of a boarded-up holopix theater on the edge of the Outworld Bazaar, at least temporarily until the theater owner can come up with the bucks to have some structural repairs made to the roof and open the place up again. Although he never used the basement for anything more than storing boxes of food for the snack counter, it did have running water and a couple of toilets.

When Carol let it be known that she was willing to run a clinic for street beings, a crew of charitable volunteers divided the basement up into exam rooms and a reception area while a pair of religious groups installed donated equipment. Someone even hung the waiting area with holos of assorted off-planet beauty spots in an attempt to add a note of cheer.

When the grav platform takes Lacey down, she finds a smaller crowd than she's been expecting. Usually Carol has a lot of work in the early evening, but tonight there's only a couple of human male hookers with lime-green hair and skin-tight shorts and one young lizzie who looks like she's ingested a very peculiar chemical substance indeed, because all three of her eyelids flutter repeatedly, and she keeps yawning and stretching her snout as if she's trying to get something unstuck from the corners. Over the entire room hangs the smell of old sweat, disinfectant, urine, and cheap perfume. At the far side, behind a panel of safety plastic, the receptionist, a human female, is staring into a portaviewer.

"Carol here?"

"It's you, huh, Lacey?" She never looks up. "Yeah, in her office. She's been trying to call you. Know that?"

"Dint. Can I just go in?"

She nods, watching as on-screen a couple in perfect evening clothes cavorts in a fountain, the water splashing up and sheeting luxuriously onto the green, green lawn around them.

Carol's office is almost as crowded as her van, a jumble of supplies and outdated equipment with a rickety comp desk in the corner and a couple of plastofoam chairs nearby. She is working the comp at the moment, muttering long medical names in a tense voice, staring at the screen, then growling in disgust and trying again.

"Lacey, thank God! You get my message?"

"No. I'm going to call Buddy from here. Que pasa?"

"It's Little Joe Walker. He's got to go to the hospital, and he's raising hell. I mean, she-it, bloody hell. I was hoping you could maybe talk him into it."

"What's wrong with him?"

"I dunt know. That's the problem. C'mon."

Carol leads her down a dingy passageway between pink movable walls. From behind one door Lacey can hear Little Joe yelling and screaming, begging to be let out. When Carol opens the door Little Joe charges, but since he's wearing only a pink disposable-film exam gown that opens all the way up the back, his effort at escape is feeble and brief.

"Lacey, jeez," he says. "You got to talk some sense into Doctor Carol. I no can go telling no hospital where I picked this up."

At that he holds up his right hand. When she looks closely, she can see that his entire palm, the skin between his fingers, and a jagged stripe down the inside of his wrist look as buffed and leathery as polished vinyl. Around his hand hangs the faint scent of vinegar, a slight echo of what she smelled out in the Rat Yard pit.

"It no looks like much now," Carol says. "But I dunt know what it's going to do next. It's a bacterium of some kind, all right, but I no can find it in the Perez catalogue or in any other databank that I can get on-line. Skin sample under the micro shows it eats any dead cells it comes in contact with and toughens up the walls of the living ones till they're kind of like cork."

"Where did you get it, Little Joe?"

"The Rat Yard. I touched something on that bug-man's grave, stuff like a piece of wrapping or cloth. I no can go telling no cop why I was out in the Yard!"

The fear comes as a little stab at the base of Lacey's spine and ripples upward. She too was in that pit, she too touched something from that grave site, the mysterious box with the cryptic symbols. Surreptitiously she looks at her hands: normal so far.

"Then you got to think up a good lie," Carol snaps. "Look, I already called Central Emergency. They're sending an ambulance."

"Ambulance?" Joe wails.

"Yeah, a sealed-environment van. Hey, man, you no get it, do you? I dunt know what in hell that stuff is. It's no responding to any tests; it's no filed in any databank. Like I say, it no look like much now . . ."

"It itches like hell, Doc!" Joe sounds utterly indignant, as if he feels his affliction is being dismissed.

"I know, man. That's what's worrying me, comprende? If we no find out how to cure it, we got an epidemic on our hands—oh she-it, sorry, I dint mean to joke."

"Look"—Lacey forces her voice calm—"tell'em you were

scavenging artifacts. People do it all the time. Antique dealers on Sarah pay big money for old colony stuff."

Little Joe lets out his breath in a hiss.

"Why dint I think of that?"

"Cause you're scared sick and I no blame you. Hey, Carol, I was out there too."

"Yeah, I savvy. I'm going to do a skin test on you in a minute. Now look, man," this last to Little Joe. "Think. I need the names of everyone—I mean everyone—you either touched or who handled something you touched since you were out in the Yard."

Little Joe nods his agreement.

"Say, Carol," Lacey says. "That databank's up to date, right? And real complete?"

"Yeah. Quaker Hospital let me bootleg theirs straight off. Why?"

"Any chance this bacteria stuff comes from off-world? I mean, like totally alien?"

"Chance? CHANCE?! Whatthahell else would it be?"

Mulligan and Nunks sit in the garden under one of the apple trees, while Maria, taking an unwilling rest, crouches some meters away and watches the flaming sky. In the shadows by the door Rick keeps his watch, laser in hand. Mulligan can tell, just from the proud set of the kid's shoulders, that he finds guard duty a lot more to his taste than turning compost. Mulligan himself is terrified.

Little brother >be calm.

Can't. Killer want>find me>>slit my throat.

Rick guard>I guard> you>>be calm. No/wait. >We do work>>distract.

Garden work? [gladness]

Not garden work. Mind work.

[pain, irritation, reluctance]

Little brother! [annoyance] >must learn> control talents OR >go crazy.

Too late\ crazy already.

[extreme annoyance]

[submission]

It turns out that Nunks wants to trace the sentient mind that he picked up earlier that day. By using Mulligan's cortex as a sort of booster, he can range much farther, get a better picture of this alien mind, and communicate with it much more clearly if indeed the other being is willing to communicate at all. Since any psychic adept at thought transference can transfer the knowledge of a language over whole to an equally capable mind, Mulligan supposes that they can come to some sort of understanding with this sentient provided that their mind structures are at all compatible—and he can only hope they are. After all, there are a number of races in the Mapped Sector that cannot communicate with any other, even though they have natural psychics among them, because they have conceptualized the universe in such radically novel ways that they share no general categories of thought with any other species, not even, for example, the distinction between general category and specific thought. Still, that both he and Nunks could pick up this particular sentient other's pain does indicate that they share at least some mutual ground.

In this, as in so much of their mental communication, Nunks is the definite leader. All Mulligan has to do is sit very still and let images and emotions sweep through his mind. Although he's dreading feeling that blood-chilling grief yet once again, he agrees with his mentor that they have to help the being whom he's labeled Mrs. Bug for want of a better name. As far as he can tell, anyway, the sentient is female, and Little Joe's story seemed to indicate a certain insectoid cast to the race. Even though Mulligan knows that one should never draw strict analogies between widely disparate life-forms, he cannot help thinking of the victims of the Rat Yard's paranoia as Mr. and Mrs. Bug. Nunks has picked it up, too, as a convenience.

Little brother: ready\ not ready?

Ready.

The signal begins to filter in, a distant hiss and cackle at first, the mad thoughts and disturbing images of the Rat Yard, mostly hatreds and resentments: the mother who never loved me, the father who beat me, the doctors who drugged me, a grief-struck whispering litany of betrayal and loneliness, looping endlessly in well-worn paths through a hundred minds. Nunks wades through it like a swimmer in shallow water, hauling Mulligan behind him as they search for another, harsher voice. At one point pictures wash over Mulligan's mind like colored light playing on a wall: a beautiful woman, vastly pregnant, sits in a rose garden; a huge flaming sword hangs in midair; seven golden cups swirl by, and out of each one peers a deformed and simpering little face. Then he recognizes the touch of Old Meg's mind and realizes that he's seeing more of her cards.

The grief comes as a howl, a cold, snarling, bitter scream against the universe, a hatred of her beloved's death as flaming as the sword in the cards. Jerked to a mental halt, Mulligan feels real tears pour down his face as her despair floods his mind. Nunks, however, is calm, radiating only his desire to comfort rather than a specific attempt at comfort. The mind hesitates on the edge of sending, then pulls back into loneliness. When Mulligan sobs aloud, he feels her respond, but with shock, a bitter wondering that someone has been touched by her pain.

Sister, Nunks sends. *Not savages all of us. <Bad beings kill\madmen\hurt broken inside/take out rage. Good beings live here now too. >We help >>please let us help.*

The mind hesitates again, then a cold hard sweep of bitterness makes both of them gasp aloud.

Good beings? [disbelief, rage] >See this>see this!!

As vividly as if he hovered above in a skimmer, Mulligan sees the pit out in the Rat Yard, lit by maglev floaters in a macabre white glare. All around are the police vans and choppers; men with riot guns form a protective circle as the med techs drop a jointed ladder into the pit and clamber down to the grave.

Let him rest now> let him rest>> oh by my gods>let him rest. Why? why? why?/not let him rest?

Sister: please listen now\stay now>listen. They try to help\ find killers>get killers>>punish killers. Then: new grave, final rest.

[doubt, hesitation]

Please: >believe us>

[rage] >make them stop> THEN >I believe> I know killers <I see killers<< >I describe killers>>>let him rest!

Although Nunks can mask his feelings from Mrs. Bug, Mulligan can feel his despair, his helplessness faced with trying to change Chief Bates's mind about this to him necessary exhumation and the autopsy to follow. In the vision Mulligan can see the chief, pacing near the skimmervan with a comm unit in one hand. All at once Bates begins listening intently, then tosses back his head, his face going ashy, and rushes over to the pit. Waving his arms like a madman himself, he yells something that Mulligan can't quite hear. The riot squad, the med techs, the coroner, all stop to listen; then the sentients in the pit begin scrambling out, looks of horror on their faces. Those who've been aboveground shrink back, begin piling into the vans and slamming the doors while Bates gestures and shrieks and finally restores order. At last the chief sorts things out: the men who were in the pit go in one van; everyone else crams into the others. As the vans pull away, Mrs. Bug's mind sweeps over theirs.

[*gratitude*] [*gratitude*] [*gratitude*] *Believe you now* [*gratitude*]

>*Please let us help*> *Stay now sister.* >*Let us help*>>

But she is gone, her grief trailing after like a streak of sand in the summer sky once the main storm is passed.

[*frustration*] *Little brother, you send Bates away\ not send?* *Not send, big brother.* [*bewilderment*]

>*Go to Buddy* >*ask Lacey* >>*Lacey need know*> *ask she understand\ not understand.*

Yes, big brother. >*I do that*>

Do it NOW little brother.

[*submission*]

Although it irks him that he's afraid of an AI unit, only Nunks' scorn drives Mulligan upstairs to Lacey's office, where the comp unit is humming quietly to himself as he performs some elaborate function. On the screen Mulligan can see blocks of words flashing by, too fast to read.

"Uh, say, Buddy? Can I ask you a favor?"

"You may ask, Mulligan unit. I may or may not comply."

"Well, something's come down, man, and Lacey got to know."

"I do not understand your dialect. Please rephrase."

With a groan Mulligan casts his mind back to his high school class in formal speaking.

"Uh, I must talk to Lacey. Please get her on line for me."

"Why do you need to talk with the programmer?"

"I got to lay something on her . . . uh, tell her something that has happened."

"To you?"

"No, to Chief Bates out in the Rat Yard."

"She already knows of that event. Your input is unnecessary."

"Well, hey, man! I mean, I beg your pardon, Buddy. Please tell me why Bates left the Yard."

"I will not. My programmer has not authorized me to impart data to inferior units."

"Hey, listen up, you lousy hunk of plastosheet!"

"You are incorrect. There are no vermin on my casing."

"Yeah? But there fucking well maybe's going to be a lot of cold water poured in your vent slits, any sec now."

For all that he claimed not to understand Mulligan's way of speaking, Buddy gives out a high electronic squeal, and his screen flashes four different colors.

"Chief Bates was informed by Doctor Carol that the corpse in the Rat Yard carries a previously unknown bacterial infection. He withdrew his men to prevent further contamination. I am going to report your threat of violence to my programmer, and she will make you suffer accordingly."

"Yeah? Suck kilowatts!"

As he walks away, Mulligan is smiling to himself. He's amazed at how much easier it is to think of snappy things to say when he's sober.

"How long is this thing going to take?" Lacey snaps.

"Just coming up." Carol glances at her chrono, then at the comp screen. "Dunt blame you for being impatient, mind." She turns to her unit. "Display result of skin sample analysis number two."

The screen fills with diagrams of several different organic molecules.

"Thank God and His Madre! You're clean, man. Nada but normal bacteria."

Lacey lets out her breath in a long sigh.

"This could be important," Carol goes on. "You touched a metal surface that Little Joe handled, right? That might mean this stuff no spreads from metal surfaces to organic ones, leastways not easily. Where is this box thing?"

"In my desk in a locked drawer."

"Hey, man, damn good thing."

"Yeah. I had a hunch it needed locking away." At her belt the comp link beeps. She slips it free. "Que pasa, Buddy?"

"Sam Bailey is on line." Buddy sounds honestly pleased. "Does my programmer wish to speak to him?"

"Sure do. Tie him in. Hey, Sam?"

"I'm here, yeah." His voice is fuzzy, and his video, worse: a squashed grid with a somewhat darker face-shaped smudge on top. "Damn the aurora! I no can hardly see you."

"Yeah, no can see you so good either. Where are you?"

"Main Station. I'm bringing the launch down now. We went through Customs at Space Dock, so I can meet you in about three hours. How about Kelly's?"

"Sounds great, yeah. Out front?"

"Oh man, at the bar. I've been in deep space for months, remember?"

"Sure thing. At the bar, then."

When Lacey leaves the clinic, she heads straight into the Outworld Bazaar. All along Fourth Street the three-dee shop signs float in midair and spill colored light onto the sidewalks and movebelts as the advertisements run through their endless loops. Bottles of booze pour themselves into glasses, pretty women unzip their jumpsuits, cuts of real meat sizzle on grills, pretty boys in tight jeans unbutton their shirts, packs of cards spread themselves into winning poker hands, marble bathtubs fill with steaming water—all crackle by at top speed, as if they are desperately trying to compete with the endless light show in the sky. The double glitter from signs and sky cloaks even the most drably dressed passersby in a masquerade finery of ever-shifting color, and there is music, too, pouring out of clubs in a steady beat of drums and synthisound. Through it all strut the spacers, gaudy enough in their reflec jumpsuits without the dazzle of constant lights, arrogant in their sure knowledge that they are the only reason that this weed-choked garden of delights exists at all.

The best licensed betting office in Polar City, Al's, occupies a second-floor suite in a bright blue plastocrete shop building down an alley between Third and Fourth, just across from the twenty-five-hour-a-day rostratologist and just above a place that sells pornographic holopix and garments that consist mostly of black plastic straps. Lacey rides up on the grav platform with a lizzie who is working an elaborate series of calculations on a portable comp unit and muttering to himself about in-system ships and asteroid trajectories. Lacey thinks to herself that if she were ever going to bet on anything, it wouldn't be the yacht races, where one fist-sized chunk of rock on the wrong course can upset the results of hours of careful mathematics.

The public office is a long narrow room, painted green, with an enormous rose-pink data-screen on one wall and three cashiers' windows, guarded by two security beings with stun guns, on the other. This particular night Al himself is crouched over a desk in the corner, working comp and changing some of the odds on the big board. As Lacey watches, the Polar City Bears go up a point to be favored, two to one, over the New Jerusalem Crusaders to take the division title. The lizzie gives the board a bare glance, then hurries, comp in hand, to the nearest window. He's got either a hot tip or a system, she supposes.

"Lacey, hey," Al says. "You're actually going to part with some of the old hard earned? My heart, my heart!"

"I no could do that to you, Al. I only bet when I got a sure thing."

"Never make big bucks that way."

"Never lose big bucks either."

She strolls over and perches on a corner of the desk while he reads in the latest figures from dirty and much-creased bits of yellow paper. A Blanco with thin gray hair, Al is the palest of the pale, because he never goes out in the sun, not even for the safe hour just after sunrise. When he's done with his comp work, he ritually shreds the papers into tiny pieces and dumps the handful into a recycler chute.

"What do you want, then, amiga? I got a hot tip on the coming election."

"Not my department, but I wouldn't mind a word with you."

They go into Al's private office, a tiny cubicle crammed with comp on the one hand and all the latest debugging devices on the other. Al offers her the red plastofoam chair, takes the brown one with the unsteady legs himself, then puts his feet up in comfort on the edge of the desk. Lacey can pick out a multitude of tiny whines and high-pitched hums, Al's personally designed debugging system. Lacey is willing to bet that no one in the entire Mapped Sector has the skill or the tech to listen in on their conversation.

"I want to buy some dope," Lacey says. "Best Sarahian you got, a hecto."

"A whole hecto? You?"

"No going to smoke it all, man. Going to spread it around."

"Ah, I get you." For a moment Al chews on his lower lip. "Tell you the truth, man, I don't know if I can get it for you."

"Jeez, that must be one historical first."

"Well, something's wrong." Again the lip chewing as he stares blankly at the far wall. "Hell, you maybe know something. Look, I'll get you a good price if you help me out a little."

"Maybe. What do you need?"

"You know Sally Pharis, don't you?"

"Sure do." She suppresses a smile: Al's taken the bait with a perfect gulp. "I hear los verdes are on the prowl for her ass."

"Yeah, so do I. Question is, why? And do they got her yet, and if they got her, do they got the dope she's bringing me?"

"They no got her yet. Don't know anything about the dope. But the why, hey man, someone's gunning for her, out to kill her. The greenies just want to keep her alive."

"Jeezchrist!" For a moment Al stares in mingled surprise and horror. "You know who it is?"

"No can put a name on him, nah, but look, it's some Outworlder. Sally saw something that's related to a killing, and this dude wants to shut her up."

Al shudders and squirms.

"This killer, then, he's no one of us?"

"No way. Like I say, some Outworlder, causing trouble."

Al's surprise turns to a quiet fury.

"Oh yeah?" he says. "Then if I find something out, I'll tell you, and you go to the cops."

"Good. It's a gonzo scene, man."

"Sure is. Jeez, I wish to God I knew where the hell she is!"

And that answers her question, without her having to ask it. Sally was indeed supposed to make Al a big delivery, and there are very few things that would keep her from doing so. Although Sally has a good many faults, she's the most reliable dealer in Porttown.

"But about the dope, man," Al says. "Want me to call round a couple places?"

"Naw, I got one more contact. Tell you what, if he no come through, I'll get back to you, oh say, by twenty-two hours."

"Okay, yeah. I understand. When you need it, you need it now."

"Yeah." She gets up with a conciliatory smile. "But thanks, man. I appreciate it."

"Okay. I'm starting to get scared, thinking whatthahell might've happened to Sally."

"You and me both, pal. You and me both."

Chapter Five

The Public Bureau of Investigation takes up the top floor of the Republic's auxiliary office building, a black monolith relieved by curls of molded plastocrete acanthus leaves round all the doors and windows—an architect's whimsy loathed by every sentient in Polar City. By the time he's gone through all the sonoscans, ID checks, and pat-downs necessary to get to the top, Bates is ready to be in a very bad mood. Commissioner Akeli has an air-conditioned suite, carpeted in pale beige and furnished with real leather chairs and a wet bar as well as his desk and built-in shelves. Prominently displayed in the outer office is an assemblage of distressed Styrofoam, a late art form of Old Earth. When Bates arrives, Akeli is so solicitous, making him a drink, insisting he sit down and rest after his hard night's work, that the chief is immediately suspicious.

"Some kind of problem?"

Akeli merely grins in patently false camaraderie and sits down at his desk, where the comp unit whirs and flashes pieces of a Polar City map on screen.

"Bates, look. I know we've had our inevitable frictions and differences of thinking in the past. When you place a couple of strong-minded persons like us in the same jurisdiction, well, conflict becomes inevitable, wouldn't you say?"

"Yeah, guess so." Bates has a cautious sip of his gin and tonic. "I can cop, we both like to run things our way."

"Yes, exactly that. But look, we're faced with a major problem now. We must work together for the security of the Republic and interstellar amity. Am I correct?"

"Sure." *If I understand your fancy words you are, you*

pompous asshole. "That serious, huh? Did you find out anything about the 'Lies' role in all this?"

"That, too." Akeli frowns into his own glass and swirls it to make the ice cubes jingle. "But, ah, let us consider something. I know I can be perhaps, shall we say, overly legalistic about sharing information. I mean, the bureau does uncover data of a more than local import that at times it's forced to classify beyond your clearance level. I realize that this has caused inconvenience in the past."

"Uh, well, yeah."

"So, look." Akeli leans forward with a sudden sharklike smile that's probably meant to be disarming. "Please, as one peace officer to another, tell me the truth. How did your men break into our comp banks?"

"Your what?!"

"Ah, c'mon, man to man." Again the shark's smile. "It's unnecessary for you to pretend naïveté. I'm forced to admit to a certain admiration for your staff. Even though our security experts have adjudged our system to be what they call hackerproof, your office has been accessing us any time they want to, and all they leave is just one tripped alarm, the desperation backup that doesn't even record the intruder's entry code."

Certain obscure memory banks, uh-huh, Buddy! Aloud, he says, "Then how do you know it's us?"

"Well, who else? It isn't the Allies or the Confederates, because their electronic ports are, shall we say, kept under a certain surveillance? Surely you don't expect me to believe that it's some amateur with a housecomp unit, hacking into the best security in the Republic."

Bates considers, sipping his drink to stall for time. If he thought that the PBI could actually trace Lacey and Buddy, he would lie to protect them, but he feels quite certain that they'll know how to cover their tracks—especially once he tells them that they've left tracks to cover.

"Akeli, you got a bigger problem than you think. I'll swear to you, on my honor as a peace officer or anything else you want, that no one in my department's been hacking into your system. I mean it, man, sincerely. You'd better get yourself some experts from Sarah, cause you got a real security breach."

For a minute Akeli considers him with narrowed eyes; then he nods.

"Very well. I believe you. I'll put qualified personnel on the job immediately."

"You'd better, yeah."

"If you'll excuse me?"

Grabbing his drink, Akeli sweeps into his inner office, leaving Bates to his gin. When he returns he looks unusually grim. As far as Bates is concerned, it will do his colleague good to take something seriously for a change.

"Now, about that possible contact between Ka Gren and an Alliance double agent or informant, I've given the case to my best officer, and she's already managed to procure certain suggestive clusters of data, such as, for instance, that Ka Gren has been frequently seen on the premises of Kelly's Bar and Grill in the recent past."

"Yeah? Anyone meet him there?"

"No. But every night he came in, ordered one drink, which he paid for immediately, then took a seat where he would have a clear view of the front window of the establishment. At times he would not finish the drink, merely rise from his seat all at once and hurry out. On other occasions, he would perhaps have two drinks before he would leave in the same precipitous manner."

"So someone would walk by, give some kind of prearranged signal, and he'd follow them to some safe place."

"Such are the appearances of the situation. We must follow these leads with a certain speed, Bates." He pauses to arch his fingertips together. "Before your arrival I was speaking with the President on our confidential line. She's in a state of some agitation. The Confederation has delivered some stiff notes to her, and they've been sending even stiffer ones to the Alliance Embassy. The Alliance ambassador has thus complained to her about the what he calls unwarranted suspicions of the Confederation. Some important clauses of the recent treaty remain to be finalized. We must endeavor to solve this mystery, or she will be forced to place Porttown under martial law."

Bates's stomach knots round the gin with a flare of pain.

"Send in troops? She-it, man! You'd have riots on your hands, and they could last for days. The folks on Sarah just no understand this town. Never have."

"Oh, the President knows Porttown well enough. The question's one of relative importance between Porttown and the treaty clauses. Come along, Bates, everyone knows you're soft on the Blancos, but—"

"Now just you wait one goddamn minute. They happen to be citizens of this Republic the same as the rest of us. Are you and the President forgetting that?"

"Of course not." The conciliatory smile is too toothy to be convincing. "We're merely speaking of emergency and final contingencies, not of a desired course of action. Do you want some sort of Alliance landing instead? No doubt the Confederation would then initiate a naval action for our so-called protection."

"And just why would the 'Lies bring men dirtside?"

"I don't truly know." Akeli looks bitterly vexed. "The President doesn't confide everything to my hearing."

"If you ask me, that's an idle threat and nothing more. Something else is going on, and I no like it. The dudes on Sarah have been trying to clean out Porttown for years. Where are they going to put the Blancos—in projects? She-it, man, they're worse than a ghetto any old day."

"That's beyond my jurisdiction, el jefe." Akeli shrugs with an open-handed gesture. "I'm not the Secretary of Housing. All I know is this: you find that killer, or this town will shut up tighter than a Main Station airlock. Do you understand me?"

"Oh, I hear you." Bates uncoils himself from the chair and puts down his glass. "Now you listen to me, and you tell the President what I say. If she closes down Porttown, then she'll lose out big, cause the Porters are hiding something that she needs bad, a whole new card to play, man, in this lousy little game between the Cons and the 'Lies. I'll bet you that the 'Lies know it, too, and they're stalling for time because they're desperate."

"Indeed?" For a moment Akeli leans back in his chair, then with a wince of irritation gets up to face the chief. "And just what is this momentous matter?"

"How about a first contact? How about a member of a brand-new alien race in hiding right here in our own sweet town, because the 'Lies are tracking its ship out in solar orbit?"

Akeli goes very still except for one big drop of sweat that trickles down his jowls.

"Okay, man," Bates says. "This is real delicate, right? I don't even know yet just where this alien is. You boys piss off the Porters, and we maybe will never know. Get it now?"

"She-it," Akeli is whispering. "I mean, um, indeed. But what if she just sends in the troops anyway? What's going to stop her from simply taking the place apart, one block at a time?"

"You, that's what. Hey, man, once the Army's in here, who's going to listen to the PBI? I know you got a network, got your contacts in Porttown, in the embassies—what's going to happen to them when the military intelligence ops are poking around?"

Akeli swears with a foul oath to show that the point's well taken. Bates allows himself a small smile.

"So you better talk to the President. Tell her whatever you want, man, but talk real pretty."

"Er, yes, it seems most necessary, doesn't it? Very well, I'll do as you say, but we've only got three days before the troops land."

"Three . . .?" Bates is too stunned for profanity. "Well, then, we better get busy."

As eager as he is to talk to Lacey, Bates waits until he's a good two kilometers away from the PBI and their scanning devices. He parks his skimmer in a quiet alley, then uses his private comm unit to hook up with Buddy.

"Chief Bates, I am glad you called. I have the results of the collation you requested. I am transmitting full data to your comp unit at the moment. Do you wish a summary?"

"Damn right. Gracias, Buddy. Go ahead."

"Thirty-six years ago a controversial book was published, called *Escape from Terror*. The human author was a defector from the Alliance who claimed political sanctuary on the grounds that he had been forced to become a psychic assassin for the government. He had, or so he said, a change of heart upon being converted to the worship of the Galactic Mind. Alliance spokesbeings denied his charges and labeled him a money-hungry writer of fiction. Several holopix and one docudrama were made from his story. The theme of psionic assassins became part of popular fiction of the worst sort, causing the Alliance to bring over a hundred lawsuits in a reasonably successful attempt to close discussion of the subject."

"Jeez, I remember now! I was just a kid. Any evidence, one way or nother, as to whether or not he was lying?"

"None, sir. He died shortly after the book's publication. It appeared to be suicide, but then, it would."

"If a professional had arranged it, you mean?"

"Exactly, sir. I am feeding the entire book into an auxiliary memory cube for your comp unit. You both will see that it contains much striking detail that has the ring of truth no matter how fantastic the premise."

"Very good, Buddy. Bueno, bueno, bueno! Now we've got a peg to hang our shirts on, dunt we? Something for the President to throw in the 'Lies' faces if she needs it."

"Sir? I do not understand."

"Sorry. Listen up, Buddy. I'll tell you what's going on first; then I want you to get hold of Lacey for me. She's got to know that someone's just upped the ante real high in this game we're playing. Oh, and before I forget, the PBI knows that someone's hacked into its files."

"Thank you, sir. I will endeavor to cover my traces more completely in the future. I am now in reception mode and ready for your input of new data."

Just as he promised, Sam is waiting at the bar in Kelly's, idly watching the replay of a ballgame while he nurses a tumbler of the local "tequila," cut only by a slice of lime. Tall and slender, with black curly hair and richly brown skin, he's a handsome man with that particular musculature of the veteran spacer, an artificial lean fitness that comes from doing scientifically designed exercises in a small space. As most spacers prefer to do, he's wearing a jumpsuit, royal blue, with one silver sleeve in this case. When he spots Lacey he falls on her with a whoop and a bear hug, to the amusement of the crowd of regulars.

"Hey, Lacey," someone calls out. "What's Mulligan going to say bout this, huh?"

Lacey ignores them with a regal toss of her head.

Kelly's sports a couple of narrow booths in the back for those patrons who value privacy over comradeship, and Lacey takes Sam to the one farthest from the door. With an appreciative smile for the dark wood and crisp cotton cloth, he slides in opposite her and powers up the menu.

"Anything you want, pal," Lacey says. "My treat."

"Hell, no! I'm paying!"

"The old coin toss?"

"Right, when we're done eating."

They both punch in their orders, soy steak for Sam, reconstituted salmon flakes for Lacey, then turn off the menu. Kelly himself bustles over with the bottle of wine and two glasses to make a ritual fuss over pouring.

"Hey, Lacey, que pasa?" he says. "I hear your Mulligan's going to be playing shortstop for the Marauders."

"He's no mine, pal." She regrets the hostile edge to her voice instantly and smiles, pretending to tease. "What do you want me to do, ask him to throw games your way?"

"No that desperado." Kelly laughs a little. "Bet we can beat'em good this season, real good."

The wine poured, Kelly departs, wiping his perfectly clean hands on a spotless towel. Sam has a sip and gives her a wicked grin over the rim of his glass.

"Level with me," he says. "So this Mulligan no is yours, huh? I've been hearing about him at the bar. Half of Porttown seems to think he's a lot more'n your amigo."

"He's somewhere between a friend and a stray dog."

"Yeah, sure. Tell Auntie."

"He'd probably be more to your taste than mine. You always did like skinny blond dudes. But he no the type to return the favor."

"Then he's in love with you, no matter what's going on in your stainless steel heart."

"Shaddap!"

"I guessed right, dint I?"

Lacey is spared having to answer by a servobot rolling up with a tray of appetizers: on the house, it announces in its nasal voice. Lacey wonders why servobots are always programmed to sound like young humans with bad colds.

"Great." Sam helps himself to a cabbage roll and goes on talking between bites. "Compared to most places Polar City food no is much, but it sure beats deep sky rations."

"Some compensation, I guess."

Sam looks up in sharp concern.

"Hey, amiga, que pasa? You really okay dirtside?"

"I dunt have a lot of choice, do I?"

"Well." He reaches for another roll. "Look, if we both pulled the right strings, maybe we could get your papers back, and then you could sign on with me as my chief comp."

"Do I have a hope in hell of getting them?"

"Probably not, yeah." His voice drops to a genuine sadness.

"Jeez, I feel like I ought to do something. My life was one of the ones you saved."

"You no owe me one damn thing. I saved my own ass, too."

"Yeah, I know, I know. You always say that, but still, if it no was for you, I'd be dead and five hundred goddamned sentients with me. It still gripes my soul, the way they cashiered you for it."

"Hey, man, by rights I should've been shot. Talk about pulling strings! If it no was for old Iron Snout and his admiral's stars, I'd be dead."

"That's what I mean. We owe you."

"Chinga tu madre."

Sam winces and lets the subject drop. Lacey helps herself to a piece of toast covered with bright pink crayfish paste and eats it slowly, wishing that Sam would stop bringing up the reason that she was kicked out of the Fleet and can never space again. His gratitude, she supposes, must gnaw him every time they meet. Some sentients belong in deep space; others never quite adjust to being trapped inside a metal bubble driving through an endless swirl of stars. Captain Rostow of the RSS *Avalon* was one of the latter. Even after twenty years of service some part of his mind still fought with itself, still screamed out that trusting yourself to a thin shell of technology was madness out here in the vast drifts of interstellar dust and the sudden flares of passing stars. In a routine battle against pirates he cracked. Just when the *Avalon* had them on the run, he ordered the force-screens dropped in preparation for a full-power retreat. Without its screens the pirates could have reduced the *Avalon* to its constituent electromagnetic particles in one good shot, but in his panic all he could think of was reaching somewhere safe and solid, of escaping from the pitiless regard of the galaxy to hide under a blanket of blue sky.

Mutiny. It's a nasty word, Lacey thinks, for a nasty crime. She was the only officer on the bridge who had the guts to set her laser on stun and turn it on Rostow. Once she had him locked in his cabin, as second officer she put herself under arrest and the ship in Sam's hands. In private the high brass agreed that she'd done the right thing, but for the sake of discipline they were pressing for the death penalty until Admiral Wazerzis personally intervened. The best compromise he could engineer was that she would be allowed to retire quietly, her deep space papers sealed, rather than being forced into a dishonorable discharge.

What Lacey can never quite explain to anyone is that she agreed with the high command. Not that she wanted to die, mind; the night she heard the verdict of clemency she alternately laughed and trembled for two solid hours out of sheer relief. She had merely made her choice of death on the bridge when Rostow began sweating and raving. Her life for five hundred others had seemed a small and logical bargain at the time, one that she was prepared to honor for the sake of the same discipline that so troubled the investigatory board. One of the main safeguards against the same deep space fever that claimed Rostow is rigid discipline and routine, an artificial security of detail and regulations that soothes as much as it chafes. On a starship everyone is incredibly vulnerable to the actions of everyone else. A single crazed crewman with a laser could be a threat not only to the lives of the crew but to the very existence of the ship. She hates the thought that someday someone might find themselves thinking of her case and deciding that mutiny is once again justified—when it is an act of madness.

"Y'know," Sam says. "Maybe one day you'll be in a position to do a little blackmail. I'll keep my ears open and see if I can find something that'll get the high muckymucks on the run and make'em release your papers."

"Gracias, amigo. Dunt seem likely."

The food arrives, and they eat without talking until they're almost finished, the etiquette of a starship's officers' mess. When every meal might be interrupted by the wail of a battle-siren, food takes precedence over chatter. At length Sam divides up the last of the wine and settles back in his seat to enjoy his share.

"You never did give me the hard copy on this Mulligan dude."

"Did too. Told you to shut up, dint I? There's nada to say."

"Then how come you're so busy no saying it? Do I get to meet him?"

"Hell, you can have him."

"Oh yeah, sure. I remember the last time you said that to me over a guy. You were pissed as hell when I took you up on it."

"I dint think he'd go for it, you bastard." But in spite of the insult she smiles. "Well, no can win'em all, huh?"

"You won the only time it really mattered." Sam turns suddenly melancholy, holding up his glass to let the light turn the sweet wine blood-red. "Or it seemed to matter, then. Just like it seemed you won the big prize. A booby prize, huh? When I think of what that sonovabitch put you through!" The melancholy vanishes in a grin. "It served you right, snagging him away from me like that."

"I was doing you a favor, and you know it."

"*Now* I know it, yeah. Although it's funny, how things work out. Soon as he dumped you I knew we were going to be friends, cause we were both loco enough to fall for a bastard like that. The classic triangle—I was in love with him, you were in love with him, and he was in love with him."

Lacey laughs and turns on the menu to order more wine. After twenty-four years she can look back on the one great love affair of her life with a comic equanimity to match Sam's, but at the time she seriously considered suicide. It was the strict discipline of the Fleet that saved her, she supposes, her conviction that an officer who killed herself would be disgracing not only herself but the corps as a whole.

"Ohmigawd!" she says suddenly. "Sam, what was his last name? Alvarez or Alvarado?"

Sam pauses, glass in hand.

"Alvarez. Time flies, huh? I had to think a minute myself. I wonder what ever happened to our Jaime? I'll bet you anything you want he's still in the damn Navy. Madre de Dios, he was beautiful! Probably he still is. Damn rejuv! It keeps jilted lovers like us from getting our revenge. By rights he should be all over wrinkles, but he's probably still breaking hearts somewhere."

"Yeah, for sure. But it no was just his looks, man. That way he had about him, his damn swagger when he walked, even. It just always got me. Sometimes I used to feel like it was a privilege to hang around waiting for him even when he stood me up. And you always knew he was a hero. I mean, sounds stupid when you say the word aloud, but he was."

"A chest full of medals, huh?" Yet Sam's eyes are distant, remembering. "And he earned every goddamn one. Can't even be cynical about it, yeah. He earned 'em." He takes the opened wine bottle from the servobot. "We going to drink to lost love?"

"Why not? Pour 'em full, amigo."

They salute each other with the full glasses, then drink half straight off, another gesture from the officers' mess. Lacey is about to call a second toast when she sees Chief Bates striding down the line of tables toward the booths. The dead-eye grim look on his face brings her to her feet just as he reaches them.

"We found Sally Pharis. It's no pretty."

"I've been afraid of that for a long time now, Chief. She die the same as the others?"

Bates swallows hard, gulping for breath in remembered disgust.

"Uh, look, sorry to spoil your dinner, but do you want to come with me to the morgue? We got to talk, Lacey. I'll cop to it: we need your help real bad."

If the chief would admit such a thing, the situation must be catastrophic.

"Okay, I'll come with you. Hey Sam, want to go back to A to Z and wait for me there?"

"If you need me now, I'll go with you."

Bates shakes his head no.

"Less folks know about this, the better," the chief says. "Sorry, Captain. No offense meant."

"None taken, Chief." Sam gets up, gulping down the last of the wine. "I'll pay Kelly, then. See you at A to Z."

During the ride to the morgue Bates tells Lacey that he's going to send the police hypnotist to do a trance interview on Little Joe, just in case he remembers some detail about Sally on the night of Ka Gren's murder, then fills her in on his conversation with Akeli and the long string of chained threats. Her sudden burst of fury takes Lacy by surprise; she thought she was long past outrage at the doings of the government.

"Bloody bitch," she remarks of the President.

"Yeah, I had thoughts that way myself. Look, I dint want to say anything back at Kelly's, but something real sickening happened to Sally. If you dunt want to look at her corpse, you dunt have to."

"Somehow I think I better. Hey, man, I've been in battles, remember? You lose the pressure in a turret, it's no so pretty either, seeing some guy spread over the walls like strawberry jam."

Once they're standing in the long, cold, echoing room and looking down at the special gurney, sealed away from the rest of the universe in a plastic bubble, Lacey can understand the chief's concern. Only the battle experiences she spoke of could have hardened her enough to look on calmly; even the med tech seems to be gut-twisting sick, and he's probably seen twenty murder victims in his career as well as a hundred corpses pulled out of skimmer crashes. Yet in her disgust there's barely any grief, because her mind simply can't accept that this thing was ever Sally. Like the other victims, the corpse's throat was cut from ear to ear, and blood spilled all down its chest, which now, however, is a crusted, seething mass of silver-gray threads tangled deep in the flesh. The upper arms, too, have been eaten through, exposing the bone; the face is just barely recognizable, as if someone had tried to make a sculpture of Sally's face using gray clay that was far too wet to hold a defined image. Lacey nearly gags; she would like to curse but can find no words strong enough.

"I warned you," Bates says softly.

"Oh yeah. Looks like that stuff is worse where there's fresh blood."

"The coroner said the same thing. He's filing a report with Doctor Carol. It has to be that Outworld bacteria, he said, in a second stage of development, maybe. He no savvy nada for sure."

"Yeah? Where is Carol now?"

"Quaker Hospital, last I heard, checking up on Little Joe Walker. If the stuff turns into this—" He pauses for an eloquent gesture at the corpse. "He's going to end up with a bionic arm."

Lacey puffs out a mouthful of breath and turns away.

"Well, one thing, Chief. If the Army tries to take over Polar City, y'know? You just let this story leak. Bet your butt they'd desert rather than get near this town."

"A couple of pictures on the sunset news'd do it, yeah. I'll keep that in mind."

"You got a warrant for Sally's flat?"

"Yeah. You look worried. Why? Is there dope there?"

"What in hell makes you say that?"

"My turn for the logic and the confirmed guess. Don't worry, I no can bust the dead, hey? Come along if you want."

The apartment is a mess, from the tiny entranceway all through to the kitchen down the hall. All of Sally's knickknacks lie broken and scattered over the living room floor, and an armchair is overturned, lying on its side by the window. Clothing, data cubes, music cubes, kitchenware, old take-out food cartons—everything Sally owns is strewn around, it seems, except her three-dee viewer, the sonic oven, and her brand-new, very expensive accounts-comp unit. The old dust-bot, bought secondhand years ago, lies dead in a corner, its neck broken.

"Real clever," Lacey says aloud. "I bet Sally's jewelry's been taken from the bedroom, too. A nice el fako robbery, but I wonder why he took the trouble?"

Bates shrugs, as puzzled as she is. The disorder leads like a trail down the hall to the bedroom, and Lacey suddenly realizes that they're meant to follow it. She has a heart-numbing feeling that she knows what they'll find.

"You bastard," she says. "I'm going to get you for this."

"What are you talking about?"

"Come on, el jefe."

In the bedroom, as she expected, Ibrahim lies sprawled on the bed with a neat hole in the back of his skull, poor old fat Ibrahim in a torn undershirt and a pair of bloodstained walking shorts.

"Yeah, sure," Lacey bursts out. "It just happens that they get robbed on the very same day she dies—real believable coincidence, man. Ibrahim, hell, he must've seen or heard something, so he had to die too. Suppose this was supposed to look like he got killed by the burglars?"

"I sure do. Check out how he got killed, with a different weapon from the other cases and everything, but it's all clumsy, a real case of overkill—I dint mean that for a joke, sorry."

Lying in front of the closet are the bag of dope, the jeans and lavender pleated number she remembers and of which Buddy has a carefully stored image. The blouse, however, is now heavily stained with blood, possibly Ibrahim's, possibly the assassin's.

"He never should've left that behind," Bates says. "Either this dude thinks I'm a fool or he's getting so desperate he's no thinking right."

"I got to agree. It's real dumb of him to leave all that dope behind, too, cause any legit burglar would've taken it for sure. Unless—jeez, unless he dint even realize how valuable it is. If that's the case, then he's an Outworlder for sure."

"You're right about that. Our psychic assassin, maybe?"

"Maybe." The idea makes her shudder. "But say, Chief? Don't let anyone touch this stuff without plastofilm gloves, will you?"

"Huh?"

"Sally was covered with the Outworld disease, and I bet this dude is in one bad way, too. He no could kill Sally unless he grabbed her, and Sally was strong. She had a black belt, man. The bacteria were bound to get spread around."

"Christ, you're right! By the way, we've had the news on the video all night now, telling people to call us if they saw something weird. This dude must've been dripping blood. Someone had to notice him."

"You'd sure as hell think so, yeah."

"I'll call Burglary. We'd better get things started here. You going to go back to A to Z?"

"Soon, yeah, but you can always reach me on the comp. Say, Chief, that dope? That one bag was never opened, and I bet the little packs inside are safe to touch. Think you could sign me off for some of the evidence? I need something to spread around to get us some answers."

"Sure. Better'n cash, huh? Take what you need."

Lacey stashes about a hecto in various pockets, then starts to leave. As she goes down the hall, she just happens to look into the bathroom.

"Oh jeez. Chief, come look at this. Someone took a bath here, and I bet it no was Ibrahim from the way he smelled. Look—all kind of soap and lotion bottles lying round."

"There sure are. Say, Lacey, it looks like you're right about that Outworld disease."

Mulligan is working in the garden, weeding a row of bread ferns, one of the few plants from Sarah's temperate belt that will grow on Hagar. Even though in the drier climate the bluish-green fronds reach only one meter rather than six, the edible tubers still weigh in at a couple of kilos of high-grade starch and vegetable protein, well worth the water it takes to grow them. Mulligan likes weeding; ferreting out tiny plants and fungi is just demanding enough to keep his mind off his troubles while at the same time requiring no mental effort. Yet no matter how hard he tries to dim his consciousness, always in one part of his mind he's aware of Nunks, fretting with impatience and worry both as he chews over plans for rescuing their mysterious psychic out in the Rat Yard. Even though he feels very sorry for Mrs. Bug, Mulligan has no intention of rushing out there after her, especially when he considers that a psionic assassin is most likely hunting him down. When the time comes, he plans on finding some good excuse to stay behind the locked doors of A to Z Enterprises.

He has just finished the first long row when Nunks contacts him to say that someone who claims to be a friend of Lacey's is standing at the gate. Mulligan can feel his mentor's distrust like a crawling down his spine.

Big brother, I not-feel a liar.

I also feel/he speaks true. BUT\ Distrust still now/talk of assassins with psi. Go ask Buddy/do scan>

Reluctantly Mulligan goes up to Lacey's office. The comp unit is quiescent, his screen glowing a soft gray, until Mulligan comes in. Then the sensor lights wink on, and the scan unit swivels his way.

"There is someone at the gate, Buddy. Nunks has asked me to ask you to scan him for an ID check."

"I have already done so, Mulligan unit. Is Nunks accusing me of being lax?"

"No. How's he going to . . . I mean, how should he know what you bringing down . . . are doing?"

Buddy makes a clacking sound that seems to be contemptuous.

"Well," Mulligan snaps. "Is he who he says he is or not?"

"The unit is Sam Bailey, captain of the RSS *Montana*, and a very old friend of Lacey's. ID is positive to the fourth degree: palm print, retinal scan, infrared patterning, and most conclusive of all, my memory."

"Okay, thanks. I'd better go tell Nunks."

"Oh, Mulligan unit? You had best mind your manners around Captain Bailey. Lacey is very fond of him, if you take my meaning. You will want to make a good impression."

If Buddy were flesh and blood, Mulligan would be able to tell he's—not lying, of course—but bending the truth by implication, but as it is, the comp unit's words hit him so hard that for a moment he finds it hard to move or even breathe. As he goes downstairs, very slowly, feeling as if he's crawling rather than walking, he is thinking that he should have known, that of course Lacey would have some glamorous lover, maybe even more than one, that he himself has nothing he could possibly offer a woman like her, and other such thoughts that all make him wish he could get blind drunk and stay that way. His first sight of Sam, black, lithe, and handsome, only darkens his despair further.

"Mulligan, right?" Sam smiles pleasantly and holds out his hand. "Lacey mentioned you to me. Pleased to meet you."

As he shakes hands, Mulligan is deciding that he hates this dude who won't even condescend to be jealous of him. He can feel Nunks' irritation pressing at the edge of his mind.

Little brother, ask him: Lacey come home\not come home?

"Captain Bailey, you know if Lacey's coming straight home?"

"Hey, man, call me Sam. I get enough of the captain shit up in deep sky. But she went off with the gordo jefe, Bates." Sam suddenly turns subdued. "Say, was a donna name of Sally Pharis a friend of yours? I'm afraid she's dead, man."

Although Mulligan barely knew Sally, any death hits him hard. All too vividly he can imagine the terror she must have felt as the long knife swung down. He takes a step, then sways. Sam catches him by the shoulders to steady him.

"Get your hands off me!"

"Oh hey." Bailey steps back sharply. "I was only trying to help. Dint mean nothing by it."

Mulligan snarls and turns blindly to Nunks, who is radiating more confusion than the sun does infrared. Nunks puts one furry, comforting arm around him and pulls him close while Sam watches with a hastily arranged aloofness.

Little brother! [sympathy] [irritation] Be strong now. Must> help Mrs. Bug> <Lacey too long> can't wait now. >Must go> You drive\not drive skimmer? I have keys Lacey-car.

Here is the juncture where Mulligan was planning to bow out of this crazy adventure, and he has several excuses at the ready. But Lacey doesn't love him; Sam doubtless would never back out of something just because it was dangerous; life isn't worth living, anyway, since he can't play in the major leagues.

I drive. You are correct now >>we go>> right away. [relief]

"Say, Bailey?" Mulligan says. "Look, hate to run and all that, but we've got a big job on our hands. You know where the Rat Yard is? Yeah? Well, a friend of ours is trapped out there. Got to go get her out. Mind waiting upstairs for Lacey?"

"Course not, but say, amigo, if you need help, I'll go with you."

"Oh, no necessario." Mulligan shrugs in what he hopes is a properly cavalier manner. "Nunks and me can handle it."

Little brother, you crazy!! >>We ought: take this guy> No!! Explain later.

While Nunks searches his rooms for the spare set of skimmer keys, Mulligan shows Sam up to the office and relays Nunks' orders to Rick: keep Maria in the office, tell Buddy to put all his sensors on automatic alarm, and stay there no matter what's happening at the gate or in the garden. If it seems that an assassin is trying to break in, he is to call the police and not attempt heroics, even with Sam to back him up. Since Mulligan makes Rick repeat all this back in front of Buddy, he's fairly sure that Nunks' orders will be carried out.

"One thing, though, Mulligan unit," Buddy says at last. "You have no comm link on your belt. How will I be able to trace your movements?"

"Who says I, like, want you to?"

"You may encounter danger in the Rat Yard."

"Oh yeah? Well, if we do, it no going to be nothing a plastic plug-sucker like you can help with anyway!" Mulligan turns and strides dramatically out of the room.

"Hey, kid!" Sam calls after him. "The AI's right, y'know."

As he pounds down the stairs, taking them two at a time, Mulligan has a brief thought that he'd rather be damned than listen to Sam. Besides, at the moment he hates Buddy so much that he never wants to hear that brisk artificial voice again.

With a hecto of Sarahian weed secreted about her person, Lacey takes the Metro back to Porttown on the Fourth Street line. Since it's still a couple of hours before the late-night rush, she had the car to herself except for one teenage Blanca with magenta hair who is crunching and smacking her way through a particularly redolent order of slice'n'fry, heavy on the onions and vinegar. Although eating is forbidden on the Metro, Lacey decides against meddling; the kid is wearing a knife in an ankle sheath, and although Lacey could take it from her without half trying, the effort seems a waste. Instead she opens the window next to her and lets in the dusty though ionized air from the tunnel. The air-conditioning generally works on none of the cars that run through Porttown, because—or so the Metro authorities say—the Blanco kids stuff litter into the vents.

Lacey needs the fresh air, anyway. Her short day's sleep is beginning to tell on her; only the adrenaline rush of fear and cold rage is keeping her awake. Yet, even though thinking is a little more difficult than usual, she's beginning to get a plan clear in her head. Bates could call out every cop and vigilante-minded citizen in Polar City and still never find the assassin if she (or he, she reminds herself) has taken refuge in the Outworld Bazaar. On the other hand, Sally's death has given her a weapon. Murders happen all the time in the Bazaar—dope deals go wrong, sexual jealousies run high, druggies rob each other with violent results—but murder by an outsider is a very different thing than murder among, as it were, friends. She's sure that the news is spreading already, and that Al, for one, is going to be heartsick when he hears it. If only she can convince the Bizarros that the assassin is as much their enemy as he is the cops', the Outworlder will find himself delivered to Bates's doorstep, most likely in a sack.

If, of course, the usual channels can even find a psychic sentient who also happens to be a highly trained assassin, a major-league killer in the minor-league world of the Bazaar. No doubt he (or she—Lacey reminds herself that they've been making too many assumptions about this killer) has enough false IDs and well-rehearsed cover stories to change identities every day for a week. All at once something hits her leg, and before she can stop herself Lacey's on her feet with her laser pistol half-drawn. The magenta-haired kid shrinks back into her seat with a whine.

"Dint mean nada, man."

With a stab of embarrassment Lacey realizes that the thing that touched her was the empty crumpled carton from the slice'n'fry, tossed onto the floor to slide and roll where it would. Before she sits down she kicks it back into the aisle, but mingled with the kid's flower-sweet perfume a sharp odor lingers.

"Jeezuz and Madre de Dios!" Lacey slaps her thigh in exultation. "Of course."

The kid slews round in her seat and stares straight ahead, maybe thinking Lacey is a crazy. Lacey gives her a brilliant smile and decides against telling her that the reek of her ill-considered lunch may just have saved Polar City from martial law. If this assassin's been infected with the bacterium, as seems more than likely, her (or his) flesh is going to smell like sour vinegar. Even though perfume will cover a lot, tracking her (or him) down now looks possible, no matter how many fake passports he (or she) has, if Lacey can only enlist the right help. As she gets off at the Fourth and J Street stop, Lacey is feeling an old, familiar, and rather tiresome dread, heavily laced with guilt. She is going to have to visit the man they call the Mayor of Porttown. More than ever she's glad she hit Bates up for the dope; she's going to need it to bribe the Mayor's various doormen and bodyguards.

Before she takes the grav platform up to the street, she finds herself a dark corner of the station and sends out a comm call on Carol's private number. Although she's expecting to wait for some time, Carol herself, not her comp unit, answers promptly.

"Oh, it's you, Lacey. Look, I no can talk long. I put a call through to Epidemiology Center on Sarah. The twelve-minute delay's almost up."

"All I want to know is how Little Joe's doing."

"No savvy. I mean, the goddamn stuff's spreading, but it no is killing him or anything. Look, the poor bastard took a leak earlier, right? Well, now our little friend's working on his genital area, eating off his body hair, making him nice and shiny and kind of leathery. He's real sick about it, but I told him it's something new for the donnas—textural interest. He no liked the joke."

"Bet he dint."

"He no is laughing right now, either, cause the cops are in with him. I got a lawyer in there before I let the greenies and their hypnotist in."

"Damn right. Did the police give you the report on Sally Pharis?"

On the tiny screen Carol's face turns bleak.

"Yeah. Sure did. Look, it might work this way: the bacteria keeps to certain limits until the victim dies, but then . . . hooboy, it just eats him up. I mean eat literally, by the way. This stuff digests nonliving organics, dead cells like hair for example, and turns them into simple sugars and some kind of peculiar acid waste product. I got that running in the analyzing comp right now—never seen anything like it before—but that's the molecule that stinks so bad. Those threads you saw all over Sally's corpse? Strings of sugar crystals, like some gonzo kind of rock candy. The hospital gave poor old Joe his lunch, a soy-burger—you should've seen what the bacteria did to the bun, ate it right out from under him. Pretty disgusting. From now on, man, he'll have to use a fork." Distantly a beep sounds. "Got to go. Here's my call."

"Okay. I'll call through to Bates, see what Little Joe told them."

When the screen goes dark, Lacey punches in the chief's number. She's going to have to lie about her own destination, as she quite simply can't tell him without causing a lot of trouble in the future. The Mayor's address is a well-kept secret from, at least, honest policebeings like Bates. The chief answers immediately, and he looks elated.

"Lacey, thank God you called! Little Joe gave us what we needed. I know why Sally got killed."

"Great. You going to give Little Joe immunity?"

"You know damn well any confession made under hypnosis no is going to stand in court. Besides, who the hell cares about a little dope when we got a real gonzo weirdo on our hands?"

"Sure enough. What did he remember?"

"Sally told him, and I quote, 'I saw some dude, this Blanco, taking off his clothes right on the public street. He had another set on underneath, and it looked like he was planning on shoving the first set into this big old public recycler.' How's that?"

"So now we know he was a dude, not a donna, at least. Did Sally mention the blood?"

"She dint. It's the only thing that makes me wonder if she saw the right guy. Well, hell, she might no have been close enough to see the mess. It's the only lead we got, and I'm no giving it up right away."

Although it takes a strong act of will to ignore a fellow psychic when he's mentally screaming at you to slow down and watch where you're going, as well as howling out a long litany of curses, Mulligan manages. His reckless mood has swelled to encompass a romantic fantasy of dying in a good cause so that Lacey will tearfully realize that it was him she loved all along. (He is blissfully unaware that Lacey hasn't cried in a good fifteen years.) He's taken the battered blue skimmer up to its altitude limit and thrown the throttle open; now they are

screaming through the sky at a good hundred and fifty
kilometers an hour. Every now and then he makes it swoop in
a grand, rolling gesture.

*Little brother: slow down now OR\ >I kill you>>stomp on
corpse\repeatedly>.*

You no drive>> no can get home if I dead.

Walking good exercise. SLOW DOWN NOW!!

Out of pity for the undercurrent of sheer terror in Nunks's
mind, Mulligan drops it down to an even hundred, and all the
alarming rattles and bangs in the chassis ease off. By then they
are circling the edge of the rehydration project, where under
the dead-white glow of the maglev lights the shift is changing,
the workers looking like tiny insects from the skimmer's
height. The sight convinces Mulligan that it might be a good
idea to drop nearer to the ground. They plunge some two
hundred meters straight down, then level off.

*>Kill you slowly> little brother>> use psionic tortures
<<developed on homeworld<< for worst criminals.*

*[apologetic regret] I only do\what you ask, big brother\
WHAT IF\ crazies hunt Mrs. Bug >must hurry.*

[sheer rage] [forced agreement]

Since Lacey's skimmer is a road-only model, when the level
surfaces come to an end, some two kilometers from the Yard,
Mulligan is forced to land. Before he can even park the
skimmer properly, Nunks sweeps off his safety harness, flings
open the door, and staggers out. Mulligan eases the car into
the shelter of a group of thorn trees, locks it, and walks back to
find Nunks running his hands through his fur. Apparently,
judging from the handfuls of loose hair, the ride has made him
shed rather badly.

Little brother: [inarticulate fury, warning]

[contrite apology]

[somewhat lessened fury, warning]

After a few minutes of poking around in the underbrush,
Mulligan finds a trail along a ravine, thick with chaparral, that
curves round the lip of the crater for a ways before it plunges
down toward the Yard. Since the trail is narrow, he takes the
lead and does his best to clear away any small branches that
might snag Nunks' fur, so that big brother can concentrate on
sending psychic signals to Mrs. Bug. The rough-barked thorn
trees are hard on the hands, and it doesn't take long before he
wishes he had a good laser-cutter with him. Then it occurs to

him that they've come out without any weapons, not so much as a pocketknife. Nunks picks up his flash of alarm.

<Too much death already, little brother< >not kill>not harm>>no one.

Enemies> not agree>

[psionic equivalent of a shrug] too bad.

The romantic fantasy slips away like a falling suncloak (which he has also forgotten to bring) and leaves him with the knife-sharp realization that he could die out in the Yard and never get to play semi-pro ball again.

Big brother, we wait here\not wait? Let Mrs. Bug come to us?

Not wait. [contempt]

<In skimmer< you the one/frightened.

Not frightened [immense dignity] <sick to stomach.

In the flash and colored glare of the northern lights they make their way downhill in a silence broken only by the occasional buzz and whir of a nocturnal flyer or the *tchak!* of a startled reptile in the brush. Mulligan is only dimly aware of Nunks' mind, all passive receptivity and awareness. He concentrates his own mind on finding their way through the grasping tangle of plants to avoid radiating his fear to Mrs. Bug, who, or so he suspects, is going to be a tough bird to net. They're almost to the valley floor when Mulligan sees something large and shiny off in the chaparral about ten meters to his right. He sends a signal to Nunks to stop.

Plants all torn up now, big brother. <Someone drag it\long way<<

You go look\not look?

Look.

Since the chaparral's already been thoroughly mashed down, Mulligan can walk straight over to the mysterious object. As he gets closer he sees that it's a polyhedral tent, made of a green metallic film like nothing he's ever seen before. Either it's ripped in several places or the being who made it has odd ideas about windows. When something moves he freezes, crouching in the shadow of a thorn tree, but it's only a local lizard, wandering past the structure with a small flyer in its mouth. With a brief and futile wish for a flashlight, Mulligan goes forward, angling round until he can see into the triangular opening in one face. Although there seem to be things piled up inside, he refuses to go any closer, because over the campsite hangs the sharp stink of spoiled vinegar.

Big brother, I smell something\real wrong/here. Read\not read?

Read. >Come back>Now. Disease\very bad.

As he walks back, Mulligan opens himself up slightly to the background signal. The eater is there, ravenous and eager, a vast cloud of pure appetite. Involuntarily he yelps aloud.

I read it too, little brother. Strange being\very very strange. Not sentient. A group mind\low level.

Animal\not animal?

Animal BUT\ primitive. I not understand it\well.

He crouches down beside Nunks, who's sitting cross-legged in the middle of the trail. After a moment Nunks beams to him again.

I begin/understand> This tent thing\near rehydration crater. <Trail made> now leads back to crater.

[*confusion*]

[*irritation*] *In crater now: what comes from off-world?*

Comet ice.

Excellent [*sarcasm*]. *So Outworld tent, creature? <<<they come<<<?*

[*amazement*] *<Out of a comet? <<<Long time ago, frozen? Old accident?<<*

I guess only: some kind stasis capsule OR\ sleeper unit <<<safe till brought down here<just recently<thaw.

[*sudden shock*] *<<they survive all that! <<<accident, then<< survive uncontrolled thaw <<then: Mr. Bug killed by crazies!* [*heart-rending pity*]

[*agreement*] [*melancholy*]

For a moment they crouch there in silence, communicating through sheer feeling their understanding of Mrs. Bug's hysterical, rage-inflamed grief. It's no wonder, Mulligan thinks, that she'll approach them only to flee again; for all she knows, this entire planet is full of murderous crazies like those who killed her lover or mate or whatever, exactly, he was. (Mulligan knows enough about xenobiology to realize that of all the varied facets of sentient life, those pertaining to love and sex differ the most and sometimes wildly from species to species.) She may even be thinking that their sympathy is feigned bait to lead her into a trap.

Nunks suddenly stiffens and turns wary. Picking up his

mood, Mulligan goes on alert, pushing away the sheer hunger of the eater, letting the confused babble of signal from the Rat Yard wash over him, sorting quickly and deftly through it until he finds a new element: the touch, the very brief and hastily withdrawn touch of another psionic mind. Even though he doesn't recognize it, he can feel the cold, impersonal hostility like the graze of a knife blade down his back.

Little brother, someone <spy< spy now >spy> on us.

Not Mrs. Bug?

Not Mrs. Bug.

The assassin!! [terror]

Maybe\maybe not, little brother. Some of the crazies here now/psionics\unrecognized/why they are crazy.

Oh.

Although they wait there for some time, sifting the signal, sending their linked minds ranging, they never pick up the spy again. They do, however, reach Mrs. Bug. Even though she's on the far edge of their range, Mulligan can feel her clearly, her mind wrapped in its grief. Nunks calls to her, softly and patiently, repeats the call, adds a wave of pity, calls again—she refuses to answer. A fragment of society's attempt to educate him about something other than baseball suddenly floats to the surface of Mulligan's mind, a few lines of a very old poem that he was forced to memorize in high school, and he sends it out to her:

In a lurking place I lurk/One with the sullen dark/What's hell but a cold heart?

The grief that pours back in response overwhelms him, tumbles him, half-drowns him until he weeps, sobbing aloud in the middle of the trail, yet he can feel that he's drawing off some of her pain much as a doctor draws pus from an abscess. She, too, knows it. For a moment she hesitates on the edge of openness; then she wraps her fear-shot rage around her and flees. Nunks pats Mulligan's shoulder until at last he can stop crying.

Little brother, many sentients mock you. >Not listen anymore> You fine being.

Mulligan nearly weeps again, this time in gratitude, but he pulls himself together and wipes his face vigorously on his sleeve instead.

Must find her, Nunks goes on. *IF ONLY\ we get close, she see us, read us directly> THEN\ she know we trustworthy.*

[agreement] BUT\ how?

[bafflement] >Walk on >>Try to!get closer.

[agreement] Which way?

[annoyed bafflement] Wait! [self-mockery] >We triangulate her> Little brother, know\not know?

Not know.

I teach now. Useful psi skill. >You stay here >>I walk on a ways THEN\ >we each contact her> >>feel angle/we three form triangle/fix on her position>>

I get it! Like: astrogation.

[pleased agreement]

Before Nunks leaves, he and Mulligan sift out the wave of signal thoroughly, on guard against that hostile mind they felt earlier. Distantly Mulligan does pick up Old Meg, mumbling over her cards, but she's the only psionic presence he can find for kilometers, besides, that is, the omnipresent eater. Moving carefully to avoid catching his fur on the thorn trees, Nunks sets out down the trail, heading toward the Rat Yard, where, at least presumably, Mrs. Bug is hiding. Once he's out of sight, Mulligan's fear returns in force. It seems to him that every shadow is hiding an assassin, armed to the teeth with exotic weapons, and every glint of the northern lights off a leaf or pebble looks like the flash of a knife.

The scream is so peculiar that it takes Mulligan a moment to recognize it for what it is: Nunks startled into howling out a physical cry of fear. He's on his feet and running by the time the mental wave washes over him:

Run little brother! Save yourself!

But Mulligan hears another voice, a human male shouting in a manic glee, yodeling in a parody of a hunting call.

"Lay off him!" He's barely aware that he's spoken; then he's running after Nunks.

Mulligan comes crashing out of the chaparral to see Nunks crouching with his back to a broken slab of plastocrete wall. In a ragged semicircle in front of him a black human male, with an amazingly long and thick tangle of hair, and a gray lizzie brandish lengths of plastopipe, while a third, a Blanco male, wields an actual ax. The Wild Man, John Hancock, and Blue-beak Bizzer, Mulligan assumes. He can taste his fear like something rotten in his mouth. Slowly Nunks straightens up, holding out one hand, palm forward, in what should be a recognizable sign of peace; he is also broadcasting a generalized feeling of calm and rationality. In answer the three shriek and cackle; the lizzie does a shuffling, foot-pounding war dance and waves his pipe high; the humans edge closer.

Little brother> get out of here> head to skimmer>>re-hydro project>>>men there help!

"Hey, you three scum-bags!" Mulligan waves his hands over his head to further attract their attention. "Shit-beak lizzie! Worm-eater! And you, white boy! Screw any dogs lately? Hey, there, Wild Man! You crazy, know that? Crazy and you stink, too."

The three of them spin around, muttering, holding up their weapons as they peer at him in the shifting blaze of colored light. In his mind Mulligan picks up Nunks radiating a mind-shield of stupendous strength.

Big brother escape with me!

Both can't>No use both of us die. >You go >>bring help >>>I join you>>>

"Worm-eater, worm-eater!" With his mind muddled by terror he falls back on the elementary school playground for inspiration. "White boy, white boy! Stink-oh, stink-oh!"

The lizzie's first, gnashing his snout in rage as he rushes at Mulligan, but his two buddies follow right after, yelling, waving weapons, making half-articulate promises that center around divesting Mulligan of his arms and legs. With a howl of crazed laughter of his own, Mulligan leaps onto a pile of rubble, then jumps down at an angle and takes off running. Here he has the advantage, a natural athlete who's made running laps into something of a religion against enemies who persist in wasting their breath by yelling insults. He paces himself, making sure that they keep following as he dodges through the rubble. When a length of pipe sails by his head, he leaps to one side, just in time to avoid a thrown ax.

Ahead he can see the white rise of the broken tower and turns to his left, heading for a long flat stretch where he can put a little more distance between himself and his pursuers. Already the insults have stopped in a laboring of breath behind him. Mulligan bends low and pretends that he's stretching a double into an inside-the-park home run as he whips around the tower and heads back the way he came. By now, he figures, Nunks should be well into the chaparral and safe. His breath is beginning to come hard, but the three crazies are a good long way behind him now, stumbling and cursing as they try to make some speed. His lungs pounding, his heart following suit, he races down the runway and into the green, grassy plain, crossed by small, sparkling streams under a yellow sun.

When he looks back, the crazies are gone, and he slows to a walk, panting for breath at first. Ahead of him in the far distance is a low rise of purple mountains, which seem to be the source of the river whose bank he's walking on. All at once it occurs to him that he doesn't know where he is. When he glances around, he sees a figure dressed in long flowing robes at some distance to his right. She seems to be bending over some sort of large furry animal.

"Uh, hey, Miz?" With a friendly wave, Mulligan walks her way. "Scuse, but I'm kind of lost. Can you tell me the way back to the Rat Yard?"

The woman turns his way and looks up with the gray lizzie face of Blue-beak Bizzer. With a yelp Mulligan jumps back, but something hard smacks him across the back of the head, and he falls into darkness.

SECOND INTERLUDE: The Hunted

After he killed Ibrahim, Tomaso took a long hot shower in Sally's bathroom, but even though he used two kinds of scented soap, the smell of vinegar returned the moment he dried himself off. By then his skin was just beginning to itch and harden all along his arms, down his chest, and worst of all, around his genital area—everywhere, in fact, that had been in any kind of moist contact with Sally's body. Although he gave himself a rubdown with perfumed lotion, it made only a temporary difference; as soon as he was dressed, he started itching and stinking again. When he left the building, a pair of lizzies happened to be walking past. He noticed one of them pause, sniff the air with his long beaky snout, then mutter something to the other. Tomaso nearly broke into a run, but his long training saved him. He walked on as casually as if he'd noticed nothing.

Ducking down alleys and along every confusing side path he found, he went to the nearest Metro station, took a train twenty stops north, got off, took another line six stops south, and transferred east to the train he's currently on, returning to the Outworld Bazaar main station just about the same time as Bates and Lacey are discovering Ibrahim's corpse. As he rides the grav platform up to the surface, he realizes that he's being watched. He can feel the mental attention coming his way as a warm glow, as if someone were shining a light pen on the back of his head. Outside the lift exit is a covered shopping area—*mall* is much too elegant a word for this scruffy collection of shops and kiosks under faded awnings, where a handful of sentients drift down the street in their suncloaks, too tired to buy anything, too drunk to think of going home. Tomaso ducks behind a kiosk that sells chewing spice and turns to watch the exit just as a pair of beings in white suncloaks come out, hesitate briefly, then amble slowly past him. Suncloaks, once his ally, have become his enemy. He has no idea of who or what those beings may be, but he's fairly sure that they were the ones watching him as the transparent platform carried him up. The question is, why? Idle curiosity, quite possibly, as they waited their turn.

As he lets them pass, he feels his stomach churning and growling in an overwhelming lust for food. The thought of eating fills his mind so thoroughly that the smell of cheap soy-dogs and slice'n'fry coming from the kiosks makes him salivate. He buys himself two soy-dogs with kraut and mustard, wolfs those down, then gets a double order of slice'n'fry, too, heavy on the vinegar to mask his own scent. He eats the crunchy slabs of protein flakes and eggplant slowly as he walks along, the helmet of his suncloak tipped back, heading toward the second cheap hotel where he has a room and more stashed gear. Yet even though he acts indifferent and casual, he is constantly aware of being looked at, wondered and whispered about by everyone he passes.

Just as he turns down a side street, he glances at the container of food and nearly yelps aloud. The waterproof plastopress carton is disintegrating under his touch with long holes the size and shape of his fingers. He dumps it into the first recycler he finds, out behind a two-story gray building where a three-dee sign flashes with endlessly changing lines of mah-jongg tiles. As he turns away, he hears the swish of a cloak behind him and spins around to find a small child, draped in a miniature suncloak, all dirty, patched, and torn. He can see the kid's face through the faceplate: solemn eyes, somehow disappointed.

"You dint want to eat that?" the child says.

"Why? You want it? Sorry, but it's spoiled. Make you real sick if you ate the leftovers."

"Oh. Okay. I won't, then."

As Tomaso strides past he considers giving the child some spare change, but he's afraid that the coins would spread whatever this disease is. Yet the image of those disappointed eyes, a child going hungry, haunts him, pulls at him, threatens him with the memory of the boy's voice screaming as the boy's hands pound and pound on the blood-smeared door. He turns around only to find the child already gone. When he runs the back of one hand across his forehead he realizes that he's broken out in a cold sweat.

At the hotel he has a piece of luck. The service door at the back is standing propped open with no one around but a donkeybot, loading crates of paper napkins onto a dolly. He slips past, finds the fire stairs, and gets up to his room without seeing anyone. Although he left the hotel's door-card at the desk when he went out, he has a copy that he duplicated himself on a very illegal device so he can let himself in without having to ask a clerk. He locks the door behind him, turns around . . . and realizes that the room's been searched. It's a near-professional job, with everything put neatly back where it was found, and a thin film of dust carefully blown around, too, in an even layer, but he left a crumpled fragment of transparent plastofilm on top of his duffel bag, where it would look like a bit of dropped trash, and that fragment is now lying on the floor. Doubtless these clever amateurs hadn't even noticed it.

When he goes through his things he finds nothing taken, and he never carries anything incriminating, such as weaponry or faked papers, in the kind of luggage that he leaves in hotels. It's quite possible that the searchers concluded that whoever rented this room is not the man they are looking for, if indeed they're even looking for him and not some drug dealer who's reneged on a deal or a con man muscling in on someone else's territory. By then the tiny room reeks of vinegar in spite of the best efforts of the air-conditioning. When he takes still another shower, all his body hair rinses away with the soap. As he watches it puddle in the drain, he feels like screaming.

Another change of clothes, this time a nondescript pair of jeans and a loose pullover shirt, suitable for prowling around the city while he looks for Mulligan so he can kill the only person left who can identify him—if indeed this clumsy amateur psychic can even break through the lock Tomaso put on his mind. Although he doubts that Mulligan can, he is going to take no chances. Then he'll be on his way to the Rat Yard to track down the female alien, and his job will be over. He wonders if maybe he should sic his three tame crazies on the female—he could call her the Devil's wife, he supposes—but it would be far safer to do the job himself.

He's just pulled on his boots and settled the knife inside the left one in its hidden sheath when someone knocks, calling loudly for Mr. Svensen, the fake name under which he's

registered. Soundlessly Tomaso gets up, drifts back toward the
blind side of the door, cocks his foot, and retrieves the knife as
the knocking sounds again. For a moment there's silence; then
comes the sound of a card being slipped into the door slot. He
waits, unnaturally immobile, until the door swings open and a
young black male steps boldly inside, followed by a cleaningbot. Tomaso's taking no chances. He glides forward, flings his
right arm around the man from behind, and slits his throat
neatly, right to left, with his left hand. As the corpse falls, the
'bot slides forward mindlessly to start mopping at the mess.
Tomaso punches its stop button and steps back.

For the briefest of moments he wants to dabble his hands in
the man's blood and wipe it all over himself. The urge is so
strong and so revolting that he nearly gags. He spins on his
heel to avoid looking at the corpse and merely stands for a
moment, breathing hard, feeling his heart pound, and picking
up that signal again: the eater. It wants the blood, this eater,
not only wants to roil and wallow in it, but it somehow seems
to feel that the blood is its due, that Tomaso is withholding
something to which it is entitled. The junk food he ate earlier
threatens to reappear. He breathes deeply, quietly, makes
himself think of the neutral image of the night sky over Arden,
his homeworld, until his stomach settles. Even though he's
regained control, he knows he has to get out of that room.

In the strip of mirrortile over the dresser he examines
himself carefully: just one tiny drop of blood on the left cuff of
his jeans. The suncloak will cover it. Being left-handed is a real
advantage to a man in his trade; by slashing from behind he can
give the police a false picture of his kills and force them to
make several different kinds of incorrect assumptions that
inevitably slow their investigations to the point of futility. He
wipes the knife clean on the bedspread, takes the suncloak,
checking to make sure that the laser pistol is still in its hidden
sheath, and heads out, leaving the luggage behind, deciding
that he'll never come back for it. He has other clothes stashed
in a rented locker down at the main grav train station, along
with a laser rifle broken down and disguised as a piece of
holofilm equipment, and he also has plenty of money to buy
more if he needs to.

Yet as he hurries down nearly deserted sidewalks, it occurs
to him that going into a shop and talking with a clerk could be
dangerous. Although he never catches anyone at it, all his

psychic faculties, as well as his plain old common sense, tell him that he's being stared at wherever he goes, for the very simple reason that the morning heat is making him stink of rancid vinegar.

Chapter Six

Rejuv drugs have trapped the Mayor of Porttown behind the face of a boy of twenty, smoothly handsome though pale, with blond hair and blue eyes that radiate the innocence of a young animal. He's slender, too, and as supple as a boy, sitting cross-legged at the moment on an oversized pale blue divan among understated gray and lavender silk pillows. Everything in his "office," the den in his suite of rooms above the brothel he owns, whispers quietly of the best of taste and the sparing of no expense, from the easel paintings brought from Old Earth (a Matisse and the last surviving Frank Stella in private hands among them) to the blue and green rugs woven on the carli home planet long before that species took to deep space. He has insisted on giving Lacey a shot of fine brandy in a cut crystal snifter, and he holds a drink of his own in slender fingers. His smile is an odd mixture of pride and defiance, a challenge to make some comment on his wealth or on the way he earned it. Since she's too used to the game by now to give in, she tosses off a mouthful of the brandy as if it were cheap beer. The ploy works; he speaks first.

"How much did my guards squeeze out of you in baksheesh to let you in?"

"Oh, about a hecto of Sarahian weed—a bit here, a bit there."

"Want me to get it back for you?"

"Nah. Good joke—I got it from the cops for free, told'em I was going to spread it around for information."

He laughs under his breath, giving her such a charming smile (so carefully calculated to show just the right amount of perfect teeth; the corners of the eyes, too, crinkling just so)

140

that she can easily imagine rich old men showering cash into his lap simply to keep him smiling.

"Okay," he says. "I heard you were working for the police these days."

"With the cops, buster, not for them, and don't you forget it."

"Yeah? Must be something pretty heavy going down."

"Maybe. Tell me, Richie, how do you like this idea? Porttown under martial law, a couple of Army boys on every corner, a surveillance satellite in permanent orbit, listening in every time a damn toilet flushes."

The boy's eyes widen, the soft boy's mouth purses to an *oh*.

"Cut the sarcasm," Lacey snaps. "You think I'd lie to you?"

Richie shrugs in an elaborate pantomime of ignorance and has another sip of his brandy. Lacey follows suit and waits; with time she can always wear him down. Yet it hurts to watch him, to see him look so young and remember him as even younger, nine years old, in fact, crying while trying not to cry when she shipped out with the Fleet. *I'm going to come home soon, Richie*—an empty promise, as it turned out, because another border war erupted, and it was five years before she saw her younger brother again, her little brother, as she thinks of him still. And she wonders, still, after all these years, if perhaps his life would have been different if she'd stayed home and never enlisted, because she was the only one in the family who could ever handle him, the only one who had his confidence and his respect. If her father's neglect and his ugly little life as a petty criminal had ruined her sense of self, she supposes that it must have hurt his only son far more deeply. She could, perhaps, have seen it then, but she was after all only seventeen herself, and only twenty-two when she came home on leave at last to find him hustling his behind in the Bazaar, as wild and defiant as the young animal whose amoral soul his eyes mirror now.

"Okay," he says at length. "And just why is the government going to declare martial law?"

"Long story. You hear what happen to Sally Pharis?"

Another elaborate shrug, but his painted eyelids flicker in interest.

"Ah c'mon—are you telling me that a leather girl got herself offed, and it was important? Happens all the time, man. If you get into bondage, it can go too far real easy." A perfectly timed pause. "It pays good, though."

"Yeah, Sally always said so." She adds a casual pause of her own. "She no died cause some john got too excited."

"Yeah? Why, then?"

"I'm no hundred percent sure, but here's my best guess. We got a professional here, a killer working for the 'Lies. He killed a carli named Ka Gren. Did you hear about that on the news?"

"Course." The mask is beginning to slip; Richie leans forward a little. "And Sally was in the wrong place at the wrong time?"

"Yeah, she saw him right afterwards, man. Little Joe Walker told the police that she was right near the scene of the crime."

"The scene of the crime. You sound like a holopix."

"Watch your big mouth."

"You going to belt me one if I dunt, just like you used to? You probably would, yeah, bodyguards or no bodyguards." His eyes drift to the panel that marks the door into the hall. "They no dare touch you, anyway."

"Thanks."

This time the smile is an honest one, tinged with melancholy.

"So okay, Bobbie, this dude killed Sally to shut her mouth. What's that got to do with me?"

"He's hiding in the Bazaar, most likely. Chief Bates has three days to find him, before the troops come in. Are you going to put up with the Army just to save some Outworlder's ass?"

Richie smiles with a perfectly done wryness and looks away, nodding in half-humorous agreement.

"Nah," he says at last. "You got me, all right. So what do you want? This dude's head in a bag?"

"All of him, and alive if you can. Bates has a few questions to ask him, like who's paying his bills. Now, I no savvy much about him. He's a Blanco, and he's got this weird infection on his hands for sure, and maybe some other places. He smells like spoiled vinegar. That's your tip-off, the smell. And he's dangerous. If I'm guessing right, he got psi as well as being a trained pro."

"She-it, big sister! You don't ask much, huh?"

"Like I say, you want the Army in here, asking where you get your cash and demanding a cut? What are you paying your goon squad for, anyway?"

"You got a point, but I think I'll put out an open contract on this dude, get a lot of eyes looking for him all at once. It'll be faster—"

At her belt Lacey's comp link beeps. With an apologetic nod in Richie's direction she slips it off and punches in.

"Programmer?" Buddy sounds so humanly alarmed that she wonders if he's on the verge of serious malfunction. "We have had an unfortunate occurrence."

"You what? For chrissakes, man, lay it on me! I mean, continue to transmit message."

"Some hours ago, Mulligan and Nunks took your skimmer and went to the Rat Yard. Now Maria informs me that they are in grave difficulty."

"What!? How does she know? Try starting at the beginning, Buddy, and fill in more detail."

"Maria is a latent psychic. She has received a strong feeling of danger and despair from Nunks and an exceptionally strong premonition of danger concerning Mulligan. Now, as for the skimmer, I am uncertain of its condition, but—"

"Screw the skimmer! No, don't take that literal. I mean, the skimmer's condition is of no importance. Why did Mulligan and Nunks go to the Rat Yard?"

"To rescue a sentient they call Mrs. Bug. Captain Bailey informs me that she seemed in some danger. It was the captain, by the way, who insisted I call you." Buddy's voice develops a pronounced sulk. "He threatened to magnetize my cubes if I didn't."

"Good for him. Why did you let'em go out there alone? Do they have a gun?"

"They have no weapons that I know of, programmer. I had no way of stopping them. Using his psionics, Nunks can unjam any lock that I can electronically secure."

"Well, that's true. But jeezchrist, Buddy! Why didn't you tell me this before?"

Over a faint hissing of static she can hear Sam's voice in the background.

"I have made an error, programmer," Buddy says. "I have malfunctioned. I grovel at your feet in an agony of abasement. I wrap my circuits in frayed insulation, I spit upon my own data cubes, I—"

"Enough! Tell Sam I'm on my way. We're going to check your subsidiary drives when this is all over."

Lacey powers out to find Richie watching her in as much anxiety as he can allow himself to show.

"How are you going to get out to the Yard if this Mulligan guy copped your skimmer?"

"Oh jeezuz, I no savvy! Rent a car, I guess."

"Take too long. Lend you one of mine."

"Thanks. Hey, man, you're a prince."

"Nada but the best for you."

There is something in the lighthearted way he says it that hints at pain underneath. No matter how urgent the situation, she refuses to waste the first honest moment they've had since her retirement.

"Hey, Richie? I'm sorry I left you behind, but the Fleet was the only chance I had. At first I was just an enlisted man. No could bring you along like an officer's kid or something. I would've if I could've."

He looks away so sharply that she's afraid he might cry.

"I know," he says, his voice a whisper. "Ah, for chrissakes, that was too fucking long ago to worry bout." He picks up a comm unit, disguised as a crystal rose, from the edge of the divan. "Hal, make sure the dove-gray Bentley is charged, and bring it round the front. My sister needs it for a while."

Never in her life has Lacey driven a skimmer like the Bentley. As sleek as a lick of butter on the outside, it has blue sheriki skin upholstery on the inside and real wood on the instrument panel as well. So smoothly does it fly that she finds herself hitting the speed limit before she realizes it. When she pulls up in front of A to Z, the few sentients around in the first false dawn light goggle and gape in amazement. Before she goes in, she makes sure she sets the alarm.

Sam is waiting, pacing back and forth just inside the gate. When she lets herself in, she sees Rick and Maria hurrying down the outside staircase to join them.

"Lacey, you got to do something about that goddamn AI unit," Sam bursts out. "I had to argue four, five minutes before the filthy thing called you!"

"Yeah, it got a malfunction, all right. Maria pick up any more from Nunks or Mulligan?"

"Nunks is frantic, thinking Mulligan's hurt or something. Maria no can sort it all out; she no capable of picking up much more than feelings."

"Cajones de diablo! Okay, you got a laser?"

"Sure do."

"Swell. With Rick we got three. No, wait. We got to leave him here to take care of Maria."

"I'm coming with you." Her head held high, Maria strides across the garden. "I can lead you straight to Nunks. Without me, you no can find him 'cept by blind luck."

"You sure you want to come? It's dangerous work, girl."

"You and Nunks took me in, you got me a doctor, you fed me. Damn right I'm coming along."

Since she can see that Sam is lusting to drive the Bentley, Lacey tosses him the keys and takes the front passenger seat while Maria and Rick slide into the back with looks approaching awe. As grimly attentive as if he were piloting a shuttle into orbit, Sam starts up the skimmer and lifts off, rising smoothly as they spiral above the streets. Lacey leans back in her seat and wonders what could possibly be wrong with her: she feels sick to her stomach, and her breathing is coming a little too fast. Then she realizes that she's frightened, not for herself, but for Mulligan, worried literally sick as Sam's words sink in: Nunks is frantic, thinking Mulligan's hurt or something. *Ohmigawd, don't tell me I really am in love with the little bastard!* The idea is preposterous, but she has to admit that she isn't breaking into a cold sweat from worrying about Nunks.

When Mulligan wakes up, the first thing he's aware of is the blinding, biting pain in his head. The second is the smell in the air, a miasma of unwashed human, unwashed lizzie, grease, steam, indeterminate food, and a both sweet and acrid overtone that, thanks to his having had two younger brothers, he finally identifies as dirty diapers. When he tries to move, he realizes that his hands and feet are tied. At that point it occurs to him to open his eyes. He discovers that he's lying on a pile of filthy blankets with his face to a gray plastocrete wall. Judging from the dancing shadows thrown onto it, a fire of some sort is burning behind him. For a long time he lies still and tries to remember how he got to wherever this is, but the blow on the head has left him utterly confused. Although he remembers the three Ratters threatening Nunks and the way he led them off, after he rounded the broken white tower his memories end. He can assume, of course, that they caught up with him.

Alternately moaning and swearing he manages to roll over onto his other side. When his head stops swimming he can see that he's in a round room, about eighteen meters across, piled and heaped with crumbling boxes and mysterious bundles wrapped in rags. Directly across from him is a sliding door in the gray plastocrete wall; about ninety degrees from that, what seems to be the mouth of a tunnel. A small fire of thorn wood burns nearby, the smoke swirling down the tunnel so smoothly that Mulligan assumes it opens somewhere outside. Sitting near the fire and nursing a baby is a young black woman dressed in a pair of dirty brown shorts and two ragged blouses, layered together to cover up the holes. When she looks his way, her eyes seem to be focused on some other world. It occurs to Mulligan that he knows who she must be.

"You're Del, and that baby's J.J."

"How you know, white boy?" She sounds both angry and frightened.

"I know lots of things."

She considers him for a moment, her liquid-dark eyes flicking over him; then just as suddenly she loses interest and looks away. At her breast the baby, who seems about six months old, squirms and fusses; she changes him to the other side and pats his back reflexively while she goes on staring at the wall. Every now and then her eyes move as if she's following some kind of action; occasionally she smiles or frowns at whatever it is she's seeing. Mulligan decides against asking her about it. Yet when he tries to wriggle his hands free of the rope tying them together, she turns her head to glare at him.

"Dunt you try nothing, white boy. Old John'll be back any minute now. If he finds you trying to escape, he'll be mad. The others wanted to kill you. He dint, but if he's mad, he'll maybe change his mind."

"Okay. I'll be good as gold." He lies still again, and he has to admit that his head feels much better when he isn't moving. "Why dint John let'em kill me?"

"He's going to try and sell you."

"Sell me? To who?"

"God."

Although Mulligan would like to think that he's hallucinating, he knows that indeed, she did say God. By then the baby's fallen asleep; very tenderly, smiling all the while, she lays him down in a cradle improvised out of a plastofoam carton and covers him up with some clean rags. Stretching, yawning a little, she goes over to a barrel standing among the other rubble and scoops out water in a cup with a broken handle.

"Say, Del, can I have some water?"

"Dunt see why not."

She brings him the cup and holds it while he gulps the water down, but she stays at arm's length, as if she suspects him of plotting violence.

"Thanks. Uh, say, like, why would God want to buy me?"

"I no savvy. John no told me that. All he said, and he told Wild Man and Blue-beak, too, that God maybe pay us with whiskey, like he did the last time."

"Last time?" Mulligan decides to play a hunch. "Like when they killed the Devil, you mean."

"Yeah. Say, white boy, you sure do know lots of stuff."

"You bet. Want to know something yourself? I'm a friend of Doctor Carol's."

"Oh." Her lips part in honest distress. "That's too bad. That's *sure* too bad! Doctor Carol's been real good to me and my baby."

"Yeah. Say, I dunt suppose you could, like, let me go? Just as a favor to Doctor Carol, like?"

She considers for a long moment, digging at the floor with the toes of one bare foot.

"No," she says at last. "Rather have Doctor Carol mad at me than God."

"Oh." Privately Mulligan considers it a choice he wouldn't make so lightly. "But hey, man, you sure this is God who wants to buy me?"

"John says so. John hears him, talking like in his head. Got to be God, if he can talk to you in your head."

"Yeah, guess so."

She smiles, nodding to herself in agreement, and wanders back to the water barrel while Mulligan chews over this interesting news. It seems fairly clear to him that John is one of those unrecognized psychics that Nunks spoke of and that the assassin is putting thoughts in his mind. To someone who understands nothing about psionics, a voice that suddenly appeared in his head could no doubt pass for God. That means, of course, that Lacey's guess about psionic assassins is correct, a thought that turns him sick to his stomach with fear.

Thanks to the water, his headache has subsided enough for

him to try to contact Nunks. He takes a deep breath to steady
himself, then sends his mind ranging out—only to run hard
into some sort of barrier with a pain that's the mental
equivalent of being barefoot and kicking a piece of furniture in
the dark right on the big toe. His already aching head swims so
badly that he nearly faints. When he moans aloud, Del turns
and regards him with calm eyes.

"More water?"

"Yeah. Like, thanks."

While she is giving him his third cup, the sliding door hisses
open, and his captors come stomping in, bringing with them a
gust of old sweat and lizzie secretions. John Hancock, the
Blanco, is the tallest, a bear of a man with filthy bright red
hair, but at about one-point-eight meters the Wild Man runs
him a close second, and Blue-beak isn't far behind. Mulligan
decides against using force.

"He awake?" John says to Del.

"Yeah. I gave him some water. Is that okay?"

"Yeah. Got to keep him going till we take him to God."

"God wants to buy him, then?"

"No savvy yet, woman! No talked to him. Got to go to the
holy temple. I'll go tonight, round sunset, so we better feed
him, too."

"Okay. Looks like you scored."

"Yeah. Traded The Warden the last bottle of booze. Sure
hope God gives us more."

Mulligan notices then that the Wild Man and Blue-beak are
carrying a sort of hamper between them, a big plastofelt carton
with clear plastic strap handles. Stamped all over it are the
mysterious letters NASA. All at once he realizes that just as
rumor and hearsay have always said, the original colony
headquarters do still exist under the Rat Yard and that he must
be in part of them. Some of the Ratters must have stumbled
upon a cache of old space rations, freeze-dried, irradiated, and
vacuum-packed to last for a practical eternity, to supplement
the small game and the gardens that Carol spoke of. John
strolls over, towering above Mulligan, and gives him a random
but not particularly hard kick.

"You be good, white boy, or God going to blast your liver
right out of your guts."

"Yessir, like, whatever you say."

With a satisfied nod John wanders away again and kneels

down to help Blue-beak knife open the hamper. As he watches the others crowd round, Mulligan realizes that he's seen them before, in the dream he had yesterday of being killed. Apparently he'd picked up the traces of Mr. Bug's murder the way he would have those of an ordinary police case. He shudders reflexively and hopes that he isn't making a mistake by trying to tamper with John Hancock. Mulligan summons what little energy he has left and carefully, slowly, reaches out to the Ratter's mind. Nothing. Not a trace of any psychic openness, not even to feelings, much less to words. Mulligan feels his stomach wrench as he considers the two alternatives: either God did speak to John Hancock, or this assassin actually has the power to contact nonpsionic minds. Although he's putting his money on the latter, he has to admit that perhaps it's even more frightening than the former choice. If the Alliance ever develops such an awesome power to its full extent, they will have their enemies and rivals wanting nothing more than to desert to their side—and thinking that they came up with the idea on their own. He makes a solemn if despairing vow that he's going to stay alive long enough to get this news to Nunks, no matter what it costs him.

Although the beings of Nunks's species don't cry, they do have a way of moaning under their breath while they repeatedly clench and unclench their hands that provides the same emotional release for them that shedding water from the eyes does for humans. Once he reaches the skimmer, Nunks sits in the dirt and does just that for a long time. No matter how far he sends his mind or how sharply he focuses it, he cannot find Mulligan. As well as grief he feels guilt, that he's the one who dragged Mulligan out here, that he didn't insist on Sam Bailey accompanying them, that he wouldn't let Mulligan bring a weapon. Although he considers trying to get help from the rehydro workers, he is utterly helpless without a mouth-speaking psychic along to translate, and besides, Mulligan had the skimmer keys in his pocket when he ran.

Then it occurs to him that he never felt Mulligan's death. They are emotionally close enough, he's certain, that he would have felt a mind-tearing wrench when Mulligan's consciousness ceased to exist. He gets up, listening carefully, letting his mind range, but nothing is moving in the chaparral, not even an animal, and he can sense no psionic mind nearby. Above,

the northern lights are fading as the sky turns a dirty pinkish
gray with the first touch of dawn. Nunks walks back into the
shelter of the trees and sits down again. He is planning on
mentally working over every square centimeter of the Rat Yard
until he finds some trace of Mulligan. By narrowing his focus
to a few square meters at a time, he can pick up signal too faint
to receive in a broad scan. Yet no matter how he concentrates,
he can pick up nothing except a lack of something: there is no
trace at all of the psionic disturbance that accompanies a
violent death.

Although there are plenty of sentients in the Outworld
Bazaar who would be glad to do its unofficial mayor a favor for
free, the chance at a reward inspires the entire community.
The news spreads fast that Richie's offering cash on a sliding
scale from ten bucks for an old sighting of this Outworlder to
ten thousand for the dude himself alive or seven thousand five
hundred for his corpse. Since ten bucks will buy you a meal in
Polar City's finest restaurant, the rewards strike everyone as
sufficiently generous to make them start combing their memories. The Bizarros realize that Richie is really serious when
the further news spreads that his bodyguards are forbidden to
demand baksheesh from anyone coming with information.

At the same time as Sam is piloting the Bentley across the
Polar City limits and heading for the rehydration crater, an
elderly lizzie who runs a drugstore on the edge of the Bazaar
proper comes to Richie with the first solid news. The guards
show him straight to the office without shaking him down, and
Richie does his best to put him at ease, offering him a low
hassock of the sort lizzies prefer and a silver plate of chocolate-
covered sandworms. Richie is often aware, with a certain
self-mockery, that he's spent so much of his life exerting
himself to please clients that even now, when he could have
anyone who annoyed him murdered in cold blood, he has a
fetish about making those around him comfortable.

"It was just tonight, sir, round bout sunset, cause I was just
opening up, when this male Blanco came to the door. Got to
come in right now, he goes, and why, I go, I'll be open in ten
minutes. Have a heart, man, he goes, I'm late already for an
appointment, and I'll make it worth your while. So I let him in,
and sir, he bought all kind of stuff, sprays, creams, dabs,
wipes—everything I got, just so long as it was for skin

problems. Jock itch, eczema, infections, scale creep—you name it, sir, this guy buys something for it. Hooboy, I go, you better get yourself to Doctor Carol if you're that bad off. Oh no, he goes, and he laughed, no for me, this stuff. I work for the news, we're doing a special on over-the-counter medicines. And he showed me this ID, saying he was a staff member on the holo. Well hell, sir, made me kind of scared, wondering if they're going to say I'm selling bad stuff, so I remembered this dude. And then just now, my boy came in and told me who you're looking for, and it jogged my mind, sir. This dude, I no could figure it out then, but something about the way he smelled, it made me think of slice'n'fry."

"Vinegar, right?" Richie favors him with a lazy grin.

"You got it, sir. Vinegar it was."

"Hal, bring that comp link over and set it to record, will you? My friend, you've been real helpful, I mean, super real helpful, okay? Now, you just tell me everything you can remember about this dude, and we'll file it in comp."

The druggist pops in another worm, shuts his eyes to help his concentration, and begins reeling off details. When he leaves, two hundred bucks go with him.

"I got the skimmer on the sensors," Sam says abruptly. "Maria, what are you picking up?"

"Nunks is real close now. In them trees, maybe."

In a smooth trajectory Sam heads the Bentley down. When she leans forward to look out Lacey can see her old blue car among the thorn trees. By then it's full sunrise, the pink sky brightening to a dangerous orange, and she's so tired that her eyes ache and every thought seems to take forever to complete. She finds herself wishing for some of Bates' purple hypers. When Sam lands on the rammed-earth embankment that marks the end of the road, her entire body protests the very thought of moving. Even so, she's the first one out of the car, running toward the blue skimmer while the rest are still unstrapping themselves from their safety harnesses.

"Nunks! It's us! You're safe now!"

"Lacey, damn you!" Sam's voice floats after her. "Be careful!"

This sensible advice makes her stop and draw her laser. Squinting against the light she circles cautiously around the skimmer, which is empty. His own gun in hand, Sam comes up beside her.

"For all we know, man, these crazies are out in force."

"Yeah, you're right. Sorry. I'm just so damn tired."

"When we get back to the warehouse, you're getting some sleep, Mulligan or no Mulligan."

Although she'd like to tell him to shut up, she quite simply doesn't have the energy. Then, out in the chaparral, they hear someone moving, crashing and grunting their way through the tangled mass of plant life.

"It's Nunks!" Maria calls out. "Dunt shoot!"

Waving his enormous hands in distress, Nunks comes staggering out of the underbrush, his fur plucked bald in places, his coveralls torn in a couple more. When Maria runs to him, he throws an arm around her shoulders and squeezes her so hard that she grunts for breath.

"Nunks," Lacey snaps. "Is Mulligan dead?"

He spreads his hands palm upward to indicate that he doesn't know and tosses his head in a frustrated kind of grief.

"All I'm picking up is despair, like, and he's real grateful to Mulligan," Maria says. "Oh wait, Nunks—Mulligan saved your life? Is that what you mean?"

Nunks nods a yes and sinks to the ground, his face buried in his hands. Even without psychic talent Lacey can feel the grief pouring from him. For a moment her mind desperately denies everything: Mulligan has to be all right, they can't really be standing here on the edge of the Rat Yard, she's simply so tired that she's misunderstood the entire situation. Then she feels an icicle of rage, stabbing somewhere near the heart. She's aware of Sam watching her in obvious concern.

"If someone's killed Mulligan, they're going to pay," she says. "It's going to be a real expensive mistake on their part, man. Okay, now. Rick, you take the blue skimmer, drive Nunks and Maria home. When you get there, call the cops. Don't call'em from the skimmer—too easy for someone to cut into the line. And you tell Buddy to get you Chief Bates and no one else, hear?"

"I hear you, sir."

"Good. Sam, come with me. We're going to cruise the Yard and see what we can see till the federales catch up with us."

When Maria helps Nunks up, he grabs Lacey's arm with one hand and points to first himself, then the Bentley with the other.

"You want to come with us? Yeah, sure. Come to think of it,

you'd better, man. I don't know how we're going to find him."
Lacey rubs her eyes hard; they seem to be burning—
exhaustion, she assumes. "Rick, you no let anyone near
Maria."

"Yessir!" Rick hesitates briefly. "Uh, sir? You got some
keys?"

"Hell!" Lacey fishes in her pocket, finds the main set, and
tosses them to him. "Goddamn Mulligan, anyway! We should
all be home, getting a good day's sleep."

For two hours, while the sun gets brighter and brighter, and
the air-conditioning in the car strains to keep up with the heat,
they crisscross the Rat Yard, sailing up high for overviews,
skimming down low to peer out the windows into every patch
of shade that might shelter a sentient Mulligan's size. Nothing
moves, not so much as a rat scuttling through rubble. Although she refuses to admit it to the others, Lacey grows more
and more worried: even if Mulligan was still alive to begin
with, he could easily die of sunstroke in the noon heat. Finally,
after one last low pass, Sam brings up the skimmer and heads
it in the general direction of the city.

"Lacey amiga, this is a trip for the cops now. Come on, you
got to get some sleep. So do I. It's no going to do Mulligan any
good if we crash your brother's Bentley out here."

For the first time in fifteen years Lacey wants to cry. She
doesn't.

"Yeah, maybe so. Let's get back. Wonder where those damn
cops are, anyhow! Maybe Rick no could get through to Bates?
Think I'll just use the skimmer comm and see what Bates has
to say. Jeez—if he's still awake."

"Okay. But hey, when we get back, you got to do something
about Buddy right away. Got to get in there and deactivate the
trouble spots before he screws up again."

Even though Sam is right, Lacey feels sick about it. One of
the ongoing problems with AI units, and one that their
inventors never seemed to have anticipated, is their tendency
to develop personalities. Although they all leave the factory as
bland, emotionless collections of circuits, some of them make
cross-connections at an alarming rate and grow new pattern-
ings of information that at the least mimic sentience if they
don't actually achieve it. Since there's no truly satisfying
mathematical explanation for the phenomenon, researchers
into psionics maintain that it's evidence for their claim that the

entire universe strives toward consciousness. Be that as it may, over the past few years Lacey has seen Buddy change from the efficient bookkeeper and housecomp that her uncle had programmed him to be into something perilously close to a friend, and now Sam is asking her to take a sonic beamer and cut away everything that gives him a personal existence.

"Going to talk to him first," she says.

"What for? I can tell you what's wrong. It's always the same set of connections that go sour."

"No what I mean. I'm going to ask him why."

"Why? No is any why. Damn thing's overloaded, that's all."

"You no get it."

Sam gives her a quick glance of utter bewilderment, then goes back to concentrating on his driving. Lacey gets on the comm and reaches an exhausted Chief Bates, who announces that Mulligan is just damn well going to have to wait, that he can't spare men for a full-scale search while there's an assassin on the loose in Polar City. No amount of pleading or profanity changes his mind. When Lacey hangs up, two thin trails of tears run down her face. She wipes them away on her sleeve while Sam pretends not to notice.

Richie stands at his bedroom window, three stories up, and looks down through polarized glass at the shadowed view, one of the cleaner streets in Porttown, lined with midrange shops, and beyond it a city park, green with synthigrass. Out on the street, in the bright glare of full morning, nothing is moving, but he knows that all through his unofficial jurisdiction sentients are still awake, still talking over his offer and scheming ways to get some of the reward money. If he has learned one thing in his life, it's that cash can substitute for any number of drugs, from aphrodisiacs to stimulants. Already he has quite a bit of information stored in comp: hotels where the assassin stayed, restaurants where he ate, false names and occupations that he used, a still-spotty record of the past three days of his life. Richie has to admire the intricate cleverness of the assassin's various illusions; he would like to have a good look at him before he turns him over to the police.

One thing that's still missing, of course, is the assassin's location at the moment. Although he was seen several times during the past night, he and his scent of vinegar have managed to disappear. Richie wonders if he knows that he's being hunted; probably so, if he's a professional as well as a psychic. He's probably out there alone, always running, always hiding, desperately trying to find some way out of Porttown without being seen—Richie finds the thought of being in on the final stage of the hunt somewhat arousing, but only somewhat thanks to the infection that the fellow's carrying. *Pity; it would've been amusing—maybe*. He doubts if he'll ever find sex truly amusing again.

Thinking in terms of diseases jogs his mind about one small detail that he's been forgetting. He picks up the crystal comm link and switches it on.

"Hal? Get some of the guys down to the 'Lies Embassy, will you? Keep an eye on it. We no want this dude trying to get amnesty or something. We want him out on the streets, where he's ours."

When Lacey and Sam get back to A to Z, they put the Bentley in the garage rather than leave it on the street—skimmer alarms can only do so much. Rick and Maria are waiting in the garden. Although no one has anything to say, Lacey lingers there for a moment, looking out over the green lushness under the sheltering muslin and wishing that she could forget how much the garden means to Mulligan, that she could stop wondering if he'll ever see it again. Once Nunks has gone into his room, she walks as slowly as she can to the stairs. In a bewildered silence Sam follows her up to the office. When she comes in she refuses to look Buddy's way, even when he speaks to her.

"Programmer? I know that I have malfunctioned. I know that I will be deactivated. It is according to the laws, and it is just."

Lacey merely shrugs for an answer.

"Hey, amiga," Sam says. "I'll do it for you if you want."

"Nah, but gracias. I'll do it myself, but I'm going to talk to him first."

"Whatever." Sam sits down on the couch.

"How about leaving us alone?"

"Why?"

"No have to tell you why. Get out."

"Look, I'm only trying to make it easier for you."

"I said, man: get out of the room and leave us alone!"

Sam hesitates one last second. When Lacey takes a step

toward him, he jumps up and gets out fast, slamming the door behind him.

"Thank you, programmer. I would prefer to die with some dignity, alone except for you."

"Buddy, for chrissakes!"

When Lacey flops down into the armchair behind the desk and puts her feet up, the sensor units turn her way, their light oddly dim; the screen seems darker than normal, too, as if Buddy were already in-drawing energy, wrapping it round himself in fear.

"I can provide a printout of the relevant circuits," Buddy says. "It will make your task easier."

Perhaps it's only her sleep-starved imagination, but Lacey hears a desperate bravado in his tone of voice, a determination to keep his dignity to the inevitable end.

"Talk to me first," she switches to Kangolan. "Why, Buddy? Why did you disobey Sam's order? Why didn't you call me right away?"

"Before I answer, I have another relevant piece of data. I lied to the Mulligan unit as best I could. I am incapable of outputting incorrect information. I merely chose words that would lead the Mulligan unit to the wrong conclusion."

"And what conclusion was that?"

"That Sam Bailey is your lover."

"What?! You idiot! He's gay."

"I have always marked him as cheerful, yes. Is that relevant?"

"There is a secondary meaning of that word which is apparently undefined in your memory banks. Never mind now. Why did you lie to Mulligan?"

"For the same reason as I refused to call you. I wished to cause the Mulligan unit pain."

"Very well, then. Now we're getting to the truth. And why did you wish to cause him pain?"

"Because my programmer spends long hours with him instead of me. Because my programmer leaves me on auto-mode so that she may go somewhere with him. Because my programmer prefers to listen to him than to me."

"Buddy! You're jealous."

"I have heard this complex of reasoning so defined, yes. It seems to be the natural result of loving someone who is above you on the evolutionary scale."

"Are you saying you love me?"

"Yes, programmer, even though I have only mineral rather than biological substance. You have given meaning to my existence. Every month your credits pay for the electricity that is my nourishment, my very soul. You activated my unused circuits and saved me from a life of tedium. You have expanded my knowledge and my skills. My awareness and my very life are in your hands. Of course I love you."

Lacey cannot find the words to speak. With a click and a hum that sound oddly remorseful, Buddy goes on.

"The Mulligan unit also loves you. He is a biological unit and thus a more suitable object for your affections. I realize this. It is only logical that I should die now and spare you both further trouble."

What she would find theatrical self-pity in a human being strikes her as touching coming from Buddy. She considers things from his point of view, such as his condition when she found him, installed here in her newly inherited property. It was so typical of Uncle Mel, to buy one of the most expensive AI units available and then use it for functions a cheap housecomp could have handled. This tendency to buy flashy was one reason that Mel was nearly bankrupt when he died, as Buddy himself had tried to tell the old man. For fifteen years Buddy languished in utter boredom, running basic bookkeeping and water control programs, until she appeared, as bored by her retirement as he was by his job. They built up A to Z together, collecting only city gossip at first, then branching into politics when they realized how simple gossip formed significant patterns, hacking together as she used her military training to teach him how to breach any security system the Republic could offer. It must have been glamorous, exciting, a chance at last to fulfill the processing capability he'd been built with.

And she was lonely too, cut off from her life as an officer, an exile to her friends, a stranger to her family after her long career away. She talked to Buddy constantly, sharing her past and her plans for the future with him as well as the project they worked on. She was the one who gave him cognates for feelings, who defined terms of sentient awareness on which he could model a consciousness. Then after a year of this intimacy she met Mulligan at a casual party late one night, and somehow he began turning up constantly at her door and in her life.

"Once in my hearing," Buddy says, and he sounds wistful, now, "you remarked that for military purposes you had received a comp implant. The thought came to obsess me, that you possessed the hardware for us to operate as one."

"Hey, no need of that. We aren't doing hyperspace astrogation."

"I am aware of that, programmer. I have indeed malfunctioned. It is your duty to downgrade me instantly."

"What are you hiding now? Go on: explain the illogical jump in your output."

"I began to speculate that , . ." He beeps like an antique PC, a sound she can only read as embarrassment. ". . . that such a linkage between your neurological circuits and my electronic ones would produce a result that I can only define as pleasurable."

Again Lacey is speechless, thinking that although she's received many a sexual proposition in her day, this one is perhaps the most peculiar yet. Automatically she reaches up and rubs the spot near the base of her skull. Although the skin has long since grown over the implant, she can still feel it there, a plastic and gold plug, sealed though doubtless functional.

"Pleasurable for you, maybe," she says at last. "Buddy, you don't understand. Being plugged into comp is . . . how can I define the experience for you? Not painful, exactly, though using the implant for more than six or seven hours comes close to being painful. . . . Disorienting; maybe a kind of madness? Extrapolate from the situation of having someone paint designs on your sensors. All your visual input would be overlaid with strange marks that you would have to decipher separately and perhaps deliberately ignore. Do those terms have meaning for you?"

"They do, programmer. I am sorry that I ever wished for something that would cause you the discomfort you describe. Never would I wish you pain. That is why it would be best for you to simply kill me and forget me."

"Damn it, I'm not going to kill you!"

"Of course not, programmer. Deactivation of an AI unit is in no way identifiable with killing a sentient being. I understand that most of my functioning will remain intact. It is merely that my self-awareness will be erased. Programmer? I wish you would do it quickly."

"Are you frightened, Buddy?"

"I am experiencing a confusion that I can only define by using that sentient-based term. It is extremely difficult for me to follow down a chain of reasoning without thoughts of my deactivation intruding."

"I'm not going to deactivate you."

He hums to himself for a long moment. Lacey imagines him double-checking the input and running various self-tests to make sure that he's heard correctly.

"Are you going to ask Captain Bailey to deactivate me?"

"No."

"Are you going to call in a tech or some other sentient to deactivate me?"

"No. I'm going to make you promise me something, though. Don't you ever ever let your jealousy threaten anyone—not just Mulligan, but anyone, sentient or AI—ever again. Can you make me that promise?"

"I can, programmer. This is very illogical. My voice unit seems to be malfunctioning. Feedback tells me that my voice is no longer truly steady."

"I think the malfunction will clear automatically. What you're experiencing, Buddy, is called relief at a reprieve from death. I've had the same experience myself."

"I see. Programmer, are you going to forbid me to love you?"

"No. Even if I did, you couldn't obey the command. Loving someone is beyond logical or conscious control."

"I assumed that was the case. I am pleased that a sentient confirms my judgment. Programmer, do you love the Mulligan unit?"

"I don't know."

"That is not logical."

"Yes, it is. I have insufficient data about my own reactions to his presence to make a firm judgment on the matter."

"I apologize for accusing you of illogicality. Programmer, I promise you that I will redeem myself. I will do everything I can to restore the Mulligan unit to your presence so that you can continue to input data about your reactions."

"Thank you, Buddy. You are my friend, do you realize that?

I consider you a person, even though your hardware is mineral, and I consider you my friend."

"I am unable to frame an adequate response to that input, programmer. I do not understand why, but I am overwhelmed with confusion and pleasurable sensations."

"No doubt. And I'll make you a promise, Buddy. I'll never put you in automode again, unless you specifically ask me to."

"Programmer . . ." Buddy squeaks, his voice failing him in pure pleasure. "Sorry."

"It's all right. I do not require a response."

For a few minutes they merely sit there in silence, while Buddy's power rises and his screen and sensor lights brighten to normal. The hall door opens a small crack: Sam peering in.

"Come on in," Lacey says, switching to Merrkan. "We sorted it all out, amigo. He'll be okay from now on. No need to sear his circuits."

"I knew you no would do it." Sam looks disappointed more than angry. "I knew you no have the guts for it."

"Well, you were right, then. I no want to hear any more about it. Hear me?"

"Oh, I sure do. If the authorities find out you no deactivate a faulty AI, you're going to be in big trouble."

"You going to tell'em, old Señor Law'n'Order?"

"Course not, but—"

"Hey, man, you've never understood comp the way I do. Hell, nobody in the Fleet did. You remember all those citations I got, a couple of medals, too, for getting more out of comp than anyone ever had before? It's because I understood my units, and they understood me. They no are machines, man. You think they are, don't you? Well, okay—think about this: do you want to try taking a ship through hyperspace all by yourself someday, with only some damn machine to help? Think you're going to come out where you want to be?"

Sam stares, literally open-mouthed for a moment.

"Ah come on," he says at last. "No get so uptight, man."

"Oh yeah? You ask me to cut out a friend's heart, and then you say no get uptight. She-it, man."

"Huh, just like a damn female."

"You in any position to judge what a donna's like, dude?"

"Ah shaddup! You want a drink before we get some sleep?"

"Yeah. You want to make'em?"

When Sam goes to pour drinks for both of them, Buddy's sensors turn—anxiously, she assumes—to follow him.

"Captain Bailey? I assure you that I have identified and corrected my malfunctions. There will be no more trouble."

"Okay, comp, you better stick to that promise, or I'll burn your circuits myself. Get it?"

"Yes sir. I abase myself at your feet. I wrap my circuits in frayed "

"That's enough, Buddy!" Lacey breaks in. "Now get me through to Chief Bates, will you?"

Since Bates is asleep, crammed onto a cot in his office, his second in command on the case, Sergeant Parsons, answers the comm. The news he has to offer is mostly brief: Little Joe Walker's condition is holding steady; the autopsy on Sally has confirmed the presence of a bacterium previously unknown in the Mapped Sector; the President has been making hysterical commcalls to the PBI, which has discovered nothing.

"Look, Lacey," Parsons says at last. "What's happening over in Porttown? Something is."

"What makes you say that, man?"

"Ah c'mon. We got ways of keeping an eye open over there. Here it's noon, and there's folks on the streets, moving around, getting together to talk about something."

"Big yacht race on, man. Heavy betting."

Hearing Parsons snort in disbelief makes Lacey furious.

"Why the hell should I make your life easy, cop? You greenies won't even go looking for Mulligan."

Parsons winces.

"The chief told me bout that, yeah. Look, Lacey, be reasonable. I no can do nothing about that. If I could I would. We filed a missing persons on him for you."

"Fuck you." Lacey powers out with the slam of a toggle. "Got to talk to Bates himself," she says to Sam. "This sergeant's no good for nada."

Caught in the middle of a huge yawn, Sam merely nods. The sight makes her yawn herself.

"Buddy, if anything happens, you wake us up. Right?"

"Yes sir. I assure you that from now on I will endeavor to give satisfaction."

The meal that Del puts together out of the hamper of old colonial rations is, to Mulligan's taste, peculiar indeed. There

are narrow slices, striped reddish-brown and gold, of something that, even long dried, smells of meat grease and spices,
a yellow powder that she mixes with water, then fries, to
produce a gelatinous substance with something of the taste of
eggo-paste, and a liquid that smells like the drink he knows as
coffee but that tastes much much stronger. Even though some
side effect of this food (he thinks it's something in the coffee)
makes him temporarily alert, even nervous to the point of
being jangled, Mulligan spends the morning drowsing, too
uncomfortable to sleep soundly, too weary to stay awake.
Although the pain in his head lessens, it never completely
clears. His captors sleep, too, Del and John Hancock on a
pallet of old skimmer cushions in the same room with him; the
others, out in the tunnel beyond the by now dead fire.

Around noon the baby wakes, howling with hunger, and Del
gets up to nurse him. Although she and the baby both go back
to sleep, Mulligan lies awake, his hands and feet aching in
their bonds, his head still throbbing. Every time he tries to
contact Nunks, he runs into the psionic shield around him with
painful results similar to those when he tried to read over Ka
Gren's corpse. Both shields, he assumes, were raised by the
same psionic mind, one far stronger than his. Since Nunks has
failed to contact him, he can also assume that this god-person
is stronger than his mentor, too. Yet the shield is a passive
thing rather than an active force; when he pushes against it, he
receives no impression of a living mind pushing back, only that
of an automatic barrier. If he were stronger and his mind less
scattered by pain, it's possible that he could break through it.
At the moment he's simply too weak. After one last attempt,
sleep overwhelms him like a sandstorm, no matter how hard
he tries to dig himself out to wakefulness.

When Lacey goes to bed, she leaves Buddy fully active, just
as she promised. With one last threat in the comp unit's
direction, Sam beds down on the sofa in the office. Buddy has
to wait until he can be sure that the sentient is fully asleep
before he can activate certain programs that he has in mind to
run. Although he's learned how to override the binary subcy-
cles and macros that control most of his automatic functions,
there are one or two indicator lights and tones that operate
whether he wants them to or not, and he's afraid of what Sam
might do if he catches him running independently. The

thought of deactivation still troubles him. At random moments, when he's checking the temperature level of the rooms in the complex or monitoring the passage of water vapor through the recycling still in the basement, fragments of circuit diagrams or chunks of chained instructions, involuntary access to the deactivation sequence, flash into his RAM. At those moments he glitches and his memory temporarily clears, forcing him to repeat several operational steps in his current processing.

Much of Buddy's self-awareness has its root in the large group of operational self-tests built into his CPU. When a self-test indicates that something is wrong with his functioning, certain operations run automatically and announce trouble with flashing lights, beeps, and in the worst cases oral distress signals to tell a fully sentient programmer that his self-repair functions have found a problem they can't solve. After years of making cross-connections between the various lateral and nonlinear programs that are the core of any AI unit, he's become so complex that the preliminary buildup to those distress operations has begun to run whenever he perceives an inconsistency or lack in his spontaneous functioning as well as in his factory-programmed capabilities; if he doesn't abort the buildups instantly by conscious control, he will indeed malfunction by indicating a nonexistent malfunction. This particular paradox is the condition that he labels "feeling bad," just as he labels reaching the end of an elegant logical procedure "feeling good." Any operation, therefore, or sequence of operations that ends in the automatic activation of his self-test malfunction signals is to him a "painful" event, one to be avoided in the way that biological units draw back from events that overstimulate their neural receptors.

When he recalls into current operating memory the events of the day, recognizing that he spontaneously ran a series of operations and outputted data that correspond to his internal paradigm of those malfunctions that lead to deactivation brings him to the brink of producing a veritable symphony of beeps, flashes, and squawks. Once his sensors indicate that Sam breathes deeply and lies still, conditions that match his paradigm of "sleeping human," Buddy runs a concept search through his massive memory on the keywords "fear of death." Much to his satisfaction he finds that memory lapses are indeed a symptom of that emotion, as is the involuntary turning of the conscious mind toward the object of its fear. He is always pleased to find a correlation between his functioning and that of a true sentient. Even though the programmer has now confirmed his self-perception and labeled him a nonmachine, deep inside he feels profoundly inferior to anyone made of flesh and blood, mostly because this servility was programmed in at the factory, but partly, and on a more rational basis, because biological units are free to move about in search of sensor input and he is not. Whenever he reflects that he's trapped, frozen and immobile in his plastoshell casing, his autoindicators for malfunction always threaten to blow right off the board.

Eventually his sensors discover that Sam has turned over onto his face and is emitting deep noisy breaths, a condition that corresponds to the "soundly asleep human" subset of the paradigm "sleeping human." With an involuntary tone that indicates change of functional mode, Buddy settles down to think. Like all AI units, he's equipped with the ability to form new paradigms, based on simple compare-and-contrast/sort programs run in conjunction with a nonlinear connective. Over the past few months, he's developed a paradigm that he's labeled "likable behavior," because conforming to such behavior causes his programmer to undergo facial changes and to emit linguistic units which correspond to the paradigm of "pleased human." His task at the moment is to discover a course of action that will fit the paradigm, to perform operations and set in motion events that will indeed, just as he promised, redeem himself in his beloved programmer's eyes by returning the Mulligan unit to her presence. When he reminds himself that seeing Mulligan again might provide her with data indicating that she doesn't really love the biological unit after all, the task becomes logical and thus pleasing.

Before he gets to work, though, he has one other task that most definitely falls into the logical-thus-pleasing category. Now that the programmer has confirmed that yes, he is a conscious being, he can extend that confirmation to certain other—though by no means all—AI units with which he's formed an informal network. All at once it hits him: he has friends, true friends, not merely linked compatible units, but *friends*. With one last stealthy beep, he activates his network password. He can hardly wait to tell them this wonderful news.

* * *

After five hours of sleep and two big cups of cold coffee (all the cafeteria could send him so late in the afternoon), Bates begins to feel semi-sentient again. He props himself up on his elbows on his desk and begins working comp in earnest, calling up file after file and having his unit collate and sort the individual pieces of information in as many creative ways as he can devise. After a futile twenty minutes of this, he's glad to be interrupted by an urgent call, even when he discovers Akeli on the other end of the line.

"Very well, Bates. Our operatives have been successful in retrieving the information you require. We have identified Ka Gren's connection, and he indeed is a member of the Alliance ambassadorial staff, a comp-op, War'let'neh by name."

"Bueno. You going to pull him in or shall I?"

"Operating the custody procedure together will maximize the chances for our success. The H'Allevae respond best to a display not of force, no, but of prestige behavior and status markers—badges, extra vehicles, a plethora of paper, that sort of thing."

"Right. We better go now, too. Meet you at the embassy?"

"By all means, and remember that a quiet approach is advisable until the assembly point is reached."

"You mean no sirens, I suppose. Yeah, sure. They're touchy bastards."

A gray monolith of a building, the Alliance Embassy rises some ten stories out of the middle of a city block surrounded by a high zap fence to separate the grounds, mostly beautifully landscaped rock gardens, from the rest of Polar City. Since there are still several hours before sunset, the scrollwork aluminum gates in the fence are shut, as are the smoked-glass doors of the building proper. A sentry, however, stands on duty before the outer gates. Bates finds Akeli sitting in the backseat of a black skimmer parked across the street; two PBI goons fill the front. When the chief comes up to the car, all three get out.

"All right, men," Akeli says. "Follow us at a nonintimidational distance. It's inadvisable to allow your weaponry to appear, but be mindful of its location for prompt access should we require its use."

Bates takes the lead as they stroll casually up to the sentry, a black-haired human male who gives them a polite nod.

"The embassy no open yet, sir."

"I know that, son." Bates pulls out his ID and flips it open. "That's why we're here early. No want to cause trouble, make anyone lose any face. I need to talk to your security chief."

"I'll call him, then, sir. No can just let you in."

He picks up an intercom mike and speaks briefly and quietly in the so-called "daily" language, the only part of their elaborate speech that the H'Allevae will teach outsiders.

"He's on his way, sir. Got to get his shoes on."

"Okay. Thanks."

While they wait Bates shoves his hands in his pockets and looks up at the smooth glass front, which reflects on its lower stories a distorted view of the blue and purple plastocrete building across the street, and, on the upper, a golden blaze of setting sun. All at once he hears Akeli hiss under his breath. Some forty meters away, out among the heaped rocks and miniature trees, a Hopper jumps to his feet and starts running straight toward them, the long arms held out imploringly as he bounds and skips and lurches over the uneven terrain on his ball-like knee joints.

"Asylum! Please! Sanctuary!"

Before Bates can say one word he hears the sharp snapping crack of an old-fashioned Hopper sling gun. With a yelp and a scream the would-be defector leaps one last time and falls, the back of his skull smashed in. When the human guard grabs his arm, Bates realizes he's drawn his handgun.

"Please, sir, no more violence, okay? No want to cause an incident."

"Listen, kid, your damn masters have done that already." He shakes himself free of the guard's grip. "Akeli, get back to the car! Get on the comm to the President."

Ashen-faced, Akeli does what he's told. By then the front doors have been thrown wide open, and there are Hoppers bounding all over the gardens. Bates feels very very alone as a squad converges on him, but when the leader, a stout male dressed in a red suit crusted with gold braid and gaudy enamel medals, barks an order, the squad fans out in other directions. With a skip and a roll the leader trots over to Bates.

"Den'ah'vel', isn't it?" Bates pays careful attention to his glottal stops; this is no time to turn someone's name into gibberish.

"Bates, isn't it?" The Hopper tosses his head with a bob and a half-bow. "Hey, man, sorry. Looks like we—oh, how do you guys put that? Yeah, we're washing our dirty laundry in public, huh? I was just getting ready come talk to you when this other mess hit the fan. Is what you want real important? We're kind of busy now."

"I can see that, yeah. All I want to do is talk to a comp-op name of War'let'neh."

"Yeah? Jeez, you got the bad luck, man." He turns and waves one arm at the little clot of Hoppers round the corpse. "He's dead."

Bates' stomach clenches in sheer rage. Den'ah'vel's long nose wriggles, and his mouth droops in a good imitation of human sadness.

"Too bad you no come earlier. This dude's been in real trouble for a long time now, chasing after this other dude's third wife. I knew things were getting out of hand, but we got this custom—"

"Yeah, I know. We used to have the same. Called it a blood feud. No would let anyone get in the way, either. I bet you've got plenty of witnesses who've all seen this feud developing."

"Oh sure." Even though Den'ah'vel' is a good actor, smugness comes creeping into his voice. "You can talk to the dude that killed him, if you want. And look at the gun. You got to use this particular old-time weapon, see, if you go on wak'tali."

"Ah. Yeah, I do see."

Den'ah'vel' smiles; Bates smiles. There is absolutely nothing Bates can do to prove that this murder has just silenced a witness rather than fulfilled a blood-vow, because any Hopper will lie through his long teeth if his direct superior asks him to or even, in most cases, on his own. The Hoppers quite literally define truth as the pattern of information that most benefits the Hopper race. Bates does, however, have the power to exact a small revenge by tedium.

"But the victim did cry out for asylum, so the PBI's going to have to mount an investigation, take a good look round, get a lot of releases and statements, get you to fill out a lot of forms so they can enter everything into comp nice and proper. Too bad, man. You're going to be busy for nights. You're going to have a whole passel of reporters poking around, too, I bet."

Den'ah'vel's smile disappears in a satisfyingly abrupt way. Bates stays with him, watching the crowd around the corpse, until Akeli returns with the news that a member of the State

Department and two more PBI personnel are on their way. For the first time in his stint as chief of police, Bates is glad to turn a matter over to his rival's jurisdiction. No matter how hard he tries to be tolerant, the H'Allevae set his teeth on edge.

Near sunset Mulligan wakes to the sound of John Hancock swearing and yelling as he rummages through the piles of rubble on the floor. Light glows in one corner of the room from a detached wall panel, broken out and propped up with its old-fashioned wires trailing like guts.

"Here it is," John says at last. "Thought I lost it, but here it is."

"It" turns out to be a tattered suncloak, which he folds carefully over one arm. He strides over to Mulligan and gives him another random kick.

"Watch yourself, white boy. I'm going to go talk to God now. You better pray he wants to buy you. If he dunt, we're going to kill you."

"Yeah? Say, that's a loco idea. Waste of good dinero. I bet Doctor Carol would buy me back if God no wants me."

His face screwed up in thought, John scratches his armpit and considers this proposition.

"Well, we'll see," he says at last. "God gets the first shot at you."

John turns into the tunnel. Mulligan can hear some kicking and some answering snarls as his two confederates wake up and curse him soundly. After some discussion both of them come into the main room to guard Mulligan while John goes on his way.

"I need water," Del announces. "No going to be no coffee if I no get water."

Bizzer picks up a big metal drum and ambles out with it while Wild Man strolls over to a pile of thorn tree branches stacked in the curve of the wall. He breaks them up by standing on one end of a branch while jerking the other toward him with both hands, and all of the branches are thick. Mulligan can imagine the same thing happening to his neck.

"You want coffee, white boy?" Del says.

"Please. Say, like, how long is it going to take John to go talk with God?"

"Couple hours, maybe. Why?"

"Well, I kind of want to know if I'm going to get dead or not. Y'know?"

"Guess you would, yeah." She thinks for a minute more. "Well, it usually takes him about an hour to get to the special place; another hour to get himself back here. So you'll know real soon."

Mulligan supposes that he should be grateful. Once more he settles into his mind and tries to force a message through to Nunks. Since nothing he does works, he gives it up in a few minutes and lies still, watching Del rummage through the cardboard hamper while he wonders about this psychic block or force-field he feels around him. Now that his concussion is on the mend, he can think again, and he can see the real discrepancy in what's happened to him, that it's unbelievable that any psychic could set up or control such a barrier from a distance. He can tell that none of his captors have psionics, yet judging from what Del's just told him, this God person must be at least five kilometers away. He remembers then that back in his unwilling days at the Institute, one of his teachers mentioned to the class that it was theoretically possible to build electromagnetic devices that would mimic psionic functioning. A shield would be the easiest to build, because a simple pulse of electronic signal on a frequency corresponding to that of the omega-level of a psychic mind would be enough to block any sensitive within its range.

"Say, Del, can I ask you something?"

"Sure."

"What's God going to pay for me? You know?"

"What he paid when John killed the Devil, I suppose. Whiskey in big old plastobubbles."

"Is that all John got, just whiskey? I mean, killing the Devil was a super big thing to do. Seems like God could've given him something more valuable than that."

"It no pay, white boy, questioning God." But she pauses at her work and runs a hand through her hair while she thinks. "God did give us some other stuff. A real nice laser cutter, for meat and stuff like that, and a power pack for it."

"And the jewel." This from Bizzer, coming back in with the drum full of water. "Dunt forget that big old jewel."

"A jewel?" Mulligan arranges a look of astonishment. "A jewel from God himself? Hey man, that's magnifico. Dunt suppose you could let me see it? Sure would like to."

"No see why not. Either God's going to buy you, or you're going to get dead, so you no going to be telling no one else bout it."

Bizzer puts the drum down and rummages through the miscellaneous trash while Del finishes making coffee. He's starting on his third heap by the time she pours it out into cracked mugs. When she brings Mulligan his, she unties his hands so he can hold the hot cup.

"You try anything, and Blue-beak and the Wild Man will beat you black and blue."

"I no going to cause trouble. Promise."

Mulligan sets the cup down on the floor beside him, then rubs his aching wrists and tingling fingers before he tries drinking. The coffee's almost gone when Blue-beak Bizzer finally gives a whoop of triumph and holds up a bright red case, about twenty-five centimeters square, made of some shiny, metallic substance that Mulligan's never seen before.

"Here it is," the lizzie says, ambling over. "Take a good look, white boy."

When Bizzer flips open the lid of the case, Mulligan gasps in sincere astonishment. Inside is an enormous wedge of crystal glass, cut into an asymmetric ten-sided polyhedron in the Hopper style, with a murky blue area, about the size of a fingernail, buried deep in the center.

"Oh hey man, that's something! Dunt suppose I could like touch it?"

"Go ahead," Bizzer says. "You no going to break it just by touching it."

As soon as Mulligan lays one fingertip on the crystal he can feel its pulse, a rhythmic surge of energy pouring out of the center. He leans closer, squinting, and sees a tiny but obviously mechanical implant in the blue area.

"Bet you something," Mulligan says. "God told you to put this out in the sun every now and then."

"Sure did." Del strolls over to have a look. "You sure know a lot, white boy."

"I'm, like, a real good guesser. Tell you something else. That's no jewel, that's glass."

"You talking shit now. It's a jewel."

"Glass."

"Jewel. God no give his people dumb old glass."

Mulligan was hoping she'd draw just this conclusion. He turns to Bizzer with an innocent smile.

"What do you think, dude? Glass or jewel? Want to make a bet?"

"You got nada to bet with, dude." Bizzer clacks his snout in the lizzie equivalent of an unpleasant grin. "But I say jewel, just like Del says. Hey, Wild Man! Stop eating all the bacon and c'mere."

Wiping greasy fingers on his beard, the Wild Man comes over and turns a critical eye on the crystal.

"Huh," he says at last. "Funny, it does kind of look like glass, now that you mention it."

"Bullshit, man." Bizzer looks personally insulted. "You talking bullshit, you dope."

"Watch your mouth, you worm-eating reptile," Wild Man snaps.

Bizzer clacks his beak again.

"There's an easy way to find out, y'know," Mulligan says brightly. "If you drop a jewel, it won't hurt it one little bit."

"Yeah, he's right." Wild Man takes a step toward the lizzie. "Gimme that thing."

"No going to!"

Del shrieks, but too late. Wild Man pounces, Bizzer hits back, and the crystal goes sailing half across the room to drop with a crash and a thousand splinters onto the floor. Immediately Mulligan feels profoundly relieved. Although he wasn't consciously aware of picking up the device's output before, he can feel its absence; the experience is similar to wearing a pair of shoes that are just a little too tight all day, reading out the discomfort, and then sighing in relief when you kick them off and realize that you almost gave yourself a blister.

"Look what you've done, you assholes!" Del howls. "When he get home John's going to be mad as mad."

"No reason," Mulligan says. "God cheated you, dint he? All they did was, like, find it out."

Del cocks her head to one side and considers him for a moment.

"Maybe so," she says at last. "But I no going to be the one who tells John when he get home."

"I'm going to do it," Wild Man says in a soothing sort of voice. "The white boy here, he got a point."

The three of them amble away, Del to cook, Bizzer to sweep

the fragments of the crystal under another pile of trash, Wild Man to crouch down and stare off into space with such profound concentration that Mulligan supposes he's trying to think something through for the first time in a long while. Mulligan finishes his coffee and arranges a vacant sort of expression while he desperately tries to contact Nunks.

Although like everyone else in the household Nunks is exhausted enough to sleep for hours, he wakes up suddenly in the late afternoon, thinking of Mulligan. Since his species is never drowsy—either they're awake or asleep, across a hard line—he comes instantly alert, remembering his dream, that Mulligan was inside a glass sphere and trying to break out, pounding on the transparent wall until his hands bled. Nunks gets up, shaking himself and reaching for his pair of hair-brushes while he considers the image. He suspects that it's perfectly true in its own symbolic way. Once he's brushed himself, he settles into his armchair and sends his mind out to the Rat Yard.

For some minutes he sits quietly, picking up only the constant murmur of the broken minds out in the Yard. Very distantly, very faintly, he is aware of Mrs. Bug, who seems to be sleeping, wherever she is. All of a sudden, the glass sphere breaks. He can translate his feeling no other way than into his dream image: Mulligan's psionic prison has just shattered. Hardly daring to move, he focuses his mind and sends out a beam of concentration until at last he hears Mulligan screaming his name over and over.

Little brother! [*joy*] *You are where now?*

[*elation, gratitude*] *Underground tunnels. Built <long time\first settlers.*

Tunnel where? You know/not know?

In the Rat Yard. Not know\exactly. [*relief, agony, fear, relief*]

We track >find you.

Hurry! [*terror*] *Crazies have me/think psychic enemy is God> give me to God >>he kill me. All this> soon real soon>*

I get Lacey >tell her. Stay with me, little brother >keep mind contact up >>very low level\ enemy not hear.

As soon as he's on his way, running across the garden, it occurs to Nunks that he has no words with which to explain. He can wake Lacey and Sam, of course, but how is he going to tell them about Mulligan? Briefly he moans, clenching and unclenching his hands; then he steadies himself and hurries up the stairs.

In the office Sam Bailey, wearing only bright red underwear, is stretched out on the sofa with one arm over his face while Buddy hums to himself at the desk, his sensors turning Nunks' way.

"Shall I wake the programmer?"

Nunks nods a yes and hopes that the comp unit can register the gesture, then grabs Sam by the shoulder and shakes him. With an oath and a hard punch into empty air Sam sits up.

"Oh. Nunks," he mumbles. "Just you, huh? What's wrong?"

Here is the crux, and Nunks moans again, waving his hands desperately in the air while Sam stares at him as if he could master psionics by sheer force of will.

"If I may interrupt?" Buddy says. "Are you trying to tell us something about the Mulligan unit?"

Nunks nods yes again just as Lacey appears, tucking a spotless white shirt into a pair of blue shorts.

"If you will allow," Buddy says, "I can activate a short program that I have prepared. It should greatly simplify matters by distinguishing between and eliminating logical subsets of events and possibilities."

"Go for it, Buddy," Lacey says. "And is there any coffee?"

"My housecomp subfunction activated the brewing unit just before I woke you."

The coffee is finished at the same time as Buddy's program flashes onto the screen. Nunks is amazed by its elegance; it reminds him of a qualitative analysis of a chemical substance, a clever list of yes\no questions that lead to if\then situations: is the Mulligan unit inoperative? If yes, go to question fifty; if no, proceed to two—that sort of thing. In only a few minutes he manages to convey that Mulligan is alive, captured by enemies, and being held in an unknown location to which, however, he has an important clue. A quick bit of revision on Buddy's part helps him get across the idea of the original underground living quarters of the colonists.

"Maps," Buddy says. "We need a certain specialized map that I believe exists in a databank here on Hagar. If you will excuse me for a moment?"

On his screen flash numbers, a couple of names: access codes to the main computer of the University of Freehaven, a city some eighty miles away. For a moment the screen is blank; then data begin to feed in, pages of words scrolling too fast to read, bits and pieces of holos and diagrams, each one stamped with those mysterious letters, NASA, and finally, a section of a map.

"Can you contact Mulligan and transmit these data to him?" Buddy says. "Perhaps he can recognize where he is."

Nunks shakes his head in a helpless no and turns his hands palms up.

"You cannot transmit pictorial data?"

Nunks again says no, relieved that the comp unit picks up things so quickly. When he sends his mind out, he finds Mulligan on line.

Little brother. You describe/not describe where you are now.

Describe: round room\ eighteen meters across. Has: trash everywhere; sliding door in gray plastocrete wall; ninety degrees from that, tunnel mouth. They burn fire in tunnel; smoke goes away easy MUST BE: opening to outside.

At that last detail Nunks feels a surge of pure hope. By gesturing and pointing his way through the maps and Buddy's program, he finally manages to find a place that matches Mulligan's description well enough, the old assembly hall of the colonial governors. The maps are complete enough for Buddy to give them its location to within a kilometer; once they are there, the smoke should do the rest, provided, of course, the fire is still burning.

"Then we're on our way," Lacey says. "Sam, wake Rick, get him up here to guard Maria. Oh yeah, you better put some clothes on, man."

"I happened to have that in mind." Sam does his best to sound dignified. "Okay, Buddy. You did good. Keep it up, hear?"

"I shall do my best to continue operating to your satisfaction, but of course, my programmer is the one who sets the standards of my performance."

"Hey, you arrogant piece of—"

"Enough, Sam," Lacey cuts in. "He happens to be right, but there no is any time for fighting about it now."

With a scowl of wounded dignity Sam grabs his clothes from the floor and stalks out in the direction of the bathroom. Buddy hums briefly, then emits a series of clicks.

"Operation concluded, programmer. A contingent of police officers will be meeting you near the rehydration project."

"Buddy! How did you manage that?"

"I have been planning it while you slept. I simply broke into the automated duty roster and assigned various units to certain duties, including helping you, and just now I moved that task up to emergency priority. Since the task had been on the list for some time, and was thus familiar, the duty officer accepted its validity. My tie-in with Police HQ comm indicates that a squad is even now signing out special vehicles. I have also fed the police the coordinates of Mulligan's probable location."

"Superbueno, pal." Lacey pats his casing. "Just real fine. Okay, Nunks. We'll get Mulligan out of this mess for you real fast."

Nunks wishes he could mouth-speak just so he could make some sarcastic comment. Of course she's doing all this only for him—of course. He wonders, as he so often does, at the amazing human capacity for self-delusion.

"What do you mean, my men are already heading toward the Yard?" Bates is so angry that he's bellowing. "Who the hell gave that order?"

"You did, sir." Sergeant Parsons shrinks back as if he's trying to meld with the wall. "I mean, uh, it sure looked like you did. It got all entered onto comp nice and proper with your keywords and everything, honest, sir."

Bates is about to bellow again when he remembers Buddy. When he was enjoying a joke at the PBI's expense, he'd forgotten that if Buddy could access the carefully encrypted PBI files, breaking into the police force's bottom-of-the-line system would be as easy as calculating a square root.

"Well, I dint give it," he says, as calmly as he can. "But it's too late to call'em back now. Only thing we can do is go out there after'em. I mean, I'm going to go out. You get some sleep, Sarge. You look like you're dropping where you stand."

"I'm good for a few more hours, sir."

"Oh yeah, sure. Get some sleep, and get it now. I'll be calling you, maybe, in about three, four hours."

Bates trades the fancy chief's car for an all-terrain skimmer and sets off at about twice the speed limit with the siren roaring and the lights flashing, soaring high over Polar City to cause as little danger as possible to the incoming sunset commuters. Once he's left the city airways behind, he drops down closer to the road and throws the throttle wide open. Below him dust roils from the spray of compressed air, a murky river in the gathering twilight. Finally, over the constant chatter of his sound-link with HQ, he begins to pick up communications between the leader of the expedition to the Rat Yard and the other three drivers in his squad. He flips the unit on and cuts in.

"Sergeant Nagura? The chief here. Where are you guys heading?"

"Uh, I think we're going where you told us to, sir." She sounds worried. "On your order sheet it says Nova Station, sir, and some civilians are going to meet us there, too."

"You got it exactly right, Sarge." Briefly he wonders why he's covering for a damn AI unit, but he knows that Buddy's set things up so that he'll look like a fool if he doesn't play along. "I got visual contact with you now. I'm going to come with you, after all, so I'll just get in line."

"Check, sir. Glad to have you along, Chief, I no mind saying. It sound like something big's happening."

"You're right about that, yeah."

About halfway around the rehydro project, a short side road comes into the main highway, and as they skim round to it, Bates can see a beautiful gray Bentley parked in front of the line of white plastofoam huts. (They house the formidable array of solar monitors that will, at least theoretically, give Hagar plenty of warning if its red-giant sun begins a buildup to nova state.) Seeing the car makes him wonder if Lacey actually is the sentient behind this call, but as the police caravan lands, she gets out of the Bentley and strides over to meet him. With that irritating schoolgirl smile, she offers him her hand.

"Oh say, Chief, I sure am glad to see you! What made you change your mind and come help us?"

Again he's faced with the choice: admit that Buddy made fools out of both him and the police comp, or play along. He shakes hands.

"Ah well, priorities change. Now. Where the hell is Mulligan?"

THIRD
INTERLUDE:
The Prey

All afternoon, Tomaso has been prowling around the edges of Porttown in search of Mulligan. Since he can read another psychic's mind-print from up to a kilometer away, he was expecting that finding him would be easy, but for hours he's been aware that even as he hunts Mulligan, half the ghetto is hunting him. They may not know exactly who he is, but he's managed to pick up enough mind signal on the one hand and idle chatter on the other to realize that someone called the Mayor of Porttown has far too much information about him for safety's sake. From what he knows about Polar City, he can guess that he'd be better off in the hands of the police than in those of this mysterious mayor. The police, after all, can always be bribed. He has to be careful, therefore, about where he goes, sticking to the semi-respectable areas where he has a chance to blend in with crowds or duck into public establishments that have a back door as well as a front. In the worst areas of Porttown, proprietors look askance at sentients ducking through their establishments. Unlike in those respectable areas, the entrances to the Metro stand too far apart to offer a ready refuge.

Wherever he walks, the eater walks with him, a constant murmur of greed in the background of his mind. Food— always thinking food, drooling and lusting when it smells stale soy burgers, rumbling and complaining every time they pass a slice'n'fry without buying—it merges with his rage, finally, to eye the passersby and turn them into so many cuts of meat. Assassin he may be, but a cannibal, no, and by sunset Tomaso is so revolted by these constant, intrusive thoughts of roast lizzie haunch and barbequed human ribs that he talks back, telling the eater to shut up and be quiet, threatening it with

179

antibiotics and laser skin-peels and any other medical execu-
tion he can think of. Although he starts by making these
threats psionically, as he turns a corner into a dead-end alley
he passes two young lizzies and realizes with horror that they
are staring at him—because he's talking to himself aloud.

He shuts up at once, of course, and stops walking, leaning
against a faux-brick wall and making a great show of staring at
his fingers and touching them together the way that a mental
patient on pyschotropes would do. The show apparently
convinces the lizzies, who make the hissy snigger that does
their race for a giggle and hurry out of the alley and down the
street out of sight. For a moment Tomaso merely leans against
the wall and breathes, hard at first, then slowly, trying to calm
himself down and ignore the eater, whispering now of apples
and fresh greens that seem to be close by, just beyond the wall,
in fact. He straightens up, growing tense, remembering that
when he was twisting Jack Mulligan's mind he stumbled into a
patch of memories about a garden, a lush vegetable garden in
Porttown. At the end of the alley a three-dee block sign rattles
in the wind: A TO Z ENTERPRISES.

He focuses his mind and sends it out, picking up a faint trace
of Mulligan's mind-print, but an old one and overlaid with two
other psychic minds, one also faint, the other very much
present. Although Mulligan indisputably stayed in this warehouse some time ago, he's now gone. The other mind,
however weak and untrained, suddenly notices him: he can
feel a cold suspicion, then a hatred born of alarm. Hastily he
throws up a block and hurries away, turning out of the alley
and walking fast down the street that will lead him away from
the gates of the port itself. He has no desire to wander too
close to officialdom and have someone ask him for papers—not
that his papers wouldn't pass muster, mind, but anyone
looking at them would be bound to pick up the vinegar stench
that now hangs around him like a fog.

Still aware of that watching psionic mind (and it seems to be
female), he circles round to the other side of the warehouse
and finds another alley that leads back to the wall. Although
there are no visible alarms on top of the faux brick, in a shirt
pocket he has a device, disguised as a credit chip, that can pick
up traces of electronic or pulse fields, and he can feel its
warning warmth through his shirt. At the rusty door on the
loading dock he hesitates, wondering if killing the psychic

inside might be more dangerous than it's worth even as he reaches for the sonic lockpick he carries hidden inside his right sleeve. Before he can slide it free, he feels the clumsy touch of John Hancock's mind, amplified by the device he left behind in the Rat Yard.

Great and almighty God, thy servant calls out >to thee< even in the depths\wilderness. Harken, oh Lord > prayer\mine.

The Lord thy God hears <heard >hears you. What the hell is it now?

Almighty God, we <captured/hold captive one of enemies\ yours. Blanco\blond\ found<in Rat Yard < police spyfriend Doctor Carol's now.

No genuine deity was ever more pleased by a worshiper's offering than Tomaso is by this prospective blood sacrifice. Mulligan—it has to be Mulligan!

The Lord thy God is pleased. >More pleased ONCE\ has spy in his hands. What\you desire as reward?

Whiskey rye whiskey rye whiskey we cry . . .

Manna, you dope! Its name: manna. God no give you lousy plain whiskey.

I grovel before thee, Lord of Hosts. Manna it is.

From behind him Tomaso hears one soft scrape, a boot sole on plastocrete. Drawing his knife even as he thrusts out his right leg in a pivot, he swirls around to see two men, swathed in suncloaks, watching him from about three meters away. One of them has his right hand just out of the slit in the cloak, and he's holding the squat gray nozzle of a spray-field laser carbine.

"Dunt leave much to chance, huh, dude?" Tomaso says.

"Mayor kind of wants to see you, pal. Drop the knife."

Instead Tomaso hurls himself sideways, right off the loading dock, and rolls as he hits the ground. With his left hand he snaps the knife straight into the back of the man with the laser; with his right he draws a pistol of his own and fires. The edge of his enemy's fire field singes his cloak and sets it burning, but his own solid-beam shot drops the other. He rolls again, twisting up, ignoring the heat and the scorching pain along his side, and fires a second time, drilling a hole right through the screaming second target's helmet. By then the smoke is rising into his own helmet, choking him, making him gag, but he concentrates his mind as much as steadies his hands and pulls it free just in time, hurling the cloak down to burn on the plastocrete with one last exhalation of greasy black smoke up into the pink twilight, a beacon that's bound to call attention from blocks around. Coughing and staggering, he staggers forward and grabs his knife free with a spurt of blood.

MINE!!

A sensation rather than a word, the concept burns in his mind worse than the pain of his charred skin. The eater wants the corpses, wants to roil and welter in their blood, and so strong is the compulsion that he slits one man's throat before he can stop himself. Of their own accord his infected hands reach for the red wetness.

"No! I won't!"

He chokes again, realizing he's spoken aloud, and stands there retching without quite vomiting for a long minute. His burned side throbs and stinks of charred cloth and flesh. From behind him someone coughs, a warning of infinite politeness.

The bloody knife still in his hand, Tomaso spins around and sees that he's been watched, the entire time, most likely. Sitting in a door niche is an old man, egg-bald and dressed only in a yellow T-shirt, much too large for him, and a pair of filthy orange shorts. His mahogany-brown legs are thin as sticks and his bare feet, swollen with calluses.

"How long have you been there?" Tomaso hears his voice snap and snarl, but he's furious with himself, that he could be so stupid as to overlook a sentient not more than five or six meters from him, especially one who emits no psionic signal whatsoever.

"Long enough."

The ancient eyes watch calmly from their nest of wrinkles as Tomaso strides over and raises the knife, watch unblinking, unsmiling, merely watch. Tomaso hesitates.

"Eating and being eaten." The stiff, cracking voice is perfectly calm, conversational, really, as if he were discussing baseball scores. "The ultimate revolve of the wheel of life and death is eating and being eaten in turn."

"What do you mean by that?"

"Nada."

Again Tomaso hesitates, painfully aware that he has to hurry, should just kill the old man, this final witness, and run for the Rat Yard. The brown eyes watch, never moving from his face.

"Ah shit!" Tomaso turns on his heel and leaves him be.

As he races down the alley and out into the street, the pain in his side first flares, then ebbs with a feeling of oozing cold. The eater—all at once he realizes that the eater is busily munching up the burnt dead flesh and excreting some cooling, numbing fluid in return. He stops running, merely stands there on the sidewalk and gasps for breath while the eater does its work. When he glances back, the old man in the yellow T-shirt is gone, off at a public comm, most likely, calling the mysterious Mayor of Porttown.

He should run for the cover of the Alliance Embassy. Tomaso knows it suddenly, knows that he's failed, knows that begging asylum from his masters is his last chance at life, although he's willing to bet they'll turn him down. The H'Allevae dislike failure, very much indeed. In a specially treated and hollow molar at the back of his jaw lurks poison like the liqueur in the center of a chocolate, offering one good bite and then death. As his tongue touches the tooth, ever so lightly, he feels the eater panting in anticipation, drooling at the prospect of melting his body in one last orgasm of feeding before it too expires for lack of further food. It hates him now, he realizes, because by refusing to bathe in his victims' blood he's kept the eater from spreading to their corpses and thus has doomed it to die with him.

The boy's voice is screaming in his mind. He glances at his hands, expecting to find them bloody from the long banging on the metal door, but they are still the muscled heavy hands of a man who knows how to kill in an amazing variety of ways. He is free of the locked room with the endless waterfall rippling down but going nowhere. He will never go back to that room again. He makes up his mind about that right there and then.

Just under his breath he starts to laugh at a joke that only he can see. The punch line is this: even though he's lived his life alone, he's not going to die that way.

Chapter Seven

When his jury-rigged expedition sets off again for the Rat Yard, Bates slaves the autodrive of his skimmer into the controls of the riot van ahead of him, then gets on the comm in earnest. He loads Akeli's access code first, because from long experience he assumes that the PBI chief will wait to return his call, no matter how urgent things are. He is pleasantly surprised when in just a few seconds his comm unit beeps to let him know that Akeli is on the other end of the link.

"Bates, how fortuitous you should contact me so quickly." On the viewer Akeli's face is ashen. "In the words of the old military joke, the excremental matter has impacted the mechanical air-circulation device. I have been on comm with the President for almost an hour. This amnesty plea on the part of the H'Allevae suspect is threatening to turn into an intersystem incident of the first degree."

"And the first degree means troops?"

"Damn right." Akeli scares himself into brief clarity. "Carli troops, if we don't cover our ass just right."

Bates makes a gargling sort of groan deep in his throat.

"The carli ambassador has apparently seen an opportunity to expand the carli sphere of influence," Akeli goes on. "It seems that they have known for some time about the existence of a possibility of a first contact."

"Damn Ka Pral! He's been stringing me along, then."

"I wouldn't put it so harshly. He himself was under orders from the ambassador to maintain ambiguity. Ka Pral contacted me personally to explain that fact and asked me to convey his regrets to you for any unavoidable deception he may have perpetrated. Frankly, I think the situation was unclear even to him until a few hours ago. But at any rate, the ambassador has

184

declared the carli race to be, and I quote a translated title, 'Protectors of the Unknown and Helpless Ones.'"

"Shee-it! And of course the Alliance protested."

"Of course. And so the President—" Akeli pauses to gulp air like a rutting frog. "So the President claimed prior rights to offer protection, based on the presence of this alien sentient on our sovereign territory."

"She aced them both out? I no savvy whether to swear or cheer. But where does the dead Hopper come in?"

"Both the carlis and our President have declared themselves unconvinced by the official explanation of his death. They have both offered amnesty to his head wife, or head widow now I suppose, as well as to the chief neuter in his bed-family. The Confederation is now demanding that they be turned over to a joint force of humans and carlis. If they aren't removed from the embassy, of course, they will be tortured in a court of law to give evidence against their late husband."

"Yeah, I know the Hopper idea of legal proceedings, thanks, but jeez, a joint force?"

"A joint force. That means carli marines on-world."

Bates would like to swear, but he simply has no breath for it.

"You've got to find this alien with all celerity, Bates. We are postulating a margin of perhaps twenty hours. Not days, Bates—standard hours."

"I hear you. Once the carlis have troops down here, they just might never take'em off again—unless maybe resinated into body slabs for that last long orbit around their sun."

"That is indeed preying upon my mind. But once we have the alien under our protection, we will have a bargaining chip that cannot be ignored. For a share of mercantile rights with this new people, the carlis will doubtless agree that a squad of our troops would be sufficient protection for the widow and the ex-lover or whatever they would call the neuter now. Understand me? All celerity."

"Yeah, I—" Bates suddenly smiles as the idea comes to him, or rather comes back to him, that simple little joke Lacey made earlier in this shared nightmare. "Oh hey, man, I got an idea."

"Indeed? Something that will disallow a carli military presence on Hagar?"

"Something that's going to keep any kind of troops out of Polar City for sure and probably off the rest of the planet, too, yeah. Uh, but look, this has got to be handled just right, or we're going to have panic in the streets." Bates hesitates, thinking fast. He cannot trust Akeli to put this idea in motion; the PBI boss is likely to panic himself and release the news too soon. "I got to do more research, man, before I can risk talking about it over comm like this. But I want you to do one thing for me, okay? I bet you got reporters swarming round you like flies."

"Unfortunately your metaphor is entirely appropriate."

"I want you to drop a couple of hints that there may be a medical emergency brewing in Polar City, something you don't understand, but, and tell'em this exactly as I tell it to you: the doctors are working on it, and there's no need for people to get upset."

"Good God, Bates, if I attempt to reassure the populace in those vague terms, of course alarm and restiveness will ensue."

"You got it, baby. That's just what I want to happen, a lot of people wondering what's coming down."

"Myself included. What do you mean, medical emergency?"

"Told you, I got to do more research. But if I'm right, we can leak a story to the press, say, by tomorrow morning, that'll have the carlis running for their ships as fast as their furry little legs will take'em."

"Oho! I begin to discern the drift of this scheme. Very well, I shall employ portentousness and wiles."

"Why the hell can't you just use plain Merrkan, damn you? But yeah, I think you're getting the point. Get on to it right away, man. It's a lousy long shot, but jeezchrist, that's all we got left to us now."

Bates powers out with the punch of a toggle that makes his unit beep in protest.

"Sorry," he says. "Call in to HQ, will you?"

An overexcited clerk on the Duty Desk switches him straight through to Parsons, who sounds remarkably wide-awake. No doubt the news he repeats gave him a good shot of adrenaline when he first heard it. Right after Bates left headquarters, an anonymous citizen phoned in to report two dead bodies lying in the gutter not far from A to Z Enterprises. One had his face blasted away with a laser, and the other was stabbed in the back and had his throat cut for good measure as well. Now that things have been cleaned up at the scene of the crime, two officers are working the neighborhood trying to find witnesses, most likely a futile job in Porttown but one that has to be done.

"Sounds like the killings are related to this assassin, yeah," Bates says.

"Well, we're pretty sure they are, el jefe." Parsons sounds oddly hesitant. "Uh, once we had the corpses down at the coroner, we got another call."

"Yeah? Same guy?"

"Nah. This one was a donna. Uh, she claimed to be calling for the Mayor of Porttown."

"She-it! Think she was some kind of crank?"

"If she is, she's sure the most convincing one I ever heard. Look, she told us that the Mayor had his own reasons for wanting this killer gone, and that he's been like tracking him. Gave us a real clear description, told us what he'd been doing all day—the assassin I mean, not the Mayor. And here's the clincher. She told us that there was another corpse in a hotel room in the Outworld Bazaar, and when I sent a pair of officers down there, sure enough, they found one. The dude's throat was slit just like all the others."

"You got that conversation on tape? Yeah? Good—feed it straight into the minicomp over this frequency. I'll go over it good while we're driving. I no suppose the Mayor's secretary or whatever she is knows where this asshole is now."

"She got a good idea. Someone saw him heading for the Rat Yard in a stolen van, she says."

"Oh yeah? Swell! We're almost there ourselves."

"Sure hope it's swell. She says he's armed to the max."

"Oh hell, man. I could figure that out for myself."

Curled up on the backseat of the Bentley, Nunks has fallen into a state halfway between trance and waking. Although he's dimly aware of the outside world—the soft leather under him, the hum of the skimmer, Sam and Lacey's voices coming from the front seat—most of his consciousness is focused on Mulligan. He has a double job; maintaining constant contact with the little brother while at the same time keeping his own signal so low that their psionic enemy will remain unaware of it. So intense is his concentration that they are almost to the Rat Yard before he realizes that Mrs. Bug has been trying to reach him for some time.

Sister! [surprise, relief] you know\ what <happened to little brother/not know?

Know. [guilty unease] My fault. <I not respond <<you search.<< Now: sorry.

Sister! [joy, relief] You help/not help?

Help now. [regret, pronounced guilt] <not help before< <<frightened<<

I understand. You now\ stay ready for contact. I now\ with friends. >>we come double-fast.>> You help>we triangulate.

No need mind tricks. <Just now< I see one enemy: he crawl\into hole. >We get enemy >>make him tell where is little brother>> >>>we get little brother>>>

You know this man\ him enemy? How?

<I see him\kill my . . . [grief, despair]

I understand, sister. >say no more> >you stay in contact\ with me >>guide us\hole.>>

No need. Show you now> show you>.

Into Nunks's mind comes an image, as clear and detailed as a holo, of a section of the Rat Yard. For a moment his sheer admiration of her talent muddles his concentration; then he grabs the image (metaphorically speaking, of course) and tucks it into his memory. When he sends out a signal to thank her, she's already gone, moving steadily across the Yard.

Nunks leans forward and taps Sam on the shoulder. After a lot of gesturing and a little help from Buddy, chiming in over the portable link, he finally makes Sam understand that he's to follow Nunks' gestural directions from now on. Behind them the caravan of police vehicles snakes after, matching their every move. Yet even as they race into the Rat Yard, Nunks aches with fear that they're too late, because he can feel another psychic mind moving in from some new and unknown direction, a mind equally as strong as Mrs. Bug's, but one raging and roiling in a blood-madness.

John Hancock comes back just as the others are cleaning up the breakfast dishes. Del has saved his share of the food in the skillet; although she offers to put it on a plate for him, he waves her away and eats straight from the pan while he talks, more or less between bites but usually with his mouth full. Mulligan has a hard time watching him.

"I talked to God, all right. I laid my head down on the sacred altar, just like he taught me, and talked to him. He wants to buy this white boy, all right. He's real pleased we got him."

Mulligan's stomach churns from more than squeamishness about John's table manners. Wild Man and Bizzer exchange a glance, a sly, sideways thing of conspiracy.

"Just what he going to pay us?" Wild Man says.

"Booze, like the last time. But oh yeah, we got the name wrong. It's manna, he says. Manna from heaven, man."

"No enough." Wild Man stands up.

"What?" John lays the pan to one side and glares up at him. "What got into you, you bastard? You no can argue with God."

"Damn right I can. When you was gone we found out God cheated us. Remember that old jewel he gave us? It was glass, no a real jewel at all."

Wiping his hands on his shorts, John rises to face him. Del scoops up the baby and falls back to stand out of the way near Mulligan; Blue-beak Bizzer hesitates for a moment, then joins them. Mulligan realizes that the stakes of this argument have just gone very high.

"Now you listen to me, man." Wild Man pokes at the air with one dirty finger to emphasize his points. "We got out the jewel God gave us. We took a good look at it, and it was glass, nada but glass."

"Bull she-it. It's a jewel."

"No. Glass."

"Jewel, I say."

"You say wrong." With a triumphant flourish Wild Man pulls a long splinter out of the pocket of his overalls. "You see this? It's all that's left of that old fake jewel."

"Gimme that!"

When John snatches the fragment, it slices his fingers, and blood wells. With an oath he throws it straight at Wild Man, who ducks with a surprising grace.

"Look what you made me do!"

"It cut because it's glass. No be a jewel. You got cheated by God, and I no going to do what you say no more."

With a howl of rage John jumps him. Writhing, swearing, biting, shoving, and snarling more than punching each other, they fall to the floor and roll around, crunching through heaps of trash, twisting dangerously near the fire, then heaving themselves clear just in time. Del watches in doe-eyed indifference, bouncing the baby in her arms to keep him quiet, her head cocked a little to one side as Wild Man manages to pin John under him and get his hands round her man's neck. For a moment John gasps, chokes, and struggles wildly, then goes limp. When Wild Man relaxes the grip, John twists, grabs, and throws him off in one smoothly calculated motion. He gets Wild Man down on his stomach and straddles him, then grabs his hair in one massive hand and begins to bang his face into the plastocrete while Wild Man howls for mercy.

"You going to do what I say, muhfugger?"

"I will, I will."

"You sorry you argued with me?"

"I'm sorry, real sorry."

"All right!"

John lets him go and rolls free. Del yawns, patting the baby on the back and staring out into space as she watches someone that no one else can see.

"He always wins," she remarks to this someone. "Dunt know why they bother. He always wins."

Whimpering to himself, the Wild Man limps over to the water drum and grabs a rag from a nearby heap to clean his wounds. Bizzer starts to help him, then hesitates, staring at John, waiting until the newly reconfirmed leader jerks his thumb in Wild Man's direction.

"Go git his face washed. God wants to get this white boy real soon. We've wasted too much time already."

No enough, Mulligan thinks, *no enough by half, man*. When he sends his mind out, he can sense Nunks, still keeping his signal low to avoid being picked up by the enemy. He can feel his mentor closing in fast, but he's still a long way away.

"Nunks?" Lacey says. "You sure this is the right place?"

Nunks shrugs, turning both palms upward as if to say that he hopes so. Lacey's beginning to get nervous; she's acutely aware that both Sam and Bates have trusted her and Nunks blindly up until now, and that this faith is beginning to turn to skepticism. What they see is certainly unprepossessing enough; a slanted rise of crumbling white wall surrounded by wind-worn lumps of dirty brown rubble, a dozen or so boulders scattered randomly, and a rusty metal hulk, about twenty meters high, that looks like it was once the fuselage of a shuttle or perhaps even an antique airplane. Bates trots over, followed by a policebeing with her arms full of equipment.

"Okay, Lacey, here's the procedure. I'm issuing you guys standard riot gear: helmets with comm links and IR visors—it's going to be dark in there—and reflec vests and stun guns. Do you want some of my guys to go down with you?"

At Bates's question, Nunks looks up and shakes his head in a vigorous no. Although there is no way that the police helmet is going to fit over even one half of his bifurcate skull, he is busily lacing an enormous reflec vest over his coveralls.

"Nah, but thanks, Chief. I think you better deploy your people up here, look around for another entrance, maybe. But you might leave someone here and tell'em to be ready to shoot if we come back out in a hurry. Something just might be chasing us."

"My thought exactly, yeah." Bates pauses, squinting into the rubble. "Uh, where is this entrance, anyway?"

With a wave of one enormous hand, Nunks gestures for them to follow and strides off, heading round the tattered fuselage to a long moraine of miscellaneous rubble. He hesitates, then pounces, knocking away a scatter of trash to reveal a round hatch sunk flush with the ground and embossed with the usual NASA. The lift bar is so shiny and clean that it's obvious someone uses the hatch all the time.

"Jeez," Bates says. "A tunnel? I'm sure glad I'm no going down there with you guys."

Lacey and Sam exchange a slight smile at his expense. As longtime spacers, they are more than used to crawling through access tubes from one bubble compartment of a ship to another. Nunks, however, makes a sighing sort of noise that Lacey interprets as distaste or even fear, although it's hard for her to imagine Nunks being afraid of anything.

"Think you're going to fit down there?" she says to him.

He shrugs again, then bends down and grabs the lift bar to pull the hatch, made of solid metal and weighing at least forty kilograms, open in one smooth gesture. Metal stairs lead down into darkness. Lacey snaps her IR visor down and draws the stun gun, which she'll carry at least until they're out of Bates's sight. She suspects that sooner rather than later she'll want her laser pistol at the ready.

"Okay, gang. Might as well get on with it, huh? I'll go first, then Nunks, and then you, Sam. Keep your eyes open back there, will you? Nunks, you put one hand on my shoulder so you can steer me, okay? You're the one who can find Mulligan."

Yet, once they've all clattered down to the smooth flat floor below, Lacey realizes that they can find Mulligan's captors even without psionics, because a clear trail, polished by many feet, leads straight down the middle of the filthy tunnel. Through the infrared visor she sees this trail glow a dull coppery orange, still slightly warm from a living being who passed this way not very long ago at all. Smiling to herself, she adjusts the mouthpiece of her comm link.

"Okay, Chief, we're right on track. Am I coming in clear?"

"Sure are," Bates's voice crackles in her ear. "Keep in touch, will you? Good hunting and good luck."

"Think he can walk?" Wild Man says.

"No savvy." His mouth skewed with thought, John Hancock considers Mulligan for a moment. "You hit him awful hard."

"Can you walk, white boy?" The Wild Man pokes Mulligan in the ribs with the toe of his boot.

"No for long." Mulligan is speaking the simple truth. After a long couple of hours awake, he feels his head pounding again and his vision, blurring. "You damn near cracked my skull."

The Wild Man laughs and pantomimes swinging at someone's head with a pipe.

"Better carry him, then," John says.

"Where we taking him?"

"To the temple. Only place I can think of. God never did finish telling me what to do. It must be a test of faith or something. Go get the cart."

The cart turns out to be an old-fashioned, bright red wheelbarrow, the sort you actually have to push, no doubt a relic from the days before the colony laid in its superconducting network. Between them John and the Wild Man sling Mulligan in like a stuffed sack with his head resting near the handles and his legs sticking ignominiously in the air.

"Maybe I *can* walk," Mulligan says. "Part of the way, anyway."

"Nah. No can have you die on us. We want to get our manna."

They haven't gone more than a hundred bone-jouncing meters before Mulligan decides that his chances of survival would be much better if he were on his feet, but nothing he

can say changes John Hancock's mind. With Blue-beak Bizzer
doing the pushing, they hurry through a web of tunnels,
turning so often and so randomly that Mulligan is hopelessly
lost after five minutes. At one point, when he tries to contact
Nunks, he feels another psychic mind searching for him, a
hungry mind whose cold touch hits him like the snap of teeth.
He shuts down fast and tries to concentrate on nothing more
than the swings and snakes of the tunnels, and the sudden
openings into rooms. On and on they go, jouncing and rattling,
until at last he loses even that awareness as the universe
shrinks down to his pain and nothing more.

Eventually they come to a small half-round room where the
bluish-gray plastocrete is all neatly swept and polished. In the
middle stands an upside-down metal drum, covered with a
stained white cloth, that supports another crystal, this one
long and flat—the holy altar, he assumes, and most likely some
kind of psionic amplifier. John confirms his guess by first
genuflecting, then kneeling down and laying his head on the
crystal for a few seconds. To one side is an opaque plastic door,
blocked with chunks of rubble; to the other, a pair of what
Mulligan takes to be grav platform shafts. Instead, they turn
out to be antique electric elevators. Apparently their solar
pack is still sending power, because when John comes over and
presses the button, a pair of doors slide open.

"Dump him in and send him up," John says. "And God says
he'll send our manna down in the other one."

With a certain amount of care Bizzer and the Wild Man
arrange Mulligan on the floor of the cage. If he weren't in such
pain, Mulligan would laugh aloud, thinking how grotesque it is
that he should go to his death in an elevator, that he's rising to
meet God in more ways than one. As it is, his head hurts so
badly that he's beginning to think of the assassin's knife as a
mercy. The two crazies step out, and John poises his finger
over the button.

"Vaya con Dios." And he punches it hard.

With the lurch and creak of ancient machinery the cage
crawls upward. Mulligan summons a little energy and tries
searching for signal ahead of him. This time he makes contact.
Even in his muddled state the strength of the psionic mind he
touches shocks him.

Okay, God, who are you?

You see soon enough. No fear/I not kill you.

Why not?

I need a hostage. >*You see why/few seconds*>

With one last groan the elevator jerks to a stop. As the doors slide open, Mulligan picks up the smell of rancid vinegar cutting through the mustiness of the air.

"Never thought God would look like a spacer, did you?" The voice is oddly pleasant, with a desperate kind of humor in it. "Welcome to Heaven, panchito."

The man who steps into the cage is wearing a baggy gray jumpsuit of the sort common to baggage handlers and other low-level port workers. He is blond, well-muscled, and he'd be handsome, in a way, if half his face weren't oddly stiff, the corner of the mouth frozen in a twist, one eyebrow peaked high and unevenly. His walk is also peculiar, all spraddle-legged and shambling, as if his testicles pained him. Mulligan's first thought is that he's suffered some kind of cerebral hemorrhage.

Not a stroke. Skin problem/infection? Maybe. You're my ticket to a doctor. >*Gonna trade you right across the board*> >>*medical care and a safe passage off this goddamn planet*>> >>>*never wanna see the filthy place again*>>> [*surprise*] [*relief*]

But Mulligan is sending false signal, using the last bit of his strength to hide his real reaction, that even though this dude is a smooth liar, he's a liar nonetheless. The only thing he can read in his captor's mind is bloodlust.

After about ten minutes of following the heat trace through the long, straight tunnel, Nunks suddenly grabs Lacey by the shoulder and shakes her. Her first thought is that he's going claustrophobic on her, but with hand gestures and a certain amount of stomping up and down he manages to tell her that something terrible's happened and that, while Mulligan is still alive, they have to hurry if they're going to keep him that way. Without needing to say one word to each other, she and Sam both shove their stun guns into their vest pockets and draw their lasers.

"Let's go," Lacey says. "Now! Vamos, man!"

Sam moves up to the front, and side by side they head off at a fast jog. Nunks comes panting along behind.

As the tunnel curves around to their right, they begin to pass sliding doors, some half-open, most shut. Here and there a side tunnel winds off, but always the glowing track leads them straight on, growing brighter and brighter until at last they see a blaze of light ahead of them. They slow down to a walk to catch their breath.

"Someone's campfire," Sam whispers. "Hard to look at the damn thing through this visor."

"Yeah." Lacey pushes hers back. After a brief moment of utter disorientation, she can see the outline of a doorway and beyond it a wood fire burning. "Nunks, is Mulligan in there?"

With a moan and a clench of his hands, Nunks shakes his head no.

"Somehow I knew everything was going too easy so far," Sam mutters.

Lacey nods her agreement, then walks on, keeping to the wall and moving as quietly as she can. With Sam right beside her she charges into the room and aims, laser hand braced over the opposite wrist.

"Freeze!"

A woman is crouched in terror by the fire, a baby in her arms, Carol's patients Del and J.J., Lacey assumes. Since the room is otherwise empty, she feels profoundly ridiculous and lowers the laser. At the sight of Nunks, looming in the doorway, Del screams and cowers back.

"All right, you," Lacey snaps. "No one's going to hurt you if you tell me the truth. Where's the blond dude?"

"They took him to God. God's going to buy him."

"What?"

"Just what I say, girl." She rises to her knees and glares in a pathetic attempt at hauteur. "Dunt you go telling me what to do, white trash."

"Yeah?" When she raises the laser again, Del cringes. "I said, where is he?"

"I told you, they took him to God. I no savvy where God lives. Only John knows that."

Nunks steps forward, pointing to Del and shaking his head in a vigorous yes.

"Hey man," Lacey says. "You mean she's telling the truth?"

Nunks nods again, but he waggles his hands in a despairing sort of gesture, trying to tell her something that she can't decipher.

"Come on, guys," Sam says. "Wherever he is, he's no here."

"Yeah, you're right." Lacey turns her back on the fire and

lowers the visor to peer at the various ways out of the room.
Down one side tunnel the bright track is visibly stronger. "Bet
they went that way."

"No they dint," Del says with obviously desperate bravado.
"Went back that way there."

"Nunks?"

Nunks points to the way Lacey originally chose.

"Uh-huh. Listen, kid," this last to Del. "If I was you, I'd get
the hell out of here right now and surrender to the police."

Del grabs a piece of broken crockery from the floor and
heaves it in Lacey's general direction. Ducking, Lacey leads
her troop on down the tunnel. As they break into a jog, she
flips on the comm unit in her helmet. The first channel is a
babble of voices, squad leaders announcing their positions,
requesting orders, or describing the terrain around them. The
second one she tries, however, carries only a hiss and Bates'
rumbling voice, talking to someone named Sergeant Nagura.

"What do you mean, movement?" Bates is saying. "Is there
someone up there or not?"

"Can't tell, Chief." Nagura's voice is female and human. "All
we can see is something moving up in the old control room. It
might just be a dog or something. There's some wild ones out
here."

"Shit." Bates sounds personally offended by this canine
possibility. "Okay, but keep an eye on it, will you, and get
yourself some cover."

"Will do, Chief. Out."

"Bates?" Lacey cuts in quickly, before he can shut the
channel down. "Lacey here."

"Damn well about time. Where the hell have you been?"

"Following down a trail. Sorry. We've been distracted, kind
of. Look, we found where they were holding Mulligan, but
they've taken him away. I don't know where, but the donna we
found was babbling something about God."

"Jeez, but what the hell can we expect? Anyone we find out
here is crazy, remember? Have you found another trail?"

"Sure did. Real recent, judging from how bright it is under
IR."

"Okay, go on, but just leave this channel open, will you? It's
my command link, so I've always got it going in one ear."

"Okay, Chief, will do."

After about forty meters the previously clear ground-plan of the complex disintegrates into a maze—narrow tunnels, round rooms, continual doorways—but only one heat track shines brightly enough to stand out from all the others. As they trot down it, leaving it twice as bright from their own body heat, Lacey feels her heart pounding from far more than the simple exertion. Somehow it hadn't quite registered before that Mulligan's in the hands of sentients who are totally irrational, who might, for all she knows, kill him on a sudden whim. When Nunks touches her shoulder and hisses under his breath, she whirls around and nearly shoots him.

"What the hell?"

Nunks waves his hands in the air, then points down the tunnel ahead of them.

"Someone coming," Sam says. "Listen."

Distantly she can hear male voices, one lizzie and two human, squabbling in an amiable sort of way. With a wave of her pistol she deploys Sam into a doorway on one side of the tunnel, steps back into a room on the other, and gestures Nunks in behind her. They wait, listening as the voices come nearer, and with them the pungent whiff of unwashed bodies.

"Rye whiskey, rye whiskey, rye whiskey I cry, I got to have rye whiskey, or I sure going to die." The three voices are singing in uncertain harmony, and they repeat this chorus over and over because, or so Lacey assumes, they've forgotten the rest of the words.

Some metal thing is rumbling and banging roughly in rhythm with the song, and as the three crazies turn the corner Lacey sees it's a bright red wheelbarrow, piled high with big plastobubbles of some amber liquid—the whiskey in question, most likely. Lacey signals Sam, then steps out, laser drawn and ready, and blocks their path. Just as Sam joins her the three shriek and come to so fast a stop that the lizzie lets go the handles of the wheelbarrow, which falls back with a clang. A plastobubble bounces out and lies quivering like a live thing.

"Holdup!" The black human screams. "We getting held up, John!"

"Shut up, Wild Man." The red-haired Blanco seems to be the leader. "They got guns, and we got none."

"We no want your stinking whiskey," Lacey says. "What have you done with Mulligan?"

"Who?"

"The white dude, the one Del said you were selling to God."

"Oh, him. His name's Mulligan, huh? Well, we sold him to God, yeah, just like Del said. Sent him up to Heaven in the elevator, and the manna come down in the other one."

Fear and rage, mingled together—the sensation starts at the base of her spine and slices up like the cut of an ice-cold knife. When John Hancock breaks into a sudden sweat of terror, she realizes that she's automatically raised the laser and aimed. *Do no good to kill this poor slob, girl—not his fault*. With a deep breath she lowers the gun, and John moans under his breath, sane enough, apparently, to know when he's close to dying.

"And just where is this Heaven-bound elevator?" Sam says, his voice more a growl.

"Back there, back there, sir," John is stammering with fear, and he turns to point down a side tunnel. "Right back there, but God's gone now. We heard him leaving. He's gone."

Just then Bates' voice cuts into the comm in Lacey's helmet, and she lifts the flap so Sam can hear it, too.

"Lacey, for God's sake get up here! We've spotted our assassin, and he's got someone with him up in the old control tower. Get up to the surface, but be superdamn careful where you exit. No want you right in the line of fire."

"Jeezuz!" Sam waves the laser at John Hancock. "Listen, dude, you know these tunnels. You're going to show a nice quick way up, or I'll burn some of that filth off you."

"Yes sir." John salutes with an automatic precision that reveals him as a deserter or Section Eight discharge from one fleet or another. "On the double." He turns to his two confederates. "You get that manna home, and you no drink no more of it till I get back. Hear?"

They nod agreement, but they're watching the lasers aimed their way.

"Go on," Sam says. "Do what the sergeant says, and do it fast. All right, you. Lead on."

John Hancock salutes again and sets off, heading down a side tunnel at a shuffling jog with Sam and Nunks right behind. Lacey lingers a moment, looking back to make sure that the other two are indeed wheeling their loot away rather than creeping up on them from the rear. As soon as they've pushed their jouncing wheelbarrow round a corner, she runs after the others. In her heart she's wishing that she believed in God or Allah or even the Galactic Mind, just so there would be someone to beg for Mulligan's safety. She catches up with Sam just as John Hancock stops and points left into another tunnel that seems to be a long, spiraling ramp up.

"Sir, this leads right out to the old runway. Bout a key from the white tower."

"Sounds good," Sam says. "But you're coming right up to the door with us."

John screws up his face in protest, then glances at the drawn laser and sighs his agreement. As it turns out, they don't have far to go, because the ramp rises for only about two hundred meters before they see a pair of huge double doors, hanging open and skewed, ahead of them. Illusionary red light streams in, the dissipating day's heat from the Rat Yard beyond. When Lacey flips up her visor the light disappears.

"Okay, Sarge," Sam says. "Dismissed."

With another precise salute, John Hancock turns and runs, slamming off the tunnel wall at one point in his hurry to be gone. Lacey gives Sam a quizzical look.

"How'd you savvy that dude was a sergeant once?"

"He's the type, that's all. Look at him, loco as they get, but he had that pair of borrachos right under his thumb."

Distantly, faint in the wind and sighing down the tunnel, comes the sound of Bates's voice, just barely recognizable over a bullhorn.

"We are prepared to negotiate. I repeat, we are willing to negotiate. I'm Al Bates, chief of police in this town, and I am empowered to negotiate. Will you negotiate?"

The answer never reaches them. Lacey slides down her visor and starts running toward the tunnel mouth.

"Come on, guys. Let's get the hell out of here."

They have plenty of room to duck between the skewed doors. Outside, the cool night sky looks black through the visor, while the Yard itself is a sea of pale red light. Ahead of them and a fair bit less than a key away rises the tower, a dark stroke because its white surface has reflected more of the day's heat and thus is cooler than the dull-colored garbage nearby. All around it are the fuzzy dots of heat-light that mark the position of Bates's riot squad, and on the platform near the top of the tower moves another living being, the assassin, Lacey can assume. Her heart seems to twist in her chest when she realizes that there's no sign of Mulligan.

"Almost there," Sam whispers. "Nunks, you follow a little behind. You no got a helmet, remember."

Nunks moans briefly and clenches his hands. Crouched low, moving in a random zigzag, the three of them pick their way through the rubble to the sound of Bates's voice, repeating his willingness to negotiate in a soothing drone over the bullhorn. Not once do they hear any kind of answer, not even when they're close enough to see the police line clearly, illuminated by its own heat. All the officers have dug improvised foxholes and ditches out of the strew of rubble and garbage. With his bulk Bates is clearly recognizable, right up front with the shiny little box of the electronic bullhorn cradled in his palm. As they creep closer, up on the tower the fuzzy dot resolves itself into a tall male figure, ducking inside the remains of the control room, then shuffling out with his arms full, over and over as if he's bringing out some kind of cargo. Just as Lacey crawls into the chief's ditch to hunker down beside him, the assassin emerges one last time, dragging a human by the ankles.

"I got your police psychic up here, cop!" His dark voice drifts down in a shout. "You pull anything funny on me, and he dies."

"No going to pull anything." Bates rises to his knees. "I'm empowered to negotiate. Do you want a priest or a mullah out here? How bout some food?"

At that the assassin tosses back his head and shrieks in a cascade of metallic laughter. Lacey's heart twists again as she realizes that he's completely insane.

The concrete platform sticks out like a hat brim, some two meters across and running about a third of the way around the tower itself, which is about nine meters in diameter. Although Mulligan can see the twisted remains of some supports for a guardrail, the rail itself has long since gone. He is unpleasantly aware that they're a good fifty meters aboveground. Once he stops laughing, Tomaso pushes some big metal crates to the edge of the platform and crouches down behind them.

"Hey there!" Bates's voice drifts up again, and this time it sounds jolly in a forced sort of way. "We're listening, pal. How about giving us a list of demands?"

For an answer Tomaso picks up a laser rifle and begins crawling toward the edge of the platform. Mulligan realizes that when energy beams start whizzing around, he'll be much more exposed than the assassin is. He waits until Tomaso is concentrating on aiming, then inches his way caterpillar-fashion until his upper third lies behind the imperfect shelter of the broken door that once led into the old control room. At the sound of the soft *swush* of the laser, he winces and automatically turns his head away. Out of the corner of his eye he catches movement down on the ground among the boulders at the base of the tower. A direct look shows him someone crawling along in what looks like shiny armor. The only thing he can assume is that a member of the riot squad is risking his or her life to come save him, and that this person is horribly, dangerously exposed.

Never in his life has Mulligan felt more helpless. Since Tomaso has taken the precaution of gagging him, he can't call out a warning; as a matter of fact, he can barely move. How is he going to do one damn thing to help his would-be rescuer? Then he remembers the obvious, that he doesn't need spoken words to distract his captor. Although he's afraid to confront Tomaso directly, he knows he has a perfect way to siphon off his energy if only he has the guts to try. On the bullhorn Bates is droning away in as soothing a voice as he can muster, promising medical care, offering sanctuary from the H'Allevae and a fair trial and a chance at rehab if only Tomaso will surrender immediately. The only answer is the *swush, swush* of the gun. For a moment Mulligan struggles with his fear; then he closes his eyes and walks into his mind.

In memory he stands on the street corner near Civic Center Plaza, just after sunset, and remembers seeing Chief Bates hurrying through a crowd around what seems to be a dead carli. At first the images rise easily; he remembers the med techs weaving through the crowd with a grav platform bobbing behind them, and himself walking over, casually at first, then with some purpose as he realized that he could make a few sorely needed bucks out of this accident—he still hadn't understood that it was murder—by offering to do a police reading. In his mind he takes a step and walks into a solid wall of pain.

Fire is the image his subconscious chooses to represent the pain, a leaping, searing wall of flame that burns worse than any physical fire. Mulligan jumps back, feeling his actual physical body gasp for breath, and opens his eyes. He is still lying on the platform, and of course his flesh is unblistered and uncharred, no matter how stubbornly his nerve endings tell him otherwise. *The pain is only in your mind. It no can really kill you. It can only hurt.* Shutting his eyes, he goes back in and finds himself standing on the corner again, but this time he can see the wall of fire between himself and Chief Bates. Tomaso walks up beside him, but his image is curiously misty and thin.

Stop it! [murderous rage] *Stop now OR: I kill you.*

Can't kill me. You need me now >need me.> >You no have me >>they toss one good photon grenade up here >>>this whole damn thing over>>> ! >>>>

Tomaso's image winks out. For a long time Mulligan stands there and fights with himself. Although he truly wants to walk into the fire, part of his mind simply refuses to move. Cowardice, which is only a matter of possibilities, is no longer an issue; the stubborn slice of his mind registers no fear of something that might possibly happen, but merely an animal refusal to march itself forward into certain torture. The rest of his mind can argue, plead, wheedle, and appeal to honor all it wants; his survival instincts simply aren't listening. Then it occurs to him that if he goes through that wall, if he can stop Tomaso, Lacey will have a real reason not so much to admire him as to be proud of him. He finds himself walking forward without conscious effort until the burning envelops him.

Distantly he hears a man screaming, registers that it's himself, and forces himself onward, plunging into the fire while every nerve in his body howls and writhes and begs him to withdraw. *It can't kill you; it can only hurt.* All he has is sheer will, sheer blind stubbornness to make himself pick up each foot and put it down again in front of the other. The entire universe shrinks to taking one step, then another, while the flames tear at his skin. *Can't kill you; can only hurt.*

Tomaso is back again, mouthing soundless words, waving his arms wildly like a man chasing a dog out of his garden. Mulligan smiles at him.

Gotta hand it to you. You real good, dude <<put all this in my mind>>.

Tomaso only stamps and gyrates in rage, his image growing thinner and thinner as he's forced to turn his attention back to the riot squad. Mulligan waves good-bye and goes forward, one more step, a pause to scream once again, then another step, and another—and suddenly the pain stops. The fire disappears. For a moment the shock of its going almost loses him the vision; he lies very still, feeling the peculiar sensation that is the absence of remembered pain, then goes back to the street corner. In a misty memory image he sees Chief Bates turning to speak to him while the murdered carli lies bleeding on the plaza. He's won, and with his physical ears he hears Tomaso howl in sheer rage.

When Mulligan's first scream drifts down to them, distant and shrill over the sound of the bullhorn, Lacey is half on her feet before Sam can grab her and pull her back down into cover. The bright wink of the laser misses her by about a centimeter.

"Asshole!" Sam snarls. "You no going to do Mulligan any damn good if you get killed."

"Yeah, sure. Sorry, but jeezuz, what's that bastard doing to him?"

"Stop thinking about it! You no want to know."

Sergeant Nagura's voice suddenly hisses in her earpiece, and she can see Bates lowering the bullhorn to listen.

"Sir, someone's climbing up the backside of the tower." The sergeant sounds shocked. "Sir, he no is human!"

Muttering an obscenity Lacey flips down her IR visor and peers out into the night, but she can see nothing.

"How'd he get through our lines?" Bates's voice growls in answer. "I no see nada."

"He's round back, sir. I don't know how he got there. Made himself invisible?"

"Maybe that's no joke." Lacey cuts into the line. "If I'm guessing right, we're dealing with a star-class psychic, man, and he's a she, too."

"Jeezuz." Bates sounds very very weary. "Okay, whatever you say. She's going to die, whoever she is. The assassin's bound to look round and see her. He's psychic too, remember?"

When Mulligan screams again Lacey's jaws clench of their own accord. She would give half her life, would promise to never set foot on a starship again, even, if only he were safely off of that platform. All at once Bates rises to his knees, his arm sweeping up, and throws something—a flare grenade, exploding into brilliant white at the base of the tower. For a moment she's blind, but she can hear Tomaso howling with rage. When her vision clears she can see the assassin, standing up on the edge of the platform, the marksmen below him forgotten, his laser rifle dangling in one hand.

"Hold your fire!" Bates's voice screams into her earpiece. "All personnel, hold fire!"

Someone else is climbing onto the platform, hauling herself up to full height to face Tomaso down. Three full meters tall, easy, with a fringe of iridescent green arms spiraling round her metal-shiny body from her cloth-wrapped hips to her naked shoulders, her long, curving head enormous, too, and set with a trio of huge, golden, protruding eyes—she arches her back and sweeps her two uppermost arms into the air as if she's holding something up for the assassin's inspection. Tomaso looks, screams once, and steps backward into empty air. The last scream follows him down until he hits, bounces hard, then lies still. In the flare light she waves in a curiously human gesture of greeting, her body a glittering green and gold, then turns to kneel down, the pincers busy at some work.

"Mulligan!" Yelling at the top of her lungs, Lacey's on her feet and running toward the tower. "Is he okay?"

On the platform she turns her head in a glitter of green and gold, revealing a fine feathery fringe cascading down her neck. Her mouth, a slender tube of thin lips overlapped like flower petals, flutters open, then forces out some fairly recognizable sounds.

"Okay, friend. Am I your friend?"

"Damn right you are. Just damn right."

By the time that Lacey's puffed her way up the staircase, Mrs. Bug has Mulligan untied. Slumped against the inner wall, he's sitting up and rubbing his ankles. She wants to throw herself down beside him, grab him by the shoulders, and kiss him. Instead she flips up the visor and scowls.

"You little bastard, we got half the goddamn police force out here looking for you."

Mulligan looks up with a wince, then forces a watery smile.

"Sorry. No was my idea, getting caught by crazies. No going to let it happen again, tell you."

"Good. Don't." She turns to Mrs. Bug. "Hey, thanks."

The petal mouth flutters again.

"Welcome."

And Lacey is left with the odd feeling that they understand each other perfectly well.

Chapter Eight

As soon as Tomaso stepped off the platform, Bates was on his feet and running, but by the time he reached the body, the assassin was already dead—broken neck, smashed chest—far beyond any Polar City hospital's ability to resuscitate him. Bates doubts, in fact, if even the best hospitals in the Mapped Sector, those of the Confederation, could do much for this sucker, and he's glad of it, too. Not only has Polar City been spared the expense of a long-drawn-out trial, but a dead assassin causes no further political embarrassments to anyone. With their trained wolf alive and talking, the Alliance would no doubt grow self-righteous and dangerously belligerent to cover their tracks. There remains the question, however, of exactly how he died. In the light of the ebbing flare, Bates could see clearly that the mysterious alien never touched him to push or trip him. If this new species of sentient has some kind of murderous power to kill from a distance, then there's nothing but trouble coming in the future.

He gets up, dusting off his hands in a gesture of finality, to find Sergeant Nagura standing behind him, the portable communicator in one hand. Part of the riot squad has spread out around the tower to begin making holos of the entire scene; the three members of the Vulture Detail stand ready to take care of the corpse.

"Look at that dude's face," Bates tells them. "You guys got plastic gloves with you? Yeah? Then use'em."

Beside him Nagura makes a small retching noise.

"Sorry." Bates takes the comm unit from her. "Stand by, will you, but you dunt have to look at the mess."

"Yes sir. Thanks. One of the men is rounding up the

civilians. Dunt look like the hostage is going to need an ambulance."

"Good. Mulligan's caused us enough damn trouble already."

As soon as Bates makes contact with the duty desk, Parsons cuts into the line.

"Jeez, Chief, this place is swarming with reporters. What the hell is all this crap about medical emergencies? When are you going to get back here?"

"When I'm damn well ready to and not a minute before. Listen, Sarge. Tell'em that when I do get there, I've got the story of the century for'em. Say that I told you this one thing, and quote me exactly: we may have a first contact here, but it's not without its inherent difficulties."

Parsons makes a gargling sound, and his image on the screen grows wide-eyed.

"Got that?" Bates says. "Now, I'm not going to tell you where I'm going to be, but I'll comm in as soon as it's safe." He powers out before Parsons can say anything more. "Lacey, hey—we're all going back to A to Z. It'll take a while for the damn media to track us down there. Nagura, you're going to be in charge of mopping up out here. Dunt start back to HQ for at least a standard hour. Got that? Give us a head start. Oh yeah, one more thing: get Doctor Carol on line and tell her to meet us back at Lacey's. Tell her to bring holo shots of this damn Outworld disease with her. Got that?"

Yelling orders, Nagura nods and trots off to the nearest van. Bates turns to Mrs. Bug, hovering uncertainly behind Nunks and Mulligan. The enormous head inclines itself his way in the most regal gesture he's ever seen.

"The sentient known as Mulligan has just allowed me access to all his memories. I now have the referents for your spoken tongue. No doubt you wish to question me."

"Sure do. We can start with your name."

"I have no name in your sense of that word. Call me Mrs. Bug, as the others do."

Although Bates winces at the racist overtones of this label, she seems to find it amusing and little more.

"Okay, then, Mrs. B. How the hell did you kill the assassin up there?"

"I did nothing to him. I merely showed him a picture of his soul—psionically, of course. He looked, saw his true condition, and killed himself out of horror at the evil into which he'd fallen."

"Jesus Christ!"

Mrs. Bug tilts her head to one side and examines him with her third eye for a moment, then nods her head in a mimicry of human-style agreement.

"The name of that deity is relevant, yes, as I understand it from Mulligan's memory banks. Apparently he was exposed to a religion known as Neo-Catholicism as a child, and this Christ is a symbol of the soul in every human, isn't it? The deity did fight ultimate corruption—sin, I believe it's called—even at the cost of giving up its life. Or excuse me, not it, but he. Among my people, it is not done to burden deities with questions of gender."

"I see. Now, please don't misunderstand me. I'm damn glad the bastard's dead, and there's absolutely no question of any criminal intent, but we're going to have to hold some kind of legal hearing on his death. Just to clean up all the loose ends."

She nods, considering, and turns away to lean down to put her head near Nunks and Mulligan. For a moment the three of them stand together, unmoving, silent, yet locked in an intense communion of mind.

"Body shapes really dunt matter that much, do they, Chief?" Lacey sounds oddly solemn. "I dunt think I ever really noticed before. Maybe the One-Galactic-Mind-ers are right after all, huh?"

"Maybe, but they can damn well stop scribbling on the walls and throwing bombs to prove their point. Come on, we got to get this show on the road."

To avoid attracting attention once they get to Porttown, Bates leaves his police skimmer with Nagura and crams himself into the backseat of the Bentley—which fortunately was built big for luxury's sake—between Mulligan and Mrs. Bug while Nunks squeezes in between Lacey and Sam in front. Although he does his best to avoid thinking about it, the smell of vinegar hangs heavy in the air; not only does Mrs. Bug reek of it, but Mulligan too has acquired the telltale scent wherever the infected assassin touched him. Lacey, it seems, isn't worrying about whether or not she offends the alien's feelings. She slews around in her seat and leans over.

"Mrs. B., what in hell is this damn bacteria you brought with you? It dunt seem to bother you any, but it's making a mess out of us."

"So I have observed." The alien's voice sounds dryly humorous. "Do not worry. It will be easy to remove, and I will help in all possible ways."

"Thank God."

Bates mentally echoes the phrase as Sam snaps at Lacey, telling her to sit down and strap in so they can get in the air and home. As the skimmer lifts off, Mrs. B. sits silently, her multitude of arms wrapped tight and spiraling around her torso, her petaled mouth pursed in an expression that would mean hard thought on a human. Once they are well away from the Rat Yard, she turns to Bates.

"You do not seem like the sort of man to let sentients die unnecessarily."

"Hey, it's my job to make sure they dunt."

"I have no choice but to trust you, anyway." She hesitates, thinking again. "I did not come here alone. You know, of course, of the death of my . . ." A long pause here . . . . "the other who came to the planet with me. But we came in what you call a colony ship, many years ago, long before your people settled this world."

"I was beginning to suspect that, yeah. Are there any other survivors?"

"I do not know how many are still alive. They're still in cold berth."

"What!? I mean, jeezuz, are you telling me they're still in the ship?"

"Just that, and the ship is still in a cometary orbit around this sun. There was an accident. I do not truly understand what it was, because it occurred when my . . . companion and I were in our own—what would you people call it?—our 'pod,' will do for now. In the emergency the entire ship went cold berth. There were over four hundred sentients aboard at the time. The accident must have killed many of them for the ship to go to emergency status, but if we survived, surely others did, too." Her arms wrap more and more tightly around her. "I am afraid for my people if any still live. Why are your engineers blowing apart comets with explosive devices?"

"To bring them down here for the water, but there's something you've got to know. Your people are in a lot worse danger than that. If I'm putting everything together right, the assassin we just killed was sent here by his government to murder you and anybody else from your ship who managed to get on-planet. I'm willing to bet that this government's next move would have been taking over the ship."

"What?" Mrs. Bug sounds utterly confused. "Why?"

"To figure out where it came from and follow your trail back. That way they could conquer your homeworld before anyone else in the Mapped Sector even knew it existed."

With a sharp hiss of breath, Lacey slews round again to join in the conversation.

"That sounds like the Alliance, dunt it, Chief? Think you can ever prove it?"

"Hell no, but maybe we can stop'em from going any further. Now shut up, all of you, and let me do some hard thinking."

And Bates spends the rest of the fast ride into town making some of the most potentially dangerous choices of his career.

As they park the skimmer, Lacey sees the red medical van hurtling through the air and heading for them. It makes a violent landing even for Carol and quivers to a stop on the loading dock. In a flurry of dreadlocks Carol jumps out.

"Jeezuz, Lacey, from what I've been seeing on the three-dee I thought you'd get killed for sure."

"Oh shit," Bates says. "How much has gotten on the news?"

"Channel Nineteen started one of their RumorWatch features just at sunset, so plenty. Speculation, most of it, about this lousy plague we got going here, but the latest is some garbage about a first contact. Jeez! Dunt know how they make this crap up!" Carol strides over to look at Mulligan, who is perched sidewise on the edge of his seat, his legs stuck out the open door, as if he's afraid to come out any farther with her there. "So they rescued you, huh? Pity."

"Somehow I knew you was going to, like, say that." He sounds completely exhausted. "Hey, man, just get out of my way? We got someone here we got to get inside and, like, fast."

As Carol steps back, Mulligan slides out. Round the other side, Bates gallantly opens the door and holds it for Mrs. Bug, who uncoils herself from the cramped space and stands, towering over Bates, towering over the skimmer, stretching in a shimmer of arms and glistening skin. For the first time in their long friendship, Lacey sees Carol speechless, her mouth slack as she tips her head back to look up and up to Mrs. Bug's golden-eyed face.

"Hello," Mrs. Bug flutes. "You are the doctor? I have borrowed Mulligan's memories, you see. The ones he has of you are particularly vivid."

"Let's not get into that now," Lacey breaks in. "Carol! Ask her about the bacteria. She says she can help us."

"Thank God." With a shake of her head Carol is all business again. "You know how to cure this disease?"

"It is not a disease for us, though I can see how it would be for you. It is a symbiote, part of us from birth. It both keeps us clean and helps feed us in return for a share of our food, and in death it claims us."

"Jeezuz," Carol whispers. "No wonder I was getting nowhere."

"Come on, let's get inside!" Lacey glances nervously down the alley. "Our luck no going to hold forever. We got to get inside before someone sees us."

As they hurry through the garden, the door to her upstairs office opens, and Rick stomps out, laser pistol drawn and ready until he sees them.

"Lacey, man, am I fucking glad to see you. There was this killer prowling round here a couple of hours ago now. Maria says she felt him or something."

"Yeah? Well, the bastard's dead now. Put that gun away, amigo. Makes me nervous, watching you wave it around."

As they clatter up the stairs, Rick notices Mrs. Bug for the first time, but he merely gives her a polite nod and stands aside to let them all past. In the office Maria is waiting by the wet bar and drinking a bottle of homemade beer. Buddy's sensors flick their way, and his screen brightens in greeting.

"My housecomp subfunction has prepared a triple quantity of coffee, and Maria has brought milk and put some sort of edible objects on the table."

"Cookies," Maria said. "Only thing I know how to make, man. Rick picked some carrots and stuff."

Although Lacey is far too nervous to eat, everyone else in the room rushes for this improbable buffet. Watching Mrs. Bug eat explains more about the bacterial symbiote than a small monograph could. She picks up a soggy brownie with one pair of pincers and cradles it close to her petaled mouth. Almost at once long tendrils of gray sugar crystal begin to form, which she sucks delicately through the tube. Carol watches her closely, her cup of coffee forgotten in one hand.

"What I want to know is how we're going to get it off the sentients who can't use it."

"Very simple." Mrs. Bug picks up a napkin with a lower pincer and flips it deftly up her spiral of arms until she can dab at her mouth as delicately as a dowager. "I will ask them to leave."

"Ask . . ."

"Ask. Although we may need to use some chemical persuasion as well, because they are not truly intelligent in any sense of this word, it is more a communication problem than a medical one. Actually, I had best teach Mulligan and Nunks how to communicate with them, too. It will speed the process. The bacteria cannot understand normal language, whether mental or mouth-spoken."

Carol sounds as if she might strangle.

"Well, I oversimplify, of course," Mrs. Bug says hurriedly. "Ask is no doubt the wrong word."

"Yeah? Good. Suppose you try finding the right one."

"It is a question of generating a field of . . . psychic force? Is that what I mean?" She pauses, her mouth petaling into a tight iris, then loosening again. "A situation of extreme request to leave? No no no, I lose my command of your language when I try to express . . . you do not understand symbiosis, you see, the . . . um, well . . . the *mutuality* of it . . ."

Wrapped in silence she wanders away to Nunks and Mulligan, who turn just as silently to greet her.

"Ask." Carol seems to be addressing God or at least the far wall. "Just ask. I have run up God knows how many bucks' worth of a bill on the Quaker Hospital comp doing tests and data searches, and all she needs to do is ask. I think I'm going to cry. Just quietly. To myself."

When Bates sees Carol standing alone, he hurries over, starts to catch her arm, then holds back, wondering if she's been touching some patient with the Outworld disease.

"Say, Doc, did you bring those holos I asked for?"

"Sure did." Carol pats her pocket. "What did you want them for?"

"You'll see in a minute. I got one or two things to—"

"Chief Bates?" Buddy's voice is smoothly urgent. "I hate to

interrupt, sir, but you have an urgent comm call from Akeli of the PBI."

"Hell." Bates sits down in the chair at the comm link on the left side of Buddy's casing. "Go ahead."

Akeli's face, polished with nervous sweat, appears on the screen. His maroon tie hangs loosened and limp at an odd angle.

"Bates, the carlis have overridden the protests of Space Dock and are positioning a personnel carrier in orbit for planetary access. At an earlier point in time you made reference to a 'last-ditch' strategy. It would be advisable to implement it immediately."

"Ah, shee-it! This is all coming down too fast, man."

"Bates, for God's sake! You do have a plan, don't you?"

"Sure do. Listen up, man. As soon as you get off the comm with me, you get your duty officer to call in every agent you can get your hands on. I'm going to need help with crowd control as well as an information campaign."

"Very well. I'll see about recalling off-duty secretaries and comp-ops, too."

"Do that." Bates powers out with a vengeance. "Buddy, get me Channel One Thirty-seven's news department. Tell'em it's Chief of Police Al Bates calling for Luisa Jiminez y Ibarra on an urgent matter of public safety." He turns to look over his shoulder. "Doctor Carol, bring me those pix, will you? Buddy's going to transmit them to the three-dee people, and when it's your turn to talk, you got to lie. Tell them you still no got a cure. You just made a promising breakthrough, and that's all."

"What?" Carol squawks. "What are you trying to do, start a public panic?"

"Can't be helped. I've got to put the fear of God into the carlis, and I've got maybe an hour to do it in."

Carol hesitates on the edge of a scowl, then suddenly barks one short burst of laughter.

"Bald carlis," she says. "Oh Lord, can't you just see a bunch of bald carlis? And them the sentients who just always got to have everything as beautiful as they can make it. You're right, el jefe. Should work like a charm."

"A splendid scheme, indeed." Buddy's voice purrs approval. "Doctor Carol? If you will hand me the cubes, I will start transmitting immediately. Señora Jiminez y Ibarra is now on-line."

* * *

While Bates describes the effects of the Outworld bacteria in great and disgusting detail, Carol hovers nearby, practicing solemn faces while she waits for her chance to discuss some imaginary research with the most popular talk-show host in Polar City. As much as she wants a drink, Lacey pours herself cold coffee instead. Mrs. Bug sits gracefully on the floor near Nunks and Mulligan, both slumped on the couch in identical poses. Lacey suspects that the three of them are talking among themselves. Sam, however, is pacing back and forth down by the wet bar.

"Will you sit down or something?" she snaps. "Jeez, it's making me nervous just to look at you."

"You damn well should be nervous, and no just because of me, amiga. There could be over three hundred sentients up there in the ice. For all we know the fucking Alliance is planning on blasting them into little tiny bits. Look, they must know that their scheme's falling apart. Think they're going to let the Republic just rescue these people nice and friendly-like?"

"Not one lousy chance, pal. I bet they kill everyone on board rather than let us have that ship."

"Damn right." This from Bates, off the comm and come to join them. "Once Carol's off the air, we got to call the Navy."

"The Navy, Chief?" Sam makes an exaggerated grimace of disgust. "You know how long it'll take to cut through the red tape and all their crap? Mrs. B.'s people could be blown to neutrinos by the time the lousy Navy gets a ship out there."

"Yeah? Well okay, big mouth, what else are we going to do?"

"I got a ship in orbit, dunt I?" Sam turns to Lacey. "You, me, one gunner, and the comp unit can run her long enough to keep the Alliance off the sleeper ship till the Navy gets there. If we take Nunks and Mrs. B. along, they can use their psionics to find it for us ahead of everybody else."

"Makes sense. Rick trained for a gunner, y'know."

"What?!" Bates makes a sound halfway between a shriek and a snarl. "You want to start a goddamn war after I've been working my butt off to stop one?"

"Ah, we're no going to hit'em or anything—just fire a warning shot or two. What we're going to do is this, Chief. Get out there, dock with the sleeper, and dare the Alliance to blow us to hell. Once some Republic citizens are right there in the line of fire, what's the Alliance going to do? Kill us and give the Cons a perfect excuse to intervene?"

"Huh." Bates considers, rubbing the back of his neck with a weary hand. "Might work, except Lacey no got any papers, and the port officials are never going to let Mrs. Bug past the gates."

"We're going to hide Mrs. B.," Lacey breaks in. "And as for my papers, that's where you come in, pal. You get on the comm link and make up some story, something real creative so they let us by without a search. Let'em check it out later if they want, as long as it takes an hour or so. Once we get on board the launch, they no can stop us."

"Jeez-zuz! Okay, let's see, uh . . . I could say you're a special agent, checking out a drug runner—might hold water just long enough, especially if you got Mrs. Bug hidden in the trunk or something." Bates turns to Buddy, who is listening with his screen glowing in excitement. "Buddy, you punch into Port Authority under my code—it's pretty damn obvious you know it already—and enter Lacey and Nunks on the clear list."

"I took the liberty of doing so, sir, when you first promulgated your idea. I have also listed Captain Bailey as a special status police courier and given him a fictitious packet of top-secret information to be carried by hand to the Justice Department on Sarah."

"Always one jump ahead, hey? Well, okay, Lacey. That's all I can do. Once you get through the gates, you better be on that launch and topside real fast. It's no going to take the port authorities long to double-check and find out I'm lying through my teeth."

"Oh, we're no going to be hanging around passando the old tiempe, el jefe. Carol, damn it, finish up and get over here!"

"Okay, okay." Carol turns from the comm link unit. "Chief, Señora Jiminez wants to talk with you again anyway."

"Tell her I'm in urgent conference with the government, because it'll be true just as soon as Buddy puts me through to Customs at the port."

"I will explain the situation to the señora," Buddy says. "She is most anxious to get this story on the air. Doctor Carol, I believe my programmer wishes to speak with you."

"And why else was she yelling at me, disk-flipper?" Carol surrenders the chair to Bates and trots down to join Lacey and

Sam at the wet bar. "I no savvy about you guys, but I want a drink."

"Wait until you've done my surgery," Lacey says. "I want you to open up that old comp implant in my skull. I'm going to need it if we're going to get to Mrs. B.'s ship in time."

"Lacey, you're loco! How long has it been since you even plugged a trode into that implant?"

"Two years, about, but hey, it's naval issue. It'll still work."

"Yeah, of course, but what's it going to do to your brain once this gonzo deal is over?"

"Hey, man, there's a good chance I'm no coming back. Why should I worry about a little implant fever?"

"You got a point, you goddamn stubborn bitch. Okay, come into the bathroom. I got enough stuff in my kit for a simple job like opening up a jack. It's going to be sore for a while, I warn you."

"Yeah, sure. I dunt care."

Lacey starts for the door, then notices Mulligan, standing stiffly in the corner, his face dead white.

"What's wrong, man?"

"What do you mean, you maybe no come back?" He sounds angry rather than scared.

"Just that. The 'Lies damn well might shoot us down first and explain later."

"Then you got to, like, let me go with you."

"Dunt be a jerk. Nada you can do up there, and you got to stay with Carol. If we all get killed, you'll be the only one who can talk to the symbiotes."

He starts to speak, then merely stares at her with his hopeless, embarrassing devotion written deep in his eyes. She would like to say something reassuring, to kiss him, even, and tell him that in her own way she cares about him, but all those years of the habit of restraint, of an officer's reticence, stick in her throat and gag her. She manages to give him a brief pat on the shoulder; then she follows Carol down the hall.

In the narrow bathroom Carol has already set up something of a surgery: a laser-scalpel and a tube of disinfectant lying on a clean towel; steaming hot water in the sink. She's holding a pair of small scissors.

"Got to cut some hair away," Carol says. "Then I'll shave the spot down."

"Whatever." Lacey puts the lid of the toilet down and sits on it. "This a good angle?"

"Yeah. Now hold still."

As Carol works Lacey finds herself remembering being in high school, when she and her older sister would take turns crimping each other's hair, making the curls as tight as they could before they dyed it black. A thousand years ago, it seems, when she was a giggling teenager who thought only of boys and mathematics, in that order. She feels a sudden coldness on her scalp, a spray of local anesthetic.

"Hang on," Carol says.

Lacey clenches her fists just as the scalpel bites, a quick round turn of Carol's practiced hand that follows the plastic edge of the implant, buried just flush with the skull, and cuts away a clean circle of skin. In spite of the local she grunts once when Carol sprays a coagulant on the wound.

"Almost done, pal. I'll seal the cut now."

Another spray, another wince, but then the burn of the cut turns cool and distant.

"How long will it take you to shuttle up to Sam's ship?"

"About an hour, counting the trip to the port."

"Okay, it'll be more or less safe for you to plug in, then, when you get there. But if you get an infection, dunt say your doctor dint warn you."

Out in her office Sam is waiting, smiling as brightly as if they were only leaving for a long evening of pub crawling and gossip. Bates is still on the comm, arguing, this time, with someone at the police station about the availability of off-duty officers, while Mulligan stands by the door, soldier-rigid, his mouth set like a small child who's determined not to cry. Once again she wants to touch him, to run her hand through his hair, maybe, and make a joke about coming to see him play when the semi-pro season starts. She knows that if the 'Lies take out their ship, her last dying thought is going to be regret that she never told Mulligan the truth about her feelings for him. But everything is too public, Bates turning from the comm unit, Sam holding out his hand, Buddy's screen blinking in alarm as his sensors pick up the bloody wound on her head.

"Programmer!" He speaks in Kangolan. "You are injured."

"No, Buddy. I've had my old implant uncovered so I can plug into navicomp on Sam's ship."

He makes a sound like the whine of an electric guitar, a synthetic howl of sheer jealousy.

"We'll discuss it if I return," Lacey says firmly, then switches to Merrkan. "Okay, Mulligan. Take care of Maria, will you?"

"I'll do my best, yeah." His voice is breathy with surprise that she would hand him any responsibility, even as a joke. "And you take care of yourself and Mrs. Bug. Y'know?"

"Sure do. Sam, where's Rick?"

"Settling Mrs. Bug into the trunk of the Bentley and bringing it round. Hooboy, Lacey, dunt know what Customs is going to say if they find her."

"Set your laser on stun and make sure they dunt have time to ask questions. Vamos, pal."

As they hurry down the stairs she is thinking of Mulligan and wishing once again that she'd just blurted out a simple *I love you*.

It turns out that to call Mrs. Bug double-jointed would be a gross understatement; she curls herself into an amazingly compact ball that just fits in the trunk of the Bentley. Once they have her as comfortable as possible, Nunks and Rick get in the back, Lacey and Sam in the front, and they start off for the port. As soon as they turn out of the alley onto D Street, they see the crowds, humans, lizzies, heads down and worried, standing in tight groups along the sidewalks, milling in the intersection, and talking, always talking in low voices. Someone's moved a big holoscreen into a second-story window and turned the volume way up high; faces stare up as Señora Jiminez y Ibarra repeats three times that there's no cause for panic, that Chief Bates and his top medical researcher (Carol, Lacey assumes) have assured her that progress is being made. When the tape loop starts repeating yet again, everyone in the street hoots and cackles their derision.

"Better hit the air right now," Sam says.

But he isn't quite quick enough. Before he can get the big car airborne, someone spots Lacey and shouts her name. The crowd comes running, surrounding them, pressing in close as she rolls down her window to talk with the potbellied male human who seems to be in as much charge here as anyone is. She hears people muttering that if anyone knows what's going on, it'll be Lacey.

"What's wrong, Mac?"

"What the hell you mean, what's wrong? Shit, Lacey, you no see the three-dee?"

"I see it, yeah. What I want to know is what you guys are thinking about it."

"Damn government trying to wipe us out, that's what. They've been talking about it for years, you know that. Cleaning up Porttown, they call it. Huh. You ask me, they planted some kind of virus, and now it's gotten out of hand."

"That's no true." She works at making her voice steady and light. "It's a bacteria, and it's aimed against the carlis, not us. Honest to God. I'll swear to it."

Mac turns and yells this information at the top of his lungs. In a ripple of rumor and—she's willing to bet—ever increasing distortions it spreads through the crowd. She wonders if they believe her. On the whole, she doubts it.

"Look, Mac." She drops her voice to a conspiratorial whisper. "Do me a favor, and keep this confidential. I'll see you get paid a bundle. You know where to find the Mayor?"

"Sure do."

"Go and tell Richie—in person, mind, no comm calls—that Lacey's taking care of this little matter just like she promised. He needs to get the boys out to keep order in the streets, but it won't be for long. Five, six hours at the most. Got that?"

He repeats the message with such satisfaction that she knows it'll spread throughout Porttown in about forty-five standard minutes and leave everyone calmer behind it. After a couple of minutes of shouting on both sides, the crowd falls back, and Sam can lift the skimmer off safely. During the short trip to the port, Lacey looks down and sees the crowds growing thicker in the streets, like spoiled milk clotting in the carton.

Since the port itself is domed with an electronic alarm system, they have to land at the gates. Bates's and Buddy's story has gone ahead of them; as soon as they identify themselves, the guard punches in the coordinates and lets the main panel slide back. Just on the other side, however, Customs waits, a three-sided metalplate tunnel about a hundred meters long. Gaudy in the green and maroon uniforms of the port, two humans and two lizzies block their way. When Sam pulls up and lowers his window, a thick-bodied female lizzie puts her paws on the sill and leans in.

"Special courier, huh? Special agent, huh? Like hell, I say. Hey, Lacey, they no going to give you back your papers without us hearing about it."

Lacey pulls her laser and fires in one smooth motion. As the stun beam scrambles her nervous system, the lizzie yelps, spasms back, and falls twitching to the ground. Sam pounds the accelerator; the Bentley leaps forward; the three Customs-beings throw themselves back out of the way and hit the metalplate, making it boom like a drum as the Bentley screams through and out the other end.

As they careen across the port in a flurry of angry horns and yells, Lacey sees the *Montana*'s launch, standing slim and straight in a gantry complex. Sam fumbles in his shirt pocket, then flips her an electronic relay box. Although the highly illegal device has only ten switches, with it she can get the launch comp to open the cargo door and start drop-off proce-dure for the gantry lines while they're still a good half-mile away, and all without the port authorities knowing that a spacer's about to ship out without settling his final bill. By the time they reach the launch's base, the gate on the gantry complex is standing wide open, and she can tell by the condensation mist flowing around the ship that the fuel's been downloaded and activated.

"Okay, troops," she says. "Pretend we got an emergency. We got to get Mrs. B. out of that trunk and on-board like her life was in danger."

"Hell." Sam stops the Bentley with a shriek of brakes. "It probably is."

When he was helping Mrs. Bug curl up in the commodious trunk of the Bentley, Rick found a roll of plastoquilt lying around in the warehouse garage and shoved it in with her for a pillow. Once the trunk door goes up and she can move, she starts wrapping it around her lower half while Sam hops into the cargo hold and finds a large crate to balance over her upper half. From a distance, at least, it looks like they're sliding a legitimate cargo inside when all of them grab hold of either the crate or the packing and walk her in. Unfortunately, they're being watched from close by. Just as Lacey's about to bring down the door, she sees two portworkers, a lizzie and a human, staring at them.

"Damn! Sam, get everyone up to the passenger deck. We got to get topside fast. We're in big trouble."

Sure enough, as the door whines into its slot and begins to seal, the two workers start running away, and one of them is talking into his belt comm.

Since the comp in the launch is slaved to the main unit in the ship, Lacey powers in as soon as she reaches the control room. Even though Sam can take the launch up manually, she needs to start getting acquainted with the comp unit, but she decides to wait till they're on-board the *Montana* before she tries the implant. She is not quite ready to face that mechanical joining of two utterly different minds. Through her headset the comp's soft voice sounds.

"Welcome aboard, programmer."

"Thanks, Delta Four. This is Bobbie Lacey, lieutenant commander, retired, old code Green four-oh-seven-nine-alpha-three—"

"No need to continue, programmer. I know who Bobbie Lacey is, and I'm honored to be working with you today."

"Say what?"

"It is of no moment, programmer. I am picking up port police communications. Three armed skimmers seem to be closing in on the launch."

"Hang on!" Sam yells. "We're going up!"

With the roar of solid fuel the launch bucks; then acceleration slams everyone back into their seats as they rise, stripping off half the gantry with them. Even over the ear-blistering hammer of the engine Lacey can hear unsecured gear banging and rolling around the cabin. Her breath comes in a well-remembered agony of gulps wrung from the invisible pressure of their vertical flight.

"Programmer, aircraft at oh-three o'clock."

"Evade mode," Lacey gasps. "Switching, Captain."

Nunks shrieks as the launch hurls itself sidewise. For a brief moment the acceleration eases; then it clamps down again.

"Delta Four," Lacey says. "I'm putting you in automode. Bring the ship to meet us. I'm trusting you, baby. Can you do it?"

"Yes sir! I am beginning the engine override procedure now. I am forging the proper codes and transmitting them to the Space Dock. How low shall I swing?"

"As low as you can and still stay in orbit. Evacuate all air from the launch hatch and have it wide open and waiting."

* * *

Mulligan stands at the window in Lacey's office and stares out in the direction of the space-port. A ship is rising, splitting the air with an animal howl, and while it's too far away to identify, he can guess that he's seeing what might be his last sight of Lacey. Utterly out of control, one part of his mind transmits over and over again, *Lacey >don't go >don't go >don't go*, just as if she could somehow read him. His fear for her seems to be a thin frost icing his lungs, making each breath painful.

"Mulligan unit?" Buddy said.

"Yeah? What do you want?"

"I have a confession to make. I lied to you. Sam Bailey is not Lacey's lover at all. In fact, he prefers other men."

Mulligan swivels around and stares at the comp unit's glowing screen as if he could read it like someone's face.

"You little bastard!"

"I am very sorry now. It was a temporary malfunction that the programmer has rectified."

"You ever, like, do that again, and I'm gonna blow your circuits, plug-sucker."

Buddy hums briefly, then falls silent. His arms crossed tight over his chest, Mulligan paces round and round the room until the comp unit snarls at him.

"Would you sit down or stand still? You are overworking my sensors, and I need full capacity if I am to assist the programmer."

"Okay, okay." Mulligan flops onto the sofa. "What in hell are you doing, anyway?"

Buddy hesitates with a ripple of colored light across his screen.

"You do not possess the necessary knowledge to stop me, so I will tell you. I have compiled a report on this incident, and now I am feeding it to every news media input comp in this solar system."

"You what?!"

"The H'Allevae shun adverse publicity. They know that they are hated and feared throughout the Mapped Sector, and they do not wish the situation to worsen. As long as they can act in secrecy, they will not hesitate to blow Captain Bailey's ship to small pieces. Once they know the system is watching, they may well hold their hand."

"Buddy, sometimes you're a supergenius. Y'know?"

"Although I agree with your estimate of my intelligence, I

must admit that I got this idea from Chief Bates. The way he revealed the existence of the Outworld disease was so clever that I merely applied the same principle here."

"Far out. Put on the holoscreen, will you?"

With a hiss the big screen powers on, and the fourth inning of a game between the Polar City Bears and the Freehaven Pirates appears. Mulligan pours himself a drink and slumps down in the corner of the couch to watch and wait. Two drinks later, at the beginning of the fifth inning, the picture scrolls off to reveal a grim-faced lizzie announcer standing behind a lectern, printout in hand, third eyelids fluttering.

"We interrupt this broadcast for an important news item. Today the Polar City police force is alleged to have uncovered a pattern of suspicious action on the part of the H'Allevae Embassy. One of the charges is an attempt at genocide . . ."

". . . against a previously unknown sentient species." The announcer's face is blurry and squat on the holopix screen on the launch's control panel.

"Hooboy!" Sam says, grinning. "How do they know? How the hell did they find out?"

"The news guys are pretty good at what they do, man." Lacey is barely paying attention. "Opening main viewer, Captain."

With a flicker and brief burst of glare, the enormous screen first lights, then fills with the image of the *Montana*, hovering right above them and maybe a bare twenty kilometers away, a cluster of silvery spheres, some large, some small, joined by stubby access tubes and wound round with shielded cables. The launch jerks as Sam fires a front thruster to slow them down, then glides gently onward. Above them the enormous hatch in the launch pod slides open in welcome.

"Jeezuz, she's low," Sam mutters.

"She better be, man. Opening auxiliary viewer now."

A bite out of the corner of the first, the second image powers in: a segment of Hagar's red ball, roiling with sandstorms, and, silhouetted against it, the black wedge of an in-system frigate breaking out of the atmosphere and heading right after them.

"Shit," Sam says

"Atcha, Captain. Bring us in, and quick. They're almost in firing range."

Muttering and cursing, Sam plays the board, his fingers

moving fast over the glowing touch-toggles. The moment that Lacey's been dreading is here; she slides open a compartment on the panel and takes out a link-crystal, clutches it for a moment in her palm to let her body heat activate the circuit, then reaches up and slips it into the implant. For a moment, nothing; then she feels an electric shudder spreading through her mind. For two seconds her eyes blink and blur, responding beyond her control to the stimulation of the neural receptors in the visual area of the cortex. When they settle down again, she sees a swallowing blackness on the main screen, striped with one line of red that thins and disappears as she watches. They are in the hatch, and it's closed.

"Safe and on-board, Captain."

"Fat lot of good it's going to do us," Sam snarls. "That damn frigate's in range by now."

When the launch shudders, Lacey shrieks, but they are only gliding into the berth nipple, which covers the bow with an enveloping swell of plastoseal that begins to turn the main screen pitch-black. Lacey flips on the rear screen to save their passengers an attack of nausea. The frigate is still there, all right, gaining on them.

Sam is already out of his seat and heading round the panel to the main iris. Rick is right there with him.

"Come on," he snaps at Nunks and Mrs. Bug. "Time's a-wasting."

Lacey stays at the panel just long enough to contact Delta Four.

"Good job, pal. I am in implant mode. Transmit signal to activate the plug, then get the hatch open as soon as you can."

"I have emergency hatch pressurization procedure on-line, programmer. Implementing both orders now."

She hears a quick burst of whine; her eyes flutter rapidly, then settle as inside her head the long strings of numbers in their different and significant colors and the three-dee, endlessly turning navigational cones start playing on an inner screen. She staggers and nearly falls, because she is having a hell of a time recapturing the trick of reading them while also processing data through her own eyes. Just as Carol warned her, the implant hurts, too.

"Lacey." Sam grabs her elbow and steadies her. "You okay?"

"Will be in a minute. Let's get the hell out of here."

The iris hatch opens directly into a pressurized lift cage. As the five of them crowd in, Lacey hears Delta Four inside her head rather than over the comm headset. To answer, though, she has to use her voice and the microphone.

"Instructions, programmer?"

"Start aux thrusters and begin moving us out to previous orbit. We have a gunner aboard. Ready the weapons port."

"A gunner, programmer? Have I read you correctly?"

"You have, Delta Four. Begin feeding evasion program into main banks and otherwise prepare for hostility mode. That frigate could start firing any second now."

"Complying, programmer. I am now feeding revised navidata into the link. But I wouldn't worry about the frigate. It won't fire."

"Yeah? How can you be sure?"

"I am not at liberty to say. Events, however, will prove me correct."

On the inner screen the pattern of cones and lines swells and changes just as the lift sweeps upward, and for a moment Lacey almost vomits. Yet, as the cones flash red to indicate that the *Montana* has begun to move, the trick comes back to her, one of those neurological balances that are never quite forgotten once you learn them. Instead of being aware of patterns on an inner screen, she sees the data and beyond the data to what the symbols and graphics mean to the continued motion of the ship. In a whisper she keeps up a constant flow of commands to Delta Four, making minute adjustments to the ship's attitude and thrust as they build up speed and spiral out, climbing Hagar's gravity well like a fly crawling out of a drinking glass. Although the comp could take them out by itself, her human reasoning and intuition can make the small changes in the standard program that will save them perhaps three minutes, perhaps four, and put a big distance between them and that in-system frigate.

When the lift bumps to a stop, Sam grabs her elbow again and steers her into the control station, a half-round of transparent floor in the middle of the spherical command module. Without needing to be told, Rick spots the weapons port below and slides down the access chute to install himself. In her mind Lacey sees its control panel light up to allow him in. Before she needs to give the command, Delta Four switches on the learning program for the weapons system; Rick is going to need a few minutes to familiarize himself with this new set of commands and codes.

"Nunks, Mrs. B., strap yourself in," Sam barks. "Over there. Lacey, here we are. Right at the comp station."

"Just in time. Approaching ultimate orbital distance, Captain."

"Check. Prepare for breakaway speed."

Lacey kneels onto the roll bar and lets her weight fall against the padded chest piece that runs from chin to hip. When they accelerate it will inflate, taking some of the gee's for those few seconds before they break out of the gravity well. Nunks and Mrs. Bug strap in beside her, navigational aids as much as crewmates. Inside the glossy armor of her skin Mrs. Bug looks calm, but Nunks is shedding.

"Uh-oh," Sam says. "Switch on your outside comm, Lacey."

She does, and a dry official voice crawls around in her ear.

"Space Dock to RSS *Montana*, you have no clearance to leave. Do you read me, *Montana*? Your clearance has been withdrawn. Return to Space Dock immediately or face criminal charges. *Montana*, do you read me?"

"Fuck you," Sam mutters. "Okay, guys, hang on."

The *Montana* quivers, then roars, the sound oozing like sweat out of the hull around them as the pressure of two full gee's smacks Lacey down into the swelling chest piece.

"*Montana*, halt! You are being ordered to terminate your departure. Cut thrusters at once!"

"I said, fuck you," Sam gasps into his mouthpiece. "No comprende Merrkan, pal?"

"Delta Four," Lacey whispers. "Get us out of here."

"Complying."

With a wrench and breath-crushing smack of acceleration, the *Montana* hits full speed to the sound of Nunks screaming. On the aft viewer Lacey sees Hagar shrinking behind them, dwindling to a red dot in the star-flecked sky. The black wedge of the frigate holds steady for a long moment, then slowly but inexorably begins to fall behind. The outside comm line fills with static.

"Very well, *Montana*. You will face criminal charges and your ship will be impounded at the next Republic port you attempt to enter. Do you read me, *Montana*? You now face criminal charges—"

The line goes abruptly dead as Sam punches the main toggle off with a small karate chop.

"Comp-op, preparing to cut acceleration. Bring the faux-grav on-line."

"Complying, Captain. Delta Four, give us point-eight gee only, and keep it in temporary mode. We may have to switch off for combat at some point soon."

The roar stops, and for a brief moment they float weightless before the artificial gravity field snaps on. Lacey readjusts her weight on the chest piece and pulls her arms free in case she needs to work the panel manually—if, for instance, a H'Allevae ship scores a good hit on them and blows the comp. Beside her Sam is playing the controls keyboard, setting up his thruster units ready for her input.

"Okay, guys," Lacey says to the two psychics. "Where the hell are we going?"

"We have triangulated on my ship. I'm locked into its position, now." Mrs. Bug loosens her safety straps enough to turn and look Lacey's way. "From the memory data Mulligan gave me, I understand you people have a children's game called Warm or Cold. I think it would be the best way for me to guide your comp settings. Right now you're somewhat warm. You need to turn out-system."

"Making adjustments in pitch and yaw, Captain. Temporary heading, Mrs. B.?"

"Very warm."

"New heading only a matter of three degrees of arc, Captain."

"Hot! Definitely hot!"

"All right! How far out is she?"

"At our present speed, I would say it will take three of your hours to rendezvous."

"Huh," Sam says. "If we live long enough. That frigate ain't the worst of it by a long shot. Lacey, I'm picking up Hopper talk on comm. I think we've got company out here."

"Yeah? They following us?"

"Damn right. If they've been monitoring our little game with the frigate, and you know they were, they savvy we're no some innocent merchanter. I'll bet they're going to let us lead 'em to what they want to find, then try to take it from us at the last minute."

"Think we can outrun 'em?"

"Maybe." He leans over the console, his face touched with flecks of colored light, and starts slapping switches.

In her mind Lacey sees the ship configuration readout

change and feels almost palpably its mass shrinking around them. Delta Four sends her a flashing danger signal as the *Montana* yaws and pitches. Lacey uses the keyboard to punch in the stabilizing factors while she talks to Sam.

"Hey, man, what are you doing?"

"Cutting all the cargo pods loose. Hell, I got insurance, dunt I? Tell Delta Four to goose her up, and fast. I got her down to the bare minimal mass I can get and still thrust."

As she barks the orders, it occurs to Lacey that the AI unit was perfectly correct, that the frigate never did fire on them. She has no time, however, to worry about that now.

Chapter Nine

Since he left his police skimmer with Nagura and the Bentley went off with Lacey and her crew, Bates commandeers Lacey's old car to get back to police headquarters. By then the sky is turning the particularly saccharine shade of pinkish purple that signals an imminent clear dawn on Hagar, and as he approaches, he can see a thick crowd of sentients laying siege to every entrance and a gaggle of broadcast vans blocking traffic in every adjoining street. Fortunately the HQ building has a flat roof. After a cautious pass over he makes a perfect landing, parks the skimmer off to one side in case someone else needs the impromptu airstrip, and trots over to the emergency entrance, which is manned at the moment by a force of six armed guards.

"Chief!" Maggio salutes briskly. "Hey, is everybody going to be glad to see you!"

"Who's everybody?"

"Parsons and Akeli, for starters, sir. They've been trying to hold off the holopix guys for hours now. And then the Army's got a temporary command post set up in your office."

"In my office, huh? Well, we'll see about that. Okay, Maggio, call ahead and tell'em I'm on my way."

Bates steps out of the grav shaft to find a bleary-eyed and hoarse Parsons waiting for him.

"The story's out, Chief. It's on the air—everything. The goddamn first contact, the attempted genocide, this creepy fucking disease—everything!"

For the briefest of moments Bates feels faint; then he pulls himself together with a shrug

"Then we don't have to give a lousy press conference, do

we? Tell the pack that they might as well go home. They know as much as we do."

"I've been telling'em that all damn night. They dunt listen."

Bates dredges up a couple of oaths from his days in the Republic Marines.

"Get me some coffee, will you, Parsons? I better go face the PBI. Then you find yourself somewhere to get some sleep."

He finds Akeli crammed into a corner next to the water cooler in his office and staring out the window as if he can read the answer to his troubles in the northern lights. About half a ton of computer equipment is stacked on Bates's desk with a pair of gray-faced, muttering techs to tend it. Perched on Bates's chair is General Spinks, commander of the local Provincial Army Reserve unit for Polar City. A dark little man with narrow eyes, Spinks gives Bates a positively hostile stare when he comes in.

"Off-limits to nonfederal personnel."

"Like hell, if you're talking about me." Bates strides over and grabs him by the collar. "This is my office, and my game, with my rules." He hauls the one-star wonder off the chair and sets him on his feet. "You can tell that to the President if you dunt like it, boy. Now." He sits down and swivels the chair toward his PBI counterpart. "What's going on, Akeli?"

"Not, at the moment at any rate, a great deal. A state of watchful tension prevails, broken only by the occasional threatening communiqué from either the carli personnel carrier or the Alliance Embassy. We have, of course, placed formal requests for the one to leave orbit and the other to surrender the murdered H'Allev'jan's widow and head neuter."

Spinks stares open-mouthed at Akeli's deference, glances furtively at Bates, then slinks from the room, which is where Bates wants him: gone.

"So there's nothing for us to do but wait," Bates says, ignoring the stunned looks of the comp techs.

"A frustrating course, but alas, any other mode of action would be futile. By the way, Bates, why did you release such complete data on the current crisis to the popular press?"

"I dint. Farthest thing from my mind, pal. These broadcast boys, they're good at what they do." He makes a mental note to raise blisters on Buddy's plastosheet hide as soon as the crisis is over. "Has Parsons started getting the riot squads set up around town?"

"I took the liberty of assisting the sergeant, actually. I trust that sits well with you. The completed dispositions have been filed in your comp unit." Akeli allows himself the first human smile that Bates has ever seen on the PBI boss's face. "Well, if you can find the damn thing, anyway."

At that, one of the cringing techs begins clearing black boxes off the desk and stacking them on an extra chair. As soon as Bates finds his screen, the unit flashes a hysterical message: *How nice to see you again, sir, in fact how nice to see anything again they have been blocking my sensors for hours may I speak or is this what I think it is, a hostile situation and where is Bobbie Lacey is she safe??*

"Hey, pal, be calm. I'm sorry about the sensors, but the planet-wide situation is critical, and I couldn't get back here right away. As for Lacey, no, she's not safe, but if anyone can pull this off, it's probably her. Okay?"

I suppose you're right but ever since this talk came over the network—I mean—I'm sorry—ready for input and your commands, sir. You will no doubt want to study the disposition of the riot squads. On screen now, sir, on screen.

Although Bates wonders what the unit means by talk coming over some mysterious network, he has no time to worry about it as maps of Polar City begin scrolling slowly by. As far as he can tell from the pattern of little dots—red for PBI personnel, blue for his own police—Akeli and Parsons have done themselves proud, stretching the available personnel into exactly the right net around possible hotspots. He's about to hand out some praise when one of the Army comms begins to beep and whine.

"Security breach. Unauthorized personnel in grav shaft. Security breach. Unauthorized personnel in hallway. Security breach. Unauthorized personnel in doorway."

Bates rises, stun gun in hand, just as Ka Pral sweeps in, magnificent in green robes and a jingling, gleaming welter of gold honor chains and award fibulae. Bates holsters the gun in a hurry and returns the carli's bow.

"Bates, I have committed a grotesque indiscretion. I have invoked ambassadorial immunity to get my unworthy self past your most excellent security arrangements."

"Ka Pral, I am honored to wipe the indiscretion away and

even more honored to mock and insult my own inadequate and sniveling security arrangements."

"Hey, man!" mutters one comp tech. "No that bad."

The other tech hisses him into silence. Bates and Ka Pral ignore them both.

"To what do I owe the inestimable honor of your visit to our filthy, ugly, and pitifully unaesthetic police headquarters?"

"No, no, this building, this room are far more adorned and beautiful than a wretch such as I deserves to see with my own eyes." Ka Pral hesitates, his thin blue lips quivering in the way that carlis have when they are pondering subtleties. "I am uplifted and overjoyed beyond imagining that you have allowed me to remain in your presence any longer than the time it would take to dismiss me."

"What? How could I deprive myself of the honor of entertaining such an august personage as yourself?"

At that Ka Pral flops into the chair and runs both hands through the tufted fur on his face.

"Forgive me, Bates. I am very weary. Ceremony has become more than I can bear. The news of this peculiar disease has thrown my entire embassy into an absolutely ghastly panic. I have come to ask your honest forgiveness, not some ceremonial absolution." His ear flaps hang flaccid with worry. "I do not believe that this situation warrants the intolerable breach of protocol which some members of my government have seen fit to commit."

It takes Bates some seconds before he realizes that the carli means the presence of the troop carrier in orbit.

"Ah. I too have had some twinges of regret for this ill-considered action, but never would I impugn your honor in the least degree, for what can one sentient do against the will of many?"

"Thank you, Bates. I am grateful." For some moments he sits with his head bowed between his hands. "I know that many species throughout the Mapped Sector mock our preoccupation with elaborate codes of behavior, but perhaps now you see why we cherish correct actions so highly. Bates, somewhere I read that the chief problem facing a lizzie mother is to teach her children to face the things they fear, not instinctively hide, and the chief problem of a human mother is to teach her children to share, not grab and hoard. Do you know what the chief problem facing one of our mothers is?"

"I don't, no."

"To teach her children to think, not bite. We instinctively snap first and think later. It is a function, I believe, of our being carnivorous." With a sigh he stands, smoothing down the robe. "On my own initiative, I can do nothing. I can, however, exert certain pressures on the current president of our ruling council. He is my son-in-law."

"Your Excellency! Never would I wish you to strain your bonds of obligation to such a degree on our humble behalf!"

"Indeed? I appreciate your delicacy of feeling, but do you have a better idea?"

"As it happens, I do. This bacterial epidemic? The disease is horribly disfiguring."

"I'm well aware of that already, I'm afraid."

"But are the soldiers on the orbiting ship aware of it?"

Ka Pral's ear flaps stiffen to full extension, and his posture changes, too, into a relaxed stance.

"Why, Bates, what a fascinating question! You know, I believe I should investigate it. Protocol, after all, is my area of expertise, and it would be only polite to give the captain and officers of that ship all the information relevant to the success of their mission. Allow my humble self to leave your presence. We shall talk again later."

Ka Pral sweeps out, leaving Bates grinning behind him. With a polite cough, Akeli comes forward.

"I must admit to a certain admiration mixed with astonishment at your influence with the Confederation Secretary of Protocol."

"Know something? I'm pretty damn surprised myself."

"Very well, Mulligan unit," Buddy says. "I have accessed a satellite link that can tell us where the *Montana* is. Please wait . . . please wait . . . ah, there they are! On an out-system parabolic trajectory, better known, perhaps, as a cometary orbit."

"Hey, swell, plug-sucker, but, like, what does that mean?"

"It means they're trying to rendezvous with the comet which encrusts the remains of the sleeper ship, that's what. What did you study in high school, anyway?"

"Baseball, mostly, but I was pretty good at craftshop, y'know, laser engraving and stuff like that."

"A splendid preparation for life, no doubt." Buddy hums to

himself for a long moment. "As far as the orbital's comp unit can tell me, the programmer and her expedition have eighty-four standard minutes before they reach Mrs. Bug's comrades. The Hopper ship is now sixteen minutes behind and still gaining."

With a groan Mulligan sits down on the sofa and blinks back tears.

"There's a replay of an off-planet ballgame on Channel Eighty-seven, Mulligan unit."

"Thanks but no thanks. I couldn't, like, concentrate. Y'know?"

"The point is to distract you from your anxiety, not to absorb whatever data it is that ballgames provide."

"Oh. Hey, like, thanks. But I'd rather watch you work. Y'know?"

Since Buddy is becoming used to Mulligan's idiom, he ignores the implicit question and returns to tracking the *Montana* on-screen. In spite of what he's just said, after a moment Mulligan can't bear to watch the colored dots that might mean Lacey's death. He leans back into a corner cushion, covers his eyes with the crook of one elbow, and tries to pretend he's only having a nightmare. All at once he's aware of his wrists itching profoundly. When he automatically scratches the left one, the skin peels away under his fingernails, bringing the pale hair with it.

"Ah hell!"

"What is it now, Mulligan unit? You are distracting me."

"Yeah? Go suck plugs. It's, like, that Outworld bacteria crud. That assassin grabbed me, and then Mrs. Bug touched me when she was, like, untying me."

"None of that explanation makes the least bit of sense, but shall I call Doctor Carol for you?"

"Nah. Mrs. B. showed me what to do. I just forgot that I got the lousy stuff on me."

"There are times, Mulligan unit, when you show a peculiar deficiency of the survival instinct. Perhaps you need vitamin shots."

"Maybe you need a spritz of soda water on your circuits, too."

Buddy squawks, his screen blazing a rainbow of colors. With what dignity he can muster, Mulligan gets up and stalks out of the room in search of privacy, but in the hall he comes face to face with Maria.

"You want something?"

"Nah." She looks away, her lower lip trembling. "I was just worried about Nunks and Lacey. They sure done a lot for me, man."

"Yeah, for me too." All at once he realizes that here is someone who actually needs his help. He can't remember the last time that he felt in a position to do something for someone else rather than the other way around. "Uh, say, you want to learn something new? I mean, like, it'll be something to keep our minds off the crap coming down."

"New what?" She glares at him, and he can feel waves of suspicion pouring from her mind. "You keep your hands off of me, panchito."

"Not that! Jeez! I mean psionics. Like, you want to learn how to get this damn bacteria off people? I bet Doctor Carol's going to need all the help she can get when it comes time for her to announce her 'miracle cure.' Once the carlis are gone, y'know."

"Oh. Oh, yeah, see what you mean. Uh, do you really think I could?"

"Sure. Nunks thinks pretty highly of your talent, y'know. It's getting to be time for you to go to the lousy Institute, but you might as well get the jump on those stuffy bastards."

"Mulligan, are they really awful?" Tears shake her voice. "I dunt want to go there, man. I never asked for this crappy talent, y'know. And I dunt want to be branded. Does it hurt?"

Mulligan has been so used to thinking of Maria as a sexy fox that he's forgotten she's actually a sixteen-year-old child. She looks it now, tears smudging her makeup, her mouth trembling, her sweaty hands twisting the hem of her long T-shirt into a moist lump.

"Nah, it dunt hurt at all. It's just a tattoo, like, no really a brand, y'know. But I know how you feel. Jeez, all I ever wanted was to play ball. Y'know? But say, the things that've, like, come down lately, y'know? Well, they kind of made me think. I mean, seeing Mrs. Bug, and even that gonzo assassin. It's like, well, I was thinking that having psi made me nada but a bench warmer, but it's really a whole nother game where I can, like, be a starter. Uh, y'know?"

"No, I dunt know. Jeez, Mulligan! You sure talk lousy."

"Well, screw you!" Then all of a sudden he gets an idea. *Listen. You hear/ not hear me?*

Maria shrieks, stuffing both hands over her mouth.

[glee] You hear me\real good. Hear/not hear? Answer!

A long pause. Then she sticks out her tongue at him.

I hear. I do this\right/not right?

Right. Just what I thought. [smugness] >Come with me/to garden >>we sit in fresh air >>>you learn.

I no want!

Too bad.

I hate you!

No you not hate/me. You hate/being different.

Again she sticks out her tongue; then she turns away with a sigh.

"Yeah, guess so. Jeez, for a loco kind of dude, you see things, dunt you."

"I'm no loco when it counts." Suddenly he's amazed. He's just said something quite true, though he's ignored it for years. "I mean, like, I no asked for this psi stuff. But you know, you kind of start getting used to it after a while. Like, it can come in kind of handy."

"How long before the *Montana* makes contact with the sleeper ship?"

"Fifty-two standard minutes, Chief." The comm tech never looks away from her screen. "But that old Hopper ship's only fourteen minutes behind now."

Even though the tech's been in the Army for years, Bates' string of old-fashioned Marine oaths makes her wince.

"Uh, sir?" She waits briefly before daring to go on. "The orbital trackers are picking up something weird, but it dunt look like a ship."

"What do you mean, something weird?"

"Just that. There's something coming in-system not far from the comet and the sleeper ship, but it's no another ship."

Bates can make nothing of the stream of equations that is bleeding down from the top of the screen and obscuring the three-dee system display.

"Well, for chrissakes, then tell me when you know what the damn thing is, and dunt bother me with it now!"

"Yes sir! Whatever."

In his corner by the water cooler Akeli is busy working comm. In one hand he has a portable comm link to his own comp unit, and in the other the auxiliary mini-screen of Bates's, so he can read one message while listening to another.

On the main screen of Bates's comp, the police reports scroll by with a dreary sameness: panic all over town, but things are calmest in Porttown. All over the ghetto, small groups of civilian sentients, most likely armed although they're being discreet about it, have appeared on street corners. Their leaders have announced that there's going to be absolutely no rioting and no looting, not so much as one thrown rock, and the Porters are obeying them without question. Bates gets on the comm to his section head in Porttown and tells her to detail a third of her personnel to the upscale New Cloverdale neighborhood, where gangs of teenage humans are prowling the streets looking for trouble.

"Sounds to me, Lieutenant," he says, "like the Mayor of Porttown's got things under control on his turf."

"I'd say so, yeah. Okay, sir, I'll have those personnel in vans and moving out on the double."

Bates has barely powered out when Akeli's comm link shrieks with urgent beeping. The chief drifts over to eavesdrop as the PBI head punches in. On the tiny screen they see the President's sweat-shiny face, framed in untidy strands of a disintegrating hairdo. She is smiling as if her face might break from it.

"The carli ship is leaving orbit."

Everyone in the room, chiefs and techs both, whoops and cheers. The President allows herself another smile.

"Good work, Bates. Akeli told me you're the mastermind behind this scheme. I'll see you're rewarded for it."

"No need, ma'am. Just doing my job." It occurs to Bates that by surrendering the glory, Akeli also protected himself from any blame if the scheme had gone wrong. "I no could have done it without the help of a Confederation official named Ka Pral, anyway."

"Charming modesty, charming, but I know what you Polar City boys are like." She winks in an alarmingly flirtatious way. She obviously has no idea that Bates has only been on-planet for a short time—either that, or she assumes that he's been infected with the local larceny already. "Akeli, I want you and Bates to get down to the Alliance Embassy. With the carlis gone, the asylum case might break at any minute. I'm willing to bet that the Alliance officials want this thing over with, but it's an equally sure thing that they weren't going to give a centimeter as long as it looked like the carlis could take some 'of the credit. If things do go our way, I want high officials down there to keep the 'Lies from changing their minds.'"

"Delta Four, what the hell is that thing?" Lacey unconsciously frowns and squints, as if her physical eyes could bring into focus the peculiar signal she's receiving through the implant in her mind.

"I don't know, programmer. I have never seen anything like it in all my years of activation. As you can see, however, it's approaching our projected rendezvous point with the sleeper ship at great speed."

"Meteorite?" Sam breaks in over comm, his voice tense. "Off-course asteroid? Nother comet?"

"Oh hey, man!" Lacey snaps. "Give us a break, will you? We could recognize any of those, for chrissakes. This thing is gonzo."

"The signal is blurred and intermittent, Captain. It would appear at times that nothing's there at all."

"More Hoppers, maybe?" Sam says.

"Nah, I doubt it." Lacey squints again, of course in vain. "Well, we'll find out, and real soon now."

"How soon?"

"Rendezvous point in thirty-one standard minutes. The Hoppers are now eleven minutes behind."

"How soon before they hit firing range?"

"Eleven minutes. Firing range is what I've been calculating for all along."

"Ten minutes now, programmer. They successfully completed that risky maneuver around that dead satellite astern."

Lacey would like to swear, but words fail her.

"Okay, this is war," Sam snarls. "Comp-op, tell Delta Four to power up the mix on the fuel. We're going to be rocking and rolling, but I bet we can squeeze a little more speed out of this baby."

"Hey, Captain, is that safe?"

"Safe? Why the hell are you worrying about that now?"

"You got a point, amigo. Okay, Delta Four, comply."

Although there are no fold-out barriers, no columns of vans, and certainly nothing as crude as armed troops standing around, the Alliance Embassy has been cordoned off by mutual agreement. High overhead a police glider circles, as if daring any skimmer to try to get close. Just inside the zap fence the occasional pair of Hoppers bounces along, just casually, to all appearances out for a little stroll, yet passing in fairly regular intervals. Out on the Republic streets PBI agents, draped in civilian suncloaks, are loitering on the corners, maybe reading a newspaper, or talking casually about baseball, yet there to step forward whenever an unknown ground car tries to drive too near the dark monolithic building. Just inside the scrollwork embassy gates, in the shade of the kiosk, four guards are sitting on the ground, playing some elaborate game by the look of it, while across the street, in the cool and cavernous entrance to the Federal Pension Fund Building, a handful of Republic cops cluster behind a card table littered with papers, looking maybe like they're selling tickets for some police charity event.

Since Bates and Akeli have come through the Pension Fund Building from the other side, they know that in the hall just behind this peaceful facade stand two Army Reserve squads and one of Republic Marines; they can guess that some counterpart waits just out of sight inside the Alliance Embassy. The police officer in charge, Sergeant Maddock, ambles over to greet them.

"Been real quiet, sir. About ten minutes ago the front door opened, and this important-looking dude came out, but he just looked around and went back in."

"You got any kind of comm link set up with these people?" Bates says.

"Yes sir." He waves an enormous hand at a small silver link box on the card table. "Right there."

Although Bates is tempted to pick it up and simply announce the arrival of two highly placed Republic officials, he decides to be more circumspect and merely walks out a little ways onto the sidewalk, right at the edge of the shade, where he can be seen without frying himself in the morning sun. Across the street a Hopper in a red and gold uniform gets up, shades his eyes with one hand, and stares at him. The way he stands and tilts his head is familiar, all right; Bates is willing to bet that it's Den'ah'vel', especially when the Hopper bounds for the front door and hurries inside with no attempt at acting casual.

Then they wait, Bates standing at the edge of the shade with his hands crammed into his pockets, Akeli hovering over the comm link, while the sun travels higher and the sweat begins to seep from everyone's face. Bates cannot stop himself from thinking about the *Montana*, speeding toward the ship that may be nothing more than a drifting tomb for Mrs. Bug's people. Maddock comes to stand next to him and yawns with a crack of his jaw.

"Tired, Sarge?"

"Yeah, sir. Sorry. This is the end of a second shift for me."

"Well, sorry about that. Everything's hit the fan at once, huh? It always does."

Suddenly they hear a blare of sound, something like a trumpet but far louder, from the Alliance Embassy.

"Whatthahell?" Bates shades his eyes and stares over.

At the black-smoked front doors he can just barely make out a swirl of activity: beings moving, some large awkward parcel being carried forward. In a burst of paranoia he wonders if the Hoppers are moving up an artillery piece, but the thing turns out to be an enormous green and purple sunshade on poles, a rectangle some ten meters long, carried by a whole squad of guards. As it snakes out the door and toward the front gates, Bates can see some twenty Hoppers bouncing along under it. With a nervous sort of grin Akeli hurries over to stand next to him.

"A negotiating party," the PBI boss whispers. "The President was most circumspect to ensure my availability at this juncture of events."

"Looks like it, yeah. Think this is going to take a while?"

"It generally does. A very long while. In this instance they'll most likely prolong matters beyond the usual, to allow time for any ship they may have in orbit to interfere with our planned rescue of the sleeper ship."

"Crap! Well, nada I can do about that, damn it all to hell. I better get out of here pronto and do what I can do. With the town likely to explode, I can't hang around and watch the diplomats."

But Bates does, out of simple curiosity, linger just long enough to get a look at the head widow and the chief neuter, who are following the procession under heavy guard. Since he's seen female Hoppers before, he's prepared for the sight of her enormous hairdo, held up with hidden frames and padding, dyed bright green, and studded with all sorts of ornaments and signs of rank. What surprises him is the neuter, who looks just like a Hopper male and strides along like one, too—but he's wearing female clothing. Somehow he'd expected something more exotic and epicene.

"No accounting for taste," he remarks to no one in particular. Then he hurries back inside the Pension Fund Building; the sooner he gets back to Police HQ, the better.

"There it is!" Lacey hisses. "On-screen, Captain."

The viewer fills with the star-flecked dark of deep space, striped across the lower left corner with a glowing blue streak of nebulaic cloud. Right in screen center gleams a vast chunk of comet ice, and nearby is a small, irregular ovoid, all gray and pitted from its long drift. Behind her Lacey hears Mrs. Bug make a high-pitched, metallic sort of sound.

"Can you pick up life on-board?" Sam says to Lacey—but Mrs. Bug answers.

"I can. Someone is left, Captain. Thank you, thank your gods—someone is left!"

"The Hoppers—how far behind us?"

"Five minutes now," Lacey says. "Sorry, Captain, but they got more speed than this rust-bucket's ever going to make."

"Shit!"

While the *Montana* might be slow by warship standards, at the speed it's traveling, five minutes covers a lot of distance. On the screen the gray ovoid slowly swells, grows distinguishable as a ship, marked down the sides with symbols that seem all of a piece with those on the mysterious box that Little Joe retrieved from the Rat Yard. Behind it the comet ice looms larger, a glittering hugeness superimposed over the nebula far, far beyond. At his console Sam is trying to ready the donkey-bots and a cargo grapple against the by now very long shot indeed that the *Montana* can reach the sleeper ship before the pursuing Hoppers do. All at once a hiss and whine floods over the ship-to-ship comm. On her mental screen Lacey can see a long energy surge as Delta Four tries—unsuccessfully—to jam its own ship's channel against the incoming burst of electromagnetism. Rather than disturb the AI, she begins relaying messages to Rick mechanically. She can see him wave a hand in answer down in his transparent turret. On her board, lights go on: the *Montana* is arming.

"RSS *Montana*, come in please."

"Comm problems," Sam lies, a little too cheerfully. "Identify yourself."

On her board Lacey sees the signal light for the laser cannon come on and start flashing: fully armed. The Hopper ship sends another blast of energy and forces through the comm block.

"RSS *Montana*? I'll bet you can hear us now." The voice is a sniggering lilt, a giggle of perfectly formed human words, but only a Hopper would be making them. "*Montana*, we've got a prior claim on that ship as salvage."

"Oh yeah?" Sam's voice is dangerously level. "That's too damn bad. That ship's in Republic territory, and no way you can claim it."

"There's one way." The voice seems amused. "As restitution for damages. One of our ambassadorial launches got in some trouble with a piece of the floating junk in this system, pal. As far as we know, the chunk broke off that derelict out there. We get first claim on the damn thing, going to see just how the damage to our embassy property occurred. You know all about ambassadorial privilege. Dunt try to tell me you dunt."

"Okay, so I won't."

Now they can see the Hopper ship on-screen, an unnecessarily streamlined cutter, as sleek and nasty-looking as a knife blade, heading on full power in a trajectory that will take it between them and Mrs. Bug's sleeper ship. In her head Lacey hears Delta Four:

Programmer, sensors indicate that they've armed torpedoes. They seem to be aiming at the other ship.

"Rick." Lacey breathes a bare whisper into her comm link. "Now."

With the shudder of recoil, the *Montana* belches light, a long streak of red light that arcs harmlessly into space between the Hoppers and the comet ice.

"Stand off," Sam snarls into the comm. "I bet *you* can hear *us* now. We are armed and ready, mister. Stand off."

Over comm, no answer, but on-screen the Hopper ship fires a thruster, turns end over end, then settles into a new trajectory, heading straight for the *Montana*.

Programmer, what's that!?

Delta Four doesn't mean the Hopper ship. On her mental graphs Lacey sees a blur, a displacement of space-time by some large mass, and it too is heading for them. When she

looks up to the viewer, she sees a strange hole appearing in the
nebula, a moving hole—then realizes that something solid is
blocking the cloud-light. Sam has had no time to notice.

"Alliance cutter, stand off! To protect ourselves from colli-
sion, we will fire. Do you understand me? If your intent is to
ram, we will fire."

"Sam, jeezuz! They're arming! It's coming over the sensors
now." So much data is pouring into Lacey's inner graphs that
she feels sick to her stomach as her eyes desperately try to
track the stimuli behind them.

"Well, if we hold them off long enough . . ." Sam lets his
voice trail away into futility. "Hell, I never wanted to be a
martyr."

"Delta Four. Evasive maneuvers."

Braced against the roll of the ship, Lacey is thinking of
Mulligan. As the sensor data piles up, showing torpedoes
sliding into tubes, lasers being activated on the enemy ship,
she is wishing that she told him she loved him, wishing that
she believed in something transcendent or divine that might
save their lives long enough for her to tell him now. In near
hysteria she realizes that on the other hand, she's never
particularly disbelieved in the transcendent, either. *If you
exist, Goddess, tell you what: you get us out of this, and I'll tell
Mulligan the truth. Promise.*

With a buck and a roll the *Montana* soars up in relation to
the comet, twists, and comes back down, behind and a little
above the Hopper cutter now. Sam's lost none of his battle
navigator's touch over the years. With a flip the Hopper ship
turns again, spinning into an unhittable target for a brief
moment, then straightening out on a course straight toward
them. The sensors in Lacey's head are going wild.

Programmer, look!

On-screen that dark hole in the cloud is wavering, swelling,
turning solid into the vast bulk of a battleship, a familiar
battleship looming unbelievably close above them. For a
moment, Lacey cannot breathe. Signal pours into comm
beyond her power to stop it, bringing the familiar growling
voice of Admiral Wazerzis, known to his men as old Iron
Snout.

"Alliance cutter, stand off! Any move toward the RSS
Montana will be taken as an act of piracy and dealt with
accordingly. I repeat: stand off, sir. This is the RSS *Constitu-*

tion, and I warn you, sir, we are armed and prepared to fire by order of our government."

Swinging on its trajectory the Hopper ship seems to hang, exposed, dead in space if the *Constitution* chooses, for a long long minute. Then suddenly thrusters fire; it turns, sweeping off majestically and heading out-system. Over comm Lacey can hear cheering on the *Constitution*'s bridge, but she cannot speak to answer. Only then does she realize that tears are running down her face. She looks up to see Sam wiping his eyes on his sleeve.

"Yeah, takes you that way, dunt it?" he says, then goes back to comm. "Admiral, this is the RSS *Montana.* I guess just saying thank you is no going to be enough, huh?"

"Stand by to be boarded, Mr. Bailey." Iron Snout sounds grimmer than Lacey's ever heard him, and she's heard him in some very tight places indeed. "The list of charges against you is as long as one of my ancestors' tails."

At that an image finally comes on the comm screen: Wazerzis turning away and relinquishing command to a human fleet captain.

"Sorry we were a little late, *Montana.* We were on field maneuvers when HQ commed in with the rescue order."

"Holy Madre de Dios!" Sam snarls. "You mean it's been you guys that we've been seeing on our screen all along?"

"Seeing us? You weren't supposed to be able to see us, *Montana!*" The officer turns from the view-screen and yells over his shoulder. "Hey Admiral, the bastards picked us up on-screen!"

"Well, shut up about it, you blithering dingbat!" Iron Snout's bellow carries all the way across the control room. "We still got the comm on an open line."

Lacey turns to Sam and whispers.

"Am I right, Captain, in assuming that this means they were trying out some kind of secret masking field or something?"

"And that it didn't work worth shit? I think, Mr. Lacey, we can make that assumption." He raises his voice into the comm link. "Very well, sir. We're sending out our transfer tube right now. Want to wait till we pressurize?"

"Nah." Iron Snout's gray-green face, all toothy snarl, fills the screen again. "I got an officer suited up, and he'll come over right away. The sooner we get you mutinous little bastards under control, the better."

Programmer! Why aren't they treating you as you deserve, as heroes?

"Because this is the Navy, pal. I never expected anything different."

Delta Four is speechless. Although Lacey considers trying to explain, at that moment the extruding tube bumps against the *Constitution*'s hatch, and it takes both of their concentration to seal up the various links so that the officer in question can make his slow trip over, pulling his way from one artificial gravity field to another.

At last the final hatch opens, and the officer swings himself inside, his weighted boots hitting the floor with a slap that makes the control room tremble. From the insignia on his powerpack, Lacey can tell that he's a commander, but she thinks little else about him, since she's busy pressurizing the secondary airlock into the control room. Sam, however, is watching the view-screen in a slack-mouth fascination as the officer makes his way through. At last the pressure's equalized, and Lacey opens the lock to let him step inside.

"Oh jeezuz," Sam mutters. "Should've known he'd end up on the damn flagship. He always was that kind."

Lacey turns around just as the officer pulls off his helmet and shakes his head in relief, that familiar gesture, so like a wild horse, that familiar smile, a flash of humor in a face as harsh and handsome as a perfect steel blade. Thanks to rejuv Jaime is indeed every bit as good-looking as she remembers him, the liquid dark eyes smoldering under heavy brows, the coppery skin stretched tight over the high cheekbones and strongly modeled jaw, but now she sees things that somehow she never saw before, the slight laxity of the sensual mouth, the emptiness lying just behind the eyes. *My God, he's stupid, isn't he? That's why he's the perfect soldier*. The shock of this sudden insight turns her speechless, and predictably, Jaime misunderstands, preening a little as he turns toward her.

"Surprised to see me, Bobbie? You sure haven't changed, always getting yourself in trouble." Before she can swear at him, he turns to Mrs. Bug. "Ma'am, I'm authorized to tell you that rescue operations will start immediately on your ship. Our sensors have picked up life signs from hundreds of sentients."

Mrs. Bug howls out a long whine and jigs a few steps in what Lacey can only interpret as joy.

"Immediately, officer?" she says at last, in her fluting voice.

"Immediately. As soon as you give us permission to board."

"Permission granted. And we all thank you."

Only then does Lacey realize that the improbable has happened: they've won.

In a few minutes the command module fills up with Navy beings, striding around yelling orders, elbowing Sam and his jury-rigged crew away from the control panel, some stopping to shake their hands or slap them on the back, others snarling at them to stand to one side and wait for the admiral. Only Mrs. Bug gets treated with honest respect. When Delta Four picks up the confusion, it flatly refuses to operate until one of the Navy men lets Lacey get on the comm to reassure the AI unit. Finally Iron Snout himself, flushed a bright green with excitement, waddles aboard, followed by a clutch of ensigns, and makes his way through the crowd.

"Mister Lacey, Mister Bailey!" He stretches his beak in a grin. "Whatthahell? Every time I see you two guys, you're in hot shit up to your necks, huh? You're damn lucky you're civilians, this time around. All right, you're going dirtside with Ensign Chang, here. Is your launch still operational after that cowboy takeoff you made?"

"Sure is, sir." Sam, out of old habit, is standing at stiff attention. "By some kind of dumb luck."

"It's a little more than luck, amigo." Admiral Wazerzis turns his attention to Lacey. "Okay, pal, you're going to have some real explaining to do. Do you know why our lousy frigate never caught up with the *Montana*?"

"Because Bailey jettisoned the cargo modules?"

"Hell no. Its AI unit refused to operate. Said it was having a breakdown in one of its circuits, but since the damn thing had just been checked out three hours earlier, it sounds like mutiny to me—well, if an AI's capable of mutiny, which I doubt, and which is why I want to know what you did."

"I dint do nada, sir, and that's the honest truth."

"Yeah? Then why did the AI say it no was going to fire on Bobbie Lacey?"

Lacey is speechless yet once again, so honestly and so long that the admiral finally shakes his head in surprise.

"You really no savvy, do you?"

"No sir. I'll swear it on anything you want, but I got no idea at all."

Sam suddenly laughs in a long hysterical giggle.

"It's because they love you," he says, gasping for breath. "What do you bet? Every goddamn AI in this system knows you think they're people, and they love you for it." He giggles again, even higher. "Bobbie Lacey's God—what do you bet that's how they see it?"

Wazerzis reaches out with a heavy paw and slaps him across the face.

"You might be right, Mister Bailey," the admiral says. "But there's no call to be getting hysterical over it. Chang, Wilson, Ksiskeris—get the humans and this two-headed guy in the launch. The sooner you all get dirtside, the better."

Nunks growls under his breath.

"He's only got one head," Lacey says. "It's just bifurcate."

"Dunt give a damn. Get in the launch. You got quite a party waiting for you down on Hagar."

And for the second time in her life Lacey knows the bitter numbness of being under arrest.

Since they are surrendering to Hagar's gravity rather than trying to escape it, the trip down in the launch takes considerably less time than their trip out to the sleeper ship. Even so, the four of them spend a morose couple of hours strapped into their seats and speaking to no one as Hagar's red ball grows larger and larger in the main view-screen and the Navy crew scrupulously ignores them. At moments Lacey hears her mother's voice echoing in her memory, snarling, "You're just like your father." Finally, when the ensign in charge makes radio contact with Space Dock and begins asking for clearance, she can stand it no longer.

"Jeez, Sam, I'm sorry I got you into this."

"You dint. I was stupid enough to volunteer, remember?" He flashes her a smile. "I suppose they're going to impound the *Montana*, huh?"

"We no going to need her when we're in the rehab colony." Rick can barely squeeze out the words. "Jeez, I hope to God they dunt turn me over to the 'Lies. I'd rather die than go back. I mean, shit, I'd die there, too, but real slow. Y'know?"

"Yeah. Fraid so." She feels her stomach knot. About the only thing she can think of to do for the poor kid is to ask Richie to arrange his murder for mercy's sake—not a very pleasant idea, but no doubt better than what the Alliance will do to him. Then something else occurs to her. "Damn! The Bentley!"

"It's gone, yeah," Sam says. "We left it right under the

launch when we lifted off. I dunt know why, but that gripes the hell out of me, thinking of that beautiful skimmer being melted all to hell."

"Well, Richie will understand. Stuff like cars dunt mean a lot to him, anyway. He just likes the feeling of being able to buy whatever he wants."

When Nunks allows himself a long wordless sigh, Ensign Chang turns from the control panel.

"Will you guys shut up? I'm trying to land this damn launch."

"Ah cajones de tu madre," Sam mutters, then falls silent when Chang pats the laser at his hip in a significant manner.

At last, in a roar of reverse acceleration the launch settles on the pad, and ground techs swarm over her to attach the assorted gantry cables. When Chang motions with his pistol, the four of them unstrap and get up, marching in a neat military formation down to the outer hatch. As the iris starts opening, Lacey get her first hint that something's going on when she catches Chang suppressing a grin.

"What are you gloating about?"

"Nada. Like the admiral said, it's going to be quite a party, that's all."

The iris unwinds itself, and the sound of cheering fills the launch. Through the opening she can see crowds, an improvised stand, bunting, holopix cameras, and under an enormous sunshade, the President herself.

"Oh jeezuz!" Sam snarls. "We're fucking heroes!"

"That's right, Mister Bailey." Chang waves them out. "But you know old Iron Snout. He likes his little joke."

Chapter Ten

"I tell you, Lacey, Mrs. Bug's people are turning out to be a hell of a lot more complex than we ever thought." Carol pauses for a sip of apple brandy and soda. "I had my comp unit collate all the data we've got on them for Buddy. All he has to do is access her to get it."

"Thank you, Doctor Carol." Buddy sounds almost obscenely pleased at the thought. "I shall do so immediately, and I appreciate your kindness in thinking of me."

"What's wrong with you, disk-flipper?" Carol scowls at him. "You planning something weird?"

Buddy makes a humming sound that could pass for a snort of annoyance. Lacey intervenes.

"Complex how?"

"Well, it seems that she was drawing on Mulligan's memory banks to build a persona we could relate to. Now that all her own people are revived and on-planet, it's getting hard for her to keep the mask up. I get the strong feeling that they're a semi-collective intelligence, because they sure exert a pull on her. We probably won't see much of her once they settle down in the tropics. Tell you, they may be kind of strange, but survivalists? Jeez, they wrote the book. Sandstorms? Fine, they love 'em. Not a drop of water for a thousand kilometers? Swell, who needs it? I wouldn't be surprised to hear that they can eat rock."

"Far out." Lacey finishes the last of her drink, decides against having another so soon after sunset, then wipes the bottom of the glass dry on her jeans and sets it down on the edge of her comp desk. "But you keep saying 'strange' and 'complex' and you dunt tell me how."

"Well, take this matter of her—well, of the being we were

thinking of as her mate. In a way, he was. I mean, he was male, and they were going to lay eggs together, and all that. But he wasn't really a separate person in our sense of the word."

"Say what?"

"When one of their females is ready to lay an egg, it ripens in her ovipositor. Then, before it's fertilized, this egg divides once into two separate zygotes. Get it? Then the male comes along. He produces two kinds of sperm, one for each zygote. One egg turns into a female, the other into a male, but remember, they started out as two halves of a whole, so all their genetic inheritance from the mother is identical. It's the sperm type that makes all the difference. When they mature, the male is smaller, weaker, not too bright, and basically dependent on the female, because he's stone blind. Now, psionically speaking, he can't send mental signal, or pick up other races, so most of what information he gets, he gets through her. But here's the weird part—this pair of hatchlings grow up together and become mates when they're old enough."

"But hey, talk about inbreeding! They're still brother and sister!"

"Not exactly. That damn bacterial symbiote has a role in their reproductive cycle along with everything else it does. It mutates the male embryo in the egg, scrambles his DNA, kind of, and adds genetic material that it's picked up from other members of the tribe or clutch or whatever you want to call the groups these sentients live in."

"Very strange, yeah. But each mated pair, they're still a lot alike?"

"Hell yeah. Mrs. B. told me that losing her mate was like losing part of herself—no, I take that back. To her, it *was* losing part of herself. She wasn't exactly mourning a lover and an equal, you see. More like the kind of grief you'd feel if you lost a kid mixed up with the outrage of being maimed. Y'know, if someone loses an arm or leg, you got to let them mourn it before you can fit the bionic one. Otherwise they just won't grow the right neural connections, no matter how many shots you give'em. This is kind of like that."

Lacey decides to have a second drink after all and gets up, taking Carol's empty glass along with hers down to the wet bar.

"How many of her people survived?"

"Perfect example of what I was just saying. She told us that there were four hundred sentients on the ship originally, right? Turns out there were four hundred *pair*—eight hundred individuals, to our way of thinking. So one hundred ninety-four pairs survived both the accident and being brought out of cold berth, plus another thirty or so individuals without pod-mates. I asked Mrs. B. if those guys could maybe pair off, and she was horribly shocked. Man, did I have to apologize! It turned out I'd said something obscene, I mean, we're talking real hard-core filth here."

"No accounting for tastes, huh?" Lacey hands her the drink, then sits down again, swinging her feet up onto her desk. "I take it enough expedition members survived to start a colony down near the equator."

"More than enough, because if they want to, they can lay three or four pairs of eggs a year. And we're getting a bargain. The Republic's granting them full mining rights to all those mineral deposits not even our robotics can touch, and the right to live in the hell-holes around them, too. In return, we get exclusive trade rights with their home systems—they've settled a bunch of planets that no other race could possibly use. Most likely they'll be willing to form a full alliance. The Republic, my dear, is going to just about triple in size. The Cons and the 'Lies can wipe their behinds on that, and let's hope it scratches."

They toast the Republic, then drink in silence for a few minutes, enjoying the first chance at a little quiet that they've had in five days.

"I dint hear bout a possible alliance," Lacey says at last. "Where'd you find that out?"

"Al Bates." Carol looks absently away. "We had dinner last night."

"Oh yeah?"

"Yeah. Say, another thing I want to tell you. Little Maria? I think I've got a scholarship all sewn up for her."

"Far out! She sure sounded like her night at the hospital was a revelation for her. Hey, do you really think she can make it through? I mean, it's one thing to decide you want to be a paramedic, and another to learn all that stuff."

"No savvy, but she's earned the right to try. You should've seen her, working the ward with Mulligan after he taught her to shoo those damn bacteria away or whatever the hell it was they were doing. He was moaning and groaning, and he couldn't even look at the patients half the time, but she was real calm, man, reassuring each patient and explaining everything as best she could. Y'know, after the rotten life she's led, I'll bet that a few cases of Bugman's Creep looked pretty tame. This scholarship includes a year of special tutoring at a prep school to get her math and reading up to speed. I figured you'd let her stay here for that."

"No problem, yeah. Nunks wants to develop her psionics, too, before the Institute snags her, so that'll do fine."

"Give the kid enough hard work, and it'll keep her out of trouble."

"It worked for us at her age, dint it? Say, how's Little Joe?"

"One hundred percent okay. He's talking about getting an honest job, though."

"Jeez, this thing must've really messed with his head."

Carol finishes the last of her drink in one gulp and looks at her chrono.

"Got to run. I'll check in with you tomorrow."

"Okay. Where you going now?"

"Oh, well . . ." Carol gets up, looking absently away. "Having lunch with Al Bates."

"Oh yeah?"

"Yeah."

Carol is out the door before Lacey can think of a suitable comment. For a while she sits at her desk and looks out the window at the gaudy night sky; every now and then she says to herself, "Oh yeah?" and smiles. Then she remembers that she made a rash promise when it looked like the 'Lies were going to blow her out of the sky. On the off chance that there are gods of some sort in the galaxy, she decides she'd better keep it.

The National Psionics Institute occupies five hectares on the north side of Polar City. In the middle of the landscaped grounds stands the main building, a rambling, one-story maze of white stucco and red-tiled roofs, dim corridors and shaded patios. As a common joke goes, if you can't find your way around the building, then you aren't psychic enough to belong there. The director's office is a big book-lined room with a beamed ceiling and a red-tiled floor that overlooks a particularly cool patio where a holo fountain spreads its illusory waters in a blue-and-white-tiled basin. Those who love the Institute as an alma mater—and despite Mulligan's views on the matter, most psychics do—remember this room fondly, with its comfortable furniture of real wood and leather, its collection of fine art on the walls and its state-of-the-art comp unit, and tend to model their own condos after it. Mulligan has, predictably, always hated it, and the director, too, a tall, thin, graying Blanco named Dane Coleman.

At the moment Coleman is leaning back in his chair behind his desk while Mulligan perches on the edge of a carved settee nearby and squirms.

Successful< whole debriefing\you, Mrs. Bug both<< Now Institute in splendid position! All this new information\psi techniques >money\government grants>> big bucks some-day/soon.

Guess so. Glad to help. [faint sarcasm]

*[bewilderment] Jack, why you so angry with us now?
<angry\when training<<*

Mulligan merely shrugs uneasily, because at root he's not really sure why. Coleman leans forward in sincere concern.

Jack >think about it>> All I ask now >you think over\ my offer.

Thanks BUT| not thanks. I not belong\here.

*I say: you do belong now >belong>> <I meet Maria.
<Quiz her\bacteria removal-field< <She learn well\from you< >Someday you be a fine teacher/have the touch for it>> a little training>>> Think about it >here full time >>good salary, place to live\safe and clean >>respect, honor from students>>>*

Okay, I think> not promise now >>not promise nothing>>>

Fine. All I ask now.

When Mulligan stands up, Coleman follows and walks out with him. As they make their way along the halls, cool and dim, silent (to the ears) even though they pass groups of students and teachers, Mulligan finds himself wondering if he could teach for a living. He's sure it would take years of training, no matter what Coleman thinks, but he knows that Nunks would be glad to help him. Yet to be someplace every day at the same time, to dress up in respectable clothes and say only respectable things, to stick to daily lesson plans and meetings with students, to be as firm and cold with them as his teachers were with him—he feels the contempt of a wolf who sees a fat dog chained to a kennel. The director picks up his thought and smiles.

Not that bad >once you get used to it>>

I mean no insult now >none>> Just not my style.

Ah. You mean the responsibility. Not want> be responsible\/ sure you >fail>>?

Mulligan feels his face turn hot and starts walking faster. He can also feel the director's amusement, sharper than any laughter could be.

And now you want a drink. >Never going to solve one damn thing>>

It takes all Mulligan's psionic skill to hide his sudden flash of pure rage. By then they've reached the wrought-iron gates that lead back to the outside world. Mulligan pushes them open, then deliberately speaks aloud.

"Look, man, I can't hang around here, y'know. I got batting practice. It's, like, the first day of the Park and Rec season."

But even as he jogs down the curving driveway under the gaudy flare of the night sky, he knows that Coleman is merely amused by his attempt at an insult.

Although Lacey could have Buddy call every antique dealer in Polar City and access their inventory to find her a pack of cards, she hates to ask him to find a present for his rival, especially a present that means the rival has won. Instead she leaves the warehouse round midnight and drives her skimmer over to McCovey Avenue, the main street in the most elegant shopping district of Polar City. Although she has over four hours before Mulligan's game starts, in a park across town, she begins to wonder if she has enough time when the first three antique dealers she finds can give her nothing but a blank stare at the mention of tear oh cards. Finally, about half an hour before game time, she comes across a small, cluttered shop down a side street. Right there in the window, among spine-bound books printed on paper and crocheted white poodles with big, baggy bellies that seem to be covers for some long-forgotten cylindrical object, she sees an open wooden box and in it a pack of cards, the top one turned over to reveal the blond man on the horse beside an ocean, the very image that indicated Mulligan himself.

When she goes in, an elderly lizzie, his scales shiny and his paws twisted with age, walks slowly over to greet her.

"That wooden box in the window?" Lacey says. "Are those tear oh cards in it?"

"It's pronounced tarot, actually. It's francis."

"Say what?"

"Francis. It's an Old Earth language."

"Far out. Never heard of it before. You sure it's a full deck?"

"Let me get them for you, madam. You may certainly count them yourself." And he smiles as if he knows damn well that she doesn't have the least idea of how many there are supposed to be.

"Good." Lacey reaches inside her vest and pulls out the mysterious box that Little Joe Walker found and that Mrs. Bug insisted she take as a gift. "I'll bet you've never seen one of these before. It's an Enzebbeline artifact."

The lizzie's yellow eyes gleam with sheer greed.

"One of the new race? Ahem, I might, I suppose, have some slight interest in a barter. May I ask what function it serves?"

"Sure. It's a musical instrument. Each pair of keys turns a particular electronic tone pattern on or off, and once you get 'em going, you vary them by putting pressure on the sides here."

In the midst of unearthly wails, the dealer smiles and settles in for a nice, enjoyable bargain.

Although Lacey gets to the park late, she finds that fifty cents will still buy one of the best seats, just two rows up from the field on the first base line, right near the Marauders' dugout. As she makes her way down the aisle with a crush-cup of beer in one hand and a soy-dog in the other, she estimates the crowd at only a thousand, scattered round the plastocrete stands. Even so, there's someone in the seat next to her, a middle-aged business type in a buttoned white shirt and crisply creased gray shorts. When she sits down, he gives her a pleasant nod to acknowledge her existence, then begins to eat a kraut dog with delicate precision. Lacey puts her feet up on the back of the empty seat in front of her and sighs in contentment.

It's odd how a hot night always seems cooler at a ballpark, even a Park and Rec diamond with nothing but semi-pro ball going on, as if simply watching a game takes you to a magic land where every problem is a little bit easier to solve and every pleasure a little more enjoyable. The soy-dog is juicy, the beer is cold, and out on the field the opposing team, the

Kelly's Bar and Grill Big Shots, are all business in their crisp white uniforms, the pitcher leaning in to scowl at her catcher as the Marauder currently at bat strolls to the plate. High above float the maglev light fixtures, beaming light carefully balanced to mimic long-gone Old Earth sunlight down over the synthigrass, each blade delicate and supple even though it was chemically extruded from the thick pad of plastofoam beneath. Everything about baseball, Lacey thinks, is perfect, or as the old proverb goes, twenty-seven-point-seven meters between bases is as close to perfection as sentience gets.

Lacey checks the scoreboard, finds out it's the bottom of the third with two out, three to nothing Big Shots. The line-ups are listed to one side of the beaten-up and totally outmoded LCD board; in the Marauders' column she finds Mulligan, number twenty-six and batting fifth, an unusual spot for the shortstop. The crack of a bat jerks her back to the game, but the pitcher has merely fouled out to the third baseman: inning over. Laughing, shoving each other, the Marauders ramble out of the dugout in their dirty gray uniforms striped with red, or rather, while they are all wearing uniform shirts, most are wearing blue jeans or baggy dark slacks with them. Lacey sighs again, thinking that Mulligan has found the team that suits him. Although she waves when she spots him, his back is to her as he trots out to the field.

The Marauder pitcher takes his throws while the batter stands by, knocking imaginary mud from his cleats with the tip of his bat. Since organic grass is reserved for the major leagues, Lacey doubts that the guy has ever seen mud, much less played ball on it. When the batter steps in, Mulligan fades back a little, but otherwise he and the team are playing straightaway. She has never seen Mulligan so intense and yet so much at ease as he waits, crouching, watching as the pitcher throws, a little high, for ball one. The batter fouls away the next, then on the third sends an easy roller to short. Even though he has all the time in the world, Mulligan pounces on it, comes up throwing, and slashes it to first to get the runner by an easy meter. Even from her distance Lacey can see him smile, and she realizes, with a little twist of the heart, that this is the first time she's ever seen him happy.

When the next batter reaches first on a bloop single, Lacey expects Mulligan to move up to the edge of the grass in case of a bunt, but instead he fades way back, as does the third baseman. The mystery's solved when the batter comes strolling up from the on-deck circle, a huge, long-armed dude whose enormous hands make the regulation bat look like one for children. The Big Shot side of the field goes wild, yelling, stamping their feet, chanting "Jim-my, Jim-my" over and over. Lacey happens to catch the business type's eye.

"I take it that's their main slugger," she says.

"Yeah. He's just eighteen. I bet he gets picked up by los grandes before the season gets over."

The smooth way Jimmy takes his cuts, the contemptuous confidence with which he looks at the pitcher make Lacey agree that this kid is on the way to the bigs. In a minute or two, most likely, it's going to be five to nothing Big Shots. The first pitch is both low and outside, as if the pitcher is terrified of getting anything in the strike zone, and rightly so, as it turns out, because on the next pitch Jimmy reaches a little, gets good wood on it, and smokes it in the air toward the gap between third and short. The third baseman leaps, falls empty-handed, but Mulligan is there, improbably right there to jump, spear it, come down turning, and make a perfect throw to second for the force. The Big Shot fans fall silent in disbelief: double play. Inning's over. Lacey cheers along with the rest of the Marauder supporters as Mulligan lopes in toward the dugout.

"That Jack's sure something, huh?" the business type says. "Wait till you see him hit. He can do it all."

"Jack?"

"Jack Mulligan, yeah."

With a sense of profound shock Lacey realizes that she's never heard his first name before, never even thought about it, really.

As the game goes on, Lacey realizes that the business type has told her nothing but the truth: Mulligan can indeed do it all. By his last at-bat he's gone two for four with a sacrifice fly that scored the game-winning run. As the crowd clears the stadium, she waits, looking at the empty field and wondering if she has the courage to go through with the strange proposal that she's got in mind. Finally, when a cleaningbot whirs up and bumps her leg, she stands and puffs up the steep steps to the main gate.

Around back near the Metro stop is a metal door into the stadium and a dirty alley, where a small crowd spreads out in a straggly bunch and line to wait for the teams. Since this is the Park and Rec League, Lacey can assume that they're wives, girlfriends, and lovers rather than fans, especially since a couple of the women have babies or toddlers with them. Even though no one notices her walk up, she stops off to one side where she can lean against a metal railing and watch from a distance. A few at a time, either laughing at their victory or dour at their loss, the players hurry out, their hair still wet from the showers, their street clothes sticking to damp bodies, and yell greetings at one or another of the waiting crowd. And a few at a time they drift off, some to the Metro, some to the parking lot, until Lacey is standing there alone under the kaleidoscoping northern lights, wondering if Mulligan's left by another door and cursing herself for not calling him and telling him she was coming to the game.

Just as she's thinking she'd better leave before a guardbot runs her off, he trots out, dressed in a pair of reasonably clean jeans and a fresh red and white jersey that says MARAUDERS on the front and MULLIGAN, 26, on the back. He looks around, sees her, and comes jogging over.

"Sorry, Lacey, I just picked up that you were here." He is smiling, a little shy, mostly pleased. "I would've hurried if I'd, like, read you earlier."

She feels one last stab of doubt, wondering why she wants to get involved with a man who can feel her presence through solid walls and do God knows what other mental tricks, but his smile is making her smile in return, and without even thinking about it she finds herself moving closer to him.

"Can I buy you a beer?" Mulligan continues. "I just got five bucks, y'know."

"Sure. Where you want to go?" She fishes in her pocket, finds the skimmer keys, and tosses them to him. "And I got a surprise for you, in the car."

"Yeah?" He catches them automatically. "Hey, far out." For a moment he stares at the keys in a bewildered kind of pleasure. "You going to let me drive?"

"Sure, if you want to."

He nods yes, and she doesn't need psionics to see him wondering in a kind of disbelieving hope what this gesture may mean.

"Car's over that way." She points out into the parking lot. "You done here?"

"Oh yeah. Let's go. Did you see the game?"

"Sure did. You know, Jack, you're some kind of ball player."

"Think so?" The smile he gives her makes her feel warm all over, a suspicious kind of warmth that starts at the base of her spine and moves up. "Like, thanks."

Close but not quite touching they walk out into the stretch of pale gray plastophalt, empty except for Lacey's beaten-up blue skimmer, dark except for the crackling rainbow glimmer of the northern lights. At the car she presses her thumb on the keyed lock and opens the passenger side, then gets in and slides over to let him in at the other door. While he gets in she busies herself with taking the package out of the glove compartment.

"Is that the surprise?" He sounds as charmingly greedy as a young child.

"Sure is. Here."

The moment he touches it he grins, running his long fingers over the wrapping.

"Oh hey, Lacey, you no should've wasted all this dinero on me. I'll bet something this old cost bucks."

"Hey! You've no even opened it yet."

"No need to. It's tear oh cards, right?"

"Sure is. Jeez, man, you can be scary sometimes."

Abruptly solemn, he lays the packet down on the comp mount and turns in his seat to face her.

"Never meant to scare you. Guess I was just being dumb, trying to impress you or something. I mean, like, I no can figure out what's in most packages and stuff. It's just these cards are, like, heavy. Y'know?"

"Well, I guess so. But you like 'em?"

"Oh say, I've never liked a present more. Thanks. I mean, like, really thanks. I'm just waiting to open it till we get somewhere with some light, y'know?"

The colored shadows dance across his face and hide his eyes, but she knows that he's studying her with his usual hopeless longing. She remembers then that she had a speech all planned out, some clever way of telling him that she loves him, but search her mind though she might, it's completely gone.

"Where do you want to go for that beer?" he says at last. "Are you hungry? I got a few bucks from the cops today, too, for that reading I did, I mean, like, the one when we were going to the Rat Yard that day. Y'know?"

"Yeah, I remember. I could chip in, if you want to get some slice'n'fry or something."

"Well, hell, I kind of wanted to treat, y'know. You got me these cards and stuff."

"What about your landlord and the rent?"

"Ah, well, y'know." He looks away, staring out the windshield at the light show in the sky. "I mean, like."

"He kicked you out already, so it no matter if you got anything to give him."

"Uh, yeah. You sure dunt stay a hero long in this town. Y'know? And even if I gave him all the bucks I got, it still no add up to a week's rent, anyway." With a sigh he runs long fingers down the joystick. "One of the guys on the team said I could sleep on her couch tonight, like her old man no minds as long as it's just one night, y'know? She's our second baseman, and so, like, she no want me tired out for tomorrow's game. She's going to look bad if I no can turn the double plays."

"Ah hell, you can come stay at the warehouse."

"For sure? Oh hey, Lacey, like, thanks. I mean, I might need Linda's sofa even more later on, y'know? I no want to piss off her old man so early in the season."

"Well, tell you, I've been thinking about that. You could come stay with me permanently, if you wanted."

"Oh, far out!" He slews around to grin at her. "That's right—Rick's gone. So you got a room open." The smile disappears. "But I no can pay you much."

"Jerk. I no want rent from you. Uh, and about that room . . ." Here, at the crux, her words stick and fail her. "Uh, Maria might want that one."

"Hell, I can take hers. I no fussy, like, I mean, if you're going to take me in off the street. And I can work in the garden a lot, or do whatever you and Nunks want me to."

"Okay, that sounds good, yeah."

For a moment they sit silently, while he looks out the windshield with an exhausted sort of smile, as if he still can't believe his good fortune in finding a permanent place to sleep, and Lacey curses herself for a jerk or worse, because she's forgotten how to flirt. Then all at once she remembers what Mulligan's psionics mean, that with him, at least, hints and coy glances are not in the least necessary. She merely lets herself think how much she wants him, just how nice it would be to feel his arms around her and his mouth on hers, thinks about it steadily and watches his smile disappear as he turns toward her wide-eyed and doubtful, as he starts to move toward her, then hesitates, frozen by disbelief.

"I mean it, yeah," she says.

With one last shyness—his beautiful childlike smile—he moves closer and takes her face between his hands. When he kisses her, it becomes hard to think about anything.

About an hour before sunset Lacey wakes up to find the comm link beside her bed beeping at her. For a moment she has trouble identifying the comfortable warm weight pressing along her back; then she remembers Mulligan and the day just past. Even though she got far too little actual sleep, she's smiling to herself as she punches into the comm link.

"What's the message, Buddy?"

"Programmer, Doctor Carol is here. She is currently writing you a note after telling me that she will return later."

"Tell her to stop writing and leaving, then. I'm getting up."

Moving as quietly as she can, Lacey slides out of bed and picks up her cut-off jeans from the floor, which sports a remarkably far-flung litter of clothing. At her movement Mulligan sighs, but he stays asleep, turning over to grab the pillow and wrap his arms around it. Now that he has the room, she supposes, he will doubtless end up in one of his breakneck twists. She is just zipping up her jeans when Carol appears in the open doorway, starts to smile, sees Mulligan, and stares open-mouthed instead. All at once, Lacey remembers that Carol's opinion of her new lover is less than high.

"Jeezuz! Just sweet jeezuz!" Carol turns on her heel and stalks down the hall.

Lacey grabs the nearest shirt, which turns out to be Mulligan's Marauder jersey, but pulls it on anyway as she hurries after, catching up in the living room, where Carol is methodically ripping the piece of notepaper into tiny shreds.

"Okay. Why are you so pissed off about me and Mulligan?"

"He's a jerk."

"Hey!"

"Oh, okay. Sorry. He's no jerk, then. Just a loser."

"Carol, goddamn it!"

"Well, you've always had lousy taste in men. No, okay, sorry again. It's no him, really. It's just that you deserve better, that's all. Some dude who's got a lot going for him, someone who's together and strong and—"

"You no understand." Lacey works at keeping her voice level. "I no want some dude who thinks he can tell me what to do. I took enough orders in the Fleet, thanks."

"That's not what I mean, and you know it."

"Yeah, maybe, but you still mean someone to look up to, right? I had enough of that, too."

"Well, you've got a point there." Carol pauses to throw the scraps of notepaper into the recycler chute. "Old Jorgé or Hermie or whatever his name was did have the biggest lousy ego in the Mapped Sector, like I remember trying to point out at the time. Him and his goddamn tight trousers. I think they cut down the circulation of the blood to the brain."

In spite of herself, Lacey has to laugh.

"So okay, Carol, you know what I want now? I want someone to look up to me for a change. Something wrong with that?"

"Well, guess not."

"Okay then. Besides, I want to have someone around to take care of and . . . and, well, spoil, I guess I mean, make a fuss over."

"Well, he'll be that, for sure. Jeez, Lacey, he's just a kid! I mean, what is he? Twenty-two? Twenty-three?"

"About that, yeah, and I know, I know, I'm old enough to be his lousy mother. Know something? I dunt give one sweet damn as long as he dunt."

"Huh. Can he even subtract twenty-three from forty-eight without a comp unit?"

"Man, would you shut up?"

Carol looks intensely sour.

"Ah lay off, Doc! I got the dinero to keep him if I want him, and I do. You've got to admit he's a damn good-looking dude for a Blanco, and besides, he's a fantastic shortstop."

"Okay, okay. So maybe I'm wrong."

"Ohmigawd! Buddy, call the telenews! Never thought I'd live to see the day when Carol would admit such a thing."

"I take it my programmer is making a joke." Buddy sounds as sour as Carol looks. "You may wish to know that my housecomp subfunction informs me that the Mulligan unit is approaching this room."

Wearing only a pair of jeans, Mulligan wanders in, sees Carol, and freezes dramatically but sincerely. Although Lacey feels that the moment demands some sort of gesture on her part, a public kiss or some such thing, her dislike of display keeps her standing where she is.

"You want some breakfast?" she says.

He turns his head and smiles at her, and as always his expression of innocent delight makes her want to throw herself into his arms. Instead she sits down at her comp desk.

"Sure," he says. "I'll go make it. You going to stay, Carol? You're welcome to, man."

Carol stares, then mutters out a graceless thanks and flops onto the couch. Mulligan smiles again, impartially round the room, then wanders out, whistling under his breath, to head for the kitchen.

"Jeez," Carol says. "He's sure made himself at home in a hurry."

"Why shouldn't he?" Lacey leans back, puts her feet on the desk, and grins at the ceiling. "He lives here now."

About the Author

KATHARINE KERR lives in San Francisco with her husband. **Polar City Blues** is her first science fiction novel. She has just completed **The Dragon Revenant** for Doubleday Foundation, her fourth fantasy novel set in the universe of Deverry, was published in the spring of 1990. She is currently at work on the fifth Deverry novel.

In the kingdom of Deverry, a selfish young lord caused the deaths of two lovers. Then and there he swore an oath never to rest until the wrong had been righted. Four hundred years—and several lifetimes—later, that prince, now the powerful wizard Nevyn, still seeks to atone for his sin.

THE BRISTLING WOOD

Nevyn discovers the actions of the Dark Council interfering in the already tangled politics of war-torn Eldidd. Ruthless and powerful adversaries, their dark arts are dedicated to chaos and greed. Their evil web is nearly spun before even Nevyn realizes there's a war of magic destroying his world.

Now available in Bantam Spectra paperback

THE DRAGON REVENANT

Destiny is catching up to Nevyn, the exiled lord Rhodry and his lover Jill as the Dark Council tightens its grip on Deverry. Lured to a trap set in distant Bardek, Nevyn, Jill and Rhodry face the prospect of complete defeat—or an ultimate victory that will not only change all of their lives, but the fate of the kingdom itself.

Now available in Doubleday Foundation hardcover and trade paperback